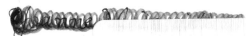

The Assassins of Tamurin

The Assassins of Tamurin

S. D. TOWER

An Imprint of HarperCollins*Publishers*

HarperCollins books may be purchased for educational, business, or sales promotional use. For information please write: Special Markets Department, HarperCollins Publishers Inc., 10 East 53rd Street, New York, NY 10022.

Designed by Kelly S. Too

ISBN 0-380-97803-2

Acknowledgments

The story about the lost needle was inspired by a description of the privations suffered by the early settlers in our neighborhood, as told by Claudia Smith in her local history book, *Gypsies, Preachers and Big White Bears*.

Mother Midnight and her school were curled up in our minds for several years after reading about a widow named Chiyome, who started just such a business in the 1500s.

Many thanks must go to Arlene McGee, Kym Dalrymple, Tony Thornton, and Colleen McKee: our friends who dropped everything in order to trek through the early world of Durdane and give us their impressions and advice.

And—as always—special thanks to Edna Jones, who had encouraged, supported, and never, *ever* questioned why we chose this path!

The Assassins of Tamurin

One

The people of my village cast me out when I was eleven. Or at least I believed I was eleven, for neither I nor anyone in Riversong knew the day or place of my birth, much less who brought me into the world.

It happened because of three sewing needles, the shiny steel kind you can buy in any town marketplace. I was supposed to take them to the priestess at the Bee Goddess's shrine, half a morning's walk from the village, so she could have her turn to sew for her family. Foster Mother wouldn't have sent me if anybody else had been available, but as it happened I was the only one she could spare. Annoyed at this, my aunt Tamzu said, "It's an insult to the priestess to send this wretched child to her, but I suppose there's no help for it."

Not to be outdone, Aunt Adumar added, "And, Lale, when you talk to the priestess—pay *attention*, you worthless girl! When you talk to her, keep your eyes on the ground. Don't gawp at her like a dead moonfish, and don't scratch and spit and pick your nose."

"I'll be very respectful, Auntie Adumar," I said. I was careful to sound glum, because if I appeared happy about my errand, she'd find some way to take it away from me. Actually, I was delighted to be going, because the priestess lived near a bee cave some three miles from Riversong, and I'd have a whole half day free of my interminable chores. So I quickly pulled my raggedy brown cloak over my smock, and Foster Mother gave me the scrap of leather with the three needles pushed through it and told me to go. Aunt Adumar aimed a swat at my bottom as I went out the door, but I dodged it.

Young though I was, I was acutely aware of how precious the needles were. I clutched them tightly and told myself I wouldn't open my fingers for *anything* until I stood in front of the priestess. Then, full of this resolve, I tramped through the village, past the fish-smoking racks and the breadnut plantation, until I came to the path that led into the forest.

The wet season wasn't far off, and a steady, lukewarm drizzle began to fall as I passed into the green gloom beneath the leaves. Around me, enormous gum trees rose from thickets of fern and brush and soared toward a gray and stone-smooth sky. I must have looked very small among those gigantic trunks, trudging along the path as the drizzle darkened my long auburn hair to a deep reddish brown. I was a lean-limbed, lanky little creature in those days, slender of foot and slim of hand, with green eyes under thick lashes.

But I didn't look exactly like the villagers, although their eye and hair color resembled mine. My complexion was pale and creamy, like the dust that powdered the forest paths in summer, while theirs was darker with a bronze cast. Aunt Adumar said my skin showed I had northern blood, which accounted for my deceitful tongue. I didn't know if northerners really were deceitful, because I had never met one, but Adumar was right about the tongue. Out of necessity, I had become an accomplished liar almost as soon as I could talk.

All went well until I reached the ford at Hatch Creek, which wasn't far from the Bee Goddess's shrine. But there I discovered that the rain had turned the ford to a rushing torrent, and I knew the pebbly bottom would be treacherous. If the current tumbled me into deeper water and I had to swim for the bank, I might well let go of the needles. Fearing this disaster, I used the biggest of the three to pin the leather to the thin fabric of my smock, under my cloak.

But despite my apprehension, I managed the ford without difficulty and went on toward the shrine. By now the rain had stopped, and although my stomach was growling, I felt quite light-hearted; perhaps that was why I neglected to make sure the needles were safe. Whatever the reason, I'd walked some considerable distance before I again felt inside my cloak for the scrap of leather.

It wasn't there. Both it and the priceless needles had vanished.

At first I was only a little frightened, because I knew exactly where I'd been. Retracing my steps toward Hatch Creek, I scanned every bit of the sodden path. I knew I couldn't miss seeing the leather, because my footprints in the thin mud showed exactly where I'd walked. And it couldn't have blown into the undergrowth beneath the trees, because there was very little wind.

But the leather was nowhere to be found, and my heart began to thud with apprehension. By the time I reached the creek, with no sign of the needles, I was on the edge of panic. Fighting tears, I stopped on the bank and examined my smock again. Broken threads showed where I'd pinned the leather holder, so I realized it had pulled from the worn fabric and slipped out of my cloak. But I hadn't found anything on the path, so where had it gone?

Into Hatch Creek. The needles had fallen into the water when I was crossing, and the rushing stream had carried them away.

My stomach turned over. I had to find them, I *had* to. My village was so poor and so far from any real marketplace that its women had to share the same set of needles, and they'd only had these for two months. Moreover, they'd had to collect every coin they possessed to buy the things from the peddler, who was the only one we'd seen in almost a year. And now my family would have to replace the wretched things, and I couldn't imagine how we'd do that. Even if another peddler showed up, he'd only sell for money, not barter, and we had no money.

Swept by waves of terror and despair, I began a feverish search downstream from the ford. The Hatch was thick with silt and running fast; it foamed around boulders, sluiced past fallen tree trunks, and boiled through tangles of sodden brown leaves. The leather would look exactly like one of those leaves, and I knew that unless the Water Lord sent me a miracle, I would never find it.

But the miracle did not occur, and by late morning I had searched all the way to the sand spit where Hatch Creek rushed into the waters of the Wing, which was a real river a hundred paces wide. As a last, forlorn hope I poked along the spit's sandy margin, but found only creek rubbish and a dead eelpout, half eaten by crabs. I was almost worn out, and a hopeless foreboding had replaced my earlier panic. But there was nothing more I could do. I'd lost the needles, and that was that.

With no reason now to go to the priestess's house, I stumbled away from the Wing and began to retrace my footsteps homeward. From the sand spit to the village was a considerable distance, and as I approached the halfway mark my steps dragged more and more slowly. Finally my misery became too much to bear, and I stopped and sat down on a flat red rock by the path. It had begun to rain again. The heavy drops made the fallen leaves on the path rustle and twitch, and in my sodden cloak I must have looked much like a wet brown leaf myself.

I sat on my rock and wept. Out of habit, though, my sobs were almost silent, for I had learned early not to let my crying attract attention. But eventually reality intruded. I snuffled, stopped weeping, and wiped my nose with the back of my hand. When I got home and they found out what had happened . . . what would they do to me?

I put two fingers into my mouth and bit them hard, so that I wouldn't burst into tears again. I could not imagine how Foster Father would punish me for what I'd done. But it would have to be dreadful, because I'd injured not only the family but the whole village by my . . . by my what? My misfortune? That was what it really was. But they wouldn't see it that way, especially Aunt Adumar. Adumar would think I'd thrown away the needles out of spite. And it might not be just Adumar who thought so. A lot of people in Riversong didn't like me. I was from somewhere else and had no ancestors; I was an extra mouth in a hungry village; I didn't listen when adults spoke to me; I fought with the other children; and I had a reputation for always being in trouble, or causing it.

Yet I couldn't put off going home forever. I stopped sniveling and peered through the distant leaf canopy at the sky. I couldn't see the sun, but midday must have come and gone, so I'd missed my chore of preparing the noon meal. That would normally be punished by a switching of my legs and no food for the rest of the day. But I suspected that the switch was nothing compared to what awaited me when they found out what I'd done.

Maybe I won't go home, I thought miserably. *I could go back to the Wing and drown myself. No one would miss me. If they could trade me for the cursed needles, they would.*

The worst of this was its truth, for to the villagers I was far less important than the slivers of steel I'd lost. I was a nobody; the aunts had assured me of this many times. No one knew who my mother was or who had fathered me. Of my arrival in the village I'd been told only this: I was just barely old enough to take solid food, when I was found in a waterlogged pole-boat that grounded early one morning in the Wing's shallows near the fish traps. With me in the boat were an elderly man, recently dead, and a woman far too old to be my mother. Unfortunately, the woman was aglow with water fever and so sick she couldn't speak. She died the same day, taking any knowledge of my origins and ancestry with her.

After the old woman expired, the question remained of what to do with me. (I later pieced this together from scraps and fragments; nobody ever told it to me all at once.) The chief shrine within the village was that of the Water Lord, and its priest was pious and influential. He knew a little sorcery but not enough to call up the woman's idu-spirit, assuming it was still loitering around her corpse, so he resorted to a day's meditation on the matter.

Finally emerging from the shrine, he informed the villagers that the god obviously wanted me to survive. First, the deity had grounded the boat before it was swept into the rapids downstream. Second, it was clearly the Water Lord who had kept me from catching the old woman's fever, since he had jurisdiction over that particular illness. So, in the priest's opinion, failing to take me in would be dangerously disrespectful, though he acknowledged that no one really wanted me—nobody had anything to spare for an extra mouth, especially when the owner of the mouth couldn't begin to repay her keep for three or four years.

Nevertheless, the god had spoken or at least muttered. So, after much discussion and argument, I went to live with a man named Detrim, who had under his roof his three sisters, his wife, and his four children. His wife, my foster mother, called me Lale, which is a southern word for "Lucky" and seemed fitting because of my unlikely survival. However, the name was also a play on the word *leyell*, which in the local dialect meant an agile green hawk that liked to thieve fish from the smoking racks. My earliest task, at four years old, was to guard these racks by shooing the robber birds away. Now that I was eleven, I was aware that the pun on my name was no accident. To my family and the village I was as much a thief as the little green hawk.

This fresh offense would only confirm their opinion of my character. Perhaps I really ought to throw myself into the Wing, but I knew that doing so likely wouldn't kill me. I was a strong swimmer, and it would be hard to let myself sink. Although, if I jumped in at the village and went through the rapids, the rocks might do it. . . .

But even in my distress I knew I'd never kill myself. Someday, when I was grown up, I'd get away from Riversong. And somehow—I wasn't sure exactly how, but I'd manage it—I'd become rich and famous. Perhaps I'd marry a Despot's son and when he succeeded his father I'd be the Despotana.

And perhaps I might even find out who my mother and father were. If I killed myself, I'd go to the Quiet World without ever knowing about them or about my ancestors. I didn't often wonder about my origins, but I now realized that I wanted to stay alive long enough to discover who I really was.

Very slowly and very reluctantly, I got up from my rock and drew the wet cloak about my thin shoulders. Then I set off for home—if that was the word for it—in the steady tepid rain.

Two

❧

About mid-afternoon I emerged from the forest into the straggling breadnut plantation that stood at the edge of the village. This plantation, along with fish, goats, swine, and a few patches of yams, provided the hundred-odd souls of Riversong with just enough food to survive and a little more to satisfy the Despot's taxmen twice a year. The village lay in Indar, one of the southern Despotates, and with the warmth and the regular rains it should have been prosperous. But in our region the soil was thin and sour and grew more stones and fireweed than it did crops.

Poor as the village was, it had become even poorer a month ago when forty armored men stormed out of the forest to the southwest. In that direction lay the ill-defined border with Kayan, whose Despot and ours had quarreled over some trifle and then made the quarrel an excuse for raid and counterraid. The Kayanese soldiers were professionals, so most of us took to the trees. The few who couldn't get away watched helplessly as we lost half our food supply and much of our livestock.

Once our own Despot got the news, he sent horsemen to pursue the invaders, but by then the Kayanese were long gone. Our fate could have been worse; they hadn't killed anyone and they hadn't taken quite enough to starve us outright. That, of course, was so they could come back another time and rob us again.

Leaving aside raiders, poor soil, and meager crops, the village was also poor because it was, quite literally, at the end of the road. Few outsiders found their way to Riversong—peddlers came from time to time, and four months ago a fabulator had wandered in and stayed for a day and a night. His name was Master Lim, and he sang his poems and stories to the music of a nine-stringed sivara. He was young and cheerful, and when I told him how I'd arrived in Riversong, he became quite interested and talked to me kindly about it, which was more than anyone else did.

But no one, not even wandering fabulators, journeyed farther than Riversong, because there was nowhere to go on the Wing's far bank. Over there, a wall of russet stone erupted from a shingle beach and flung itself toward the clouds; it was some seventy feet high and marked both Indar's southeast border and the edge of civilization. Beyond the rock wall rose thickly forested hills where only jungle barbarians lived. Beyond these, in the far distance, were mountains whose peaks bore caps of white.

The road to the village, which was really only a grassy track through the forest, came from the north. Long ago—at my age I was only vaguely aware of how long—the village had been a real town, and the road had a reason to go there. Scores of boats had carried freight on the Wing in those days, and they all used the Riversong Canal to bypass the rapids downstream. Traces of the canal's now-silted-up channel still remained in the scrub forest near the rapids, and some weedy rubble showed where the garrison's castella once stood. But only its foundations remained, for the building stone had long since been put to other uses by the villagers. The wooden warehouses on Riversong's waterfront had likewise rotted away, and the sturdy wharves of another era had been replaced by ramshackle piers like long-legged water insects.

In the old days, Riversong's merchants had built big houses in the town, but with one exception these were of wood and had decayed into the past along with their owners. The exception was a sprawling mansion that, being stone, had survived. We called it the Stock House, because its two largest courtyards contained a goat pen and a swine byre. Scattered around this building were the houses where we lived, built of dry-laid red stone and roofed with overhanging thatch. The doorways and windows were small, and at night we closed them with shutters of plaited reeds.

As I trudged down the muddy lane past the Stock House, the rain was tapering off to a mist and the sky was brightening. But hardly anyone saw me come home, for at this hour the men and the older boys were at work in the fields or on the river, while the women and girls were indoors at their perpetual dough making, cloth weaving, beer brewing, child nursing, and the myriad other tasks that made up their lives.

Including darning and sewing, with needles. Ah, the needles. I'd been telling myself all the way home that the loss wasn't as terrible as my fear suggested. But I didn't quite believe this, and I rehearsed, for the hundredth time, how I would present myself as the innocent and injured party.

Finally I arrived at my family's house. It was neither the best dwelling in the village nor the worst, having four rooms and a roofed cooking porch at the back, handy to the privy. A pauxa cote built of poles and woven reeds stood at one side, and I could hear the sleek brown hens gabbling to one another as I approached the doorway.

When I got inside, I'd have to face three of the family—Foster Mother Rana, Aunt Adumar, and Aunt Tamzu. Foster Father Detrim would be out on the river, fishing with his eldest son, Burad, who was nineteen. The other son, Chefen, with Kefsen the youngest of the aunts, had gone downstream this morning to cut cane for the kitchen fire. There were no uncles; Kefsen and Tamzu had been widowed by a fishing accident on the Wing and had never married again because they were so clearly barren. Adumar had doomed herself to spinsterhood by her merciless tongue.

I squared my shoulders and entered the house. Inside was the common room; just within was the square stone pillar of the ancestor shrine, with the carved box where the ancestors' ashes were kept, a pinch for each ancestor. Some of the ash in the box belonged to Foster Mother Rana's youngest son and her only daughter. They had died of breakbone fever not long after I washed up in Riversong, and the fact that I had waxed healthy while they had died was another source of family resentment, especially to Aunt Adumar. Adumar sometimes muttered that if I'd had the decency to catch the fever and die, Rana's children might have recovered. I thought this was probably not true, but I was careful not to argue about it, because Adumar had a brisk way with her long wooden spoon.

The room's two windows admitted a watery light. Aunt Tamzu and Foster Mother Rana were slicing yams on the chopping block and Aunt Adumar was at the plank table, flattening breadnut dough into rounds ready for baking. They wore the everyday dress of the village's adult women: short sleeveless jackets and calf-length wraparound skirts, both garments woven of bast fiber and dyed a deep tan. All three looked up as I entered.

"Ah," Adumar said, and shook her graying hair away from her forehead. She flopped a dough round onto the pile of unbaked loaves. "So you're home, are you? Home *at last*, I should say, you lazy, useless good-for-nothing!"

I was in serious trouble, and that added a spice of satisfaction to Adumar's sharp voice. She was a tall, spare woman, and as she dusted flour from her long hands, the backs of my legs tingled with painful apprehension.

"Speak up, Lale," Aunt Tamzu snapped. Tamzu was as gaunt as her sister, and through her eyes a malicious, narrow intelligence glowered at the world. She detested me almost as much as did Adumar.

I risked a glance at Rana, who was watching me glumly. Unlike her sisters-in-law, she occasionally showed me a little warmth: a pat on the head instead of a swat, a smile when I tried to make a child's joke. But the aunts ruled her, and she never intervened on my behalf when they were at me. Indeed, if she'd had a bad day with them or with Detrim, she was happy to apply the switch to me herself.

"Where were you, Lale?" Rana asked. Her voice was angry, though not as angry as Adumar's.

I burst into tears, not altogether feigned. For more drama, I fell to my knees, hung my head, and sobbed piteously.

"What's the matter with the child?" Tamzu exclaimed. My behavior had startled them. I'd sometimes cry during a bad switching, if only to make them think I'd been punished enough, but otherwise I never let them see me weep. I hoped that breaking down like this would make my story all the more convincing.

Adumar clamped her fingers on my shoulder and dragged me to my feet. "Stop it, this *instant*. Stop your blubbering, girl!" She gave me a tooth-rattling shake. "What are you going on about?"

"Soldiers," I sobbed. "At the ford over Hatch Creek. I couldn't stop them."

Rana gave a frightened exclamation and Tamzu blurted, "What soldiers? Coming this way?"

"I don't know. There were three of them. They talked about a boat. I don't know where they were from." My sobs redoubled. I was still frightened, but I felt things were going pretty well. "They made—they made me—" I lapsed into choked snuffles, which gave me a chance to see how they were reacting. Their faces wore peculiar expressions, which I interpreted favorably.

"What did they make you do?" Adumar demanded. She sounded odd.

"Auntie, they made me lose the *needles*. They caught me and they kept asking where our silver was in the village. I said we didn't have any money—we're so poor. But they just *laughed* at me. Then they hit me. I was afraid they'd *kill* me. They had swords, like the ones who robbed us before."

"You're sure there were only three?" Tamzu said in a worried voice. "It must have been a scouting party. But how did they get upriver, if they were from Kayan?"

"Didn't you *hear* her, Tamzu?" Adumar exclaimed furiously. "The little wretch has lost our needles! That's what she's trying to make us forget with this drivel about soldiers!"

"But, Auntie, it's true! They were *there*!"

Adumar shook me again, eyes narrowed. "Then why didn't they slit your gullet? They knew you'd warn us."

I hadn't prepared for this one. "I got away," I said desperately. "They chased me but I got away."

Rana said, "Maybe they didn't dare go after her. She says there were only three of them. Or maybe they were bandits. Not soldiers at all."

"Then which were they?" Tamzu snapped at me. "Soldiers or bandits?"

My hopes rose. Rana and Tamzu at least were nosing into my net. But before I could go on, Adumar said: "So you lost the needles while they were chasing you?"

"Auntie, I couldn't help it! I was running downstream and I fell and I think I lost them then in the creek." I burst into tears again.

"I don't think so," Adumar snapped. Her fingers tightened painfully in the hollow of my shoulder. "I think this is not what happened at all."

"But, Auntie, I swear it did! I swear it on the shrine of the ancestors!" And if they didn't like my false oath, they'd just have to put up with it. They weren't *my* ancestors.

"They're not your ancestors," Adumar said in a voice like a grindstone. "They wouldn't have you in the family, you little liar. You're a deceiver and a blasphemer—calling on our shrine to witness your lies. No soldiers would be upriver of us. There *were* no soldiers—you threw the needles away out of spite! You knew how much they were worth." She took a shuddering breath. "Those needles were the price of my brother's boat." She looked wildly around, took two swift paces to the corner, and seized one of the heavy canes that Detrim used to drive swine. Then she turned on me, hefting the stick in a white-knuckled hand. "You've ruined us, you little *shegesh*. And you did it on purpose."

"I didn't, I didn't," I cried, terror surging through me. That stick could break my bones. "Please, Auntie, it's the truth. I swear it. They were chasing me. If I'd stopped they'd have killed me."

"Small loss," Adumar said in a terrible voice. My knees were weak as sand. I turned to flee but Adumar's talons seized me by the hair, hauling me upright so that I was half dangling by my tresses. I shrieked and rose on tiptoes to stop the pain.

Before me, the doorway darkened as a man filled it. It was Detrim, back early from the river.

"What's this?" he asked in his reedy voice. "What's going on? Who's been trying to kill who?"

"You'll kill the little wretch yourself," Adumar said furiously, "when you hear what she's done." She let me find my feet but kept her grip on my hair. I stood very still. I could not imagine what Detrim might do to me. Perhaps he *would* kill me. If what Adumar said was true, I might just as well have burned his fishing boat. He might not care much about his sisters or his wife, but he cared about that boat.

"What? What's she done, then?" he demanded, scowling down at me. Detrim had large round eyes and a pursed, thin-lipped mouth above a tiny chin; he had always reminded me of a hatchet-fish. Now the resemblance wasn't funny. Hatchetfish had long sharp teeth and plenty of them.

"She's tossed away the needles she was supposed to take to the Bee priestess," Adumar said. "They're lost for good."

Detrim's eyes got bigger and his lips drew back from his teeth. "She *what?*" he said in a strangled voice.

"She threw them away," Tamzu piped up. "She threw them away, but she won't admit it."

"Or she lost them," Rana suggested diffidently. No one paid her any attention.

"I didn't," I wailed. "Soldiers came. They chased me and the needles fell. I couldn't go back or they'd have killed me. Foster Father, that's what happened, please believe me—"

"She's lying," Adumar hissed, giving me a shake. "What would soldiers be doing upriver, if they were from Kayan?"

"Where did you see them?" Detrim demanded. His sinewy brown hands were twitching. "Where were they when you ran away?"

"At the Hatch Creek ford," I got out in a choked voice. "I was on the way to the Bee Goddess shrine. I ran downstream to get away. To the sand spit. Their boat was there."

Detrim said slowly, "Burad and I rowed past the spit at midday. There was no boat. There were no soldiers."

A pit had opened at my feet and I was falling into it. A buzzing filled my head and my sight darkened. Knowing I was lost, I blurted, "But they were *there*. You just didn't *see* them, Foster Father."

His thin lips writhed. "The needles. You lost them."

"I—" I began desperately, and then Detrim's fist was flying toward me. I flinched and his knuckles glanced from my left cheekbone. Half stunned, I twisted in Adumar's grip but could not break it. Detrim was roaring curses, his bunched fist drew back, and I screamed and wrenched myself aside. Detrim's blow missed me and hit Adumar in the stomach. She lost her breath with a vast gasp, let go of my hair, and doubled over. I lunged for the doorway. Detrim seized the hem of my cloak, but it pulled from my shoulders and I half fell into the street. Then, mindlessly, I ran toward the river. Detrim was yelling for someone to stop me, Tamzu screaming a shrill echo as they took up the chase. Some fleeting idea of jumping into a boat and shooting the rapids flashed through my mind, but Detrim was too close; I flew around a corner and ran for the woods. Women's heads were popping out of doorways and windows.

"Stop her!" Tamzu shrieked. "She's ruined us—"

I hurtled around a pauxa cote and without warning slammed into a man's midriff. The man yelped. I gasped, and as I tried to collect myself, his burden of cane slid from his shoulder sling and knocked me flat on my face. Before I could scramble away, the heavy bundle had rolled across my legs, pinning me to the mud.

"Curse you, Lale," Chefen snarled. "Watch where you're going!"

"Hold her!" Detrim came up, spattering mud. Behind him trotted Tamzu and Rana. Stumbling after them, bent over and still fighting for breath, was Adumar. I saw my aunt's eyes and wished I had not.

I tried to get up, but it was already too late. Chefen had been in exactly the wrong place at exactly the wrong time. He grabbed my upper arm and held me with a grip like a mooring rope. Half crushed into the dirt, all I could do was lever myself onto one elbow. A small crowd was gathering, mostly women and children. The latter stared at me wide-eyed, without a single jeer or catcall. Their silence only added to my terror. The afternoon sun had come out, and the thatch of the houses was beginning to steam.

"You, Feriti," Adumar wheezed at a woman standing over me. "You were supposed to get the needles after the priestess. But now you won't."

"I won't? Why not?"

"Because Lale lost them!" Adumar shrilled. "Everything else we've had to suffer, and now this! She's a curse on us all, the little demon. She's been bad luck for everyone since we pulled her out of the river! Better she'd gone into the rapids!"

I saw their faces change. I'd seen them harsh before or angry or cold and indifferent, but I had never seen them become less than human. Their eyes were like the eyes of the boar we kept in the swine byre. The furies they'd stored up against one another, against the soldiers who had robbed them, against the thin soil and the bad crops and the Despot's taxmen at last boiled over.

Feriti began it. She kicked at me almost tentatively, as if unsure of what she was doing. Then she did it again with more conviction. I moaned but no one protested, so Feriti kicked me harder. This time she hurt my ribs, and then Adumar kicked me and another woman did and then another and it hurt, it hurt a *lot*, and I heard someone screaming and it was me, *Please I'm only eleven please please please I didn't mean to oh please* but they were all screaming too, mad, demented, and went on kicking me, kicking me until I was bleeding at the mouth, blood on my tongue hot and salt like tears, curled up now with my arms over my head so they couldn't reach my stomach and then, oh horror, fingers clutching my hair, straightening me so they could get at my belly and my eyes, not just bare feet and fists now, but thick canes from the firewood bundle—

Shouts through the din. I was barely conscious now, but I heard the priest's voice bellowing, *Stop stop it's blasphemy.* The grip on my hair vanished, and I could curl up again as the kicks and blows slowed little by little, faded away like rain diminishing. One person kept at it, two kicks at my face, the priest's voice, *Adumar leave her be I warn you.* And finally it stopped, and so did I, sliding away into silence and darkness, into a place that lay deeper than the riverbed of my dreams.

Three

✦

I was alive but seemed dead. I walked, but no one saw me. I spoke, but no one heard me.

Even the smaller children, when I held one by an arm, waited silently for me to let go. If I persisted or if I threatened anyone, an adult or an older child would intervene and remove me bodily. But they didn't look at me or speak to me. If I went into a house, I would be picked up and put outside as if they were shifting a piece of wood. They didn't even try to hurt me when they did it.

As for the beating, it didn't leave any lasting damage. The Water Lord's priest had kept me in the god's shrine for five days, but during that time no one came to look for me. That was a relief, but I reckoned I'd have to go home eventually, and I dreaded it. I didn't think the village was through with punishing me, and the knowledge made me feel sick and frightened. I asked the priest what was going to happen, but he refused to answer.

On the fifth day, when he saw that I could walk without a limp, he told me that I was to suffer the punishment called Negation of Being. I knew nothing of this, so the priest had to explain it. It was, he said, my penalty for lying, blasphemy, false swearing, and *shegeshvai*, the crime of stealing from a kinsman. Kin theft was worse than simple theft, and in places like Riversong *shegeshvai* was a very serious matter. Adults could have a hand off cut for it, and repeated offenses could bring death.

But, the priest went on, the Goddess of Mercy did not permit the mutilation of a child. Moreover, the Water Lord had preserved me from death when I was a baby, and if I needed killing, the god himself would arrange it. But I must be punished for my many offenses, and inflicting the Negation of Being was within the village's rights. While I remained in Riversong, I would be allowed food enough to sustain my life, but that was all I would receive. Otherwise, as far as the village was concerned, I would cease to exist.

Then the priest fell silent. He would never speak to me again nor would anyone else; my punishment was forever. To the people of Riversong, I was as good as dead.

But for the first few days of being deceased, I thought I must have fallen into the lap of Our Lady of Mercy herself. Nobody hit me or shouted at me, and Rana put out a dish of food for me once a day. Since I couldn't enter the house, I slept in the cooking porch, wrapping myself in my ragged cloak, which I retrieved from the midden where somebody had tossed it. When I was thirsty I drank from the butt beside the Stock House, and if I didn't get enough food from Rana, I slipped into the breadnut plantation at night and ate some of the fallen nuts raw.

And best of all, I did not have to work. The thing that puzzled me was why more people didn't get themselves punished by a Negation on purpose. It seemed a fine life, as long as you didn't mind being outside all the time.

I spent much of my time at play, and several days passed very happily. Sometimes I pretended I was Vahir, the maiden in the old tale who could conjure a hat of invisibility—this was very apt, because I did seem to be invisible. Or I played at being a place god, as if I were one of the minor spirits that liked to associate themselves with particular locations: a woodland glade, an old house, a tree, a bridge, a waterfall. But nobody made the usual small sacrifices to me, so the place god game wasn't very realistic. I liked being Vahir better.

Once I pretended I was an ancestor spirit, but it turned out rather unhappily. As everybody knows, you're most likely to encounter one of these on your birthday, provided you call them with the proper rituals. It so happened that Feriti had her natal day shortly after I was Negated, and for revenge I decided to present myself at the end of her ritual, as if I were an ancestor, and make nasty faces at her. I hoped I'd make her scream or even faint.

It didn't work out that way. I plastered my face and hair with white dust as a sort of ancestor disguise, then listened outside her house until she'd finished the chant and I smelled the musky offering smoke. Then I jumped up and peered through the window, with a horrible leering grimace on my face.

But she wasn't looking at me. Instead she was on her knees, praying as fast as she could to *something* near the ancestor shrine. And I glimpsed it, too, as solid as Feriti was: a young man I'd never seen, wearing peculiar clothes, frowning down at her. I saw him for no more than an instant, but his presence startled me so badly I ran away and hid in the Stock House. It took me some time to get used to the fact that I'd seen an actual ancestor, even if it belonged to somebody else. It wasn't common for people to meet such a spirit, even on their birthdays and even with the rituals, and I was astonished that I'd seen as much as I had. But then, after I got over my fright, I felt a wave of sadness. I didn't know my birthday and never would, so I could never summon a spirit of my bloodline to give me advice or encouragement.

I moped over this for a day, but then tried to restore my spirits by imagining I was a different person entirely, a girl who looked like me but was someone else. This was an old game, one I'd enjoyed since I first discovered I had an imagination. Instead of drudging in poor shabby Riversong, I lived in one of the rich cities of the north. There I was no foundling, but the beloved daughter of a great and respected bloodline. My father was handsome and brave, and my mother was beautiful and wise, and they loved me very much. We lived in a big house with sunlit courtyards and a secret garden luminous with flowers. Just like the people in Master Lim's stories, we ate from plates of gold and drank from cups of crystal; my gowns and jackets were woven of gossamin patterned in purple and red and lilac, and my skirts rang with tiny silver bells. Everything in that world was lovely, and now I could spend as much time there as I pleased, because nobody yelled at me to stop daydreaming and get to work.

But despite such delights, after six or seven days I began to tire of having no one to talk to. Even the younger children wouldn't acknowledge my presence, except to steal a sidelong glance at me, and finally I realized that being invisible was not as wonderful as I'd thought. Then I began to have awful nightmares, in which I turned into a ghost and had to walk the earth instead of going to the Quiet World where I belonged.

And then I woke up one morning and realized, for the first time, what Negation really meant. It meant that I would be alone until I died.

In that instant, terror overwhelmed me. I ran through the village lanes, crying out for someone to notice my existence. Then I tried to go inside my old house. I got into the common room, where Rana sat with her face turned away. But Adumar hit me without looking at me; and Kefsen, Burad, and Tamzu silently picked me up by the arms and legs and threw me into the lane. Then they closed the door.

I lay there in the mud under the overcast sky, and after a while a soft drizzle began. The rain fell on me as people walked past; some stepped over me as if I were a length of cane, and I didn't move for a long time.

But when the drizzle stopped and a pale silver smear in the clouds showed that midday had come, I made myself get up. Then I stumbled around to the rear of the house, where I sat down on a stone. Rana and Aunt Tamzu were in the cooking porch, simmering fish and greens in a clay pot for the midday meal. A stack of flatbread, baked that morning, waited in a straw basket. I dully considered going and getting in their way, but I knew nothing would come of it.

Then I thought: *I have to leave here. I have to go somewhere else, where people won't do this to me.*

Before my Negation, the idea of leaving would have scared me, even though my life in Riversong was so difficult. But now I realized my loneliness would madden me until I killed myself or until I did something that would justify my being put to death. That was the purpose of Negation; the person either died or ran off, and the village was rid of them one way or the other.

I don't want to die, I thought. *I'm only eleven. But I'll die if I stay here. And they'll be happy about it, and I don't want them to be happy.*

All right, then, I'll leave. Maybe I'll die somewhere else, but at least someone might talk to me before it happens.

I couldn't just walk away, though; I'd need supplies to sustain me until I found a village where I could beg or work. To start off, I'd head for Gladewater, some two days' walk along the road to the northwest. If I couldn't find anything there, I'd keep going; according to Detrim, there was a town named High Lake somewhere beyond Gladewater. He'd been there for a few months as a young man, when he was impressed into the Despot's army.

And beyond those two places lay the great world and all its countries. I knew a little about that world, knowledge I had gleaned from the half-comprehended tales carried by the infrequent wanderers who found their way to Riversong. I knew that the villagers and I were of the race called the Durdana, and that our empire of Durdane had once been great but was now broken and cast down. I knew that there had been no Emperor of Durdane for a hundred years—only the Despots, who governed a dozen petty states in the south of our ancient realm, and the Sun Lord of Bethiya, who watched over his larger domain in the north. I knew also that our ruin had come at the hands of the people we called the Exiles, and that they still ruled half the lands of the old empire—the Six Kingdoms—and that neither Despot nor Sun Lord had the power to drive them out.

But I had no clear understanding then of how vast my world really was. Our empire had once stretched fifteen hundred miles from east to west and a thousand from south to north, and beyond those borders lay other places and peoples yet: the wintry northern chiefdoms of the Daisa and the Huazin; the archipelagoes of the Chechesh, the Khalaka, and the Yellow Smoke Islanders in the western ocean; the Country of Circular Paths, the Bone Tree Kingdom, and Narappa-lo on that ocean's far shores; and in the east, the brooding and barbarous realm of Abaris. And there were others beyond these, but so far away that they were more like rumors than real places and had no names.

If I'd known more than I did, I might have been daunted at the prospect of leaving. But in my innocence, I felt that the whole world was mine to discover, if I were daring enough to seize my opportunities with determined hands. My fortune, I told myself, lay in rich foreign places, not here in this wretched village where the road ended.

Excitement flooded me at the prospect. Why had I ever imagined I had to stay in Riversong until I died? My Negation was a blessing in disguise. I'd never have thought of leaving my old life, unless this punishment had befallen me. Losing those needles was perhaps the luckiest thing I'd ever done.

So tomorrow morning I'd leave. No, not tomorrow morning— Suppose something happened to change my mind? I'd go today, this afternoon.

But I had to be practical, so I thought about what I'd need. Two days' worth of provisions would sustain me as far as Gladewater, but I should make it three to be on the safe side. I had my cloak and my smock, and I could take a length of cane to serve as a walking stick and a sort of weapon. As for footwear, I didn't need any; I'd gone without it all my life, and my soles were tough as boar's hide. All I had to do, then, was get my hands on three days' worth of food. Smoked fish and breadnut meal would be the best choice;

I could wrap them in the broad leaves of the butterfly acacia to keep them dry and carry them in a fold of my cloak.

I got up off the stone and walked along the lane until I stood in front of the Stock House. The sky was clearing, and small ribbons of warm blue showed through rents in the cloud. The rapids growled softly from the Wing, like the rumble of distant drums.

I drew a deep breath and shouted, "Pay attention to me! I know you can hear me, even if you pretend you can't. I'm going to do something now. When I tell you what it is, you'll want me to do it."

I paused. All Riversong seemed to be a huge listening ear.

"I'm going to take some fish and bread from some of you. I know I'm not supposed to, and I know you can beat me for it, but I want you to let me take enough for three days. Because then I'm leaving. Forever. You give me three days' food now, and you'll never have to feed me again. I won't come back. I swear that on the name of the Water Lord, who preserved my life. If I do come back, you can kill me."

Another pause. Riversong still listened. "I'm going to come for the food, then," I shouted into the humid afternoon. "Then you'll be done with me."

I realized that my hands were clenched into fists. *O Lady of Mercy*, I prayed, *make them give me what I need.*

I set off along the lane, intending to begin at Detrim's house. When I went around to the back, no one was in the cooking porch. The basket of bread was gone. The fish still simmered in the pot but I had no way to carry a portion of it. I'd have to go inside and look for what I needed. They might throw me into the street, but given what I'd promised, they might not.

But before I could try this, Rana came through the house doorway. She carried a woven bag with a strap, worn but still serviceable. It was the bag she used when she went clam digging in the Wing's shallows. I stared at her in puzzlement, and then Rana looked up, and for the space of three heartbeats I gazed into her eyes. She opened her mouth as if to speak, then closed it. She put the bag on the earthen floor of the porch, then went back inside and shut the door.

My sight blurred. I stumbled into the porch and picked up the bag. It smelled fiercely of old clams, but in it were three rounds of bread and a bundle of smoked eelpout wrapped in leaves. It was enough to keep me walking for a whole day, and the tight weave of the bag would keep out the rain.

I didn't understand why Foster Mother had been so generous. I got a lump in my throat at first, but then I thought: *Ah, but it's just to make sure I leave, so she'll never have to see me again. That's all it is.*

This made me even more sad, so I pushed the thought from my mind and slung the bag over my shoulder. Then I got a length of stout cane from the firewood pile and set out for the next house. The people there had left a few scraps outside the front door. I packed them away and moved on.

It was the same at the next house, and the next. Before the sun had moved much farther, I had all I needed. I went to the edge of the village, where the road began and ended. It ran northward away from me, toward the mysteries of those distant lands.

I settled the bag on my hip, took a firm grip on my staff, and walked out of Riversong forever.

Four

꙾

By the second morning of my great adventure, my enthusiasm for it had somewhat waned.

I'd slept, or tried to, in a thicket by the road, under a leaky roof I wove from the big round leaves of a butterfly acacia. Showers came and went, and when the night wasn't full of the patter and hiss of rain, I heard noises: hoots of night birds, the *chirr* of crickets, the guttural creak of tree frogs.

But I was used to these natural sounds and wasn't troubled by them. What did scare me a bit was the thought of being visited by something from the Quiet World. For that realm, as the village priest had taught, is separated from our human one by less than the thickness of a leaf, and in the dark of the night, those thin partitions become thinner still.

And just as our world has its fearsome and hungry beasts, so does the Quiet World—not only demons and ghosts but also nameless things worse than these. Fortunately, however, our ancestors reside there, too, and with the help of the Beneficent Ones they protect us from such evils as best they can. But such protection can fail, and in the middle of the night, in the middle of a forest, I was very worried that it might—especially since I didn't know who my ancestors were, and could only pray to Our Lady of Mercy that they'd notice me anyway and keep me safe. Perhaps they did, for nothing came whispering and sighing out of the rainy blackness to trouble me, and toward dawn I fell into a broken sleep.

Finally the light woke me. The forest had emerged from the darkness, dripping wet and hung with mist. Sodden and chilled, I jumped up and down on the road's rough turf until I'd warmed up a little. Then I ate sparingly of my dried fish and bread, drank from a pool that had collected in the hollow of a rock, and set off into the drab morning.

In a while the clouds parted in the east, and the sun poked rosy fingers through the rents. But the growing brightness did not cheer me much, for I was beginning to realize how utterly alone I was and how uncertain my future had become. However, there was nothing to do but go on, so I tried to bolster my spirits by imagining all the wonderful things I might do once I reached Gladewater.

But after a few miles I decided that Gladewater, being just a village, would be too small a compass for my ambitions. I'd stay there only long enough to get a new supply of food, and then go on to the town of High Lake, where there would surely be opportunities for a clever and resourceful person such as myself. I'd become rich and successful in no time, and I'd ride back to Riversong on a horse—an animal whose appearance was hazy to me, since I'd never seen one—and show everybody how stupid they'd been not to recognize my talents.

Such bright pictures sustained me till mid-morning, but at length my mood changed again and I began to feel very low. What did I have in the world? A few scraps of food in a smelly sack, a cloak, a smock, and a length of cane. And my wits. I was no longer sure how much my wits were worth.

I tramped onward nevertheless. The sun went in; more rain fell;

the sun came out. The air was humid and thick, full of the smell of greenery, damp bark, and the fragrances of the wet-season blooms that grew beside the road: honey hibiscus, cinnivar, white glory, silverfoil. But I was too downcast to take much pleasure in their beauty, though back in Riversong I'd delighted in their hues and scents.

After a while I came to a place where the road cut sharply around an outcrop of stone. And there, just beyond the bend, was a blaze of red and orange, like a great fire frozen by sorcery. It was a flame magnolia.

I'd never seen one so ancient and enormous. It had impressed other people as much as it did me, for beneath its flower-weighted limbs was a stone pillar with niches cut into it, and in the largest niche was the round plump face of a place god. His stone features were old and worn, but I could still make out the cheerful grin below his mustache and his bushy eyebrows.

I had knelt and was sprinkling a few crumbs as an offering for him, when a man strode around a bend in the road ahead. I stood up quickly, but I didn't flee into the trees although I knew he might be a bandit. Maybe I thought the place god's presence would protect me. Also, I had nothing worth stealing.

I watched him approach. He wore a straw hat, loose knee-length tan trousers, and a sleeveless brown tunic. A short sword dangled at his waist, and on his back he carried a pack. His hair was brown and fell unbound to his bare shoulders.

And slung over one of those shoulders was the slim leather case of a musical instrument. I stared at it in disbelief, and as the man came nearer I burst out, "Master Lim?"

Recognition dawned on his face and he exclaimed, "Why, it's young Lale, isn't it?"

"It is. What are you doing here, Master Lim?" I couldn't imagine why he'd be on his way to Riversong. He'd gotten only his keep, and scanty keep at that, during his earlier visit.

"And what are you doing here, young mistress?" he asked, grinning. "I'm a wanderer, but I didn't know you were one, too. Have you run away, or are you on an errand?"

I thought it better not to mention my Negation, and said, "I'm running away to find my fortune. I'm going to become rich and powerful and famous."

Master Lim threw back his head and laughed. It was a happy, warm sound. He had a wonderful voice, and I was old enough to know that he was a very handsome man.

"I see," he said. "But aren't you afraid they'll catch you and drag you back to Riversong to scour the pots?"

"They won't," I told him. "Nobody cares if I'm gone. And I don't have any ancestors in Riversong, so I didn't belong there anyway."

"Are you going to look for your ancestors, then?" Now he sounded as if he took me seriously. "As well as make your fortune?"

I hadn't thought much about my real parents since I left the village. But they were there nevertheless, shadowy, in the back of my mind. "I think so. Someday."

"Hm," he said, and gazed south along the road. "And are things any better in Riversong?"

"No. Everything's worse," I answered emphatically, in the sudden hope that he might come to High Lake with me. With that, great possibilities flashed through my mind—me, playing a sivara, wandering the world with him, singing.

"They won't be able to feed you," I added. "That's another reason I left. I was always hungry."

He removed his gaze from the road and inspected my face. I couldn't work out why he was looking so intently at me, but I gave him my best, most-trustworthy grin.

"Well," he said, "in that case, there's not much point in going on, is there? But here's a thought. I need an assistant, somebody who can help me by collecting from my audience, maybe learn to dance a little for the stories. How would you like to join me and see a bit of the world?"

I couldn't have asked for more. I looked at the place god's benign face and thanked him for his gift.

"I'd like that," I said nonchalantly, as if I were used to such offers. "Of course I'll go with you." And at the same time I thought, *Maybe I shouldn't ask him yet if I'll get paid.*

"Good, that's settled." He squinted up at the sky. "We'll go on for a way, and then we'll stop and eat something. Or are you hungry now?"

I was, but I wanted to start out before he changed his mind. So I told him I was fine and skipped off beside him, with a final silent thanks to the place god under his burning tree.

I soon discovered that, unlike all the other grown-ups I'd known, Master Lim seemed to enjoy talking to me. I'd told him, during his previous visit to Riversong, how I'd been found in the drifting boat, but I told him again because he seemed interested, and then I chattered about lots of other things. He listened carefully, nodding from time to time and making suitable noises of alarm or encouragement. I was quite out of breath by the time we stopped to eat.

By then it was early afternoon. We sat on a fallen tree by the roadside, and unwrapped my bread and smoked fish and his biscuits and some of his journey cheese, the kind that doesn't spoil even in hot weather. He'd been telling me about High Lake, but suddenly, just as we began to eat, he broke off and said, "Well, I've got another idea. What do you think of becoming a learned woman, Lale?"

I was so astonished I lost my tongue and could only stare down at the grass by the log, where some lucky ants struggled with a morsel of fallen fish. "What?" I said at last. "I can't even read."

He didn't reply. I heard a brief buzzing hiss and a soft *thunk*, and then Master Lim made a peculiar noise like *Uuuh*, as though he'd suddenly let all his breath out.

I looked up at him. Protruding from his left eye was a long slender stick with feathers on the end. Master Lim sat very still for a moment and then, as I watched in speechless shock, he toppled slowly backward into the grass. The arrow swayed a little as he hit the ground and then he just lay there, staring one-eyed at the clouds, with his legs draped clumsily across the log. There was hardly any blood, just a couple of tiny rivulets trickling across his temple and into his long brown hair.

I couldn't even scream. I put my hands to my face, and sat paralyzed as two men came out of the thicket on the other side of the road. One held a bow with an arrow nocked, the other a long curved knife. They were barefoot, ragged, and dirty and looked starved. The bowman's face was pocked by some old disease, and the man with the knife had a walleye that pointed outward, so that he seemed to be looking in two directions at once.

They approached almost timidly, as if Master Lim might yet leap to his feet, draw his sword, and fillet them like a pair of fish. In fact I couldn't believe he wouldn't. But I'd seen enough of death to know that he would never sing his way down a road again.

"Sit still, girlie," the walleyed man said. "Don't go running off now, till we see what you've got in that bag. If you try to scoot, I'll put an arrow in your back, understand? Is he dead?"

The bowman said, "Dead as old leather," and slung his bow over his filthy tunic.

I began to scream then, and wouldn't stop until the bowman hit me across the cheek. It wasn't a hard blow; I'd had harder from Detrim, but it stopped my shrieks and I began to sob with hopeless grief. I was too frightened to run away, and in any case my legs wouldn't have carried me.

They ignored me while they stripped poor Master Lim of all he'd owned. I couldn't look, but I heard them sounding pleased over the sword and arguing about how much the sivara would bring. Then they got around to me. They took my bag, the only gift Rana had ever given me, all my food, and even my walking stick. The walleyed man then grabbed my cloak and was going to rob me of that, too, but the bowman said, "Leave it, she's got little enough."

"What for? What do we care?" the other demanded. But he stopped.

The bowman looked at me and said, "I had a daughter near your age once. Wasn't your father, was he?"

"No," I croaked. I had no idea what they were going to do next. We Durdana didn't sell or buy human beings, but I knew other nations did. Maybe the men would take me far away to Abaris or the Yellow Smoke Islands and sell me there.

"Who was he?" the bowman asked. "Uncle? Something else?"

"My friend," I whimpered. "He was my friend. He could sing and play music and you killed him!" I was suddenly beside myself with fury, enraged at what they'd done, at the waste of it, and I screamed, "You killed him for nothing! Nothing!"

They looked away as if shamed. I didn't know it then, but they were probably farmers driven off their land by hunger and violence, as desperate as me and likely no more evil.

"He should have been more careful," the walleyed one said sullenly. "You can keep your cloak. Go on, run off now. We won't hurt you."

"You already have," I said wretchedly. "Let me keep his sivara for him, at least."

They stared at me as if I'd taken leave of my senses. Then, without another word, they turned and hurried into the forest the way they'd come.

After they were gone, I cried over Master Lim. When I ran out of tears I arranged his body with as much dignity as I could; at least the bowman had taken the arrow away, so I didn't need to attend to that. I had neither the tools nor the strength to bury him, and I had no fire to burn a lock of his hair for the ritual ashes. But I whispered some prayers and scattered some flowers over him, hoping their beauty would help his idu-spirit find rest in the Quiet World.

Mid-afternoon had come and gone by the time I finished. I now wanted to curl up near Master Lim and sleep for a long time, but I knew I had to go on. We had just begun to eat when the bandits came, so my belly was almost empty, and it would remain so till I reached Gladewater. Even then I'd have to work before somebody would feed me, so I had no time to lose. I left poor Master Lim behind, and tried not to think about how the carrion birds, which were already gathering overhead, would treat him once I was gone.

For a long time all I could think of was how close I'd come to a new life and how two stupid and worthless men had swept it all away. If I'd felt glum before I met Master Lim, I felt worse now, and was so wrapped in my misery that at first I didn't notice the faint sounds from ahead. When I did, I stopped short and listened. The road was so twisty that I couldn't see what was making the noise, but it sounded like people thumping the ground with heavy wooden mallets.

I wasn't going to be surprised again. I slipped off the road and hid in some tassel bushes, through whose slender leaves I could see without being seen. The noises got closer and louder till I felt the earth quivering under my bare knees. Suddenly, from around the next bend, came a throng of at least thirty men, wearing armor lacquered in hues of tan and slate blue. On their heads were spiked helmets, and they rode enormous brown animals whose tread made the ground shake, and I realized, with terrified delight, that these must be *horses*.

I knelt behind my bush, rigid with indecision. The men didn't look like bandits, and I was desperately hungry. Also I had nothing left to steal, at least nothing that people like these would want.

And then I saw, in the middle of the riders, two grown women and two girls. That made my choice for me. I scrambled from behind my bush and jumped into the road, almost under the hooves of the lead horse.

I didn't know about horses then, and bedlam followed. The animal whinnied with alarm and shied violently, almost pitching its rider from his saddle. The other mounts, taking fright from the first, reared and pranced and tried to run off into the bushes. Horrible curses seared the air as the riders struggled to control their mounts. Terrified of the flailing hooves and the bellowing men, I threw myself to the ground and wrapped my arms around my head.

The racket died away, replaced by the nervous stamping of the animals and the mutters and snarls of the men. I gingerly raised my head and saw a number of iron-tipped lances pointed at my face. The blades looked very sharp.

"What in the gods' name do you think you're playing at?" It was the lead rider, the one whose horse I'd frightened. He was a big man with sweeping russet mustaches and a strong, hard face. He'd have been about Detrim's age, but my Foster Father had never worn such gear as this. The hem of his armored tunic had gold edgings, his helmet spike was gold, and his sword hilt was set with bright jewels. I realized to my horror that I'd almost unhorsed the leader of this amazing band. He must be a very mighty lord to wear such riches, and I'd already made him mad at me.

I struggled to my knees and he saw I was a child. He lowered his lance, as did the others. I spotted some suppressed grins, and my hopes rose a little. They might give me something to eat after all.

"My lord," I quavered, "I'm sorry I frightened your horse, if that's what it is. I didn't mean to. I didn't know it was so easy to scare them." I had noticed vaguely that he spoke not quite as I did. I didn't realize then that I was hearing the accents of the north.

A couple of the grins widened. In the corner of my eye I saw the women watching me. One was a small round lady of bland appearance and early middle age, wearing a brown traveling duster and a broad-brimmed leather hat to keep off the rain; the second woman was young enough to be her daughter and very beautiful. The two girls, who were not much older than I, regarded me curiously, as if I were some exotic forest animal that had jumped out of the thickets for their entertainment.

And then I noticed that they were paler of face than the villagers who had surrounded me all my life. They didn't look quite like the people of Riversong. In fact, they looked like me.

I was so flabbergasted I couldn't say a word. The horses tossed their heads and waved their long silky tails and peered sideways at me. Several were short, sturdy-looking beasts that bore huge wicker panniers. Others, longer in the leg, were obviously spare mounts, since they carried no burdens. There must have been nearly fifty of the creatures.

The lord scowled down at me from his vast height and said, "Where's your village, girl? Are we nearly at the Wing?"

"N-no, you're not, great sir," I stammered. "It's almost two days farther on. I've been traveling and I'm hungry because some—"

"But is this the road to Riversong?"

Why would people like these want to travel to such a place? "Yes, great lord. I come from there."

He began to speak again, but the small lady said, "Ekrem," in a quiet voice, and he instantly fell silent. Then she edged her mount toward me, and as I saw how Ekrem moved from her path, I realized that it was not the gilded and armored warrior who led these people but this unremarkable woman with the round kindly face.

I was still on my knees. "Get up, girl," she said. I obeyed. It would have been hard not to; her voice, though soft, had a compelling power.

"What's your name?" she asked.

"Lale, honored lady."

"Family name?"

"I don't have one, honored lady. I'm a foundling. I have no ancestors."

Her green eyes narrowed slightly. "You have the look of a northerner."

"I might be, ma'am. I was washed up at Riversong in a boat. Nobody knows where I came from."

"Ah. Why are you so far from your village?"

"I left, honored lady. They wouldn't give me enough to eat. I'm going to High Lake to find something better."

"Are you, now?" she asked. And then she said, "Have you met a man on this road? He is a fabulator named Lim. You will have seen him in Riversong some months ago."

At this reminder of poor Master Lim, I burst into tears; I

couldn't help it. Then, through my sobs, I told her what had happened. She listened carefully and her round face became hard as I wept out my story.

When I sniffled into silence she said, "And your name is Lale, and you came to Riversong in a boat, and you have no family."

I nodded. Her eyes never left my face. I wanted to ask how she knew Master Lim, but it seemed impertinent when she and I hadn't been properly introduced. So, remembering a phrase I'd heard in one of Lim's songs, I ventured, "Honored lady, may I have the honor of knowing who it is who addresses me?"

Her mouth twitched at one corner. "Where did you hear that manner of speech?"

"From Master Lim, honored lady."

She said, "There's nothing wrong with your memory, is there?" And then she said, "Since you ask, I am Makina Seval, the Despotana of Tamurin."

A Despotana? Plunged utterly out of my depth, I could only goggle at her. She looked so little like a ruler. Where were the jewels, the scarlet and gold gossamin, the great carriage? Or the look of majesty and the regal bearing, for that matter? Aunt Adumar, if you'd washed her hair, would have resembled a Despotana more than this short, plump woman. And I'd never heard of a Despotate named Tamurin.

But she paid no attention to my discourteous stare and said, "Ekrem, have her ride with one of your men. We'll find Lim."

Before I knew what was happening, I found myself squashed between a soldier's armored chest and his high saddle front, and he was telling me in very strong terms not to grab for the reins even if I was falling off. An instant later the horses were thundering down the road with me clinging desperately to the pommel, and Ekrem out in front with his lance at the ready. I realized the two girls must be riding as hard as the men and I felt a stab of envy. I wanted to be able to ride like this, too.

I had never realized that horses could cover ground so fast. In a tenth of the time I'd needed to walk the distance, we were round-ing the curve where the log was. A cloud of snail kites and carrion hawks poured into the air and I felt sick, knowing whose flesh they'd been at.

We halted. Master Lim was still there, but I didn't look closely at what was left, because I wanted to remember him handsome and alive, and not dead and horrible. My soldier dumped me onto the ground and I sat by the roadside while Ekrem went to inspect the remains. I heard the Despotana say, "Nothing?" and Ekrem answer, "No, my lady, they took his last stitch."

He cut a lock of Master Lim's hair for the ritual ashes and set some of his men to digging a grave. Nobody paid much attention to me, but they didn't tell me to go away either, so I stayed put. Then other soldiers began unloading the pack horses and I realized they were setting up camp. The sun was now well into the west, rain clouds were gathering again, and I wondered if the Despotana might be gracious enough to give me shelter as well as a meal.

The soldiers were very quick and practiced. In short order the horses were tethered in neat lines, the roadside had sprouted tents, cooking fires were alight, small iron cauldrons had appeared on tripods over the flames, and I smelled herbs simmering. My mouth watered. Surely they wouldn't begrudge me a little something, if only for telling them what had happened to Master Lim?

I'd already noticed that the two girls had been watching me. Finally they came over to where I was sitting. I didn't know how to act toward aristocrats of my own age—or of any age for that matter—and, besides, I was tired. So I didn't act particularly respectful but simply nodded and said, "Hello."

They were dressed in traveling clothes much like the Despotana's, but wore no hats. One seemed about a year my senior, the other a bit older than that. Both had straight brown hair trimmed into sleek helmets, beside which my long tangled mane looked like a pile of underbrush.

"Hello," the older one said. The stockier of the two, she had a round face like the Despotana's. "I'm Sulen. This is Dilara."

Dilara was thin and sinewy, her eyes dark green on each side of an upturned snub nose. Her mouth was a touch too large for her chin, which was square and firm. She eyed me thoughtfully. I eyed her back.

"Are you running away from home?" she asked in a manner that suggested she knew all about such undertakings.

I nodded. Their accent was like Ekrem's. "Are you the Despotana's daughters?" I asked.

They looked at each other and laughed. "We're not her bloodline," Dilara said, "so we're not really her daughters. But she *calls* us her daughters, and we feel as if she's a mother to us."

Mystified, I stared from Dilara to Sulen and back. "I don't understand."

"We're her students," Dilara explained. "She has a school. It's for girls like us, and like you. You see, Sulen and I don't have any ancestors. We're orphans."

"You *are*?"

"Oh, yes," Dilara told me. "But in the school we have lots of sisters, because every one of us is an orphan, and none of us knows our bloodlines or our ancestors. But it doesn't matter, because we're our own family."

"And we learn all *sorts* of things," Sulen said. "When we get back to Tamurin I'm going to be studying *The Dream Pool Essays* and the *Analytical Dictionary* and *The Spring and Autumn Annals*!"

"Where's Tamurin?" I asked her. I wished wretchedly that I wasn't so ignorant, so that I could be in such a school.

"You mean you've never heard— All right, it's up north, by the sea. A long, long way from here. As far as the mouth of the Pearl River."

Even to me, this made no sense. "But why are you so far from home? Why are you going to Riversong? There's nothing there for anybody, let alone a Despotana."

"We don't actually know," Sulen admitted. "But it's been exciting. On the way here we stayed with three different Despots at their palaces. She brought us with her—and Tossi, too—because she said it would further our education."

"Did you know Master Lim?" I asked.

"No," said Dilara. "We didn't even know he existed. But I guess we're going home, now that she's found out he's dead." She turned her gaze to the cooking fires, where the Despotana was speaking with Ekrem. "He must have been important for her to come all this way to look for him. She's never done something like that."

"Maybe she was just tired of staying home." Sulen leaned toward me and lowered her voice confidentially. "You see, Mother's a widow. Once she lived in Kurjain. She had a son there but he—"

"Shut up, Sulen," Dilara interrupted. "Nobody wants to hear about that. Look, here's Sertaj."

The soldier came up to me and said, "Girl, you must speak with the Despotana now. When you come to her, show respect. You may call her either 'honored mistress' or 'honored lady' or 'ma'am.' "

Sulen, Dilara, and I followed him to the largest tent, which was of a fine, close-woven fabric dyed deep crimson. The Despotana sat in front of it on a small collapsible stool. The beautiful young woman, who must be Tossi, sat cross-legged on a cushion next to her. The sun, low in the west, sent copper bars of light through the trees.

I bowed to the Despotana, touching the fingertips of both hands to my throat. Then I stood quietly, kept my gaze on the ground, and waited for her to speak.

After what seemed a long silence she said to me, "The men who killed Master Lim will be found. Not soon, perhaps, but I will find them."

"I'm glad, honored mistress."

She tilted her head a little to one side. "Do you want to go back to Riversong, Lale?"

"No, honored mistress." I looked up at her, hoping for the best.

"Hm. You're not a stupid girl, are you?"

"I'm not sure, ma'am. I don't think so."

"Do you know how to read?"

I shook my head, wishing with all my heart that I did.

She said, "I have a school for girls like you, Lale. For girls who have no ancestors. Do you know what I say to such girls?"

A small crack opened in the darkness of my heart and admitted a tiny ray of light. "No, honored mistress," I whispered, "I'm afraid I don't."

"I say to them, 'You shouldn't worry that you have no ancestors, because you *are* an ancestor.' Do you like the sound of that?"

The crack widened and more light poured through. "Very much, honored mistress."

"For now, please dispense with 'honored mistress' and such. It wastes time. Do you want to learn to read?"

Not even in my most bizarre fantasies had I ever imagined I might possess that secret. "Yes. Oh, yes!"

"Then you may come to my school, Lale, if you wish. Your belly will never be empty under my roof; and as for your mind, it also will have as much as it can hold. You will know as much as a learned magistrate of Kurjain, if you can contrive it. Would you like that?"

The darkness in me was burnt up in a flame of rapture. I managed to squeak, "Yes!"

"You'll travel with us, then," she said. "This is Tossi, my first and best student. If she tells you to do something, you will do it. And these are Dilara and Sulen, who I see have already introduced themselves. They're girls at my school, just as you will be. They can't give you orders, but pay attention to what they tell you. Go with them now and eat your supper. Then we must all sleep, for we're heading for Tamurin in the morning."

Sulen and Dilara grinned at me. They had no ancestors, no more than did I, but somehow it didn't matter. I was in the middle of a forest, among strangers I had known for less than half a day, and for the very first time in my life, I was home.

But what I did not know was that our meeting, which looked

so much like chance, was not chance at all. Many years would pass before I discovered what lay behind that encounter on the Riversong road: that the Despotana had been searching for me, without pause and in perfect secrecy, from the time I was six years old.

Five

꩜

(M)y education began the next morning, as we set out for Tamurin. I felt very grown-up in the clothes Dilara had lent me, for this was the first time I'd discarded a child's smock for adult garments. I had a tunic of pale linen with blue dragonflies around the hem and a garment I'd never seen before—the loose, calf-length divided skirt that Durdana women wore for riding. There were blue dragonflies on the skirt, too, and I had a straw hat and a duster to keep off rain and mud. I didn't want anything on my feet, but Sertaj said I had to wear boots with a heel, to keep from being dragged if I fell off my horse, and Sulen lent me a spare pair that luckily fit well enough.

The first thing I learned was that horses were not boats. I'd imagined that guiding the animal would be much like steering a boat, and I'd overlooked the fact that the creatures had minds of their own. I was given the least skittish of the spare riding mounts, but the chestnut mare did not take to me, nor I to her. Despite the coaching I got from Dilara, the wretched creature insisted on barging off the road to nibble leaves, and I nearly fell off a dozen times in my efforts to dissuade her. So, about mid-morning, I was consigned to the back of a placid and unadventurous packhorse. My humiliation and chagrin left me almost speechless for a while, but Dilara and Sulen didn't snicker as I'd feared they would; instead, they rode alongside me and told me I just needed more practice.

Rain came and went as we trotted along, but my duster and hat kept me marvelously dry and warm. Dilara, Sulen, and I formed our own little group, while the Despotana and Tossi rode some yards ahead; around us the soldiers formed an armored, moving wall. About midday we reached Gladewater, and as I gazed around the place, I realized that it was nearly as poor as Riversong. If I'd had to make my living there, I would have starved.

But now I was on my way to High Lake, and Dilara said we would reach the town by nightfall. I could hardly wait to see it, although Sulen sniffed and said that High Lake was a run-down place and not nearly as big as the city of Chiran, where the Despotana's school was. That turned our talk to the school, and soon I was getting very uneasy—how could anyone be expected to learn so *much*? But Dilara and Sulen seemed to manage tolerably well, as far as I could tell, and I decided I'd probably do no worse.

The forest thinned as we traveled, and the road became a little broader, with occasional remains of pavement jutting through the turf. After a while I asked hopefully, "What happens after you learn all you're supposed to learn? Does the Despotana find you a rich man so you can get married?"

"I'm not sure," Dilara said. "Tossi is the oldest of us, and she's not getting married. I don't think so, anyway. She told me that Mother Midnight says we shouldn't bother about— Oh!"

Sulen had twisted around in her saddle and was making shush-shush gestures, but she was grinning. Dilara giggled, and I said, "What's the matter? Who's Mother Mid—"

I shut up as I realized she meant the Despotana. Then, lowering my voice, I asked, "Why did you call her that?"

"We all do," Dilara told me. "But we don't say it if she can hear. Usually we call her Mother, or if we're speaking with her, we call her ma'am. Her Midnight name—it's kind of a joke. It's because of the story."

"What story?"

"It's in *The Book of the Pearl Garden Mistress*. Don't you know it?"

"No." I'd never even seen a book, but I was determined not to admit it. "I can't read, remember?"

"Then I'll tell it to you tonight before we go to sleep. All right?"

"All right."

"You'll learn to read just fine, too. I'll help you."

I felt better for her promise. I was already coming to like Dilara a great deal, with her pert grin and her nimbleness and her quick, nervous gestures. And I sensed that she liked me as well. For the first time in my life, I seemed to be making a real friend.

We rode on through the rain-washed day, with only a brief rest in the late afternoon. Well before then I was saddle sore and too tired to talk much. Dilara's and Sulen's chatter also diminished, and eventually they both looked as weary as I felt. But neither grumbled about being tired, so I didn't complain either—though back in Riversong I'd never kept quiet when I was uncomfortable, even if piping up earned me a cuff on the ear.

The ground rose slowly as we approached High Lake, the lowland forest giving way to scrub meadow with scattered stands of bead trees, gums, loquats, and wait-a-bit thorn. The loquats were in fruit, and when the sun looked out from behind the rain clouds, the clusters of small bronze globes shone like metal. More people lived in this region than around Riversong, and during the afternoon we passed through two farming villages. One was as miserable as Gladewater; the other was abandoned, its roofs falling in and its gardens choked by weeds. But every so often we saw big fortified manors, with tilled fields all around them, and scores of men, women, and children stooping among the furrows with their hoes. I asked what the manors were. Sulen said they were the homes of wealthy landowners, and that the people in the fields were the tenant laborers who worked the fields for them.

Not all these workers were of my race; some were Erallu, the people that had inhabited these lands before we Durdana came. I could tell, because they were small of stature, with bronze skin and long blue-black hair adorned with copper rings. The priestess of the Bee Goddess in Riversong had been an Erallu, but she was the only one I'd known. Clearly they were more common here.

We reached High Lake as the first fireflies began to sparkle in the dusk. The town didn't have a wall, which disappointed me because I'd wanted to see one. Sertaj told me this was because the place was only half a day's march from the fortress garrison at Shiragan, the capital of Indar's Despot, and so was reasonably well protected. To discourage malefactors, a gibbet stood on the edge of the town, a pair of corpses dangling from the crosspiece.

The town's civic boundary was marked by a ceremonial gate that consisted of two tall posts and a curved lintel. The vermilion paint on the lintel had almost all worn away, and its exposed wood was silvery with age. By one upright was a place god shrine, with a lichen-stained tile roof and a gnarled wooden image in the central niche. I thought of the shrine by the flame magnolia, and of Master Lim, and I was ashamed at how quickly I'd stopped thinking about him. So I whispered a prayer to Our Lady of Mercy, to ask that Master Lim might be happy in the Quiet World and that he might be allowed a new sivara, or whatever instrument a fabulator's spirit used.

Then I saw how the town got its name. We rode past some acacia trees and suddenly there was Myriad Mirror Lake, a great plain of water that glittered indigo and copper in the setting sun. Fishing boats scudded across it, sails white against the wooded green hills rising from the far shore. The breeze blowing off the waves smelled of cool water and citrus.

Sulen, who had a tutorial streak in her nature, now decided

that she must pass on to me what she'd learned about High Lake. She told me that before the invasion of the Exiles, which brought about the Partition and the end of the old Durdanian Empire, the place was a famous resort town. Wealthy families of the empire's southwestern prefectures used to come to these forested hills to escape the hot season, and the richest of them built villas of spectacular magnificence along the wooded shore. But after the Partition, the southern part of the empire broke up into the Despotates, and many rich families became poor or died out. Eventually their mansions fell into ruin, just as the Stock House in Riversong had done. But a few of the town's palatial inns remained, among them the one where we were to stay tonight.

An inn! I'd never imagined I'd sleep in one. I desperately wanted to ask Dilara what it was like, but I'd already displayed enough ignorance for one day.

As we continued along the esplanade, Sulen went on with her lecture, pointing out the remains of the famous parks and floral displays of the town, now forlorn with neglect. We passed shrines to Father Heaven and his consort, the Bee Goddess, and one to the Lord of Starlight. Although they had graceful domes and spacious sanctuaries with columned porches, they looked worn and old, and the two priests I saw wore shabby robes.

Beyond the gardens were the buildings of the town itself. Its streets were busy even at sunset, mostly with Durdana but with a few Erallu among them. Petty merchants called their wares from beneath the awnings of their stalls; people haggled for fresh fish, loquats, plums, and rounds of bread sold cheap at the end of the day. A barber shaved a man in a porch; a public scribe, pen in hand, huddled with a worried-looking young woman over a sheet of paper. Lanterns like yellow moons glimmered at the street corners and over the stalls, their light wan in the early dusk.

At length we reached High Lake's main square. The buildings around it were two stories high and sided with overlapping boards, their windows covered by patterned latticework. All had verandas and balconies with elaborately carved and painted balustrades. Above the buildings' ornate eaves the roofs varied in design. Some were low pitched and drably shingled, while others rose with a curving sweep like a hawk's wing and were covered with red and blue tiles.

At first I thought the square magnificent, but very quickly I realized that its wonders were less than they appeared. Most of the square's paving remained, but in the side streets many flagstones were missing. The alleys between the buildings were thick with refuse and smelled worse than the middens of Riversong. Many of the carvings on those elaborate balconies were broken, and their paint had mostly worn away. Shingles and roof tiles showed gaps, and I realized that many of the buildings, even those in the center of the town, were falling into ruin.

But I was used to tumbledown places, so the shabbiness didn't take me aback. What did surprise me was the effect our cavalcade had on the townsfolk. The Kayanese soldiers had terrified me during the raid on Riversong, but this was my first experience of the fear that commoners everywhere in the Despotates had of armed men, even those who were behaving themselves. Many people vanished as soon as they saw us, scuttling away down fetid alleys or sidling through the nearest doorway. A few bolder ones stayed on the verandas and watched us sidelong as we passed, our horses' hoofs clattering and the lance pennons waving above the troopers' helmets. Most merchants hurried to close their stall shutters at our approach, although some of more courage called out, "Noble lord, noble lady, fine cloth, fine silver, fine wares" as we went by. But nobody got too close to the horses, and our soldiers were clearly ready to use their lance butts on anyone who did.

We left the square and rode farther along the esplanade. Eventually we came to a big wooden building of two stories, secluded within a stone-walled compound on the lakeshore, and unlike the town it still possessed a faded magnificence. A tall sign by the compound gate had writing on it, which Dilara said announced the inn's name: the House of Lofty Grasses.

The gate stood open. Ekrem led our party into a large courtyard with stables left and right. A man was lighting a cluster of lanterns that hung on a pole in its center. Attendants appeared, and a huge-ruffed watchdog with an iron collar barked angrily from its cage. Then an elderly woman came out of the inn and bowed repeatedly to the Despotana, and before I could blink I was inside the inn, up a flight of stairs, and in a dim corridor paneled in dark wood. A door opened and closed and I found myself with Dilara and Sulen in a high-ceilinged room of—to me—stunning opulence. Lamps in wall sconces burned with clear yellow flames. The walls were smooth plaster painted in alternating panels of cream and red, and on the polished floor were thick mats and a pair of sleeping couches, each a size for two people, with coverlets of a fine green fabric. Next to each couch stood a low table with washbowls, ewers, towels, and a basket of ripe citrines. A tall, latticed window looked toward the lake, fading now into darkness.

I must have gaped at my surroundings, for Sulen said, "Oh, Lale, this place isn't all *that* wonderful. Wait till you see the Despot's palace in Shiragan. We stayed there on our way south." She giggled. "He liked looking at Tossi, so I bet he'll want us to stay there again. I think he wanted to keep her."

"Why didn't he?" I asked. "A Despot can do anything he wants, can't he?"

They both laughed, though not nastily. "Don't be silly," Dilara said. "Of course he can't. We've got safe passage from him and the other two Despots between here and Tamurin. Molesting any of us would ruin his honor."

"Oh," I mumbled. Until now I hadn't wondered how the Despotana could be traveling so freely through another ruler's domains. If Kayan's Despot put his nose into Indar, for example, our Despot would slice it off at the neck.

"Look," Sulen said, and I recognized the tutor's tone, "it's like this. Tamurin isn't at war with anybody. Mother doesn't bother

other Despots and they don't bother her, even though Tamurin is a rich place."

"Why don't they?" I asked, lowering myself gingerly to one of the couches. I was very saddlesore and extremely hungry.

"Because Tamurin's got a lot of mountains and our pikemen are very fierce and they all love the Despotana. A general from Brind tried to conquer Tamurin back in the old days, just after the Partition, and he lost his whole army. Also, the other Despots hope that if they're nice to Mother she'll help them if they're attacked by another ruler, for example, or if there's a rebellion."

"Does she do that?" I asked. Dilara had lost interest in the conversation and was washing her face.

"Not so far. But she might. Also, each of them hopes she might marry him, so he'd get Tamurin along with her."

"*Is* she going to marry anybody?" I asked in dismay. I didn't like the idea of some man telling the Despotana what to do, and maybe having a say in my education.

"Not very likely," Sulen answered, with a snort of disdain. "I don't think she likes men very much. Don't you know what happened to her?"

"No. What was it?"

"Don't get started on that," Dilara said as she dried her face on a towel. "You sound like our history tutoress. Can't it wait till after supper?"

Sulen ignored her. "Mother's bloodline name is Seval, but she was married into the Danjian family and had a baby son. Her husband's father was Sun Lord of Bethiya, so she was of very high rank indeed."

"Bethiya?" I said, trying to imagine how she'd ended up being the Despotana of Tamurin, and failing.

"Yes," Sulen went on. "Her husband was to be Sun Lord, you see, after his father died, but his enemies assassinated him. So the old Sun Lord named Mother's little boy as his successor."

This was my first introduction to the complicated dynastic affairs of Bethiya's rulers. I listened patiently.

"They lived in Kurjain," Sulen went on, "where the Danjian bloodline had been feuding for years with the Tanyeli, the other great bloodline of Bethiya. That was because the Tanyeli thought they had the better claim to rule, and there were a lot of assassinations on both sides. Then, soon after Mother's husband was murdered, the two clans started fighting in earnest. They ended up almost exterminating each other and the old Sun Lord was killed. Mother's little boy was murdered, too, during the fighting, but she survived because she wasn't in Kurjain when it happened."

"Oh," I said. "What happened to her then?"

"She went to Tamurin, for her safety, and married its Despot. Then he died of a fever and she became Despotana. Then she started her school. That was seven years ago. Tossi was her first student. There are thirty-nine of us now."

"So who became the Sun Lord? There *is* one, isn't there?" I had visions of a vast empty palace with no one at home.

"Yes, of course there's one." Abruptly Sulen seemed angry. "He's sixteen years old now. But he's a usurper, and anyway, he doesn't really rule Bethiya. The Chancellor does. The Chancellor's a very wicked man, you know. He pretends to justice, Mother says, but he's really a cauldron of vipers. He could have kept her baby from being killed but he didn't. In fact, he made sure the Danjian and the Tanyeli would wipe each other out, so he could put the usurper onto the dais and then have his own way in everything. Mother hates him. We all hate him, don't we, Dilara?"

"Yes," Dilara said. "Now, can we *please* find out when we're going to eat?"

We women didn't dine in the inn's common room with the soldiers and other guests but instead were taken to a private chamber with paintings of herons and wild geese on the walls. It was a quiet meal, not because the Despotana forbade conversation but because we were all weary. I watched Tossi so I'd know how to eat in an approved manner, and remembered not to spit bones and pits onto the floor. One thing I found strange was the food spear, an instrument I'd never seen. It looked like a tiny fish trident. You used it to convey morsels to your mouth, which I decided was a very good idea, as it kept one's fingers from becoming greasy.

When we'd finished eating, the Despotana sent the others from the room but told me to stay. I sat quietly, gazing down at my dish. It had a blue rim and a white center with yellow grasses painted on it.

"Lale," she said, and I looked up at her. I saw again that the Despotana was a very ordinary-looking woman, no longer young, not yet old. There were lines at the corners of her small mouth, she had tiny wrinkles at the corners of her eyes, and there was a tracery of gray in her hair. She could have been any of the stall vendors in the streets of High Lake. But, oh, her wonderful voice. It was rich and smooth as the honey of the Bee Goddess. When she spoke, I could do nothing but listen.

"I've been watching you," she said as she studied me. "Did you know that?"

I did. I'd been aware of it all day. But my years with Detrim's family had taught me never to be open about what was in my mind, so I hesitated, unwilling to admit that I knew how close her scrutiny had been.

"Lale," she said, seeing my hesitation, "now that you have been accepted into my school, you are my daughter. I will forgive my daughters all transgressions except two. One of these is lying to me."

I'd been about to do exactly that, and I shuddered inwardly at my narrow escape. I said, "I knew you were watching me, Despotana."

She tilted her head a little and pressed two fingertips to her mouth. I later learned that the mannerism meant she was thinking.

"That was perceptive of you," she said at last. "I'm pleased."

I felt a warm flush of gratification. She was happy with me, and more than that, she had told me I was her daughter. No one had ever told me that.

"However," she went on, "I am now going to give you your first lesson in deportment. Do you know the precept in the *Noon and Midnight Manual* that says, 'A closed mouth catches no flies?' "

I'd heard the saying, but didn't know somebody had written it down. "Yes, Despotana."

"I have noticed that you're a chatterbox, Lale, but I know why this is the case. Do you?"

"No, ma'am."

"It is this. All your life you have talked as fast as you could, to keep people from detecting your private thoughts. In the *Compendium of Important Military Techniques*, this is called the strategy of distraction."

I opened my mouth and closed it again. I'd never thought about why I talked so much. But what she said made sense.

"The technique is admirable," she went on, "but it fails in the face of a clever enemy who refuses to be distracted. Also, it grates upon the ear. So, beginning tomorrow, Lale, I want you to speak less and listen more. I already know you're quick-witted and re-sourceful. You don't have to prattle on, as you did today, to convince me of this."

"Yes, ma'am," I said humbly. I felt shamed at my behavior yet deeply relieved that she still thought I was worthy of her school.

"Do you have any questions about this?" she asked.

One sprang to mind. "Well . . . please, ma'am, what's the other thing you won't forgive? I don't want to do it by accident."

She gave me one of her rare smiles. "I doubt you could commit that fault at your age, but I'll tell you nonetheless. The second thing, Lale, is disloyalty."

"Oh," I said.

"The *Golden Discourses of the Five Elder Sages* tell us that dis-loyalty is among the worst of the Eight Iniquities. Disloyalty overthrows the natural order and causes all things to descend into confusion. Therefore it is to be avoided at all costs."

"I won't be disloyal," I told her stoutly, "ever."

"I'm sure of this, Lale. But let me tell you why loyalty is so important for my daughters. It is because they don't know their bloodlines; and so they have only me, each other, and the school. For this reason you must always be loyal to the other girls, who are your sisters, and to the school itself, which is your home, and to me, since I have become the mother of you all. Nothing is more important than that loyalty. It gives you a family, Lale, and to be disloyal is to break that family apart. A girl who is disloyal not only has ruined herself but has also turned on the only family she will ever have." She paused and then added softly, "It has never happened, but such a girl would be sent away. She would never see her sisters or me or Tamurin again. She would be as alone as she was before she came to me."

I felt such fright at this prospect that I could hardly speak. Eventually I managed to whisper, "I'll never betray you, Despotana."

"Of course you won't," she said cheerfully. "I only want you to know the rules. Give me your loyalty, daughter, and you give me everything. Do you understand?"

"Yes, ma'am."

"Now it is time you went to bed. We'll be riding again at dawn."

I glanced at the single honey cake remaining on the serving board in the table's center. She saw me and said, "Take it with you, if you like. Dilara has a taste for them."

"Thank you, ma'am," I answered. I took the cake, said good night to her, and slipped away to the bedroom, where Dilara and Sulen pounced on me.

"What did she want? What did you talk about?" they both demanded at once.

I left out the part about being a chatterbox and said she'd told me about loyalty to the school. Dilara chewed the honey cake and nodded, a fierce look in her eyes. "Mother's right," she said. "Nothing's more important than that. A girl who betrays the others throws away everything. Being sent away is too good for her."

On this note we put out all the lamps, except the one on the low table next to Dilara's side of the bed, shucked our clothes down to our breechclouts, and slid under the coverlets. Sulen took one sleeping couch and Dilara and I ended up in the other one, which was just how I wanted it.

Sulen was one of those people who can fall asleep instantly, and did so. But Dilara and I whispered and giggled for a while, despite our fatigue, and at length I said, "You were going to tell me why you called the Despotana Mother Midnight."

"Oh, that," murmured Dilara. "All right, here's the story, the way it is in the book. Be quiet and don't interrupt."

I snuggled down beside her and listened. The story was about a girl named Aysel, whose parents ruled a great and rich kingdom. She was stolen away at birth by an evil sorcerer, and he put her with a family that treated her most shamefully. Then there was a golden fish in the story, a fish that could talk, and a long journey with many hardships, and at the end of the journey Aysel came to the house of Mother Midnight in a deep forest on the highest mountain of the world.

"Why was she called Mother Midnight?" I asked drowsily.

"Because she stood at the place where today and tomorrow meet, and looked both ways, and knew everything. Don't interrupt."

She went on to tell how Mother Midnight told Aysel who her family was, and Aysel returned to the kingdom and revealed herself, to her parents' great joy, and the evil sorcerer was found and put to death.

"And afterward they all lived as they wished," Dilara finished, "for as long as they wished it. And that is the end of the story."

I pondered. "So you call the Despotana 'Mother Midnight' because . . ."

"Because she gives us a family, just as the Mother Midnight in the story did for Aysel. And also because she knows everything—

she's very learned, just as learned as any scholar. And someday she'll help us defeat a truly evil sorcerer, the Chancellor in Bethiya."

"I wonder who *my* evil sorcerer was?" I mumbled, my mouth under the coverlet.

But Dilara didn't answer. She was very, very slowly easing herself up on one elbow.

"What are you—"

"Shh," she breathed, and I fell silent. I carefully lifted my head and peeked over her shoulder.

A furry brown basket vole was sneaking along the floor next to the wall, nose twitching. It was interested in our boots, to chew the leather. It was about the length of my hand, not including a short fuzzy tail. They were vermin, but pretty ones, with their soft pelts and black-ringed eyes; some children in Riversong had kept them as pets.

Dilara's hand crept out and took a citrine from the fruit bowl. The vole crept on, sniffing. It began to gnaw the sole of my boot and I heard the scrub of chisel teeth on leather.

Dilara's arm moved like a whip. The citrine shot across the room, slammed the vole against the wall, and bounced away. The little creature, stunned, lay on its side with its flanks heaving.

Dilara was out of bed in a flash. She picked the vole up by the neck, so it couldn't turn and bite her, but it was too dazed to defend itself.

"Put it out the window," I said. I was rather awed; I was a good shot with a stone, but Dilara was either very lucky or a lot better than I was. In the other bed, Sulen seemed to be coming awake, but then she snorted, rolled over, and fell silent.

"It will only come back if I let it go," said Dilara. She took the vole's throat between her fingers, and, with a single twist, neatly snapped its neck. "There," she said, in a matter-of-fact voice. "Now it won't bother us again." She crossed to the window and dropped the small corpse through the lattice.

Then, yawning, she came back to the bed and slid under the

coverlet. "I'm tired," she said, "and we'll be leaving at dawn. We'd better go to sleep now, Lale."

"All right," I answered, and closed my eyes. Almost immediately, Dilara's breathing deepened as she fell into a sound sleep. I spent a few moments feeling sorry for the vole, and then I followed her.

Six

❧

Tamurin! In my memory, my first sight of Mother's realm has
never faded. I need only close my eyes to see again, on the far side
of a broad valley, the mountain ramparts of the Despotate soaring
toward the clouds. I could hardly wait to reach them, for I felt that
my new life would not truly begin until I was safe within their
rugged embrace.

Over the thirty-odd days of our journey I had become good
friends with Dilara and Sulen, and we chattered incessantly as we
rode. Our relationship with Tossi was different, and not merely because she was several years our elder. She was not unfriendly, but
she maintained a cool reserve with everyone except Mother and
rarely spoke to us—or to anyone, for that matter. Dilara said she'd
always been like that, because of something horrible that had happened to her before she came to Mother's school. I asked Dilara
what it was, but she didn't know; and I certainly wasn't about to
ask Tossi.

I also got acquainted with Sertaj. He was the junior man of the
escort, though he seemed very grown-up to me, with his armor

and weapons and his muscle-corded arms and sweeping mustache. He was the fourth son of a landowning family in a village near Tamurin's capital of Chiran, and his skill with horses and archery had secured him a place in the Despotana's personal escort. This escort was called the Green Heron Guard, because of the insignia that appeared on its battle standard. It was a hundred and twenty men strong, but when the Despotana set out for the south, she had taken only its best thirty troopers, a sign of her friendly relations with her neighboring Despots.

For a day and a half we rode across the valley, the mountains looming ever nearer. I was now a very long way from Riversong, for I had seen my native Indar fall far behind as we rode into the Despotate of Brind, and then left Brind behind for Guidarat. I'd seen thatched roofs change to shingle or tile, timbered houses and barns replace those of plastered mud brick, and bullocks and dray horses at work in the fields instead of marsh oxen. I had now eaten beef, carrots, leeks, and wheaten bread for the first time, and I now knew that the north had four seasons, rather than the three I was used to. I'd grown up with the south's rainy spring, dry summer, and the cool of its harvest; but here they didn't have harvest, but autumn and winter instead.

Northerners also wore more clothes than people in the south. Women put sleeved bodices over their tunics, and men wore not only loose trousers and shirts but also overtunics. In cooler weather they added long jackets or mantles and, on wet days, rain cloaks. Some better-off adults wore knee-length hose and shoes or boots instead of sandals.

Most people dressed simply, but at the courts of the Despots, and among the rich landed families and the big merchants, things were different. I knew about luxury now, for the Despots of Indar, Brind, and Guidarat had made us their guests, and wealthy people along the way had been eager to have a Despotana under their roofs for a night. Such people wore clothes of fine linen or shimmering gossamin, in hues of cobalt blue, crimson, yellow, silver, midnight black, and sunlit gold. Woven or dyed into the fabrics were intricate designs of flames, running water, clouds, bees, swallows, and long-finned fish. As for jewels, the price of any of the women's necklaces would have fed Riversong for a year.

But I was too young to realize who paid for this glittering sumptuousness. I did not think about the bent and aching backs of the Erallu and Durdana field hands, on whose labors our hosts grew rich but who had almost nothing for themselves. I did not wonder why the towns and cities through which we passed were so ramshackle and decayed, while the palaces of the Despots and their families glowed with opulence. Nor did I wonder why so many farming villages lay abandoned or sunk in poverty, though they lay within sight of the splendid manors of the local magnates. In short, I did not see how the riches of the land and the people were being sucked into those few greedy mouths, as a man would suck barley beer through a hollow reed and leave the jar empty of all but sodden husks.

Late one afternoon we came to the edge of Guidarat and the southern border of Tamurin. If I had been a moon stork, the bird that flies higher than any other, I could have seen the Despotate laid out before me, like a plump, beckoning finger that stretched two hundred miles northward into the sea. On the finger's eastern side was the Gulf of the Pearl, the great bay into which the Pearl River flowed after its thousand-mile journey from far inland. To the west lay the Great Green, the world's ocean, in whose waters rose the archipelagoes of Khalaka and the Yellow Smoke Islands, home of spices, pirates, and burning mountains.

The border was marked by the narrow but swift Banner River. A stone bridge once carried the road across it, but the arches had fallen long ago into the rushing torrent. Sertaj told me that the bridge had been broken on purpose, during the Era of the Warring Emperors, to help defend against an invading warlord from Guidarat. The banks of the Banner being so steep at that point, we had to go upstream a mile to reach a ford. I'd expected a welcoming party and was a little surprised that no one had come to the border to meet the Despotana. I didn't know then how much she preferred invisibility to display.

At the ford I finally put to Dilara the question that had been puzzling me for some time. In a low voice I asked, "Why isn't Mother afraid that somebody might rebel while she was away? It happens in the stories, you know, the wicked general betrays his lord and kills him at the homecoming banquet."

Dilara snorted. "Nobody would dare."

"Why not?"

"They just wouldn't, that's all. Everybody's loyal to her. The people and the soldiers and the merchants, everybody. You'll see when we get there."

"Oh," I said, and left it at that. Loyalty was still a new idea to me, but I found it comforting that such a thing could exist, having known so little of it in Riversong.

The air grew colder after we crossed the river, and colder still as we climbed toward Crossbone Pass, the mountain gateway to the settled part of Tamurin. No one was on the road but us, and the only people we saw were a few herdsmen pasturing their curly-horned sheep on the upland meadows. A peaceful place Tamurin might be, but they kept well away from us. The only other signs of humanity were occasional stone watchtowers, with signal beacons at their summits. But none of the beacons flared to life as we approached; the towers were abandoned and derelict.

We camped for the night at the top of the pass, which was a narrow cleft overshadowed by monstrous cliffs, and the next day began the descent. As the air warmed I found myself in a country of steep-sided green valleys, and through each valley ran a stream or small river, watering fields already lush with young wheat and millet. Little shrines to place gods were everywhere, and there were bigger shrines for the Beneficent Ones and the Lord of the Dead. I saw a really beautiful one to the Moon Lady that had silver crescents painted all over a dome of dark blue tiles.

In Tamurin also were the manors of big landowners, and people toiling in the fields around them. But there were no abandoned farms, and even the small villages looked prosperous. During the two days it took to reach Chiran, we passed through several such places, and to my surprise the inhabitants didn't make themselves scarce. Instead they came running out to cheer the Despotana, and often they threw flowers.

And so at last I came to the valley of Tamurin's capital, Chiran. The city stood about a mile from the sea, and rambled across three broad ridges that reached out, like spread fingers, from the valley's flank. From a distance it was a jumble of high-peaked roofs clad in red tiles and gray cypress shingles, but as we drew nearer I could make out carved wooden eaves, painted gable ends, and high verandas with columns colored red and blue. Scattered everywhere were striped awnings; a trio of wooden fire-watch towers, slender as pines, rose high above the roofs. And surrounding everything was a stout wall of russet brick, dotted with stone towers, zigzagging uphill and down like a great red serpent.

A river, the Plum, flowed seaward past the city, and there was a bustling port at the foot of Chiran's river walls, where the river emptied into an estuary. Thronging the water's fish-scale glitter were boats and ships: plump fishing lorchas, their nets hung to dry in the rigging; waterspoons with slatted sails outspread like ladies' fans; slender periangs resembling long-necked black geese, their boatmen balanced in the stern against the long sculling oars. There were also a few big freighters, the ones that sailors call "pelicans" because they carry so much cargo. These had several masts and high, pointed sterns, and they loomed over the smaller craft like marsh oxen over a flock of paddling ducks.

I was accustomed to riding into towns and cities by now, and considered myself an old hand at travel. Even so, my entry into Chiran was a confused swirl of scents and sounds and images, for word of the Despotana's return had leaped ahead of us, and as we rode through Ten Fragrances Gate the narrow streets had already filled with people. Most were Durdana but with a salting of Erallu and some races I'd never seen: one was black-haired like the Erallu, but much darker of skin and larger of frame, while another might have passed for Durdana except for the pale gold hair worn in an elaborate coif. A third was thin-lipped, flat-nosed, with russet skin; others, from their features or coloring, were of mixed blood.

But whatever the race or blend of races, everybody had seized the excuse to celebrate. Long multicolored banners waved jauntily above the crowds, noisemakers banged and clattered, thick sweet incense smoke wafted from temples and shrines, drums thumped and boomed, dogs barked, flutes shrilled, and people called blessings on the Despotana in the names of all the Beneficent Divinities.

Dilara called to me over the uproar, "See? They love us!" She was laughing with delight, and, as for me, I was ecstatic. They were cheering the Despotana, and since I was one of her daughters, I felt that the cheers were partly for me, too. I'd never been so happy in my life.

Chiran was a fortress city, and the Despotana's palace was a fortress within a fortress. It was named the Citadel of Serene Repose, but everybody just called it Repose. It stood atop the highest and broadest of the city's three ridges, and overlooked the port and the estuary of the Plum. We reached it only after a long ride, for the street wound back and forth as it ascended the ridge, and I kept looking down on roofs that had been above me earlier. The crowds thinned as we climbed, and the air, happily, got fresher. Chiran smelled no better than any of the other cities I'd been in, although it was in much better repair than most of them. Indeed, when we finally topped the ridge and I had my first sight of Repose itself, I saw that everything was fresh and bright, as if newly scrubbed, polished, and painted.

Because this was to be my home for the next several years, I took a good look around while we rode through Prefect's Square toward the gate. The square was paved with cobbles, and on three sides of it were large houses where the Despotana's ministers and senior magistrates lived. On the fourth side rose the fifty-foot walls of Repose, built of red brick and capped by white stone parapets. Tall, gilded flagstaffs stood in niches in the walls, and from their peaks flew heron banners that swirled and danced in the breeze from the sea. Above the walls was the uppermost story of a very large stone building with tall windows flanked by red shutters, most of which were flung open.

"That's where *she* lives," Dilara said, seeing the direction of my gaze. "High up in the palace, just like Mother Midnight in the story. The school's on the far side of the compound. You'll see when we get in."

We rode through the fortress gate. Here was the courtyard, the five stories of the palace rising on the right and a wall to the left that must, from the neighing of horses, have stables on its other side. In front of us was a lush, tree-shaded ornamental garden, with white graveled paths and pools of water like silver mirrors. Beyond this were several stuccoed buildings with steeply pitched roofs; each had large windows with fretwork lattices and red shutters. Behind them, at a good distance, rose the fortress's far wall.

"That's the school," Dilara said, pointing at the buildings in the garden. "Everybody's at lessons now, but you'll meet them when we eat dinner."

And so I came to the School of Serene Repose, where my life as a scholar, or so I thought, began.

My memories of the school are unfaded. Here is the fabric of Repose itself: the parapets overlooking the harbor, the rough, comforting touch of their white stone warmed by a summer sun. Here are the high-ceilinged schoolrooms, with their plaques bearing aphorisms from the *Golden Discourses* and poems from the *Book of the Sapphire Hall Master*. I can smell the fragrance of grilled fish in the refectory and see pale sunlight burnishing the oiled paper that sealed our dormitory windows against the winds of winter. Here are the spring mists hanging over the stables, ripe with the damp smell of horse dung, and here the courtyards and passages of Seaward Yard, where the fortress spilled down the north slope of the ridge in a maze of bakeries, baths, armories, and storage magazines.

Like any ancient stronghold, it had several ghosts, like the old

man who occasionally appeared in the laundry house and the little hound that trotted along the west battlements when dank autumn fogs billowed in from the sea. Only one specter was of the
frightening sort; she'd been the wife of an imperial magistrate who
unjustly executed her because he wanted to marry his mistress.
The poor lady haunted Beacon Tower and the wall adjacent and
often appeared on the anniversary of her death, when she was especially angry. There had been several priestly attempts to release
her from her torment, but she was a very stubborn ghost and nothing worked. I saw her once, from a distance, and it was not nearly
distance enough.

Repose was a big place, and months passed before I became
completely familiar with it. We girls didn't have full run of everything, of course. We could not go near the barracks where Ekrem's
men lived, nor down to the armories; also parts of Seaward Yard
(though not the baths or the laundry house) were off limits, as was
the palace building itself. We could go anywhere else, though, provided we didn't leave the circuit of the fortress walls.

But we didn't spend all our time within Repose. There were excursions to the country for riding lessons, and every second market
day a group of us went down to Plum Market next to the harbor,
where we inspected the merchandise for flaws or adulteration and
learned how to haggle if we hadn't learned it already. This was because our education had a very practical bent to it. By the time her
students were sixteen, Mother expected them to know how to run
a large household, from cleaning to brewing to cooking to weaving
and sewing, and along with that to know every trick that a cheating servant or tradesman might get up to. We had a Domestic Tutoress who made sure we learned these skills.

But all that came later, for the first two things I had to learn
were reading and writing. I was lucky in that I had a knack for
them, which was a profound relief. But then I must not give myself too much credit, for we Durdana have the simplest way of
reading and writing in the world. The people of Abaris, for example, have myriads of signs for ideas and sounds and whole words,

and a student there needs years to learn their proper use. But we have just thirty-two signs, each of which stands for a different sound, and by arranging these signs on paper, we preserve the sounds of our words for the ears of others. With this advantage I learned to read in less than a month, and from then on there was no stopping me.

All Mother's students were Durdana by race or close to it, just a handful having some Erallu blood. To teach us we had eleven tutors, nine of whom were women; these were well-educated ladies of good family who had come on hard times through widowhood, war, or other bad luck, and had found a home in Repose. Six were Tamurines, two came from Guidarat, and the ninth, to the awe of us girls, was from great Kurjain itself. She was the Tradition Tutoress and taught deportment and manners; she appeared to know the *Golden Hall* precepts and the *Noon and Midnight Manual* by heart, and she was very, very strict. Our Arts Tutoress was more fun, since she taught us the games that well-bred women played: Twelve Lines, Courts, Crossing the River, and the like. I was not very good at them, especially the classic Twelve Lines, which was very simple to learn and very difficult to master. As any scholar will tell you, it is the purest and most perfect of all games that are played with pieces on a board. Mother was extremely good at it; she loved games of all kinds and especially those that turned on strategy rather than on luck.

Our two male tutors made up the eleven. They were retired magistrates and taught us geography and mathematics, and were almost as severe as the Tradition Tutoress. The Mathematics Tutor also instructed us in reckoning by the calendar. I found working with dates to be tricky at first, since I wasn't good with numbers. In Riversong we never paid much attention to exactly what day it was, because we lived by the rhythm of our crops and of the solstices. But now I had to get used to the Sun Calendar and learn that a year had twelve months of thirty days apiece, and that each month was made up of six "hands" of five days each. And then there were the extra five days at the New Year that didn't belong to any month, but were for the Solstice Festival and therefore sacred. I'd always known about the festival, since people celebrated it everywhere, but the rest of the calendar had always been vague to me. And I'd never even thought about year dating, which we Durdana calculate from the founding of the city of Seyhan, long ago at the beginning of the Commonwealth. So I was somewhat surprised to find that I'd been living in a year with a number and hadn't known it.

But now I could record the date of a most important event. It was this: on the twenty-third day of Early Blossom, 1306, not quite two months after I came to Repose, I received my very own surname.

Detrim's family had a surname, but because I was a foundling I couldn't use it unless they adopted me—and they never did. But Mother was the Despotana, who had the power to bestow not only official titles and ranks but also actual names. The surname she had selected for her daughters was Navari, which in an archaic form of our tongue meant "wanderer." So I became Lale Navari, and was very pleased and proud about my new identity. To go along with it, Mother also fitted me out with an official birthday. She gave one to every girl who entered the School, according to the day and month we arrived at Repose. Mine was 10 Furrow, while Dilara's was in the fifth hand of the summer solstice month, 27 Hot Sky.

Thus equipped with a name, a birthday, a family, and a mother, not to mention being well fed and well clothed, I began the happiest time I'd ever known. Mine was a big family; when I arrived there were nearly forty students, and by the time I left there were still that many, plus another two score who had completed their training and moved on.

Of course it was not all harmony. With so many girls living cheek by jowl, there were furious rivalries and snarling fights and storms of tears. But each of us had arrived at Repose friendless, destitute, and starving, so nobody could claim ascendancy of rank over anyone else; in that way we were all equal. So beneath the

squabbling and childish insults a close bond persisted, strengthened by our shared surname and by the wretched pasts we'd all
endured. I had my share of quarrels, but they never amounted to
much, at least after I gave one girl a bloody nose for suggesting I
was stupid. I never even waited for her to finish her insult, I just
hit her three times as hard as I could, even though she overtopped
me by a hand span. After that, I got all the respect I wanted.

As for Dilara and I, our friendship deepened steadily, and by the
time Hot Sky rolled around, it had become a sturdy bond. We
were sisters in the school, of course, but it went beyond that. We
were so attuned that we might have sprung from the same womb,
and we never doubted that we would be friends as long as we
lived. Sulen was jealous, because she'd imagined herself to be Dilara's chief confidante, but Dilara and I made a circle of two that
excluded all others.

My status rose because of my friendship with her. This was because most of the girls, even the older ones, were a little afraid of
Dilara. She was very strong and very agile, and like the rest of us
had learned how to fight in a hard world. But no one else possessed her aura of dangerous efficiency, as if she were a blade that
could slice through any armor. I had seen this aspect of her in the
inn, when she snuffed out the life of the basket vole with such
matter-of-fact precision. But she was not fully aware of this men-
acing side of her nature, nor of the effect it had on people. Or at
least I don't think she was, though she had a secretive streak and
might have hidden such an awareness even from me.

Dilara's story, which I had learned by the time we reached Chiran, resembled that of many of the girls in the school. She was
fairly sure she'd been born in Dirun, a coastal city across the Gulf
of the Pearl, but her parents had either abandoned her or died. All
she knew was that she had no relatives. For the first nine years of
her life she had lived with a potter's family, kneading clay and carrying charcoal for the kiln. Then the oldest son began to abuse her,
so she stowed away on a Tamurin-bound ship and ended up on the
streets of Kalshel, where a magistrate took her up for thieving. He

saw in the waif a possible candidate for Repose, and sent her to
Chiran instead of placing her into penal servitude. Mother agreed
with him, and Dilara had been her student now for three years.

So that was the School where the river of my life had washed
me up, just as the Wing had washed me into Riversong: the
fortress-palace of Repose, crowded with soldiers, servants, officials,
teachers, and students.

And one other: Nilang.

We all knew Mother kept a sorceress. This was normal, since
Despots usually employed someone who, they hoped, could compel the powers of the Quiet World to act for their benefit. Most
such adepts were men, however, and Nilang was therefore unusual. The name Nilang wasn't foreign, though, so I assumed her
native one was something else. She'd entered Mother's service several years prior to my arrival at Repose, and came from the Country of Circular Paths, far across the waters of the Great Green.
Apparently she'd been on the run from her homeland, for reasons
that remained obscure, and her pursuers finally caught up with her
in Chiran. What happened next was equally obscure, but Mother
had ended up giving sanctuary to both Nilang and her handful of
followers, and turned the pursuers out of Tamurin. The followers
vanished a while later, but where they went or why, nobody
seemed to know.

We rarely talked about Nilang, however, and then only in un-
dertones. A real sorcerer is not like your neighborhood spirit summoner, who consults spirits on behalf of people afflicted with
illnesses, evil dreams, or possession by ghosts. Despite the name, a
summoner has only a suppliant's status in the Quiet World and
must humbly ask for help rather than command it. But a sorcerer
is different, for where a summoner must petition, a sorcerer can
compel—although exercising such compulsion can be a very per-
ilous undertaking indeed.

Consequently, while everybody gossips about a summoner's doings, there is little such prattle about sorcerers. Idle talk might invite their attention, and that is an interest that only a fool would

welcome. Not that most self-styled sorcerers were as dangerous as they made themselves out to be. Even the ones who served Despots were often no more than convincing charlatans, and equally often were merely people with a tiny occult ability who knew how to make it appear a huge one. But, as I was later to discover, Nilang was one of the very few whose talent was real, significant, and skillfully used.

I first met her in midsummer, about three months after my arrival at Repose. We had one half day in every hand that was free of schoolwork, and Dilara and I were in the courtyard between the classroom wing and the refectory. We were making a kite to fly from the fortress's ramparts, where a brisk wind always blew from the sea. I was busy with a glue pot when a young man in the green-and-silver livery of the palace staff appeared. He looked me up and down and asked if I were Lale.

"Why?" I asked, impudent as ever. "Who are you?"

"Feras the undermessenger," he said. "You have to come with me."

I showed him the glue pot. "See, I'm busy."

"The Despotana says you are to come," he told me with a frown. I instantly handed the pot to Dilara and followed him.

I had not yet been inside the palace, but that was where we were going. Its five stories of gray stone rose far above me, all its shutters and lattices thrown wide because of the heat. Above the roof the heron banners coiled lazily in the sea wind, and the gilding at the eaves gleamed as yellow as the sun. The courtyard smelled, as it always did in summer, of dust and warm stone and flowers.

We ascended the seven broad steps to the porch; the big lacquered doors to the interior stood open. I peered around, and as my eyes adjusted to the dimness I saw a long room with carved and padded benches arranged along its walls. Several doors led off the hall, and from its far end rose a staircase.

"We go up," Feras said, and led me toward the stairs.

"What does she want?" I asked, in a half whisper, because the palace was so silent.

"She didn't tell *me*," he said. "Save your breath—it's a long climb."

It was, because we went all the way to the top. Long straight corridors, paneled in dark wood below cream-colored plaster, opened off the stair landings, lit dimly by windows at their far ends. Beginning at the third floor, these had clear glass in their lattices. I marveled at this, for in those days even the thick, whorled windowpanes that you could barely see though were very expensive.

On the fifth floor the staircase ended, and we went along a corridor to a door painted with reeds and blue swallows. I could smell incense, and under it drifted the burnt-leaf scent of sweetcup smoke. I knew the latter smell because some of the Riversong villagers had used the drug.

Feras stopped at the door and tapped on it. A woman's voice, not Mother's, said, "Enter."

Feras gingerly lifted the latch and eased the door open. Then he grabbed me by the elbow and pushed me through the gap. The door thumped shut behind me.

I found myself in a light, airy room at a corner of the building. The walls were painted with the most wonderful landscapes, and in them were birds and animals such as I'd never imagined. A wooden chest stood under a window, and in the center of the room was a low table of blue and white marble. Four straw mats and some kneeling cushions were arranged on the floor around it.

But all this held my attention for only a heartbeat, for a woman was sitting by the table, cross-legged on one of the mats. She was as small as Mother and near Mother's age. At first glance she could have been an Erallu woman, except that her eyes were not narrow and black. Instead, they were big and round and of an intense sky blue, their color a startling contrast to the bronze of her skin. Nor did she wear Erallu hair rings; instead, her black hair was coiled high on her head and fixed there with silver combs. Her face was triangular, with a wide forehead, high cheekbones, and a pointed chin.

I bowed with the fingertips of my left hand at my throat, as the Tradition Tuteress had drummed into us. The woman on the mat fixed those enormous azure eyes on mine, and I felt a quiver of apprehension. She seemed to be seeing all the way to the back of my head.

"I'm Nilang," she said. "You're Lale."

"Yes, mistress," I squeaked. The sorceress's voice was high and brittle, not pleasant on the ear. Her words were accented, too, just at the edges. But even in my unease I was puzzled. If this was where a sorceress lived, where were her books, her bottles of weird substances, her arcane instruments? Even an everyday spirit summoner owned such things. I decided they must be in the wooden chest under the window.

"Sit," she instructed, pointing at the mat on the opposite side of the table. I edged across the polished floor and obeyed, covertly examining her clothes as I did so. Instead of the customary skirt and bodice she wore a loose, high-collared robe, in vibrant hues of orange and indigo, woven of the finest gossamin. Her small slender feet, peeping from beneath its hem, were bare, and her toenails were painted gold. I nervously wondered where Mother was, and hoped she'd put in an appearance.

Nilang stared at me and then reached across the table to touch my forehead with a warm fingertip. I flinched slightly and she withdrew her hand.

"Do you think I'll hurt you?"

"No, lady mistress." I lowered my gaze to the table, on which stood a blue porcelain jug and two matching cups, and beside these a bronze incense burner. A silver pipe sat on a wooden rest beside the burner; it had a long stem and a small bowl, and from the bowl wafted a tiny thread of smoke that carried the scent of sweetcup.

Nilang picked up the pipe and drew on it thoughtfully. Then she exhaled and replaced the pipe in its rest. The tendril of smoke wavered and vanished as the drug burned out.

"Are you afraid of me because I'm a sorceress?"

Unlike the villagers I'd seen smoking sweetcup, she didn't look as if her mind had gone somewhere else. She was very much *here*, and her blue gaze bored into me. Under that scrutiny, any thought of lying fled.

"Yes, lady mistress," I told her, from a dry mouth.

"You don't need to be afraid. You're under *her* protection. Therefore you're under mine. Do you understand?"

"Yes, lady mistress." I hated sounding like an imbecile who had only three words in her head, but what else was I to say?

"It's a hot day," she observed. "I want to talk to you, but first we must drink to keep off the heat. Here."

She poured for me from the blue jug. It contained fruit juice— citrine by the color and fragrance. I took the cup and waited politely while she poured her own. Then we both drank. The juice was cool and I was thirsty, and I finished it more quickly than the Tradition Tutoress would have liked. It was delicious, not just citrine but something else, a hint of peach perhaps. Nilang gave me more, and this time I sipped.

She began asking me questions. Not difficult ones, just about Riversong and my life there. When I told her how I'd left, she seemed amused and said, "I see that the Despotana hasn't misjudged you."

This was gratifying, although I was becoming terribly sleepy and was finding it hard to follow the conversation. My voice didn't seem as if it really belonged to me. Oddly, I wasn't troubled by this; in fact it seemed rather amusing, and I giggled, which I realized vaguely was very rude. But I was *so* sleepy. . . . I wondered if Nilang would mind me curling up and dozing for a while.

The wish somehow transformed itself into the deed, with me lying on my side on the mat, a cushion under my cheek. Nilang was still murmuring to me, but I didn't pay much attention to her, because I was so interested in what I was seeing. The room was still there, but the painted landscapes on its walls had become perfectly real, and I knew beyond a doubt that if I stood up and approached them, I would find myself among those mountains, clouds, and marvelous animals.

After a while, they became translucent and then diminished into swirls of blurry colors. Then, for some reason, it seemed a very good idea to think about the other me, the girl I'd always imagined as living in a rich household with a handsome, powerful father and a beautiful, wise mother. So I did, and the house and my parents were very clear and vivid, just as if I were really there. And as I wandered through the halls and cool shaded rooms, I was faintly aware that I was talking about what I was seeing, that Nilang was whispering questions and I was answering them. I wondered why she was doing this, but it didn't upset or annoy me, because I liked talking about this wonderful place I was in.

But little by little it faded as my drowsiness grew deeper, and little by little I drifted away from the vision, and as I did so I heard Mother's voice. But I couldn't understand what she was saying. I tried to speak to her and ask her what she wanted—and why she was with me and Nilang—but my tongue would not obey me. And then my eyes closed, or perhaps they were closed already, and I fell asleep.

When I woke, the light showed it was late afternoon. I was still in Nilang's room, but now I lay on a soft sleeping pallet with a gauzy coverlet over me. I was thirsty and I had a slight headache, but otherwise felt rested and refreshed.

I turned my head and there was Nilang, still cross-legged at the table, writing on a sheet of paper. She looked up as I moved and gazed at me attentively.

I suddenly realized that I had committed a dire breach of etiquette. "Mistress," I said around a sticky tongue, "forgive me. I didn't mean to fall asleep, I—"

Nilang held up a small hand. "Too much sun," she said. "It can take one without warning. The best thing is to drink water and rest. Here."

She took the goblet that stood by her elbow and gave it to me. I drank the contents quickly, being much too parched to sip in a ladylike manner. As I handed it back, memory flickered.

"Yes?" Nilang asked. "What is it you're thinking?"

"I was dreaming," I said slowly. "About a house and . . ." I stopped. I had never shared my imaginary life with anyone, not even Dilara.

"They were very clear dreams?"

"I think so." Now I remembered that Nilang had been whispering to me. Or had I dreamed that as well? And had Mother been with her? "Were you and the Despotana . . ." I ventured.

"Yes?"

I suddenly lost interest in the subject. It wasn't that I was reluctant to think about what had happened, I just couldn't be bothered. It wasn't important enough to think about. What was important was to go back to Dilara and get on with the kite, so we could finish it before dark.

"Nothing," I said. "Please excuse my discourtesy, mistress."

"Too much sun often causes vivid and unsettling dreams," she told me. "If you experience them again, ask to see me. Are you feeling well enough to go back to the school?"

"Yes, lady mistress."

"Come with me," she said, getting to her feet, "and I'll take you down."

She left me at the palace's main door, and I made my way back to the courtyard. It was empty now, except for Dilara and Sulen. To my annoyance and disappointment, Dilara had almost finished the kite, and Sulen was helping her attach the harness.

"Where have you *been*?" Dilara demanded as I came up. "We were afraid you were in some awful trouble with Mother."

She sounded so worried that I instantly forgave her for going ahead without me. I said, "Nilang wanted to talk to me."

Their eyes got big. "What about?" Sulen asked.

"She wanted to know about Riversong," I said. "Then I got sleepy and she let me have a nap. Then she sent me back here."

"That's *all?*" Dilara said. Clearly, she'd hoped for something more alarming and interesting—Nilang changing me into a bird, for example, and letting me fly around the palace until she changed me back.

But was there more? Yes, the dreams. But thinking about them seemed more trouble than it was worth. The memories of them kept flickering out of my reach, as if they were small silver fish that eluded my fingers even as I touched them.

"That's all," I said. "She looks like an Erallu, except she's got blue eyes."

"Why did she want to know about Riversong? She never asked me or Sulen where we came from."

"I don't know. Maybe she was just curious about the south."

"Maybe." Dilara hefted the kite, resplendent in its scarlet paper. "Do you think the glue's dry? Maybe we can get this thing into the air before supper."

Seven

❧

(M)other herself gave us our history lessons. During the next couple of years I discovered that I liked learning about history, even when we studied from such dull classical works as the *Historical Mirror of the Empire* or *Annals of the Commonwealth*.

Through this I began to understand why my world was as it was. Like every other child, I'd picked up the stories and legends of my race: how we Durdana came in ships from a snowy land far across the sea and sailed far up the Pearl River until we found the place appointed for us by the Bee Goddess and Father Heaven. There we built our first villages in what was to become the ancestral heartland of our realm, Durdane.

How long ago we began to plough those fertile river lands, no one really knows. However, the *Annals* suggest that we had lived there for a thousand years before the Founder established our chief city and named it Seyhan the Luminous. Ever since, our years have been dated from Seyhan's foundation, more than thirteen centuries ago.

But in those days, Mother taught us, we were not ruled by Emperors or Kings, for the Founder created not only Seyhan but also the Commonwealth. Thus we had no monarchs, but governed ourselves through the Clan Assembly, which was made up of the adult men of all the recognized Durdana bloodlines. The Assembly elected the year's magistrates, appointed our generals when we needed to defend our lands (which was often, for a long time), and attended to the Commonwealth's business, such as taxes.

We were a very prolific people. As the centuries passed, we became a multitude, planting our fortresses and cities south of the Pearl, as well as eastward toward the Juren Gap and westward to the sea. The Erallu and the other tribes we encountered often fought us, and there were bitter wars. But in the end we always overcame our enemies, and most of them eventually adopted the ways of our Commonwealth, which gave them laws and civilization. Even the Erallu, who resisted us most fiercely, finally became much like us.

"And then what happened?" Mother asked, looking around the schoolroom.

It was a breezy spring morning, and in the school courtyard the bark of the red willows was turning to crimson. I'm not sure if it was my second or third spring at Repose, but I know it was the month of Early Blossom, for there were garlands around the windows for the Lantern Festival.

Mother's gaze glided to me. "And then, Lale?" she repeated.

I pushed my stool back, stood up, and folded my hands. "Ma'am, the leaders of the Clan Assembly became disloyal to the Commonwealth and to the Durdana. A few men gathered all the power into their hands and abused the proper traditions, but soon their greed and treacherousness made them quarrel with one another. These warlords dissolved the Assembly and began to fight among themselves, each with his own army. This was the beginning of the Civil Wars that destroyed the Commonwealth. They lasted fifty years."

Mother nodded. "And how," she asked, "was this disloyalty and treachery resolved? Sulen?"

I sat down and Sulen stood up. Beside me, Dilara yawned surreptitiously. She was not fond of history.

"In the year 337 after the founding of Seyhan," Sulen began in
her singsong voice, "General Kirsal Brenec called a new Assembly
and fought the traitor warlords in its name. He crushed them,
whereupon the Assembly, seeing the ruin inflicted by the Civil
Wars and wishing for a strong leader who would bring order to
Durdane, asked him to take up the rule. He refused three times,
but when they asked him the fourth time, he accepted. So the
Clan Assembly proclaimed the Empire of Durdane, with Kirsal its
first Emperor, to govern in the name of the Assembly and the people. And the Commonwealth was no more."

"Exactly," Mother said. "And from this we learn a principle.
What is the worst iniquity in the governance of a state?"

"Disloyalty," we chorused, "to those to whom we owe our good
faith."

"You are correct. Adrine, explain how such disloyalty applies to
the destruction of our empire."

Adrine was my age but had been at the school six months less.
Some would have called her ill-favored, what with her blemished
skin, lank hair, and thin lips, though I thought she was merely
homely. She was one of those colorless people who escape everyone's notice until something very bad or very good happens to
them. But in class she always knew the correct answers.

"Yes, ma'am," she said. "In the year 1152 of the imperial reckoning, the Emperor Bartuin ascended to the dais. But disloyalty
was rife among the magistrates and the generals, and before long
the prefects of Anshi and Kayan rebelled. Then the prefect of
Indar declared himself Emperor, saying that Bartuin's claim to
the dais was false. This led to the Era of the Warring Emperors,
which ended a century ago with the Invasion of the Exiles and
the Partition."

As Adrine continued, my imagination took over. I saw the empire blackened with the smoke of burning fortresses and cities; I
gazed on the march and countermarch of armies, shuddered at

massacres and betrayals. Across all Durdane, the generals and imperial pretenders fought and murdered one another, each craving to ascend to the emperor's dais in Seyhan.

And then, in the Year of the Five Emperors, came the great catastrophe. The Githans to our northeast were driven from their vast grassy plains by barbarians even more barbarous than they. Calling themselves the Exiles, because of their expulsion from their homelands, myriads rode through the Juren Gap, looking for pasture and plunder in the tottering empire. The Emperor who ruled then at Seyhan, called Daquin the Iniquitous, paid them to fight for him against the other four pretenders, and multitudes of Durdana died under their spears. But worse was to come, for when Daquin and his barbarous allies finally destroyed his rivals, the Exiles under their king, Pakur One-Eyed, turned on him. At the Battle of Mualla they butchered the last imperial army and Daquin with it.

"Yes," Mother said, as Adrine paused. "You may sit down. Lale—*Lale*, are you asleep, young lady?"

She must have spotted my faraway look and assumed I wasn't paying attention. "No, ma'am," I said.

"Suppose you tell us the rest, then."

"Yes, ma'am," I said, and began to recite from the *Historical Mirror*. "After Daquin's death, the Exiles under Pakur tried to overrun the Durdana lands that were still free. These were the nine imperial prefectures south of the Pearl River and the two prefectures north of it, Tamurin and Bethiya. But the wars had weakened the barbarians, and the prefect of Bethiya held them off for a time, until Pakur suddenly died. After that, his sons fought over his conquests until their stolen realm broke up into the Six Kingdoms of Jouhar, Lindu, Seyhan, Suarai, Mirsing, and Ishban. But those Six Kingdoms still enslave half of our old realm in the east, as they have for a hundred years, and we can have no Empire of Durdane again until they are destroyed."

"Excellent. You've done your work well."

I resumed my seat, pleased by her praise. Our lesson then went on to examine the century that followed the Exile invasion: how Durdane remained broken in half, in what we called the Partition, and how the old imperial prefectures came to be governed by local rulers, who styled themselves Despots.

But there was one exception to this: the rulers of Bethiya, who called themselves Sun Lords and not Despots. They did this because "Sun Lord" had once been the title of the Emperor's heir apparent, and they considered themselves the true successors to the imperial line. As for the Despots, they did allow some precedence to the Sun Lords, though not because they formally recognized the claim. It was because Bethiya remained the most powerful state among the free Durdana realms, although it was still not powerful enough to defeat the Six Kingdoms.

Mother, who had listened carefully as we recited, now paused. Through the open window came the twitter of the wine finches sunning themselves in the courtyard.

"And who," she asked at last, "is the Sun Lord now?"

"Terem Rathai, the usurper," we answered.

"Yes. The one who took my son's place. My son, who might have been your brother, who was to be the Sun Lord. His father's bloodline was the highest in Bethiya, and it was his right. But they murdered him, the Tanyelis did. Murdered my son."

We all knew this. It had happened in the year I was born, and it wasn't only Mother who had told us about it. Our Tradition Tutoress had drummed into us what had happened that autumn day, when the two great bloodlines of Kurjain fought to the death and the ornamental cascades in the palace gardens ran red. But what Mother told us next we had never heard.

"I was not there, or they would have slaughtered me, too," she said, "but I know what happened. I still dream of it. . . . I am on the Water Terrace and I see it all. The Tanyeli retainers are through the gates and the arrows have stopped flying, but they have spears and swords. My brother fights them, back to back with my husband's cousin, until blades pierce their hearts. I hear my sister-in-law scream and beg for her life as she flees, and there is my son's small face in the bundle she carries, my son crying out for me. And then a swordsman cuts her ankles through, and when she falls he stabs them both, and my little boy is silent forever."

She was trembling, though her face remained calm. But she had gone very white.

"Mother?" someone whispered into the silence.

"It was Halis Geray," she said. Her voice lost its beauty and became harsh and cracked. "*He* did this. *He* killed my son. *He* contrived the destruction of my husband's family, and of my own, and of the Tanyelis. He did it so he could replace my son with a boy of inferior bloodline. And why? So he could seize the Chancellor's robes for himself, and rule as regent."

She closed her eyes, then opened them. A little of her color had returned. "So now the usurper Terem Rathai calls himself Sun Lord. But does his ambition, or the ambition of his Chancellor, end there?"

We were back on familiar ground. "No, ma'am," we answered.

"What is the intent of these tyrants? Adrine?"

"To rule all the Durdana outside the Six Kingdoms. To take everything for themselves, just as the Exiles did."

"Yes. And if the day comes when Tamurin is conquered and Chiran falls, the tyrants will execute me amid the ruins. And because you're my daughters, they will kill you as well." Her face, which had gone hard, softened suddenly. "But, my daughters, remember that Father Heaven and the Bee Goddess hate traitors. If we're vigilant, they'll help preserve us, although we must never underestimate our enemies. Halis Geray the Chancellor is very cunning, and the Sun Lord has paid close attention to his lessons. Why do I say they're cunning, Lale?"

"Because the Chancellor has deceived the people of Bethiya into thinking that Terem Rathai is the legitimate Sun Lord, although he's not."

"Precisely," Mother agreed. "And by that same cunning, the people think the Chancellor is a just and able magistrate, even though he is violent and treacherous, and has the blood of my son under his fingernails. So when you hear that the Chancellor feeds the poor, remember that he would starve them if it would serve his purpose to do so. Likewise, if you hear that the young Sun Lord rules justly, remember how he came to the dais. Of the Eight Iniquities, treachery and murder are the worst."

She stared at each of us in turn. "But I must remind you again: never say such things outside these walls. Who knows who might be listening? I do not want to be poisoned because of a careless word, so this knowledge must remain our secret. But what, do you suppose, is the best way to keep it hidden? Dilara?"

My friend said, "The best way to keep secrets is to seem to have none, because then nobody bothers to look for them."

"Yes, exactly," Mother agreed. Then, as if we were coming to the end of a normal lesson, she asked, "Are there any questions?"

There were not, and she dismissed us. We trooped out, but not as gaily as we usually did. For once, we had seen past Mother's imperturbable calm, into the fury and grief that ate at her vitals, and glimpsed the craving for revenge that had rooted in that rich, dark soil. Unknown to us, that obsession ruled all she did, and I suspect that even then it had begun to drive her mad. But I would have been outraged if someone had suggested such a thing to me.

As we crossed the courtyard, Dilara muttered, "Someone should kill them both. The Sun Lord and the Chancellor."

"Of course someone should," I agreed. "But who could do it?"

"Maybe I could."

"Don't be silly. How would you manage it? Someone would already have done it, if it were that easy. Wouldn't they?"

"I don't know," Dilara said, and with that we went in for our dinner.

According to the birthday Mother had bestowed on me, I was fourteen when Master Luasin and his company of actors came to Chiran. She announced their visit only about four hands before it happened, and the palace staff went into a great fluster, with

Mother's steward and the chatelaine yelling into servants' ears at all hours of the day and night.

Not to be outdone, the Literature Tutoress decided we must present a selection from a classical piece for Master Luasin. Because I was tall and slender and had a notable talent for mimicry, I got to play the male character Unsal, the evil moneylender in *The House of the Magistrate*.

I was now of a stature to be convincing in the part, for I'd shot up in the past year and had to look down into Mother's face when I spoke to her. My freckles had disappeared and my hair had become a deeper auburn; I wore it at shoulder length, tied back by a blue ribbon.

As for the rest of me, although I had become a woman, I still showed little of the shape of one, being composed mostly of knees and elbows. Dilara hadn't quite matched my height, though she was older than me; on the other hand, she'd acquired some modest curves. I myself wished for the figures of some of the other girls. Kidrin, for instance, who was now fifteen, already had the feminine proportions of the Moon Lady, and I envied her.

Dilara laughed when I first told her this. We were at a riding lesson in the hills south of Chiran and had halted to rest the horses. The other five students were a little way off, though we were all under the watchful eye of our Heron Guard escort and the even more watchful eye of our Equestrian Tutoress.

"What's funny about wanting curves?" I asked.

"Curves?" she asked derisively. "Why would you want to be all bulges? When Kidrin's horse trots, she bounces all over the place."

This was somewhat exaggerated; Kidrin was womanly but didn't approach the lavish endowments of the Bee Goddess. "Well, what about finding husbands?" I demanded. "Kidrin says it's easier if you're curvy. She says a man doesn't want a woman who looks like a veranda pillar."

Dilara eyed me. "Why are you thinking about husbands all of a sudden?"

In truth I hadn't been, or not really. From what I knew of marriages, especially Rana's to Detrim, husbands had little to recommend them. Still, marriage was what most women did, and most men, too. Indeed, in the three years I'd lived in Repose, Mother had found well-off husbands for several of her daughters, once they were seventeen and had finished their education. This was fortunate for them, since it was usually difficult for either a woman or man without known ancestors to make a good marriage. Even the girls who had to leave Tamurin for new homes in distant places knew how lucky they were.

We had one great advantage, though, of which other foundlings could only dream: the very best teachers had trained us in the domestic and cultural arts, and in those we matched any great merchant's or landowner's daughter. The men who married Mother's girls were perceptive enough to put ability and intelligence above ancestry; and while they didn't get a helpful clan of in-laws, they did get a connection to the ruler of Tamurin. This was valuable, since everyone knew how the Despotana doted on her daughters. Furthermore, she provided a dowry, not lavish but not mean either. So, although I wasn't aware of it at the time, her reputation as a savior and teacher of orphan girls had spread well beyond Tamurin, and she was considered to have gained great merit with the Beneficent Ones, especially with Our Lady of Compassion.

"I wasn't thinking about husbands," I told Dilara. Then I remembered certain reflections I'd had about Olaban the new Heron Guard trooper, and my ears got warm.

"Well, *I'm* not going to marry anybody," Dilara told me. "I'll get Mother to set me up in a trade, the way she did Jathen. I could be a perfumer. Or a weaver—I'd really like weaving."

Actually, going into a trade was as possible for us as marriage. Not all of Mother's girls wanted husbands—some because they had suffered at men's hands, others simply because of temperament—and Mother was perfectly willing to accommodate them. After they completed their educations she arranged for their training as a book copyist or a seamstress, or the like. Once they'd mastered their craft, she set them up in their own establishments, sometimes in Tamurin, sometimes in neighboring Despotates. We almost never saw them after they went away, but occasionally Mother would read us the letters they sent her. Some had gotten so good at their trades that they were becoming wealthy. Some had married after all and were happy, or said they were.

However, not every girl went into a trade or married; for a select few, Mother decided on a religious vocation. This was because she was a devotee of the Moon Lady, and had endowed a sanctuary for the deity up north, at a place called Three Springs Mountain. Being in the wilds, it needed to be supplied from Chiran, and every so often a train of pack asses, escorted by half a dozen Heron Guardsmen, set off from Repose for the highlands. Tossi had already gone there to serve the goddess; in fact, she was the very first of us to do so. Mother chose one or two girls every year to join her, and it was considered an honor. Honor or not, it didn't interest me, but I reckoned that Mother knew I wasn't the religious sort, and so I never worried about finding myself at Three Springs.

"I'd like a trade, too," I said. "Why don't we go into one together? We could get rich twice as fast, with both of us working at it."

"We should try that," she agreed. "When it comes time, we'll ask Mother if we can train together. What do you want to do?"

"I want to make books."

"How tedious. A copyist?"

"No, a real printer. You know, with the carved wood blocks and the press, like we saw in town last year." There was one licensed printer in Chiran, and I'd been fascinated by his manufactory with its stacked reams of wheat-straw paper and the smell of ink and binding glue. He'd had six text cutters at work that day, all meticulously carving whole pages onto blocks of wood. Each letter was reversed, of course, which made the carving very difficult. When a block was finished, he'd put it in the press and squash the paper down on it, and when he lifted the paper there was the whole page. Nobody could hand-copy a book that fast, although cutting a page into the wood was very slow, and if there was one mistake, the whole page had to be carved over again. He got a lot of business from Mother, since he printed all the books we used in the school.

"I don't want to do that. You know how books bore me."

"Well, maybe we can think of something we'd both like," I said. "We don't have to decide for quite a while yet."

We got back to Repose just before the evening meal. We clattered through the main gate into the fortress, turned left at the gardens, and rode into Horse Yard where the stables were. And there the unexpected met us: Master Luasin had arrived, two days early.

I reined in and stared. Five big covered wagons with tall spoked wheels stood in the center of the yard, surrounded by stable hands and strangers. Our grooms were still unhitching the horses, enormous golden beasts with white manes and tails. Kidrin cooed at the sight of them, but I'd never been much interested in horses except as transportation; what I found fascinating were the wagons. They were boat shaped, as though they were built to float across rivers. Three of the five had windows covered with translucent sheets of horn to keep out dust and wind, making them resemble houses on wheels, which in fact they were. The wheel rims and spokes were crimson, as were the axles and fittings. Gold scrollwork was everywhere, and on their sides were the most wonderful paintings—soldiers in silver armor who fought under clouds of arrows; great ships flying before the wind on storm-black seas; glittering processions that climbed toward mountaintop cities; and, most fascinating of all, a tall robed woman who gazed imperiously at me from her jeweled throne.

"You like them, do you, young mistress?" asked a voice below me.

I looked down to see a man by my stirrup. He looked old to me then, but I suppose he was barely forty; he wore plain traveling clothes and was very tall. His nose was big and hooked and his eyes were set close together on each side of it, and unlike most Durdana men he had a short beard, russet shot with gray. I thought him extremely homely.

"Yes, sir, I do like them," I said, minding my manners.

"Which one the most?" He sounded not at all patronizing but as if he really wanted to know my opinion, and with that I found him not quite so homely after all.

"I like the woman on the throne," I told him. "Who is she?"

"Ah, that's the Empress Maylane. You'd know of her, from your studies."

I was never loath to display my learning, so I said, "She held Seyhan against the usurper Derjad, while her husband, the Emperor, was imprisoned in the Yellow Smoke Islands. But she freed her husband at last and brought him home through many dangers. Then there was a great battle against the usurper, and she and the Emperor died in it, side by side. But before Maylane fell she killed Derjad, and Derjad's army fled. It was very tragic. But their son took the throne, and afterward he brought peace and happiness to Durdane."

He grinned. "I see you pay attention to your teachers. That's the story in an oyster shell." He lost the grin and regarded me thoughtfully. "Would you like to be such a woman?"

I blinked. It seemed a bizarre idea, but on the other hand it would be beautifully sorrowful, and people would read about me in the histories.

"Maybe," I said cautiously.

"Always a wise answer. Anyway, it's a good story, so a lot of people have written about it. We play Ristapor's *Maylane Unyielding*, which to my mind is the classic of all the forms."

"Indeed," I answered. "I look forward to seeing it."

He gestured at the wagons. "And so you will. Now, if you'll excuse me . . . Ah, my apologies. I'm Master Luasin. And you?"

"I'm Lale Navari," I stammered. Here I'd taken him for some minion, and instead I'd been talking to the greatest living master of the High Theater. In my confusion I added unnecessarily, "I'm one of the Despotana's students."

"I gathered as much," he said, "from your erudition. Now I must . . ."

He waved vaguely to me and made off. He walked oddly, as if his ankles were stiff.

Dilara said, "That was *him*? He doesn't look like I thought he would."

"No," I agreed, "he doesn't." I gazed at the painted empress. She gazed back at me. I tried to see my face in hers, but of course I couldn't.

Master Luasin's company presented not only *Maylane Unyielding* but the cycle of three history plays called *Loyalty*. *Maylane Unyielding* came first, to my delight, because I wanted to see an empress at war.

None of us knew exactly how a High Theater drama looked and sounded. Our Literature Tutoress had taught us that it used poetry, song, and mime and that it included paintings and tableaux, but that wasn't the same as seeing it. And our attempt at *The House of the Magistrate*, though we were terribly earnest about doing a selection from the classics, didn't really fill the eye with its magnificence.

Our theater studies were exclusively of the classics, but Mother had allowed us to see a few works of the common drama down in the city, to round out our education. In that type of theater there was a lot of action, usually punctuated by street songs, not all of them polite. The dialogues were slangy and fast and often very witty, and the plots were frequently blood drenched, with people being executed and murdered all over the place. Our Literature Tutoress considered it extremely low, not, I think, because it could be bawdy and violent, but rather because ordinary people liked it so much. Hers was a common opinion among the well educated, who held that the popular plays were vulgar, the acting execrable, and the performers defective in both morals and character. Some of them *were* defective in these ways, which naturally made them all the more interesting.

The High Theater enjoyed a far more elevated reputation, and

Master Luasin was an artist of its very first rank. This was because the classical drama was very old and stately, and told stories of honorable people who were beset by villains of dreadful power and malice. Because the plays always taught a clear moral lesson, High Theater performers were considered quite reputable, and Master Luasin's were deemed the most reputable and accomplished of all. His company was under the patronage of Yazar, the Despot of Brind, and normally resided in Istana, Brind's capital, but it was so excellent that it customarily traveled to Kurjain every summer, to perform for the Sun Lord and for the powerful and rich of Bethiya's capital. This was the first time the company had come to Tamurin, and paying Master Luasin to do so must have cost Mother a pretty sum.

There were ten people in the company: six were actors, while the other four and Master Luasin managed the staging, the music, and everything else. They all kept pretty much to the quarters Mother provided for them, but I did manage to catch one of the stagers in Seaward Yard; she was a stocky woman with big hands and heavily muscled forearms. I made the mistake of asking her how they got their wagons through the steeps of Crossbone Pass.

She laughed. "By the Lady of Mercy, that would be a long thump and bump from Kurjain, wouldn't it, by the overland road? If you can call it a road any more. No, my dear, we came mostly by water. By boat down the Short Canal from Kurjain to the Pearl, then by lorcha to Dirun at Pearl Mouth. Then we loaded ourselves on a pelican and sailed across the Gulf to your Despotana's port at Kalshel. And a bit longer after that, and here we were."

"Oh," I said, embarrassed at sounding ignorant. Kalshel was on the other coast of Tamurin, and was connected to Chiran by a well-maintained road that ran across the peninsula. If I'd thought clearly, I'd have realized that Master Luasin would come that way, because Kalshel port was how the merchants of Tamurin traded with the mainland to the east. Commerce from the southwest coasts, and from the offshore archipelagoes, went through Chiran—though not without first enduring the attentions of Mother's customs agents, as did all the goods shipped through Kalshel.

Mother's palace had a private theater that dated from the imperial days when Repose was the residence of Tamurin's prefect. Master Luasin's stagers needed several days to bring it to the condition he demanded, but at last it was done, and the afternoon of *Maylane Unyielding* arrived.

We students, our tutoresses, and Mother with several of her senior officials, made up the audience. We sat on the four tiers of cushioned benches that rose above the theater floor; before us, positioned to catch the best light from the tall windows, was the stage. Its sides were closed off, to conceal the performers' entrances and exits, and a filmy hanging stretched across its rear; the fabric was translucent and behind it I could make out the first landscape of the play, painted on a curtain of gossamin. To the stage's right was the musicians' gallery, already occupied by a woman with a double flute and a man with a sivara.

We students settled ourselves quietly on the benches, with the icy gaze of our Tradition Tutoress ensuring decorum. Mother went down to the small altar by the stage, where she lit a cone of incense to the Sun Goddess, the patron of artists. We all prayed to the goddess, and Mother returned to her seat.

There was a silence of a dozen heartbeats. And then, with five perfect notes of the double flute, the gauze curtain folded itself upward and there before us, real as life, was the Stone Flower Garden in Seyhan Palace.

And the play began.

Everyone knows Maylane's story, but few have seen the drama performed in the old manner, and fewer still have seen it in such perfection. Master Luasin declaimed the poetry of the narrative parts in a voice so deep and resonant I didn't believe at first it was him. The gossamin paintings that illustrated the story glowed like cascades of jewels, every one more gorgeous than the last: the burning mountains of the Yellow Smoke Islands, the imperial necropolis of old Seyhan, the pearl-inlaid bedroom of the Empress, the sunlit and terrible battlefield of Maghara.

And the singing! It sent chills through me, especially when the women's voices rose above the men's, like many-hued birds soaring in the winds that blow far above the earth. And as Maylane and her husband approached their fates, I could hardly hold back my tears, for I knew that although they never lost hope, there was no hope for them.

But most of all I watched the actress who played, no, *was* Maylane. Her name was Perin, and in her imperial regalia and actress's paint she was unutterably beautiful. I fell completely in love with her. I wanted to be like her, to be glorious and passionate and stand before a multitude and make them mine, just as she'd made us hers. And when she died at Maylane's moment of victory, I wept.

In fact I think everybody wept, though I'm not sure about the Tradition Tutoress. Dilara certainly did; as the last notes of the last melody died away, she buried her face in her hands and sobbed. As for me, I stared with tear-blurred eyes at the stage, wishing in my deepest self that it had been me there, being Maylane. For I knew at last what I was going to do with my life. I was certain of it, in a way I'd never been certain of anything.

I was going to be an actress.

Over the next few days, Master Luasin presented the plays of the *Loyalty* cycle. I liked them, even if they didn't overwhelm me as had the story of Maylane, and I watched Perin every instant she was onstage, with my resolve to emulate her growing by the hour. But because Master Luasin kept his people at work almost all the time, I never got a chance to speak to her until the morning after the *Loyalty* cycle finished. That was when we presented our selection from *The House of the Magistrate* to Master Luasin's company and the whole school.

By this time, the prospect of Master Luasin being in our audience had reduced both the Literature and Arts Tutoresses almost to nervous collapse. Fortunately, they'd had the sense to use a scene with mostly declamation and mime, with just two songs and no instrumental part, so the performance went tolerably well. At least, nobody giggled during it, and everybody applauded at the end. We all mingled afterward, and I finally got to talk to Perin.

She wasn't quite as beautiful out of paint and costume as she was in them, but she was still very lovely. And quite young, not much past twenty. Flushed with my new experience, I marched up to her and told her I wanted to be an actress, and asked how I should go about becoming one.

To her credit, she didn't even blink. Instead she said, "You played Unsal, didn't you?"

"Yes, Mistress Perin."

She pursed her mouth a little. Then she called past my shoulder, "Guyal, come here." To me she said, "You are . . ."

I'd forgotten my manners. I was behaving just as I had years ago in Riversong, pushing in wherever I liked and chattering until somebody aimed a swat at me.

"I'm Lale, Mistress Perin. I apologize for being so forward, I—"

She gestured impatiently. "Better than being backward. No girl gets anywhere if she makes herself part of the scenery gossamin. Guyal, this is Lale. She played Unsal."

This was to the sivara player, a thin man whose eyes were on a level with mine. He had some foreign blood, for they were gray eyes, and his hair was closer to copper than auburn.

After contemplating me he said, "Ah, yes, Unsal. Did you know your voice is very good?"

I hadn't. The Arts Tutoress had said it wasn't the worst she'd heard, which might have signified anything.

"Does that mean I could be an actress?" I blurted.

They exchanged glances, then looked me up and down. Perin said to Guyal, "Well, she maintained the presence of her character, didn't she? Loose at the edges, but the center was strong."

Guyal nodded. "Possible, possible." To me he said, "How hard are you willing to work?"

"Very hard," I told him hopefully. "All the time."

"Then you might manage it someday," Perin said. "I started in Master Luasin's theater school in Istana when I was eighteen. That was a bit late to begin, but I managed."

My ears pricked up. "I didn't know he had a school," I said.

"Oh, yes. He's even expanding it, because he's trying to start a second company to go along with this one. But it's going slowly. It takes so much money."

If I had been older and more experienced, I'd have realized from this that Master Luasin had come to Repose with more in mind than his performance fee—he was looking to Mother for money to finance his dream. He got what he wanted, too, although he should have considered more carefully what she might make him do to earn it.

"Well, then," I said, trying to sound nonchalant and confident. "Someday, perhaps."

Perin smiled, dazzling me, and then the Literature Tutoress came up and wedged me out of the conversation. But I didn't care, for now I had the beacon of Master Luasin's school before me, and it seemed the perfect answer to my ambitions. I'd never been quite sure how to achieve them, but now the means was clear: I'd become a High Theater actress. I'd certainly become famous and probably rich, and everyone would talk about me. It was, I told myself, only a matter of time.

Eight

❧

By the time Master Luasin departed, not only I but half the other girls in the school wanted to be actresses. But the passion was fleeting, and by summer's end everybody's interest had waned.

Except mine. My fascination with the craft endured, and over the next three years I relentlessly pestered our tutoresses to let us put on plays from the High Theater. Often they yielded, successes that I smugly credited to my persuasive tongue. In this I was wrong, for it was Mother who was behind their compliance. She was engaged in a very deep game, Mother was, and my awakening talent—for I did have talent, and it was considerable—had played into her hands in a way she could scarcely have expected. I had been part of her game from the day she caught up with me on the Riversong road, and now she had a much better idea of the kind of game piece she might make of me.

But all I knew was that Mother took a flattering interest in my increasing skills and praised me for them; I basked in her attention and glowed with pride when she told me, for example, that my singing had moved her. I loved her so deeply that I worked as much for her approval as for my own pleasure in the craft.

But one day, when I was sixteen, I overreached myself. I had got it into my head that we should stage *The Orphan's Daughter*, a slightly risqué comedy from the popular drama, and I tried to persuade the Literature Tutoress to allow it. She recoiled in horror, as I should have foreseen she would, and refused. Angry over this, I sought an audience with Mother and complained not only about the decision but also about the tutoress.

This was a serious mistake. I thought of myself as Mother's favorite student, and thus expected her to see the matter my way, but this was not at all what happened. In a brief, painful, and humiliating audience, she told me that my teacher's authority flowed from hers, and that in rebelling against the authority of the Literature Tutoress, I was rebelling against Mother herself. I must ask her forgiveness immediately and never do such a thing again.

It was a very frightening rebuke. My greatest terror was losing Mother's love, and disloyalty was the shortest path to that abyss. I was well aware of how far I'd strayed from the path of proper conduct, and I apologized abjectly both to her and to my tutoress. But in spite of my contrition I still felt deeply thwarted, and for some time afterward a tiny coal of anger burned far down inside me.

As for my future, I'd made no secret of wanting to go to Master Luasin's school after I'd finished my basic education. Mother knew my goal, although she refused to comment on it, just as she refused to comment on any girl's prospects until she judged it time to do so. Dilara, however, had no interest in the stage and still wanted us to be weavers. We had angry arguments over our future together, although we always made up again afterward. Finally we agreed to stop fighting over it. We'd wait until our schooling was complete and then see if Mother could help us decide what to do.

There was more to our lives than schooling. We celebrated the Solstice Festival that led up to the New Year, when Chiran blazed with torchlight processions. Then there were the holidays like the Lantern Festival and the Fragrance of Nature Festival, as well as the feast days of the gods and goddesses.

For such occasions we learned dances like the five-string dance with its sedate steps, and the lazy thrush, which despite its name left you out of breath. And Kidrin surreptitiously taught Dilara and me the tassel dance, during one of the Plough festivals. It was fun but very unseemly, and I don't know where Kidrin learned it—she wouldn't tell us, but it certainly wasn't at the school. I think it belonged to her life before she arrived.

There were also bad times. One hot, dry summer the spotted fever broke out in Chiran; several hundred people died before the cooler weather of autumn brought relief, and the deaths didn't abate until the new year. The crowded old necropolis outside Chiran's east gate filled up, and Mother had to get a new piece of land purified for the spate of burials. The masons ran out of tomb markers, and at one point people were dying so quickly that they had to go into common graves, to the great distress of their families.

Because of the pestilence Mother kept us at home, but two of us fell sick anyway. The first, sadly, was the earnest and scholarly Sulen, and despite all Mother's personal physician could do with infusions and poultices, and despite the efforts of the best spirit summoner in Chiran, she died. We other girls hoped that Nilang might help her, but Nilang was not at Repose (her absences were sometimes long and never explained) and she did not return until after Sulen's burial.

Mother put our classmate into a tomb in a special corner of the old necropolis that she had set aside for such purposes. Some years before, she had also consecrated an ancestor shrine for us, and we burned a lock of Sulen's hair for the ritual ashes and put them into the shrine's spirit box. Of course, it wasn't an ancestor shrine in the true sense, because we weren't sisters by blood, yet it meant a great deal to us all.

But as we left the shrine after the ceremony that morning, I began to feel unwell, and before the day was out, I, too, had fallen ill with the fever. Mother moved me into a room in the palace, and for the next seven days she never left my side, although she risked the sickness demons herself by remaining with me. She laid cool cloths on my burning skin and dribbled water through my cracked lips; she sang to me and murmured words of comfort. When I shook uncontrollably with the fever chills, she lay on the bed beside me and held my trembling body tenderly in her arms. No mother could have done more, and many would not have done as much.

Finally, on the night that the palace physician and the spirit summoner despaired of my life, Mother sent them away and called Nilang to join her in my room. I was very weak and must have appeared to be asleep, but I was more aware of my surroundings than they realized. Also, perhaps because of the fever, my hearing seemed preternaturally sharp.

"You must do something," Mother said. "Drive the illness out of her."

Nilang's voice answered, "I can compel some of the creatures of the Quiet World. But the fever is not of that world, it is of our own, and its nature is not subject to my art."

"You will try, nonetheless."

"Trying will do her no good. It may do her ill."

"I cannot lose her," Mother said. "Already she has been years in the making. Try."

"I protest."

"Protest as you like. But remember that you are bound to me and how you will suffer if you prove disloyal."

A silence. Then Nilang said, "I will attempt it. Stand aside."

Another silence, and I smelled a fragrance like that of burning incense but not quite. Then I sensed motion by my bed, and a fingertip touched my brow. I was so aflame with the fever that it felt like ice.

The only thing that happened then, for what seemed a long time, was that Nilang whispered to me. I could not understand the words, for they were in a tongue I did not know. But gradually, as she whispered, the sounds began to take shape, as if I could see them through my closed eyelids, and I realized that her whispers had opened a passage to some other place, and that this place was the Quiet World. I glimpsed improbable skies, some of them night black but spanned by vast whorls of starry radiance, others blue with day yet bearing many pale moons like diadems of pearls. Under these heavens lay eerie landscapes. Some were bright and wondrous, as if cut from jade and sapphire and crystal by some magical jeweler, but others were as evil and ghost haunted as an ancient field of massacre, and these sickened my very spirit.

And then, in one such foul place, a creature lifted its ghastly head, and I saw that it knew of my presence.

Terror seized me, but I could neither move nor cry out, for Nilang's whispers had bound me tighter than manacles of iron. Yet the beast, if it was a beast, felt no such constraint. It slouched nearer; it stalked me. Spiritlike, it had no clear form, but within it swirled all the shapes of my darkest nightmares. And somehow, as if I perceived its awareness, I knew that it hungered after me. That hunger flooded me with horror, for I knew what it foretold: I was to be eaten alive, but I would find no release of death while I was devoured, and afterward I would live on within the beast, shrieking at what had happened to me.

Nilang's words now struggled to keep my stalker at bay. It feared her, but not enough, and her power could not halt its relentless advance along the passage she had opened. I wailed a silent prayer to the Lord of the Dead who ruled this realm, and to all the Beneficent Ones, and to all my unknown and nameless ancestors. But still the creature came.

And then a woman's soft voice, not Nilang's or Mother's, said from a place I could not see: *Go back. It is not her time.*

The beast quailed at the sound, and Nilang instantly hissed a sharp word. The passage contracted and snapped shut, taking the creature with it. I suddenly lay in my bed again, as sick and fevered as ever, hearing Nilang's breath rasp in her throat. I opened my eyes; she was staring down at me, her lips tightly compressed, brows knit. When she saw me wake, a flicker of relief passed over her face.

"What?" Mother asked. She was not in my line of vision, and I was too weak to look around. I shut my eyes again.

"She will not die," Nilang answered. Her voice was without emotion.

"So you do have the power," Mother said harshly. "Why did you tell me you couldn't cure her? Are you playing some game of your own?"

"I did not say I have cured her, because I have not done so. What I said is that she will not die. But we are lucky that she is still with us. While I searched for a healing instrument, a *khnum* attempted to subsume her."

A long pause. Finally Mother said, "I see. And if it had?"

"She would appear as if sleeping, but she would no longer be within her body. Eventually the body would die."

Mother's voice became worried. "She appears to be sleeping now."

"The creature failed," Nilang said. "There was an intervention that enabled me to close the nexus. It is from that intervention that I know the girl will live. It was an ancestor, I think, and no doubt one of hers."

Sick as I was, I felt a tenuous comfort at this. An ancestor in the Quiet World knew me and had helped protect me from something very nasty.

"And you say she won't die."

"It is not her time," Nilang answered.

A faint sigh of relief. "You may leave us."

When Nilang had gone, Mother lay down by my side. I drowsed for a while, then found myself half awake. Summoning all my strength, I whispered, "Mother?"

"Yes, Lale?"

"I won't die. I promise."

"No, child. You're safe here."

"I love you, Mother," I breathed.

"I love you, Lale. Now go to sleep and get well."

I obeyed her, and by midnight my fever had broken and I was sleeping normally. But several days passed before I was strong enough to leave my bed, and during that time I thought about what Nilang had done. Mother said nothing of the incident, and I began to wonder if it was only a fever dream, so finally I plucked up the courage to ask her about it.

"Yes," Mother answered, "I summoned her, and she did what she could. What do you remember?"

I told her about the creature and the rescuing voice. She nodded and said, "All men and women have ancestors in the Quiet World, even if we know nothing of them in this one, and so cannot summon them here. But you already knew this, Lale—the matter is examined in the *Discourse on the Eight Divinities and the Ineffable.*"

"Yes, ma'am. But it's still a surprise to find that it's real, instead of just something in a book."

"You are not the first to make this observation," Mother answered in a dry voice. "But sorcerers dislike any gossip about their doings, so I strongly suggest you do not speak of this to anyone, not even Dilara. Now, what else do you remember?"

I hesitated. I wanted to ask why and how Nilang had bound herself to Mother, but that would resemble the gossip Mother had warned me against. And Nilang was very clearly no one to be trifled with. So I merely said, "You told Nilang I had been years in the making. What did you mean?"

"Ah," she replied smoothly, "All my girls are years in the making, Lale, from the time I find them until they are ready to go out into the world. You are no exception. That is all I meant."

I believed the lie, of course; she'd already given me so much, why would I not expect the truth as well? And as it happened, on the day I left the palace to return to the school, she gave me something more: the news that the murderers of Master Lim were dead. She didn't tell me why she'd avenged him, or what he'd been to her, and I sensed it would do no good to ask. But she'd kept the promise she'd made to me after he died, and I was grateful to her on Master Lim's behalf.

It did not then occur to me to wonder at how long an arm she had, to pluck two such distant birds from their perch. But in my heart, I believed that Mother could do anything, so I suppose I expected nothing less.

My teachers deemed me fully educated soon after I turned seventeen. Being no scholar, Dilara finished at the same time I did, although she was a few months older.

The completion of a girl's studies was marked by two occasions, or three if she decided to take her Universal Examination. This last was rigorous affair of several days, during which she must write authoritatively on history, literature, and the natural world, as well as develop an argument and support it with both rhetoric and fact. Finally, she must be able to compose poetry in four of the seven formal modes.

Only a handful of Mother's students elected to take the Examination. It was very difficult and of no benefit to a woman except that it enhanced her reputation for intelligence and culture. But I thought this enhancement might prove useful, since I intended to move one day in intelligent and cultured circles, so I asked Mother if I might try, and she agreed.

As I wrote my papers, I was vividly aware that I was following a very ancient tradition, for the Universal Examination had long been used to select talented men for government office. The Examination was created by the great Emperor Jadurian, who disliked the way that imperial relatives and the rich military aristocracy passed these offices down to their sons, without regard for ability or merit. This had led to corruption and serious abuses of power, which he resolved to end.

So, drawing on the precepts of the *Golden Discourses*, Jadurian suppressed the magnate families, broke the power of the soldier nobles, forbade the inheritance of government positions, and established the Universal Examination to allow men of any origin—not women, of course—to ascend to the highest magistracies. After that, neither wealth, land, nor an ancient family name gave anyone the right to rank and power; the only path to these now ran through the gateway of the Examination.

This worked so well that our view of precedence became very different from that of other nations whose aristocrats and soldiers stand next after the ruler. We do consider the ruler to be supreme, but directly beneath him is the magistracy, followed by the farmers (since they feed everyone) and only then the soldiers. At the bottom, socially speaking, are the merchants, though if they're rich they may have great unofficial status—money is as good as magisterial rank, if there's enough of it.

But during the Era of the Warring Emperors and the Exile invasion, the soldiers got themselves back into the saddle. By my time, all Durdana rulers were warriors or descended from warriors, and all the great land magnates came of military bloodlines. Still, the tradition of the Universal Examination remained so strong that anyone who wanted to rise in the service of a Despot must still undergo a version of it. But the times had so corrupted the tradition that only the sons of the new nobility managed to pass. Their families had grasped power and were not about to share it with upstart offspring of merchants, craftsmen, or farmers.

Mother's examiners, though, were scrupulously fair when dealing with her students, and to my surprise I passed with Meritorious Distinction, the second highest grade. I was especially proud of this because I'd done better than most male candidates would, whose usual grade was third or fourth.

The second of the three occasions was a ceremony before the whole school, when the girl received an adult's seal ring with her name engraved on it. Soon after that came a private dinner with Mother, during which her future was assessed.

To Dilara and me, this third occasion was the most important of all. Most of us had a pretty good idea of where we were headed, either because of some particular skill or because a husband was in the offing. But while Dilara and I didn't believe that Mother had looked for husbands for us, she'd given us no hints about our future.

I hardly recollect the ring-giving ceremony, since the events of the following day so overshadowed it. What I do remember begins with the next evening, when Dilara and I were on our way to our celebratory meal with Mother. Her tradition was to banquet her graduates a pair at a time, and she had instructed us to attend together.

It was the month of Late Blossom, close to the beginning of the Boat Race Festival. The afternoon had been sweltering, and in spite of the sea wind the evening was little cooler. The yellow lilies in the gardens drooped, and the very stones of the palace seemed to sweat. Dilara and I wore new clothes: linen shirts under stiff bodices with blue and silver embroidery and long skirts printed with flowers. We were both very nervous, not because we were dining with Mother but because our futures would be decided before we slept again.

"It's so *hot*," Dilara muttered. She brushed a strand of brown hair from her damp forehead. "I wish we didn't have to dress up like this. I'm sweating so much the dye will run."

"Maybe it'll be cooler inside," I suggested as we climbed the steps to the palace's lacquered doors. A nondescript man was leaving as we went in. I'd noticed quite a few such men, and a few similar women, come and go over the years. Mother had landholdings throughout Tamurin, and I supposed that these were estate understewards bringing her news. One person we rarely saw around Repose, though, was Nilang. Sometimes she didn't appear for a month at a time. But then she'd turn up, doll-like, looking down from a palace window or drifting like a tiny daylight apparition along the ramparts above the harbor.

Within the palace, the thick stone walls kept much of the heat at bay. A servant met us in the anteroom and escorted us to Mother's private quarters on the topmost floor. I'd been there several times over the years, because Mother would invite a few of us in for meals or for visits, during which we would compose and recite poetry for her, sing classic songs or play a flute or sivara, or simply divert her with wit and conversation. We did our best to live up to her standards, since both we and our tutoresses suffered if we failed to meet them.

We were ushered into her private dining chamber. Unlike the enormous banqueting hall on the ground floor, it was an intimate place, with a round table and only six chairs. Windows on the seaward side admitted late afternoon sunlight and a brisk breeze, and I felt the perspiration dry stiffly on my upper lip.

Nothing had changed since my last visit. Mother's tastes were not austere, and the clutter of alabaster carvings, ornamental fruit stands, and other curios made the room seem smaller than it was. A Twelve Lines board was set up by the windows, the pieces showing that Mother had a game in progress. In one corner was the Moon Lady's blue-lacquered cabinet shrine, with the silver statue and crescent gleaming in the niche. At the statue's feet a votive lamp burned with a pure clear flame.

Mother stood at a window, gazing out to sea. She turned to us, and we each presented an appropriate bow.

"My newest ladies," she said in that wonderful voice. "Look what marvels my two daughters have become."

Dilara and I responded with another bow and polite assertions of our unworthiness. Then we sat down at the table.

Mother was no more austere with her food than her furnishings. We began with prawns in clam broth, accompanied by leek soup. Then there was grilled breast of river hen with apple glaze, accompanied by pickled cucumbers and mock lettuce, and a puree of chestnuts and spices. After this came a layered honey pastry containing almonds and walnuts. And, as on every Durdana table that could afford it, there were rounds of bread and an oil sprinkler, and a dish of finely ground salt.

At school meals we drank only boiled water, as directed in the *One Thousand Golden Remedies* which prescribes boiling to drive out sickness demons. But this evening Dilara and I each had our own ceramic jug of young wine, the fragrant vintage of last autumn's grapes. We drank it well watered, since only sots take their wine neat. We'd all been taught the reason for this in our sixteenth year, when each of us had been required to become intoxicated, under Mother's supervision. This was so we'd know what drunkenness felt like and how treacherous it was.

The meal would have been more comfortable for Dilara and me if we hadn't been so nervous. Worse, Mother never once spoke of our future as we ate, and good manners forbade us to mention it. So we talked of other things, including the recent news from Kurjain, the capital of Bethiya. Apparently the Sun Lord had at last married the woman to whom he'd been betrothed when a boy. Her name was Merihan, and she'd taken the title of Surina; this title, like that of Sun Lord, came down from ancient days and was the formal honorific of the wife of the Emperor's heir—another example of how the rulers of Bethiya considered themselves the legitimate imperial successors, even if they couldn't get rid of the Exiles.

"Dangerous times are coming," Mother went on, as she mixed water into her wine. "Halis Geray schemes in secret to bring Tamurin and the other Despotates under the rule of the Sun Lord. Ardavan, the new Exile King of Seyhan, is an unknown but is said to have ambitions against Bethiya. And to our southeast, Abaris waits, hoping for easy pickings if Durdana and Exile exhaust and cripple each other. We all play a game: move an army here, send an ambassador there, put a word in this place, another in that." She gestured at the game board by the window. "In Twelve Lines, if you don't like the way it's going, you can clear the pieces and begin again. But in the contests that rulers play, all moves are irrevocable."

Her small mouth tightened. "And this is the look of the larger board, as I see it. We've had a long time of peace in the Despotates and the Kingdoms, except for the usual border raiding. But I think it won't be long until the quiet ends—three years, five perhaps. Then there will be war."

We'd all been taught how important it was to understand what was happening in the world, and normally we would have been interested in this. But while we did our best to converse intelligently, we knew our fates were to be decided before the evening was out, and by the time the servants left us to ourselves, Dilara and I were rigid with tension.

After their footsteps died away, Mother looked at me and then at Dilara. And then she said, "Well. This is the time, I see."

I stared down at the polished wood of the tabletop. But I barely saw it. Would she send me to Master Luasin? I prayed fervently to all the Beneficent Ones that she would.

Mother said, "Lale and Dilara, each of you now has a choice. That's a luxury that few people are given in these difficult times. But I've watched you carefully for a long while, and I think you both deserve it."

"Thank you, ma'am," we answered.

"I'll tell you each the first part of your choice. Listen quietly until I've finished."

She turned to Dilara. "There is a man in Dirun," she said, "who saw you last year at the Ripe Grain Festival. A day ago he came to Chiran and informed me that he wished to marry you."

Despite her training, Dilara's mouth fell open and a choked gasp came out of it. Of all possible futures, this was the one she most despised. I went cold all over, then hot. Not only would we be separated, she'd be sent far away across the Gulf of the Pearl. I might never see her again.

"He's a city magistrate rising in society," Mother continued, as if she hadn't noticed Dilara's stricken face. "He may eventually go to the Despot's court. He needs a wife who will not embarrass him, and he does not concern himself overly about bloodlines. It would be an excellent match for both of you."

"Yes, Mother," Dilara whispered. Her gaze was blank, as if she saw into the dry and barren years that lay ahead.

"Lale."

My earlier nervous anticipation had been replaced by dread. If such a disaster had befallen Dilara, what awaited me?

"Yes, Mother?" I croaked.

"You might do well if you remained here, Lale. The Tradition Tutoress is elderly, as you're aware. She would train you in all she knows, and in a few years you would assume her place."

This was as bad as I could have imagined. The Tradition Tutoress didn't like me, and I didn't like her. How could I spend years under her thumb, being bored to madness by the minutiae of ritual, custom, and etiquette, the details of proper dress for all occasions, the honorifics by which one addressed this official or that? I'd be a dried-up husk, just like her, before I was twenty.

"Yes, Mother," I whispered, from an aching throat.

"Or," she said, "you may both have another choice, one I give to very few of my daughters. I am allowing you to choose it together, because I know that you are the best of friends and that you would prefer to stay together if you could."

She paused. I felt as if my ears must be sticking straight out from my head, I was listening so hard.

"It is this," she went on. "You may to go to Three Springs Mountain, to join Tossi and the others there as devotees of the Moon Goddess. Take a few moments to think before you answer."

I stared at her. It was rude, but I was helpless to do otherwise, for of all she could have offered us, this was the last I'd expected.

I did not want it. I knew it was an honor, but I had no bent for the religious life and neither had Dilara. How could we sincerely devote ourselves to the goddess's service, droning the prayers day in and day out, performing the daily, monthly, and seasonal rites, eating dried fish, coarse bread, and pickles? Would we have to spend all our lives at the shrine? Perhaps so—neither Tossi nor any of the other girls who joined her had ever returned to Repose, even to visit.

Withdrawing from the world, even in sacred service, was not the future I had in mind. But I *had* to accept one of the choices Mother had given me, and so did Dilara. To reject both would be the deepest filial ingratitude, both insulting and disloyal.

But choosing Three Springs did have something to be said for it. I wouldn't have to become the Tradition Tutoress, to start with; and if Dilara chose the same, we could stay together. Also, I sensed that the choice would please Mother, and pleasing her was always very near to our hearts.

I did not quite realize, then, that she had really given us no choice at all. She knew us better than we knew ourselves and knew we'd choose anything other than marriage or tutorship, especially if it meant we wouldn't be separated. She needed us both, me because of who I was, and Dilara because of her perfect loyalty and her ruthlessness, and she had made very sure that we would choose as she wished. Without each other present, Dilara or I might just possibly have hesitated. Together, we did not hesitate at all. We looked into each other's eyes and, without speaking, agreed.

I said, "Mother, we accept the service of the Moon Lady."

"I'm so glad," Mother exclaimed. She rose from the table and embraced us, and the fragrance of the sandalwood scent she wore filled my nostrils. I was bitterly disappointed, but she was so happy with us that I could not let my feelings show.

"I made no mistake in choosing you as students," she said. "Few can hope to reach the condition of the superior man or woman, but you'll be of that company, I can see." Her face grew serious. "Soon you'll begin a time of very hard work, but you're grown women now, and you'll thrive on it. And make no mistake, you'll be well repaid for your faithfulness to me and to the school."

I hoped she meant that we wouldn't stay at Three Springs for good, although I could hardly say so. But Dilara was more direct.

"Do we have to leave Repose forever?" she asked. And at her words I realized how much I'd be leaving behind: the protective ancient stones of the fortress, my friends, my sisters, the teachers who had so painstakingly transformed me from an ignorant and unmannerly child into a cultured young woman. And especially Mother. How could I live without her to nurture me? I was an adult now, but I still needed her.

"Not forever," she assured us with a gentle smile. "How could I ask that of you? Of course you'll see me again, and no doubt you'll see some of your fellow students as well. Of that I'm sure."

She kissed us both, then said, "You know there comes a time in every woman's life when she must take leave of her mother. That has to happen, or she remains a child in a woman's body. But you'll always be in my most secret heart, my dearest daughters."

I gazed on her small plain face, and loved her as I'd never loved anyone; in that instant I would have died for her, and she knew it. As Dilara would have died for her, and she knew that, too. And so we three were gathered into one perfect moment, there in that beautiful room in the palace of Repose: the woman who was our mother, and the woman who would betray her, and the woman who would not.

Nine

❧

Three days later, glum and apprehensive, Dilara and I reached Three Springs.

Six Heron Guard troopers, with a pack train of supplies needed at the sanctuary, accompanied us to our new home. The place was northeast of Chiran, in a range of peaks so worn by time that their forested heights held snow only in winter. Nevertheless, the way there was very rugged, and even the tough upland horses of Tamurin found the going difficult.

The sanctuary's buildings clung to a mountainside dense with beech, cedar, and evergreen oak. It hadn't originally been a religious establishment. In the days of the empire it served as the summer residence of Tamurin's prefects and was actually called Three Springs Mountain, after the height on which it was built. It was a very suitable place to withdraw from the world; nobody had lived in that stretch of the highlands since the Partition, and Mother's late husband's grandfather had declared it a hunting preserve, with ferocious penalties for trespassers. The region was also said to be haunted by emanations from the Quiet World, which discouraged wanderers and the curious.

We arrived in mid-afternoon. The steep, overgrown track entered a small clearing, not much more than a broad ledge on the mountainside, and there before us was our new home. At the sight of it, Dilara exclaimed, "Holy Mother of Mercy!" and gaped. So did I.

Before us was a stone wall with a sentry tower above its narrow gate. Beyond the wall rose the mountain's upper flank, an enormous cliff of pink and gray stone, thickly garlanded with rock cedar and spindly shrubs. In the cliff face was an immense cleft that stretched all the way to the distant summit.

The buildings of Three Springs nestled into this cleft. Constructed of black wood and russet stone, they rose in four levels above the clearing, each level like a step of a gigantic staircase, with the roof of each building forming a terrace for the one above it. A waterfall tumbled down the cliff beside the cleft and plunged into a pool at its foot. It was so beautiful that despite my unhappiness, I could not help but respond to it. If I had to endure the religious life, I thought, there were much worse places than this.

Still gawking at the heights above, we rode through the gate into a courtyard. It was a paved oblong with stables, a vegetable garden, a small orchard, and the building that formed the sanctuary's bottom level. This had a single door lacquered in red, with doorposts and arch carved most whimsically with birds, tortoises, and fish. Several windows looked into the courtyard, but their lattices prevented me from seeing if anyone was watching us.

We dismounted and unloaded our satchels. Our escort took our horses and the baggage animals away to the stables.

"Where *is* everybody?" I said.

"At their prayers, of course," Dilara answered grumpily, although I couldn't hear any singing. "Just like we're going to have to do." She glanced up at the courtyard's outer wall. "But there should be guards, shouldn't there? There must be somebody to keep off robbers."

"Maybe the Moon Lady does it," I suggested. Even in these dangerous times it was a rare bandit who would attack a shrine of the Beneficent Ones, and it was particularly foolish to offend the

Moon Lady. You might find yourself facing the Moonlight Girl, whose mere touch could bring despair, madness, and self-murder.

"Maybe," Dilara agreed doubtfully. "But—"

The door opened and a woman came out. It was Tossi. She'd changed in the six years since I'd last seen her, but I'd still have known her anywhere. She'd cut her flowing brown hair short and had become leaner, but the leanness only made her huge dark eyes more striking, and it had refined her oval face into a grave loveliness. An air of authority hung about her, as if she had become used to giving orders. A life of devotion clearly suited her.

I bowed and said, "Mistress Tossi, Mother sends her greetings and hopes that you and everyone here are well."

She smiled, which she had almost never done when I knew her at Repose. "We're very well," she said, looking us up and down. "You've changed, Lale. You, too, Dilara. Not girls anymore but women. And very lovely ones."

This was so unlike her I blinked in surprise and blinked again when she said, "Mother has given me the charge of Three Springs, but we're all sisters here, so you must call me Tossi, or Sister Tossi. Agreed?"

"Of course," I said, wondering if life at Three Springs might not, perhaps, be as awful as I'd feared.

"Come with me now," she said, "and we'll go and meet the others. They're all expecting you."

I settled my satchel strap more comfortably on my shoulder as Tossi led us inside. Dimness enveloped us; we were in a small bare anteroom decorated with faded murals of hunting scenes. A masonry staircase ascended at the far end.

"This is the stair to the Second Terrace," Tossi said as we began to climb. "We keep supplies and such down on the Lower Terrace, and the kitchens and baths are on the Second. The Second is where we eat, too. The Third Terrace is where you'll be taking your lessons. We sleep on the Fourth Terrace, by the top of the waterfall. It's very lovely up there."

"Lessons?" I asked. Were we going to have to study *theology*? My spirits sagged, for I'd hoped to be done with school. I could only imagine what Dilara must be thinking.

"Oh, yes. You have much to learn. But we'll discuss that later."

"How many girls are here now?" Dilara asked.

"Let me see. With you, it's eleven students, plus me."

We reached the top of the stairs and entered a large room containing dining tables and stools. The window lattices were open and admitted a warm breeze scented with mountain camellia and cedar. Here, the wall frescoes, faded to soft pastels, portrayed men and women at a banquet, and thanks to the Arts Tutoress I recognized the paintings as dating from the later empire. Their formal simplicity and cool colors were quite different from our modern preference for lavish detail and vivid hues.

"This is the refectory," Tossi said, as we passed through it to enter a corridor on its far side. I smelled fried peppers, hot oil, and stewed fowl, and realized I was famished. Through an archway was a long kitchen with iron pots and griddles on a tiled stove set into the wall under a chimneypiece. Nobody was there, but a door in the far wall stood open and through it I glimpsed the green of a small herb garden.

"Supper's on its way, as you can tell," Tossi said as we gazed hungrily at the gently steaming pots. "Neclan and Gethriya are cooking it. We all take turns."

A dark-skinned Erallu man came into the kitchen from the herb garden. I assumed he was a servant, but then Tossi said, "Sisters, be pleased to greet the head instructor at Three Springs. His name is Master Aa. Master Aa, these are our new students, Lale and Dilara."

Less and less of this made sense, including Master Aa himself. I'd never heard such a name, and a closer look told me why. He was not an Erallu as I'd thought, but a real foreigner, clean shaven, with a flat bony face and very small ears. His tunic left his arms bare; they were as thin as the rest of him, but whips of muscle glided under the dark skin. And his eyes were sky blue, like Nilang's.

He presented us with the half bow of a teacher to a pupil. In return Dilara and I gave him a full bow, and I said, "We're very honored to meet you, Master Aa."

"I look forward to our useful relationship," he answered. "It will be a labor of privilege to instruct you." He had a very strong accent and a quirk of using Durdana words in a way that was almost, but not quite, exact. Still, I found him easy enough to understand.

But instruct us in what? I asked myself.

Tossi didn't explain but led us onward past an archway closed by a heavy door. She gestured at it and said, "The baths are in there. All our water comes from the falls—there are pipes from the old days and they still work, so we've got it on all four levels and we don't have to carry it."

Running water! Even in Repose we hadn't had such luxury. There were basins and pipes in the palace, but they hadn't worked since the Year of the Five Emperors, when somebody's army wrecked the aqueduct that brought water to Chiran. No one had ever rebuilt the aqueduct, so Repose used wells and the towns-people purchased water from water carts, or lugged it up from the river if they were poor. And as in most other cities, the public baths of Chiran had been closed for a long time.

But life seemed better organized at Three Springs. My spirits rose a little, then sank again as I remembered I was going back to school. But what under heaven would someone like Master Aa teach us?

"Up, again," Tossi said and we began to climb another staircase. From above I heard a sudden burst of women's voices and felt a stab of anticipation.

The staircase took us up to a pillared porch. We emerged into it like the three daughters of the Water Lord rising from the ocean, and before us was the Third Terrace. It was grass covered, but in patches the grass had been worn to bare earth, as if by the passage of many feet.

And there our sisters waited for us. The instant we emerged from the porch they cheered, and a moment later were all around us: Kidrin, Temile, Merrin, Tulay, Neclan and Gethriya who had deserted the kitchen, along with all the others I'd never expected to see again. I almost wept for happiness.

After a while the excitement died down and Temile, who had left Repose only three months before, said, "Well, I bet you never thought you'd find yourself up here."

"No," I said, "we didn't." I saw now how lean and fit they all were. They wore loose shirts of plain unbleached linen and equally loose calf-length trousers of the same material. Everybody had bare feet, and everybody's hair was cut to shoulder length or shorter. Kidrin and a few others wore headbands to keep stray locks from their faces. If these were devotees of the Moon Lady, they didn't resemble any I'd ever seen.

Dilara looked equally puzzled. Finally she said, as they all stood and smirked at us, "Well, how much time every day do you have to spend at prayers?"

Everyone burst into laughter. Dilara flushed angrily, but I thought: *This doesn't look like what Mother said it was.*

Kidrin said, "We go turn and turn about at it, both to please the Lady and because Mother likes her. But it's only a couple of days a month. The rest of the time we're studying."

"Studying what?" I burst out. "For pity's sake, what's going on at this place?"

"You mean you haven't guessed?" Kidrin asked, her pretty face full of mischief.

Merrin grinned. "We do this to everybody who's new," she said, "and nobody ever guesses right. Can you?"

"No," I answered in frustration.

Dilara, never one for banter, demanded, "Tell us, then."

"We can't," Kidrin said. "You have one more step to take. Then you can know everything. But that step has to come first."

"What is it, Tossi?" I asked. I was dying of curiosity.

"Soon," Tossi said, and led us away.

She assigned Dilara and me to a room in the students' residence, two buildings that snuggled against the cliff on the Fourth Terrace, with a courtyard garden between them. The garden had not only flowers and a pair of big mist trees, but also a small fountain. In our room were two sleeping platforms and two cedar storage chests, and Dilara and I each had an oil lamp. The residence was the old servants' quarters, delightfully cool in summer but so cold in winter, as I came to find out, that it made one's bones ache.

When we had unpacked our few belongings, Tossi said, "Before I can tell you anything of what we do here, there is the step that Kidrin spoke of."

"Tell us what it is," Dilara pleaded. I hoped it might keep until after supper, whatever it might be, because I was famished.

"Come with me," Tossi said.

Mystified, we followed her down to the Second Terrace and into a tall building that clung to the cliff face. Within was a big room, three walls of which bore landscape paintings in the Late Northern style. On the fourth wall, facing the high windows, was a marvel: a huge mosaic map of the whole breadth of our empire as it was before the Partition, including the major cities, roads, rivers, canals, and mountain ranges. Even at Repose I had seen nothing to compare with it.

"This was the imperial prefect's banquet hall," Tossi explained, as we stared at the mosaic. "We use it now as our classroom."

Indeed, there were benches and writing tables arranged near the stone dais where the prefect's chair of state must once have stood. Near the dais was a door into another, shadowy chamber, and out of its dimness came a girl who wore iridescent gossamin of crimson and blue.

It was not a girl. It was Nilang. My heart skipped a beat, and Dilara gave a soft exclamation of surprise.

The sorceress halted and studied us. No one spoke. I could hear a bellbird somewhere in the forest, singing his soft, chiming song.

Nilang said, "This is to be your initiation into the Three Springs School. If you refuse it or fail it, you cannot enter the service of the sanctuary and must leave."

"Could we go back to Repose then?" Dilara asked, a little hopefully.

"No. You will be sent far away and given a trade. But you will never see Three Springs or Tamurin or the Despotana again. Is that clear?"

Painfully so. "Yes, Mistress Nilang," I said for both of us.

"You accept the initiation?"

What else could we do? She was giving us no time to think it over anyway. But what kind of service to the Moon Lady could demand such rigors as this?

"We do, Mistress Nilang," I answered.

"Sit at the table, then."

We obeyed. Tossi came with us, and, standing by our bench, she said, "Dilara and Lale, there is a hard road ahead for all the sisters of Three Springs, and soon it will be ahead of you. That road will take you to places you have never seen, and on it you will do things you never imagined you would do. Danger will breathe on the back of your neck, and much of the time you will not know who is your friend and who is not. Your only allies will be your skills and wits.

"But the merit will be great. You'll help Mother keep Tamurin safe, and so ensure the safety of the school and of your sisters. There's no greater achievement than that, and no higher loyalty."

I reflected fleetingly that wealth would be an ideal companion for such merit. But before I could pursue the thought, Tossi turned to Nilang and said, "Begin when you wish."

She left us, and I heard the hall doors close behind her. Nilang drew an incense burner from her robes. At first it didn't seem to be alight, but as soon as she set it on the table, it began to smoke. I smelled the same odd, incense-like fragrance that had hung in the palace sickroom years ago when she'd opened the Quiet World to me, and I felt a stab of unease.

She said, "Fix your gaze on the smoke."

I did so. It wafted gently from the burner, like a small, unquiet ghost.

Nilang tilted her head forward and breathed it in. I wondered how she could do that without coughing or sneezing. The scent was making me oddly light-headed.

"Soon," Nilang said, "you will be learning things that the Despotana wishes to keep secret. You must never talk of these things except to your sisters in arms, those who have also undergone this initiation. Even if an enemy torments you to make you speak, you must refuse. Even if it means you must die, you must still refuse. Do you understand?"

Her voice had become low and soft, and I wondered why she didn't speak like this all the time, because it was very soothing, so soothing that my anxiety was ebbing. I had become wonderfully relaxed and very drowsy.

"I understand," I said. My voice seemed to waft across a great distance.

Nilang inhaled the smoke again and murmured, "You are good and loyal students. But what if you were not so good, not so loyal?" Her eyes were blue and deep. I saw myself far down in them, as if I looked into a still millpond. "Do you know what would happen then?"

"No," Dilara breathed.

"I will show you," Nilang whispered.

She closed her eyes and her face grew lined and strained. Then her lips moved, as if she spoke silently to some unseen audience, and, despite my strangely relaxed state, my skin turned cold. She made an odd gesture with her right hand and let it fall palm upward on the table.

I stared down at that hand. There seemed to be nothing in it, but at the same time there *was*, and a tiny, wakeful part of me suddenly wanted to scream and run away.

Nilang slowly closed her fingers, as though she squeezed or crushed a thing invisible. The light falling through the high windows failed, as if night approached with unnatural speed. My calm vanished as an unspeakable foreboding crept over me; it was like being gradually immersed in icy water. My limbs grew weak, as though my blood were being slowly drawn out of my veins. But I was paralyzed where I sat and could not so much as whisper.

Nilang's fingers tightened into a fist. A soft, dull moan emanated from the air, and things like shadows began to form in the corners of the hall. I watched, horrified, as they grew into a throng that drifted toward the table, blotting out the great mosaic map, the darkened windows, the painted walls. For a few moments I dreaded that I was slipping into the Quiet World again.

But then I knew that I was not, and that what was happening was worse. For Nilang was drawing these terrible shadows from that world into our own.

They were unlike the creature that had wanted to devour me but no less ghastly. There was an eerie, nauseating luster about them, as if they were not really shadows at all but some species of diseased and disfigured light. They were shapeless, but it seemed to my appalled gaze that they might assume shape at any moment, and above all I did not want to see what might congeal out of those swirling, semi-luminescent vapors.

They crowded about the table but did not come quite within an arm's length, and I understood that Nilang's will held them in thrall. But furrows of tension deepened around her mouth, and even in my haze of fear it occurred to me that she might lose control of them. For I knew that she had once almost failed me, and that I had almost been devoured, and the thought turned my bowels to water. Worse, the things were in *our* world now, and the ancestor who saved me before might not be able to aid me again.

Her eyes still closed, Nilang said, "I have asked you to swear your silence. Do you so swear, that you will die rather than break it?"

My tongue would barely move but I whispered, "I will," and Dilara made a strangled noise of assent.

"My wraiths have heard your oath," Nilang murmured. "If you betray it, they will know and they will come for you. You'll see them from the corners of your eyes, you will feel their wings at your mouth, and you will feel them within your flesh. Sometimes they will leave you for a little while, and you will think you are free, but always they will return to feed on you. And they know how to keep you alive, so that you will be a long time dying; and before you die you will have clawed out your eyes and bitten off your tongue and lips and fingers, and you will be mad."

I tried not to look at the shadows. I imagined, or perhaps did not imagine, that I heard faint voices, sweet and merciless.

"Do you understand this?" Nilang asked.

"Yes," I croaked.

And Dilara whimpered, "Yes, mistress."

Nilang opened her blue eyes, made a complicated gesture before our faces, and said, "Enough." Her sudden movement startled me, as if I'd been asleep and she'd rudely shouted me awake. Instantly the shadows faded, withdrew into the room's corners, and seeped away. The evening light returned, and with it a soft, forest-scented breeze. I was damp with the sweat of fear, though the fear itself had fled, as if dismissed by Nilang's word and gesture. But I knew a curse when I heard it, and I knew I'd do anything rather than bring this one down on me.

"You've passed your initiation," Nilang said. Her voice had regained its usual harshness. "With it comes something else. Are you listening carefully to me?"

I didn't at all like the sound of this "something else," so I listened very carefully indeed.

"Because you have felt the wraiths," she said, "you can now experience certain other emanations from the Quiet World. From time to time, I may need to speak to you from a distance, and it is by this means that I will do so. These emanations are under my control and you need not fear them, although their character may cause you some discomfort. You will be trained to recognize such sendings. Do you understand?"

"Yes, Mistress Nilang."

"Good." She clapped her hands and called out loudly, "It's done."

The door opened and Tossi entered the hall. She surveyed us and then said to the sorceress, "Well?"

"The Despotana has two brave young women here," Nilang said. "I've seen strong men disgrace themselves under the same test. They'll serve her well."

"I'm so glad," Tossi said, her face suddenly radiant, and she hugged us both. I was so happy I almost wept. Dilara and I had been tested, and we'd both passed. It made me feel proud and superior, as if we'd found a place among a secret and exceptional few. Which, indeed, we had.

"Come in, everybody," Tossi called, and instantly the others burst into the hall, surrounding us with laughter and praise. The memory of the wraiths was suddenly far away, and when I looked around for Nilang, she had gone.

"Scary, wasn't it?" Neclan said. "Don't say it wasn't, because it scared *me*. But you're all right now, aren't you?"

"We're fine," I said. "But now can we *please* find out what's going on here?"

"You still haven't guessed?" Temile asked. "How slow of you."

"For pity's sake," Dilara burst out, "stop it! Tell us!"

"Tossi?" Kidrin asked, and Tossi nodded. Kidrin paused dramatically, like an actress about to deliver a killing line.

"Three Springs," she said, "is a school for spies."

"It's *really* a school for spies?" Dilara asked.

It was early evening, not long before supper. Tossi and Dilara and I were sitting in the courtyard garden of the Fourth Terrace, under the mist trees that were now coming into golden blossom. Beyond the terrace's stone balustrade was the view: the deep shadowy cleft of the valley, whose far wall was a mountain clad in forest, and beyond that another peak and then another, all the way to the northern horizon.

"That's exactly what it is," Tossi replied. "We call it the Midnight School, partly because of Mother's nickname and partly because we keep it wrapped in a very secret darkness. The Heron Guardsmen who bring our supplies know it's more than a sanctuary, because they help the departing girls get on their way. But they don't know much else, and they're oath bound to Mother not to ask questions or talk. They also know Nilang's involved, and *that* would bridle their tongues, even if their oath didn't."

Mother, she went on, had founded the Midnight School the year after I came to Repose. Tossi was the senior of its first three students, and there were five instructors to teach them, headed by Master Aa and his wife. In the five years since, seventeen young women had completed their training and gone out into the world to be weavers, perfumers, bakers, and owners of wine shops. And to work for Mother.

"Where?" I asked.

"Here and there," Tossi said with a smile. "You only know that kind of thing when you need to."

"But why?" Dilara wanted to know. "What's it all *for*?"

"Knowledge," Tossi said. "People think that arms, men, and wealth are power—and so they are. But without knowledge, these can be lost between one dawn and the next. An army can be destroyed because it doesn't know where its enemy lurks. A besieged city falls because its governor doesn't know his second in command has been bribed to open the gates. A merchant is ruined because he doesn't know his competitors have conspired against him.

"So, you see, strength without knowledge is brittle and easily broken. But even a lesser strength, if it's multiplied by knowledge, can overcome a much greater power. We are Mother's eyes and ears in the world; through us she gains the knowledge she needs to protect Tamurin from its enemies. Particularly, as you know, from the Sun Lord and his Chancellor but also from the other Despots. Though she does have friends among the Despots, and she helps them occasionally with what she knows."

"But how do we get such knowledge?" I asked, feeling very inadequate. "And how do we send it to her? How do we know what she wants?"

"You'll be trained. For example, when you're out in the world, instructions will be sent to you from time to time. But you won't hear from Mother directly. A man may come to your shop, for example, and hand you a letter folded in a certain way, and you will give him a report. Or a woman will say certain words you'll recognize, and you'll go to a tree in a certain place to collect a message. Perhaps the message will tell you what information you are to obtain, or perhaps it will instruct you to carry out a particular action on such and such a day."

Suddenly struck by the solution to an old mystery, I exclaimed, "Was *that* who Master Lim was? One of Mother's secret messengers?"

"Exactly so," Tossi replied. "Although I still have no idea why she sent him so far south. She doesn't tell me everything she's doing, you see. Just as much as I need to know. It's better that way."

"But then it's not only us who work for Mother," Dilara said. She sounded disappointed—as I was also, for I wanted us to be completely exclusive. I remembered the nondescript people who came and went from Repose and realized they were the counterparts of Master Lim. But I didn't want to be like *them*.

"By no means is it only us," Tossi said. She leaned forward and her tone became emphatic. "But remember this: All rulers are at war all the time, even while they claim friendship and brotherhood with other rulers. These are secret wars, hidden from almost everyone, but their victories and defeats can overthrow a ruler in a night or destroy his army in an afternoon. We of Three Springs are by far the most important of Mother's soldiers, because we are the hidden warriors in the thick of the fight, the ones who do the hardest work, the most dangerous, the most desperately needed. All the others—the men who carry the messages, the women who leave you a purse of coins—can be replaced. But you can't. To Mother, every one of you is a gem beyond price, because it is you who slip into the most carefully hidden sanctuaries of our enemies, to learn the secrets they dare not breathe even to themselves. In doing so you protect us from defeat and ensure our victories."

"But how," Dilara asked, "are we to do such things?"

"You'll be trained, as I said. That will take between one and two years, depending on your aptitude and any special skills Mother may want you to learn." She turned her gaze to me. "You, for example, Lale—when you leave here, you'll probably be going to Master Luasin's school in Istana."

After several moments, during which I tried to find my tongue. I said, "I *will*?"

"I think so, if your promise as an actress holds true. And, Dilara, while you may not become a weaver as soon as you leave the Midnight School, a fine loom awaits you someday. I believe that's what you want."

Silence fell. A flock of wine finches flew down into one of the mist trees and settled in the branches, twittering. The evening sun turned their violet plumage to crimson and purple, rich amid the flowers' gold. I stared at them, contemplating the fact that I might become an actress after all.

"You'll also be trained to fight," Tossi went on. "That's what Master Aa and his instructors are for. When they've finished, not even a veteran swordsman of the Sun Lord's guard will be able to touch you. That's why we have no guards here; we don't need them.

"But there's something else you must know, and it's this: To defend oneself, one must sometimes kill. You will learn how to do that, too, silently and without blood or struggle. You are to be not only spies but also, if need be, assassins."

If the rest seemed strange, this last was unimaginable. I'd heard Sulen crying out in the sickroom before the fever took her, and I'd seen two or three criminals hanged in Chiran, so I knew what people looked like and sounded like as they died. But the possibility that I might someday kill someone seemed as remote as the ruby mountains of Narappa-lo.

"Assassins?" Dilara said. She sounded curious rather than surprised. "We might really have to kill somebody?"

"You might. But all this is for you to learn later. Ah, there's the supper gong. Come down with me and we'll eat together."

That night, as Dilara and I lay in our beds in the darkness, I said, "Do you think you could really kill somebody?"

A pause. Then she said, "Yes, if I had to. There are people I'd like to see dead, people from the time before Mother found me. I think I could do it, if I knew I'd never be caught. What about you?"

I remembered Riversong and its villagers, and Feriti and Adumar who would have kicked me to death if the priest hadn't stopped them. I remembered all the others who had bullied me, hit me, starved me, and called me a useless good-for-nothing and a thief. I hadn't thought about them for a long time except fleetingly. But now a breaker of rage swept over me and I saw Adumar with a knife in her belly, her eyes staring in shock, blood sliding out of her mouth. I saw Feriti choking her breath out in a hemp noose, and Detrim with his head lying beside him in the dirt.

Astonished at my fury, I tried to drive it back into its lair, and more or less succeeded. My heart slowed and I unclenched my fists.

"Well, would you?" Dilara prompted.

"Yes," I said.

Dilara emitted a low laugh. "But I doubt if Mother would let us do away with somebody just because we were mad at him. She'd have to order it, wouldn't she?"

"I suppose." I pondered this. I reckoned I could kill if I were defending myself. But could I take a life only because Mother said I must?

Then I realized that Mother would order only the deaths of our enemies, so obeying her would be the right thing to do. Moreover, we were soldiers in a secret war, and war made the whole business different. Nobody thought soldiers did wrong because they killed other soldiers in battle. In fact, the more enemies a soldier dispatched, the more highly his officers and fellow warriors thought of him.

"Maybe it'll never happen," I said. "Maybe we'll just have to find information for her."

"Maybe," Dilara murmured.

"I wouldn't mind that," I said. "It might be fun."

"It might be," she answered, then fell silent. Through the open window I could see stars. I thought again about Riversong and that made me think about being a foundling and about my real mother and father. I rarely did this any more, although I vaguely recollected that searching for my family was one reason I'd left Riversong. Maybe, once I was out in the world, I could try to find out who I really was.

But then I realized that even if I did find my real blood, I wouldn't dare tell them I was their daughter. Being at Three Springs had already given me too many secrets. I could never risk betraying Mother, even by accident—and not just because of what Nilang's wraiths would do to me if I did. It was because I loved Mother so much.

I would never find my parents, anyway. It was a big world, and there were so many people in it. My only small comfort was to remember that I did have ancestors, because Nilang herself had said that one had helped save me in the Quiet World. Back when I was fifteen, I'd twice secretively tried to summon that ancestor, but nothing had happened and I'd never tried again.

"Dilara," I whispered, "do you think about your mother very often?"

But Dilara only snored, and after a while I fell asleep.

Ten

❧

Discipline at Three Springs was very strict. We rose at dawn and meditated for an hour before breakfast, no matter how our stomachs complained. Our instructors took these sessions seriously. Master Aa's wife, Mistress Ipip, supervised them, and she would apply a light cane smartly to the shoulders of anyone who dozed off.

We had five instructors, of whom Mistress Ipip was the only woman. Like Nilang, they were of the race called the Taweret, from the Country of Circular Paths. I believe all five were related, although I never understood exactly how, because they calculated kinship differently from us Durdana. Cousins appeared to be more important kin to them than brothers or sisters, and uncles and fathers seemed indistinguishable.

These five were, in fact, the followers whom Nilang had brought to Chiran several years previously, when Mother gave her sanctuary from her enemies. She was related in some manner to both Mistress Ipip and Master Aa, and they and the other three were devoted to her. Tossi told me they'd all been condemned to death at home and that Mother had offered them sanctuary and protection in exchange for their service.

At least, this was what Tossi said. But I remembered, or thought I remembered, that Mother had obscurely threatened Nilang on that fever-ridden night when I saw the Quiet World, and that there might be more to the arrangement than Tossi let on. But then I told myself I'd misheard Mother's words, or more likely imagined them in my sickness. It was not possible, I thought, that Nilang would serve Mother unwillingly, for surely not even a Despotana could place such a powerful sorceress under duress.

Nilang spent a lot of time at Three Springs, for she was the chief instructor there, and this explained why she used to vanish from Repose for such long periods. I was always nervous around her because of the wraiths, and I wasn't the only one who felt this way; none of us, even Tossi, was ever fully at ease in Nilang's presence.

We all had to learn to recognize her sendings. They were eerie, especially since the voices did not come through our ears but seemed rather to emanate from within our heads. The first warning of one was a tingling at the back of the neck and a numbness of the lips, after which we would perceive the manifestation.

This was weirder than it sounds, because of the caprices of the entities she employed. Once I was confronted by a fringed salamander that took on a child's face, delivered Nilang's words, and scurried away. The things were capable, however, of bearing only the simplest messages; they were like those southern birds that can learn to imitate, but not understand, a few words of human speech. As a result, messages of more than a simple phrase had to be committed to paper, and for this we learned various Taweret codes and ciphers.

Sendings were useful, though, and one day, egged on by the rest of us, Kidrin asked why we students couldn't learn to do them ourselves. At this, the sorceress gazed silently at the poor girl until she began to look quite frightened. Then Nilang said, "Because none of you has the talent, and even if you had, you would need twenty years to learn it, as I did."

I soon learned that Nilang was versed in much more than sorcery. In order to survive in their turbulent realm, Taweret lords spied with feverish intensity not only on their enemies but also on their allies and their rulers. Those who prospered did so by constructing vast and intricate webs of observers, agents, double agents, and assassins. Nilang, a cousin of such a magnate, had become highly skilled in such clandestine work, and she and her five companions had served him with their own special skills of combat, concealment, treachery, and subterfuge.

Of course, Mother was no stranger to spying—no Despot was—but Taweret practices were far more sophisticated than those of the Durdana. So Mother recast her methods according to the Taweret mold and Nilang's advice, and thus the Midnight School was born.

Our studies were interwoven with rigorous physical training, but strength and endurance were merely the foundation of our craft. As the months passed, I learned to make fire with a rawhide thong and three sticks, to take game with snare and bow, and to eat well in a winter forest. I learned to climb sheer rock walls using my fingertips, toes, knees, and elbows; to walk along a rope fifty feet above the ground; to use an inflated sheep's bladder to support myself through a long swim. I could throw a hunting javelin or a climbing grapnel and almost never miss my target, although Dilara, somewhat to my chagrin, never missed at all.

We also became adept in the Taweret modes of fighting without weapons. There was nothing honorable or fair about this form of combat, the ideal being to strike lethally from ambush. Surprise and speed were of the essence: a foot broke a leg; an elbow, a rib; a stiffened hand crushed a windpipe.

Weapons were not neglected, however. Many Durdana women, especially those whose husbands spent months away from home as mariners or traders, had swords or spears in the house and knew how to use them. But our training went far beyond that. We learned the long knife, throwing knife, short sword, short halberd, long spear, bow, quarterstaff, and others. Some of those others were quite strange, being Taweret devices: weighted chains, fighting sticks, the hand trident, and clawed gloves. I was good at chain work and delighted in tangling my opponent at the knees, sweeping her off her feet, and finishing her off with the edge of my hand.

But all this training was a tool, not an end in itself. Nilang taught us that the real foundations of our success must be concealment and deception, not combat. If we had to use our fighting skills, it meant an enemy had detected us, and this was next door to failure. Being detected was not, as Nilang put it, *elegant*, even if we got away unscathed. We would have exchanges like this with her:

"Kidrin! What is the pinnacle of elegance in our profession?"

"Mistress Nilang, it is as follows. That we act without being detected, so that the enemy does not know who has carried out the attack against him. He is befuddled and does not know whom to blame."

"Wrong! You are lax in your application! It is that the enemy does not know that there has *been* an attack, until he discovers that his strength is dispersed, his defenses nullified, and that he is suddenly in the hands of his enemy." She turned to me. "Kidrin's position, however, has an element of virtue. Lale! Tell us why."

I said, "Because, in the world as it is, the pinnacle is the ideal and therefore difficult to achieve. Thus, while we should strive for the ideal, we must not always disdain the less elegant solution. Through reaching too high, one invites failure."

"Well put. In other words, if there is no paved road up the mountain, we must make do with the sheep track."

She also taught us that men were particularly vulnerable to young, attractive women. They could easily be induced to boast about their knowledge and power and in doing so reveal what we wished to discover. And since men did not normally perceive females as dangerous, even those who were well guarded against assassination would often let a woman approach within killing range. But achieving this might, she warned, involve some erotic dalliance.

This aroused giggles from those of us who had fluttered over the young soldiers of the Heron Guard and the junior palace clerks, and scowls from those, like Dilara, whose pasts had given them a distaste and contempt for men. Back at Repose, Kidrin and several others had clearly enjoyed male attention, but I think it was their power over the men they enjoyed, not the attention itself, because they never let things go very far—not that they could have, for our tutoresses had always watched us very closely, and Mother kept a vigilant eye on us as well. As for my opinion on the matter, it was simple: I would never leap into any man's bed unless I was doing so for a very good reason, and I would leap out of it just as fast if the reason vanished.

A more congenial subject was deception. People usually see what they expect to see, instead of what is really in front of them, and we helped this tendency along with disguises of appearance, stance, action, and voice. For me, with my flair for acting, this was wine and meat. I was also a very good mimic, and I used to scare the other girls by sneaking up behind them and screeching at them in Nilang's voice and accent, a trick that Dilara found excruciatingly funny.

Along with everything else, Nilang taught us about poisons. She had a plot of ground near the little orchard in the Lower Terrace in which she grew various plants. Some were native, but others were not; I suppose she had carried their seeds with her when she fled her homeland.

Nilang's garden was an odd place. It was not fenced, but no rodent or insect ever touched a leaf or stem of it, and even the bees, protected though they were by the Goddess, would not go near some of the flowers. One especially subtle poison was prepared from the root of one bush and the sap of another; either alone was harmless, but if consumed together they killed swiftly. A twist was that you could administer the two ingredients some time apart—at breakfast and at the noon meal, for example. If you did this, the symptoms were of a failure of the heart, so that the poisoning might go unsuspected.

෨

As the months passed and young untrained women arrived, older trained women departed to begin their clandestine careers. Mother placed a few, quite openly, as tutoresses in prominent families, representing them as recent graduates of Repose while concealing their time at Three Springs. But most she sent to live quietly in the cities along the Pearl River, as sandal makers, public scribes, seamstresses, glass and pottery merchants, basket weavers, and the like. Their lack of family connections might cause some neighborhood comment, but so many bloodlines and clans had been fractured since the Partition that such unattached women were common. Furthermore, we were trained not to attract attention, and to deflect it if anyone became too interested in us. Finally, each of us memorized a false personal history, to which we could turn if we needed to conceal our connection with Mother.

It was through us that Mother knew so many secrets, and she used that knowledge both to enrich herself and to extend her power. She knew in advance when to buy cheap and sell dear, and thus acquired secret control of a dozen trading firms up and down the Pearl River and along the western seacoast. She used us to find out who in the Despots' families and in the magnate clans were most hostile to the Sun Lord, and these she helped toward greater power, sometimes by removing others who stood in their way. My Three Springs sisters were adept at causing the accidents and illnesses that accomplished this, but more often they simply arranged for the local authorities to do Mother's work for her. Nobody was more suspicious than a Despot, and forged documents, with some false evidence and a little judicious perjury, can lead the most upright of men to the scaffold.

The daughters she married off directly from Repose were also her tools, though not wittingly. Once in a while a Three Springs graduate might make a sisterly visit to such a wife, and by careful questioning find out about certain legal, political, or financial matters. Sometimes the wives could be induced to influence their husbands in directions useful to Mother. Some of the husbands had tastes above their income, and if the wife could negotiate a loan from Mother's coffers . . . well, so much the better, but the loan would never be quite paid off and the man would be firmly in Mother's debt, and in her grip, thereafter.

Such were the skills we learned at the Midnight School. All were directed to one purpose: to protect our home and our family in a world that grew more dangerous every day. For us, in our innocence, that purpose justified an unthinking obedience to Mother; we never thought to ask whether we *ought* to be doing these things, or whether we might be better off doing something else. Fear of Nilang's wraiths was only a small part of it; we served Mother because we wanted to, and because we loved her. It was almost impossible for us to imagine doing anything else. So we were all perfectly loyal, until Adrine came up the mountain.

She arrived at Three Springs about six months after I did, but she was no longer the self-effacing, nondescript girl who had always known the right answers in class. Her skin had cleared, her hair had a new gloss to it, and her figure had become more womanly. She was also more vivacious, at least for her. I never got to know her, though, because she was at the Midnight School for so short a time—less than two hands, I think.

By chance, the incident happened while Nilang was away at Repose. Dilara, Neclan, Tulay, and I had been sent into the forest for three days, to test our winter survival skills, and when we trudged back through the gate at Three Springs we found uproar, or as much uproar as Tossi would permit.

The instant we entered the Lower Terrace, Master Aa and Instructor Shefenwep stopped us, told us not to talk to anybody, and escorted us to the little room from which Tossi managed the school's business. Then they left. Tossi stood behind her worktable and scrutinized us carefully. Her face revealed little, but I sensed that she was very angry indeed, and almost as alarmed.

She said, "When did you last see Adrine?"

The four of us, dumbfounded, looked at her and then at one another. Impatiently, Tossi repeated, "When? Lale! Answer me!"

My confusion grew. We seemed to be under some suspicion, and I couldn't imagine why. "The morning we left," I replied. "She was eating breakfast."

"Did you talk to her?"

"No. She never talks much. You know how she is."

"*Do* I?" Tossi snapped. "Tulay, when did you last see her?"

The same thing: at breakfast. That was the way of it with all four of us, and we told Tossi so. I was alarmed but also a little angry at being treated with such suspicion.

Finally Tossi said, "And you didn't meet her in the forest? You didn't help her?"

"Help her do what?" Dilara snapped. "We didn't see her, so how could we have helped her do anything? Why won't you tell us what's happened to her?"

Tossi eyed each of us and then abruptly sat down on her stool. "She's run off," she said. "It was sometime last night. We found the rope she used to get down from the wall, and some of her things are gone. You were out at the same time, so I had to question you. I didn't really think you'd helped her, but I can't overlook anything."

This passed belief. "But why?" I blurted. "I mean, why would she run away?"

"Jisrin thinks it's a man," Tossi said. "She told me Adrine took to writing poetry before she left Repose, and she saw some of it. There were three or four love poems that used a man's name, but that's common in the nine-seven form so she didn't think anything of it. She didn't notice, unfortunately, that it was the name of one of the Heron Guard troopers."

"A man?" Dilara exclaimed. "Poetry? Adrine?"

I shared her incredulity. If I'd been asked who among us was most likely to lose her head over a male, I'd have picked Kidrin without hesitation. But Adrine? It was hard to imagine that her colorless character concealed such sentiments. It was just as hard to believe that a man would notice her long enough to feel the same way. Which only shows how little I knew about such things.

"Yes, a man," Tossi agreed wearily. "If Jisrin's right, his name is Lahad. Do you know who he is?"

"He took service with the Guard last year," I said. "I remember him because he got a kite out of a tree for me in the courtyard garden." He'd seemed a very ordinary young man and had barely spoken to me, except to tell me his name.

"Do you think she's gone back to Chiran to find him?" Tossi asked.

"She's not a fool," Neclan said. "I don't think she'd run unless she was expecting Lahad to meet her near here. It's a long way to Chiran and she'd never reach him before she got caught."

"And she must know we'll be looking for her," Dilara said in a cold voice. "I bet they'll try to get out of Tamurin altogether. Maybe down to Guidarat, through Crossbone Pass."

Tossi stood up. "She's got to be stopped. Tulay, get four of the senior girls together, and horses. We'll try to catch her on the track. And ask Instructor Harakty to get a horse ready for himself, too. I have to send a message to Mother."

They brought Adrine back a day later. Jisrin was right; she'd run away because of Lahad and had met him a few miles down the mountain. They hadn't traveled much farther than that because Nilang's wraiths got her. The couple had then attempted to hide in a cave, but Adrine's shrieks betrayed them. Lahad tried to fight, but the girls and Instructor Harakty made short work of him and left his body for the forest scavengers.

The wraiths were giving Adrine a respite when they brought her back, but even so I had never seen a face so stark with fear. Tossi ordered her to be put into a storeroom on the Third Terrace, and immediately sent a message to Mother to say the boy was dead and Adrine taken and to ask what we should do with her.

For the next few days, Tossi took Adrine's meals to her, although the food came back untouched. She wouldn't talk about what she saw in the storeroom, but Nilang's wraiths were paying regular visits, to judge by the dreadful noises that seeped through the thick door. I couldn't understand how Adrine had hoped to elude them. Maybe she'd believed that love would be her armor or even that the wraiths were mere bluff. But it was clear that they weren't bluff, and that love was no protection at all.

Mother's instructions finally arrived, and Tossi assembled us in the reception hall to hear them. She had the letter with her, the seal broken. I remember that the morning was bright and cold, winter sunlight glowing through the thick oiled paper we'd glued over the window lattices.

"Mother reminds us—" Tossi began, and broke off. I couldn't tell whether her voice had cracked from distress or from anger.

She swallowed and began again. "Mother reminds us that our secrecy is our strongest defense and that Adrine has compromised it. Furthermore, she did this knowingly and willfully. She has committed both desertion and treason, and cannot be trusted anymore. She is a soldier who has run away from the battlefield and, worse, who has risked laying her general's plans open to the enemy."

Tossi stopped again. Then she said in a flat voice, "For these reasons, Mother declares Adrine no daughter of hers and condemns her to death."

It seemed as if a silent shudder passed through all of us. No one spoke, though Jisrin made a soft noise.

"However," Tossi went on, "Mother is disposed to be merciful. The wraiths will kill Adrine slowly. But she may avoid this if she chooses to take poison."

Tossi fell silent and folded up the letter. It was as if she were folding up Adrine's life at the same time.

I didn't know what to think. I'd believed that while the world might be full of faithlessness, we at Three Springs were different, that we were steadfast and incorruptible. That was one of my deepest beliefs, and I clung to it as a child clings to its mother's breast. Adrine had violated that belief, inflicting a bitter, shameful wound. But at the same time I wondered why Mother could not be merciful. Had Adrine betrayed us so utterly as to deserve death? She hadn't told anyone about us except her lover, and he was dead. Moreover, he was dead because of her. Was that not punishment enough?

Dilara interrupted these thoughts by asking, "When will you tell her about the poison?" Her voice was cold, betraying not a qualm about Adrine's fate.

"Now," Tossi said. "But Mother's instructions are that we draw lots for it."

So Neclan brought broom straws and Tossi broke one short and left the others long, then held them out to us. I drew the short straw.

I went with Tossi to the storeroom. For once there was no sound from within, but I imagined Adrine, huddled in a corner of that small dark prison, waiting for the wraiths to come for her again.

Tossi was looking anguished and sick, and I was sure I looked the same way, because that was how I felt. She handed me the two ceramic vials, the double poison that Nilang favored. "After you explain it to her," she said, "come out, and we'll leave her alone for a while."

"Tossi," I ventured.

"What?"

"Why can't she have another chance? She didn't betray us to the Sun Lord's spies or anything like that. She never intended any harm to Mother."

Tossi bit her lower lip, and I knew she didn't want this to happen any more than I did. But she said, "Would you have her die of the wraiths, then?"

"But Nilang commands the wraiths. Maybe she could make them stop, and then we could help Adrine see why she was wrong to run away. Then Mother might forgive her. Doing this to her is such a waste. Why can't we at least write and ask?"

I wondered if Adrine could hear us, and was crouching at the door in an agony of hope and fear. Tossi hesitated, but then she said, "She's sent her orders. We have to obey them."

"But . . ." I cast desperately about for words that might persuade her. "But maybe Mother needs more time to think. You know . . . you know she's been grieving for her son and family for years. And you know how grief can make people do strange things, things that seem a little mad. So maybe, about Adrine, she's, well . . ." I trailed off, frightened at where this was leading me.

"Are you serious?" Tossi said incredulously. "Do you mean to suggest that Mother's *mad*?" Her face went hard. "What foolishness is this, Lale? She's not mad. You're on the edge of lunacy yourself, if you believe such a thing."

"I don't believe it at all," I said hurriedly, appalled at myself for even thinking it. "I just, well, I don't want Adrine to die."

"Nor do I. But Mother knows what she's doing. She always does. Now go in."

There was nothing more to be said, so I drew the door bolts. In the back of my mind was the memory of my own encounter with the wraiths, and I did not want to set foot in that storeroom. But I had no choice, so I opened the door and entered, and Tossi shut it behind me.

Because of the room's tiny windows, the interior was dim. The smell of vomit and sewage was very bad. I blinked, letting my eyes adjust to the poor light, and took shallow breaths. Adrine was slumped on the floor by the far wall, on a heap of filthy blankets. In spite of myself I recoiled at her appearance. I would not have known her.

"Lale?" she whispered.

"Yes. It's Lale. What—" I almost said, *What have they done to you?* but caught myself just in time.

"Have you come to help me?" she asked in a soft, broken voice.

By now I didn't want either to help or harm her. I just wanted to escape from the horror before me.

"Mother wrote to us," I blurted. "You have a choice. The wraiths or poison."

She stared at me as if stunned. I realized she'd been hoping, even now, for Mother's forgiveness.

"Poison?" she asked at last.

I showed her the vials. "These. They act quickly if taken together. It won't hurt."

"She won't pardon me? She won't send Nilang to . . . to stop them?"

"No." I hoped she wouldn't start pleading and begging. But she was stronger than that. I suppose Mother had seen that strength, or she wouldn't have sent her to Three Springs.

"Oh," she said, and in that soft word was such a weight of loss that I could have wept. With so much against her, she had found a man to love. She must have dreamed of it hopelessly, in silent yearning, and suddenly it was hers. It must have seemed a miracle. And now this.

"Adrine, why did you do it?" I asked.

"I loved him." She shuddered. "I'd thought and thought about it, about us escaping together. And even with what I was thinking, *they* didn't come for me. So I told myself they weren't real, and when we were running away I thought it was safe to tell him what I'd been doing here. They came for me right after that. If only I hadn't told him, if only I'd believed Nilang . . . Did you know they try to make you bite your tongue off?"

Speechless, I stared at the lacerations and the crusted blood around her mouth. There were scratches and scabs all over her. I could see them through the rags she'd made of her clothes.

"I've stopped them so far," she whispered. "But I think it will be my eyes now. That's already starting. I ripped my nails off on my . . . but that's just . . . you see, it's the fear. It makes you scream and it—"

She took a deep, trembling breath and said, "Give me the poison. I want to die before they come back."

I was supposed to leave the vials with her, but her fingers were so maimed she couldn't open them. I drew the stoppers and held the poison to her broken lips, and she drank it down without faltering. Then I helped her to her pallet and got her to lie down. I wanted to go but could not bring myself to desert her.

"How long?" she asked.

"Soon." I prayed to Our Lady of Mercy that it would be.

"Will you stay with me until I . . . until it's over?" She sounded both fearful and diffident, as if she were too frightened to let me go, but at the same time didn't want me to think her a nuisance.

"Yes," I answered. "I'll stay."

She closed her eyes. "I'll see Lahad soon, won't I? I'm sure he's waiting for me."

"Of course he is," I agreed with an aching throat.

Adrine fell silent. The poison took longer to act than I'd expected, and I was starting to worry when she suddenly gasped and clutched at her breast. Stupidly I said, "Is it—"

"It hurts," she gasped. "Oh, Lale, it, oh sweet Lady of Mercy oh it hurts it hurts—"

Her back arched and she screamed. Then she slumped back onto the pallet and rolled her head from side to side. Sick with horror and pity, I seized her hands in a futile, stupid gesture of comfort. But in her agony she didn't notice. She drew a sobbing breath, held it, let it out, drew another. Her eyes stared into mine. I couldn't meet them. I wanted to scream, too. *Die*, I thought, *please die and get it over with. Please.*

She shuddered, then went limp as her last breath flowed from her. I thought I sensed her idu-spirit rush past me on its way to the Quiet World to find Lahad, and I hoped fervently that that was where she'd gone. She would make a very unquiet ghost if she lingered.

After a while I closed her eyes and slowly got to my feet. Then I called out, "It's done."

Tossi entered and joined me in looking down at the poor, ruined body. Eventually she said, "You didn't have to stay, you know. I said to leave her alone."

"She wasn't always a traitor," I mumbled. "I stayed because of that."

"She didn't deserve it," Tossi said.

The next day we buried Adrine beneath a camellia tree outside the walls. Then we burned a lock of her hair, but because of her crime the ash couldn't go back to Repose to be placed in our ancestor shrine. Instead we scattered it on the mountain wind, which we hoped would blow her away and prevent her ghost from troubling us.

After she had gone under the earth, Tossi instructed me to dispose of her belongings. There weren't many: a leather bag, a scarf, a copper necklace, a comb, and some hairpins. Nothing about them was memorable, just as there had been nothing memorable about Adrine herself, except her wretched death.

I knew nobody would want any of her things—they had a sad, doomed air about them—so I decided to bury them near her, as a sort of offering. I gathered them up and was slipping them into the leather bag, when I felt something at the bag's bottom. It was two sheets of paper, folded small. I opened them, glanced at the first neatly written line, and discovered I was reading Adrine's love poetry.

I almost put the papers back then and there. I knew how flat my own poetry was, and I imagined that hers would be no better. But then I read the next line, and the next.

There were four poems, in the very difficult three-nine-three lyric mode. I was no poetess and never would be, but I'd been trained to know the bad from the good, the merely good from the splendid. These were splendid.

> For ten days I have not seen you.
> Now you return from the river,
> You kiss my mouth,
>   And make me drunk as wine.

I read them all several times, realizing sadly that in executing Adrine we had killed a poetess of the first order. What might she have achieved if she'd lived? I couldn't imagine why she'd kept her talent from everyone, including the Literature Tutoress. It would have saved her, if she'd let it. Mother would never have sent her to Three Springs, if she'd known the greatness of Adrine's gift.

But there was nothing anybody could for her now. I told no one what I'd found but instead took her belongings to the grave by the wall and dug a hole for them beside her.

At the last moment I couldn't bear to let her words go into the dark. I took the papers out of the bag and slipped them into my jacket, begging her forgiveness if this was displeasing to her. Then I covered up everything else and went away.

The next day Tossi summoned me and said, "I heard Adrine say to you that the wraiths came, but only after she told the boy about us and about Mother."

I nodded. I'd puzzled over this. I'd supposed, from the ambiguity of Nilang's words about the wraiths, that merely fleeing Mother's service would bring them after you. This seemed not to be the case.

"You will keep this to yourself, Lale, but running away will not alone awaken them. Nor will thinking incorrect thoughts, such as imagining that one might run away. But if you speak our secrets to someone who has not shared our initiation, that act will summon them."

"But then," I asked, worried about this vulnerability, "what's to prevent somebody from running off, if all she has to do is keep her mouth shut?"

"The fact that we'll hunt her down and kill her," Tossi said grimly. "Adrine was doomed, even if she hadn't been so stupid as to betray us."

With this cold comfort, I promised I'd keep the knowledge to myself, and Tossi let me go. That afternoon she had the storeroom door walled up as if to obliterate the memory of what had happened there.

A couple of months went by, and we left off talking about the execution. Later, we stopped thinking much about Adrine and how she died, and eventually our lives went on as if she had never set foot in Three Springs. By the time a year had passed, she might as well never have existed at all.

But I kept her poems, never showing them to anybody, not even to Dilara. And I almost never allowed myself to remember how I had wondered whether Mother might be, if only sometimes and just a little, mad.

Eleven

❦

Three important events occurred in the year 1314, in the month of Early Blossom. First, I completed my training at the Midnight School. Second, Mother gave me leave to study with Master Luasin in Istana. And third, Ardavan, the young Exile King of Seyhan, overran and annexed Jouhar, the realm of his uncle to his west.

Dilara and I were now the senior students at Three Springs, the girls preceding us having departed on Mother's business. I was soon to go as well; in fact, we received the news of Ardavan's conquest just before I was to leave for Istana.

It came up with the supply train, in the form of a letter from Mother. She sent such dispatches regularly, and we were expected to pay close attention to them. We could not do our best work, she believed, unless we understood the dynastic and military affairs of the world beyond Tamurin's borders. To this end, Tossi led a discussion of each dispatch, during which we considered the motives and intentions of kings, ambassadors, generals, despots, and, of course, the Sun Lord and his Chancellor.

The day after the letter arrived, Tossi summoned us to the banquet hall, where we gathered under the mosaic wall map of the old empire. I listened with growing excitement as she read the dispatch to us, for it was by far the most dramatic we'd ever received.

Mother had mentioned Ardavan in earlier dispatches, and we'd studied the Exile kingdoms, so we knew this young King's background. Ardavan was in the direct bloodline of Pakur One-Eyed, the ferocious leader who crushed the power of the Durdana a hundred years ago and founded the first Exile realm. Following his victory, and to add bitter insult to the catastrophe he'd already inflicted on us, Pakur took our beautiful and ancient capital of Seyhan for his own chief city.

Then, after he died and his conquests broke up into the Six Kingdoms, the region that contained Seyhan became the Kingdom of Seyhan. Because the city had been Pakur's capital, its Kings claimed precedence over the other five Exile rulers, who, naturally, paid not the least attention to the claim. From time to time a King of Seyhan would try to bring the other kingdoms under his sway so as to reunite Pakur's conquests, but nothing ever came of it.

Pakur had been preparing to finish us off when he died, and only the ferocious struggles among his six sons and their heirs saved us. But we Durdana had been so weakened by the wars that we could not take advantage of their struggles to recover what we had lost. Thereafter, although occasional border squabbles broke out, we and the Exiles had avoided a major war for a century, not because we didn't hate and despise each other, but because neither side was united or strong enough to risk an attempt at conquest.

As the years passed and we and the Exiles became accustomed to the stalemate, we began to exchange embassies and envoys. Trade grew between us and the Kingdoms, although their monarchs would not allow our merchants on their territory; all buying and selling had to be done at designated border points or at tightly controlled port towns along the Pearl.

Among their nobility, it eventually became fashionable to ape our ways. They read our literature and adopted our method of writing, and their Kings used what remained of our imperial bureaucracy to administer their realms. But they never relaxed their savage grip on the Durdana who had fallen under their sway. There were so few Exiles, compared to the population they had conquered, that they didn't dare to. They governed by terror and the threat of terror, and they did so very effectively; massacre was the ordinary punishment for rebellion, or even the threat of it.

When Mother's dispatch reached Three Springs, Ardavan was twenty-three. Already he had acquired a reputation for severity and for his pitiless methods of assuring his power. On ascending the throne at his father's death, he executed his two younger brothers on treason charges; he next arrested his sister and her husband and put them to death, along with their young son. His mother also died suddenly. Publicly it was said that she fell to an illness, but the rumors were that she had committed suicide from grief.

The *Golden Discourses* strongly condemn kin murder, for we Durdana know that the well-being of any realm, as well as our own day-to-day happiness, depends on the nurturing of family bonds. But the Exiles felt no such compunction, and the rulers of the Six Kingdoms murdered their relatives frequently, indiscriminately, and without remorse—although no Exile King would kill his mother, the one exception to such ruthlessness.

In this way, Ardavan was no different from his fellow monarchs. But on the evidence of the dispatch, he was much more inclined to war than they were, and a lot better at it. A month and a half ago, he suddenly moved his army from Seyhan to the north bank of the Pearl, and there he collected Durdana slave-labor gangs and began to construct barges.

This was startling behavior for an Exile ruler. The Pearl had long been neutral territory, because the Exiles had never understood ships; their crude attempts at river piracy after the Partition had brought them only disaster. We Durdana might be no match for them on land, but they couldn't beat us on the water, and after a time they prudently left the Pearl to us. Later they even forbade the building of boats along the Pearl, except for fishing skaffies.

The north shore towns and cities they ruled consequently fell into poverty, and smugglers flourished, though they risked dismemberment if caught.

Ardavan's sudden willingness to venture onto the water horrified the neighboring Despot, whose domain of Panarik lay directly across the Pearl from Ardavan's busy barge builders. The King clearly intended to extend his power across the great river, a thing not attempted even by his ancestor Pakur.

Or so everybody thought, including Ardavan's maternal uncle, the King of Jouhar. So when Ardavan suddenly turned and marched into that realm, he caught the uncle's forces unprepared. In less than a month he had routed them, and his army stood at the gates of Jouhar's capital, whereupon the uncle foolishly led his remaining forces out of the city to do battle. But his officers and men, foreseeing certain defeat, murdered him the instant they were outside the gates and offered Ardavan the throne. He graciously accepted. The conquest of Jouhar was complete.

"So," Tossi said, gazing at the mosaic wall map. "Ardavan now rules two of the Six Kingdoms. What will everybody else do about it?"

Like Tossi, I examined the map. There was our peninsula of Tamurin, and to its east the Gulf of the Pearl; on the far shore of the Gulf lay Bethiya. Beyond Bethiya was the Exile kingdom of Lindu and beyond that, Ardavan's newly annexed dominion of Jouhar.

"If Ardavan overruns Lindu next," I said, "he and the Sun Lord will stand eye to eye. There will be nothing between them but the Savath River, and that's easy enough to cross. Will the Sun Lord let Ardavan come so close without attacking him?"

"But will he need to attack him?" Jisrin asked. "The other Kingdoms might combine against Ardavan, to keep him from gobbling them up one at a time. They might do the Sun Lord's work for him."

"Or," Tossi observed, "they might see Ardavan as a new Pakur, and then all would combine against us."

"Yes, but we Durdana might win this time," Tulay said, with a tinge of excitement. "Bethiya's armies might drive the Exiles all the way through the Juren Gap, and get our old lands back!"

"And then what would happen?" Tossi snapped. "Can you imagine what the Sun Lord would do after he drove out the Exiles? Do you think that would be enough for him? No, it wouldn't. He'd go after the Despotates next, and pick us off one by one. And there goes our freedom—we'd have the emperors back, and the empire with them, and then what do you think would happen to Mother and to us?"

This was too obvious to need comment, but Dilara said, "Still, maybe Tulay's not so far off the mark. The Sun Lord *might* give the Exiles a bloody nose—in the past two years he's practically doubled the size of Bethiya's army. And Bethiya has cavalry horses these days, good ones and lots of them."

This last was very significant. The Exiles' great strength was in their horse lancers and mounted archers, while we Durdana preferred the remorseless battering ram of an infantry army. But the Sun Lords of Bethiya, whatever their other failings, had realized years ago that they needed a powerful cavalry of their own. Ever since, they had been improving their herds both with native stock and with animals bought—or stolen—from the Exiles, and by adapting the Exiles' cavalry tactics to Durdana purposes. This present Sun Lord had continued the work more vigorously than ever.

And the Sun Lords of Bethiya had never made any secret of their ambition to reunite the Durdana people, nor of their conviction that they were the legitimate heirs of the imperial power. And suddenly I knew, as surely as if Father Heaven had whispered it in my ear, that we Durdana and the Exiles were going to war. I could not suppress a shiver.

"What's the matter?" Dilara asked me in a low voice. "Have you got a chill?"

"No, it was something else. Remember back when we had our last dinner with Mother at Repose and she said there'd be a big war within a few years? I think this is the beginning of the road to it."

"I bet it is," Dilara said. Her face suddenly lit up. "Lale, everything's going to change! Everything! And we'll be in the thick of it! It's going to be so *exciting*!"

Her blazing enthusiasm kindled mine, for she was right. We *were* going to be in the thick of it. My sisters and I would trouble the sleep of Kings and Despots, and of the great Sun Lord himself; because of us, armies would march and thrones would tremble. I practically bounced up and down on my stool at the prospect.

And if I worked everything just right, I reminded myself, I could probably become rich and famous into the bargain. My dreams were nothing if not expansive.

Dilara and I were much gloomier two days later, when I had to leave for Istana. We had been together for eight years and had grown into adulthood side by side. She was the first friend I'd ever had, and although I'd been sociable with other girls in both schools, those friendships had come and gone. But my intimacy with Dilara had never wavered or diminished. She and I were as near as branch and bark.

"You won't forget me?" she asked, trying to smile. We were in the little courtyard with its mist trees and stone benches; the wine finches were there, too, chirping and squabbling among the leaves. Tossi and the others were down in the Lower Court, waiting to see me off. Knowing how close Dilara and I were, they'd left us alone to say our private farewells.

"Don't be silly," I said. "How could I forget you? Anyway, we'll see each other again. It may not even be that long. Maybe Mother will give you an assignment in Istana."

"I *wish* I knew where she's going to send me," Dilara said grumpily. "There was nothing in the dispatches that came last night."

"I'm sure you'll know soon," I told her. But we both knew also, though we didn't say it, that if Dilara did go to Istana for some secret purpose, I'd never know she was there. It was against the rules.

"I hope so. Oh, Lale, I'm going to miss you so—"

She didn't cry because she never did. But I got the sniffles and Dilara put her arm around me.

"We're soldiers," I said eventually, wiping my eyes with the back of my hand. "I shouldn't make so much of it. It's not forever."

"No, not forever. We'll have fun together again. Maybe, when the wars are over, we can go somewhere and just be ourselves." She gave me her old sideways grin. "You can be an actress in some despicable low-class theater and I'll weave gossamin robes for rich ladies, and we'll have a house and live in it and let the rest of the world go by. And Mother can come and stay with us whenever she likes."

It was such a wonderful, ludicrous vision that I burst out laughing. "You're mad," I told her.

"No," she said. "The world is mad, but we're not." She squinted at the rising sun, a hand's breadth now above the eastern horizon. "You'd better go. But I won't come down. I'll watch from here and wave before you get into the trees. Remember to look."

"I will," I said huskily, and embraced her before hurrying away. Down the stairs I went. So many times my feet had trod their cool stones; not a step was without its memories.

My other sisters were on the Lower Terrace, waiting for me. I said good-bye to them all, to Tossi and the two newest girls and the older ones, and to Master Aa and Mistress Ipip and the other instructors. Master Aa said, "You are very good, very well trained, one of the best. Do not forget the exercises, though. Always do the exercises."

"I promise," I told him.

Then I embraced Tossi, who hugged me and said, "Now, Lale, you really must go."

The Green Heron escort that had brought the supply train up the mountain was waiting for me. The same six troopers had been coming for years and I knew them by name, but they were always very taciturn—not surprisingly, given the oaths that bound them and their wariness of Nilang. An especially silent one named Jassar was to escort me across the Gulf of the Pearl, and it would, I realized with a sigh, be a journey without much conversation.

I mounted a gray gelding, and we all rode out through the narrow gate, my sisters calling their farewells. As we cleared the gate's shadow, I turned to look up. Far above, on Three Springs' topmost terrace, her white bodice a shining speck in the early morning light, Dilara was waving to me. I waved back as hard as I could. Then tears blurred my vision and I rode under the trees, and she was gone.

Opinions differ on sea travel. Many people dislike it because of storms, shipwreck, and possible attack by pirates. The food is usually boring or even outright bad, and then there is the probability of seasickness.

But I loved every moment of it. When Jassar and I rode into Tamurin's eastern port of Kalshel, and I saw the ship that was to take me across the Gulf of the Pearl to the mainland, I could hardly contain my excitement. As a young lady of education and breeding, I had to appear composed and unimpressed, but under my cool demeanor I was aquiver with anticipation.

We left our horses at the stables of the city garrison, hurried down to the port, and were aboard the vessel by the fourth hour of the sun watch. She was a cargo pelican rejoicing in the name of *Celestial Diadem*, broad beamed and slab sided, with a long overhanging stern and a blunt prow carved with a garland of stars. Being a Gulf trader, she wasn't as big as the ocean-going pelicans I'd seen in Chiran's Plum Harbor, and she had three masts instead of four or five. But I'd never been on a real ship, and *Celestial Diadem* seemed very big. She carried washed fleeces, aromatic cedar planks, and kegs of preserved cherries, so she didn't smell as bad as ships often do. Her crew was mixed, the officers and half the men Durdana and the rest Ris Rua and Yellow Smoke Islanders, with one amber-eyed Khalaka for variety.

I went up to the bow as we sailed past the twin beacons at the harbor entrance and out into the Gulf of the Pearl. As soon as we cleared the long stone breakwaters, the wind strengthened and *Celestial Diadem* began to pitch and roll to the long swing of the sea. The motion, the wind's rush, the roar of the waves, all exhilarated me. Spray dashed cool on my face and I tasted the ocean's salt, like tears. Ahead of me stretched the blue horizon, and waiting beyond it was the mouth of the Pearl, and Istana and Master Luasin's school and all my future.

Jassar and I were the only passengers, and he was seasick, so I passed our brief voyage pretty much alone. As the end of the second day approached I went up to the bow and gazed into the watery distances ahead, thinking about where I was going.

I knew I'd be successful. I'd known that ever since I trudged out of Riversong, and so far everything had worked out just as I'd hoped. But now I was entering the real world, far from Mother, Repose, and the Midnight School, and my choices were up to me.

For example, nobody would stop me if I wanted to take a lover. As for the possible results of such dalliance, Nilang had taught us how to avoid children, and had given me a selection of potions and salves for this purpose, which I carried in a secret compartment in my traveling chest.

I thought about the possibility of lovers as the wind blew my hair around my face. I'd known since I was fourteen that I was comely enough to make men look over their shoulders as I went by, which pleased me. But given the memories of my own childhood, and knowing what had happened to many of the girls in the school at men's hands, I wasn't inclined to trust them a thumb's breadth.

And in any case, taking a lover was as yet mere theory to me. I'd never had that particular experience, nor even the opportunity for it. Still, I knew I could charm a man if I needed to, and I that I could appear to trust him if necessary. And I knew how the bouncy part worked, since it was part of our schooling. Every Durdana girl is taught about the art of lovemaking and how it can lead to both pleasure and children. Girls with families are instructed by their mothers or aunts, and every youth is similarly taught by his father or uncle. And while it's a source of much humor, especially around the time of the Plough Festival, we believe beneath our laughter that the act is sacred, since it is how Father Heaven and the Bee Goddess created the world. We don't look on it as do the Exiles, as something dirty and shameful and not to be spoken of. Nor, unlike them, do we regard a woman's virginity as her most precious asset, and it is therefore no real disadvantage to a Durdana girl if she chooses to discard it before marriage.

But I knew very well, from Adrine's example, how love could lead to calamity. I couldn't imagine being that foolish, but I decided, as *Celestial Diadem* heaved with the waves, that I'd better be careful anyway. High Theater actresses sometimes married but more often had lovers, and I might find myself in situations where I'd be expected to take one. I had all the normal inclinations of a healthy young woman, and I was a little worried that I might be tempted. But I told myself sternly that I would never, never, let such inclinations affect my judgment. I had far too much to lose, and I wasn't going to ruin my life for any man.

I felt much better once I'd settled this. And just as I did, I saw something out on the horizon: a hazy gray line on the blue rim of the Gulf.

"What's that?" I asked a sailor, who was splicing a line nearby. "A storm cloud?" A storm would be an exciting way to end my first sea journey.

He squinted, then grinned. "No, mistress," he said, "that's not a cloud, it's land. We'll lie offshore at anchor tonight, 'cause we don't want to thread the shoals in the dark. But you'll be walking dry tomorrow."

The city of Dirun lies at the Mouth of the Pearl, on the river's south bank, in the Despotate of Guidarat. North across the river's estuary is the territory of Bethiya, but the shore there is low and swampy and supports only a handful of fishing villages. Dirun therefore has the great advantage of being the first landfall for vessels making for the Pearl. However, the lower reaches of the Pearl are so wide and deep that even the biggest pelicans can navigate all the way upstream to the city of Sutkagin, which is on the Bethiyan shore of the river. Above Sutkagin, freight has to be carried on smaller river lorchas, so the city is also a transshipment depot. This gives Sutkagin its own special advantage, and its merchants and those of Dirun have engaged in a furious commercial rivalry for centuries.

I was up early next morning as we sailed into the Pearl's estuary. The breeze was light from the west and the ship moved easily across the waves, which were tawny brown with silt and touched with pink where the dawn caught their crests. This disappointed me a little, since I'd always imagined the Pearl as a sparkling blue river, with necklaces of white foam where its waves broke in the wind. But otherwise the sight was everything I could have hoped: the sky crimson and gold and azure, the broad expanse of the Pearl with the low, dark line of the north shore to my left, and to my right the green hills of the south bank. And there was Dirun, its walls russet and cream in the morning light, the old prefect's palace on the hill in the city center, and along the waterfront a thicket of masts and spars.

Jassar was still indisposed and hadn't risen yet, but one of the ship's junior officers happened to be on the foredeck with me. He asked if I'd ever been to Dirun, and I admitted I hadn't. It was his native city, and he told me how, back in the old days, it had sent fleets of great ocean-going pelicans to trade on the most distant shores of the Great Green, returning with rare spices, tortoiseshell, coral, musk, aromatic woods, and the marvelous gem that looks like clear glass but cannot be scratched, even by the hardest jade. They were voyages that took years, he said, and although many ships never came back, the ones that did could make their owners as rich as Despots. But no such fleets had sailed now for a century and more, he said, and added sadly that Dirun was no longer the glorious place it once had been.

I saw, as *Celestial Diadem* glided though the fortified entrance of the commercial port, what he meant. The great basin could have held three ships for every one that was moored at the quays, and many of the waterfront warehouses were derelict, with huge gaps in their roof tiles and the harbor gulls swooping in and out. There were enormous stone slipways where Dirun shipwrights had built the great long-range ships for the ocean trade, but these were empty and moss grown. Three new vessels—two gulf pelicans and a river lorcha—were under construction near the port entrance, but you could have fitted them all onto one of the old slipways.

Jassar recovered from his seasickness once we reached the calmer waters inshore, and joined me as the ship came alongside the quay. I wanted to go ashore and look around the waterfront, but he said we were to be met. Frustrated, I sat on a companionway roof to watch the crew unload. We might, I reflected irritably, be forced to dawdle here for hours, wasting time that I could much better spend in exploration.

The seamen had barely got the hatch covers off, though, when a man came up the gangway. He saw Jassar and me and picked his way toward us among the ropes, hatch boards, and shouting sailors. He was a lean, bony-faced fellow of about thirty, dressed without any suggestion of either wealth or the lack of it. But I noticed that he had very watchful eyes, and at his waist was the narrow scabbard of a scathata, the expensive and nimble blade favored by Durdana cavalry officers.

He stopped in front of Jassar and they sized each other up. They must have approved of what they saw, for they bowed courteously to each other and the man said, "You're from the Despotana in Chiran?"

"We are," Jassar answered. "And you?"

The man removed a thin wooden tablet from his jacket and handed it to Jassar, who glanced at it and gave it to me. I inspected the man's bona fides, found them in order, and gave the tablet back.

"I'm Birek Artaj of Wayfarer's Guard," the man said. He bowed to me and touched his throat respectfully; it wasn't every day he'd meet a Despotana's adopted daughter. "I am at your service, Lady Mistress Navari."

I said, "As I'm also at your service, Master Artaj. You're escorting me to Istana?"

"Yes, mistress. Our lorcha leaves in the morning, and Master Luasin has been notified that you are on your way. I have made arrangements for Master Jassar to sail back to Tamurin in two days."

"I'm going to Istana by water?" I asked hopefully. I'd discovered that I liked boats very much.

He nodded. "We'd need four men to guard you by land, Mistress Navari, and that's expensive. The river's a lot safer, especially since I know the lorcha's master."

"Is there anyone else in our party?"

"There will be one other lady," Birek said. "Very well-bred and respectable, and already known to Wayfarers' Guard—she's traveled under our protection before. She's going home to Istana."

"She is?" I asked. This was out of curiosity rather than surprise, for even during the troubled days of the Partition women traveled almost as freely as men, and they did many other things as well. In fact, we Durdana women hold up half the sky, as the *Golden Discourse on Manners and Customs* says, and we mention this often enough to prevent Durdana men from forgetting it.

Still, long-distance travel, especially on land, was a lot more dangerous during the Partition than under the empire. Consequently, enterprising merchants had set up security firms that provided armed guards on contract. The best such firms would guarantee to escort a beautiful woman, with a casket of pearls and a trunk stuffed with gossamin robes, from anywhere to anywhere in the Despotates or Bethiya, without harm or insult to herself or her possessions. They almost always made good on their promises, although such a level of protection, for one person, was very expensive. More usually, a group of people traveling the same road would hire an escort together, and so defray the costs. The Wayfarers' Guard was such a firm and had a fine reputation. It also provided a dispatch service for those who needed to move letters safely and quickly, and who could afford the steep rates for doing so.

What I didn't know about Wayfarers' then, and neither did anybody else except Mother, Nilang, and the Wayfarers' supposed proprietor, was that Mother owned it. I suppose I should have worked this out for myself, since the advantages were so obvious: Owning Wayfarers' allowed Mother to conceal the movements of agents like me among those of innocent clients, and its couriers could carry her dispatches and orders along with legitimate messages. And into the bargain, Wayfarers' turned a fat profit to help finance her other activities.

"What sort of business is the lady in?" I asked, hoping it might be an interesting one.

"The wine trade, I believe," was Birek's disappointing answer. He looked up as the seamen swung a net stuffed with bales of wool over our heads. "Now, let us all three get ashore, and we'll go to the hostelry for breakfast."

I won't dwell on the time I spent in Dirun, first because I was there for only a day, and second because it wasn't a very interesting place. But I did notice that the decline I'd seen on my way to Tamurin years ago was in Dirun as well: Its once-magnificent public buildings were neglected and dirty, and a third of the city was abandoned to the hordes of desperately poor who worked for a few coppers a day at the docks and shipyards. Somewhat better off were the shopkeepers, middle-grade merchants, and craftsmen of the city's western quarter, who at least had something of their own to show for their labors.

These were the many, but there were also the few. On the hillsides, above the squalid rookeries of the lower city, rose the walled compounds that protected the mansions of the rich, all guarded night and day by heavily armed retainers. But for every man or woman who lived in those graceful halls, among those cool, shaded courtyards and galleries scented with flowers, a hundred sweltered in the heat and stink of the lower city.

Everybody knew that the common people had been better off before the Partition, but the equally common belief was that the disasters of the past century and a half were to blame for our decay. We did not realize how much of the blame lay with the Despots and the Sun Lords, and with the soldier-aristocrats who spread ruin as they pursued wealth and power. Hidden in the dismal record of their petty hatreds, their ferocious avarice, their treacheries and their brutal little wars, was the story of our decline. It had continued for a hundred years, this slow decay, our world slipping inexorably toward an abyss that few among us could perceive.

I was among the unperceptive, however, so during the next few days I was as cheerful as could be, watching the world go by as we sailed upstream aboard the river lorcha *Radiant Sunrise*. I shared a tiny cabin in the stern with Birek's other client, a chubby woman twice my age. But I didn't have much to do with her, as she spent most of our voyage working through a collection of account books. Her eyesight was poor and she used a round, polished crystal to make out the writing in her ledgers. I'd seen such things, because Sulen had needed one in the last year before she died. But grinding a crystal was very expensive, and this one was three times the size of Sulen's, which made it uncommonly valuable. My curiosity at last overcoming my manners, I asked her how she'd come by such a treasure.

"Oh," she said, looking up from her ledger and squinting at me, "it's not a crystal. It's glass—there's a glass founder in Kurjain who makes them. See?"

"Really," I said, examining the polished disk. There were no flaws or bubbles in it at all. "I've never seen glass so clear."

"My husband says it's new, something they do to it while it's melted."

"Ah," I said. "In Kurjain."

"That's where it's from, yes. They do all sorts of new things there nowadays. The Sun Lord encourages it. But I don't suppose you know much about Kurjain and the Lord Terem, being from out there in the west."

One of our strictest rules was never to speak ill of the Sun Lord; you never knew who might be listening. So I merely said, "It's true Tamurin's far away from Kurjain, but we do hear of the Lord Terem's justice and generosity to his people. He is certainly very admirable. And perhaps I'll visit Kurjain someday and see all these new things."

"Perhaps you will," she said, and screwed the glass back into her eye. Then she rather rudely returned to her accounts, especially since I wanted to ask her about those other new things. So I found Birek and got him to play a game of odds and evens with me for pebble stakes, and won every pebble he had, without cheating even once.

Twelve

❧

We reached Istana after a fast passage of seven days, the speed owing to the moon being nearly full; the river masters will sail at night if there's moonlight, because they can see to navigate safely. I'd hoped to stop at Sutkagin so I could visit a Bethiyan city, but we passed it after nightfall, and I only saw the distant glimmer of its lights across the water.

Istana more than made up for the loss. In imperial times the place had been very large, and, although the suburbs outside the walls were now mostly abandoned, it was still home to some eighty thousand people. But what impressed me was Istana's prosperous air. It was the only place I'd seen since leaving Tamurin that didn't look dilapidated.

The first reason for this was the Long Canal. Durdane is a land of canals, for the best way to move heavy loads over long distances is by boat, and we Durdana have been constructing waterways for a very long time. Istana was fortunate in that the Long Canal joined the Pearl beneath its walls, and there the Despot's tax collectors waited with tally and ledger. Not a scrap of cloth, a sip of wine, or a length of spice cane moved from a canal boat onto a Pearl River lorcha without paying a levy to Yazar, the Despot of Brind.

This gave him a lavish income, for even during the Partition there remained an appetite in the north for the luxuries of the south, and most of these luxuries traveled up the Long Canal. The cargo boats were called slippers, both because of their shape and because they were built narrow to slip through the canal locks. On the Long Canal, a slipper could travel four hundred miles south to the border of Indar, assuming that the various Despots along the route kept the channels and locks in repair. (They were careful to do this, because they liked imposing transit taxes). Then, when the slipper reached the southern end of the Long Canal, it could sail across a small lake and enter the South Canal. Using this, it could eventually reach the Wing River of my childhood, although it would still be a long way from Riversong.

The canal trade was the first reason for Istana's air of wealth. The second was that the city was Brind's capital, and Yazar had lavished much attention on the place. He was famous both for his love of beauty and for his generosity to artists, so much so that even the canal revenues could not cover his expenses, and he was perennially in debt.

Yazar came of the Demirak bloodline that had bred fierce soldiers for the past several generations. He'd been on Brind's dais for nineteen years, having won a violent succession struggle that burned down a quarter of Istana. After he won, he suspended the civil laws and summarily executed most of his surviving opponents, often along with their families; others fled before his men could haul them off to the military courts. His behavior attracted little comment, being common in such situations, although the *Discourses* speak most vehemently against such barbarism.

Once he'd removed the threats to his position, however, Yazar put aside savagery and ruled more or less by the laws. At bottom he preferred building things to knocking them down, and to this end he spent money as if it grew out of the earth. His wife was equally spendthrift, and determined to prove herself the fashionable equal of any Despotana in Durdane. She had even founded a school for orphan girls, to show herself as charitable and compassionate as Mother.

Yazar and his Despotana had no children, however, because he preferred men to women. He was also unlike other Despots in that his favorite leisure pastime was carpentry, rather than the more usual pursuits of hunting or horse racing. He built, among other things, a small, graceful pavilion in the palace gardens, where he liked to dine with his collection of artists and actors. Because of Yazar, Istana had attracted many such people, and the city in its way was as cultured as Kurjain. And with Master Luasin in residence, it could claim the finest High Theater company remaining in the world.

Yazar thought so highly of Master Luasin that he'd lent him the old prefectural residence, to provide living quarters for his actors and theater students, as well as space for the training and rehearsal stages. Adjoining the prefecture was Yazar's opulent new palace, and he allowed us to walk in its splendid gardens whenever we liked, a privilege extended to few.

We were very comfortable in the prefecture. The place was laid out in the manner of imperial times, on a north-south axis, with the family quarters arranged around a large inner courtyard. This courtyard had a garden with plum and pear trees, a reflecting pool, and a fountain. The large three-story building on its north side contained—among elegant formal rooms now left to dust and moths—the students' stage, a larger rehearsal stage, and a small theater once used for the prefect's private enjoyment. Adjoining it were accommodation wings with verandas, where both students and full-fledged actors lived. On the south was the outer courtyard, where the servants' quarters were, along with the stable, kitchen, storage magazine, the baths, and the porter's lodge at the main gate.

The theater school was doing well by the time I arrived, and had produced its first crops of trained actors. Some had already sought their fortunes elsewhere, but Master Luasin was nevertheless able to maintain two full theater companies. The Younger

Company remained at Istana year-round to regale Yazar, while the more experienced Elder Company did the summer tour up in Kurjain, under the supervision of Master Luasin himself. He and they had already departed for the north when I reached Istana; his deputy, Mourken, a man of combustible temperament but great ability, was in charge of our training.

Master Luasin's ambitions, as so often with brilliant artists, were greater than his resources. Unfortunately, while Yazar was lavish in his support of the theater, he was not unreservedly so. Consequently Mother was financing Master Luasin with secret payments from her own treasury, and had been doing so since his visit to Chiran when I was fourteen. The amounts weren't large, not enough to make Yazar wonder how Master Luasin did so much with so little. But they put him very firmly under Mother's control, which was the real reason for her generosity.

I am sure that Master Luasin also served Yazar as an agent and reported to the Despot what he saw during the Elder Company's travels. But he also sent this information secretly to Mother, along with similar gleanings about Yazar and Brind. Even the easygoing Yazar would have asked sharp questions if he'd known this, and this was Mother's second hold over Master Luasin: She could destroy him in a moment, if she chose to, by revealing his spying.

Mother thus had no trouble getting me into the theater school, and she paid Master Luasin well for my training. If I'd shown no acting talent, I suppose she would have found another plausible way of moving me to the desired position on her game board; she was a very astute player of games, was Mother. But I did have talent, and consequently the game board looked just as she wanted it. I am sure that Master Luasin knew I was more than I appeared to be, but except for his aesthetic ambitions he was a man of good sense, and kept his questions to himself.

My first full month in Istana was Hot Sky, and the city sweltered. Usually there was a breeze off the Pearl, but it was not as cooling as the sea winds of Chiran, and at sundown it dropped to a zephyr. It was on one of those suffocating evenings, when the city smelled of river water and wilted flowers, that I first took a life.

I had been unsure how my fellow students would react to me, given that I was the protégé of the Despotana of Tamurin. There were ten of us, including me, of whom three were women. Some had already performed on the popular stage, others were from families with artistic backgrounds, and one was a leather merchant's youngest son with more talent for song than for dressing hides. None of them had much money above what they needed to eat, drink a little, and pay for their training.

I was much better off, since Mother had sent a generous note of exchange with me, which I banked with the Wayfarers' Guard office and drew on as I needed. I was deliberately vague about my resources, though, and I lived as the others did, allowing them to believe that Mother kept me on a tight financial rein. Pretty soon they accepted me, showing in this the best quality of artists, which is that they judge you on your abilities and not your bloodline or wealth.

On the other hand, while most artists are indifferent to rank, they also tend to be self-absorbed, spiteful, envious of each other's successes, and as likely to cooperate as rats in a sack. We theater students were no exception, being arrogant by nature and having the usual braggadocio of youth. However, we had a certain fellowship through being collectively at the mercy of Master Mourken, and we got along well enough to spend much of our spare time together, both within the school and outside it. I tended to be the leader in our city excursions, since I was at least as brash as the men and more inventive.

On the night I first killed a man, five of us had gone to a punch house near the prefecture. The palace quarter was quite safe because of the Despot's patrols, and it was in this punch house that we spent most of what spare time we had. I remember it because of its peculiar name, which was the Frolicking Stoat.

Punch houses had recently become fashionable in Istana, espe-

cially among the youthful smart set. You could buy wine or dis-
tilled spirits in them, but their specialty was punches, made from
water boiled and cooled, and then flavored with various nectars
and syrups. One popular type had the elixir of a southern bean
added to it. If you drank it in the evening you'd be awake all night,
but it was very useful for perking one up in the morning after one
had made a night of it.

There were no such nights for me, though, partly because I
didn't like being drunk and partly because drinking might make
me drop my guard. Even in my most carefree moments I never forgot that among these not-yet-professionals I was already a professional, in ways that none of them could be allowed to suspect. For
this reason I liked punch houses, because nobody expected you to
swill wine in them, and I could relax as much as I ever did.

On that particular evening, the Stoat was crowded and fear-
somely hot, and I had the inspiration of going to one of the lower-
class places by the river docks, where it might be cooler. That was
an unsafe neighborhood at night, but after some debate I persuaded everybody to go. There were five of us, after all, and we had
our belt knives, although these were not much use except for cutting meat and bread.

We left the Stoat and headed for the river. A full moon hung in
the sky, and bats squeaked faintly as they hunted through the thick
air. Many people, made restless by the heat, were out and about,
and we encountered a crowd around the doorway of a fried-fish
shop. In the darkness—foolishly, we didn't have a lantern—we got
ourselves mixed up in it. After some confusion I disentangled myself and followed the dim shapes of the others into the darkness of
the next street.

I was thinking about a part I was to act the next day, and I'd
gone a few dozen yards before someone ahead of me spoke. But I
didn't recognize either his voice or the one that answered, and
with a shock I realized that I'd been following the wrong people.

I stopped. I was on a narrow street, whose second-floor balconies shut out the moon and most of the stars. Above me, only a

few seams of dim orange betrayed window shutters with lamps behind them.

What to do? I didn't know this quarter of Istana, but I could tell
it wasn't among the better ones. I considered trying to find my
companions, but decided it wasn't worth it; I would be better off
going home. So I turned around and went back along the street
until I found the crowd outside the fish shop. I skirted it and hurried into the alley through which I'd come with the others. Or I
hoped it was the same alley. I was now going in the opposite direction and everything looked different.

At the next corner was a wider avenue, and I heard a fountain
off to my left. Here I could see the stars better, and the position of
the Hammer told me that the prefecture must lie to my left. I set
out in that direction, keeping to the shadows along the walls. Dogs
barked and I heard the dusk watch drums sound the fifth hour. It
was getting late. I stepped in something mushy the street cleaners
had overlooked, and swore because my shoes were nearly new.

Finally, after a few more alley intersections, I worked out where
I was—not far from the palace quarter, so I'd be home in no time
at all. I was so sure of myself I began walking in the moonlit part
of the street, so I could see if I were about to tread in anything unpleasant.

Abruptly a man stepped out in front of me, not two paces off.
I stopped, smelling the wine on him.

"Come here, woman," he said. He had a young voice.

"I'm not a whore," I said. "Let me go by."

"I'm not after that," he said, taking another step toward me. He
raised his right hand and I saw the glint of moonlight on a leaf-
shaped blade. "See this? Keep quiet and give me your money."

Nobody had threatened me with violence since Riversong, but
I felt neither angry nor frightened, just very alert. Without thinking about it, I shifted my stance to the guard position.

"Leave me alone," I said. "Go away."

"I'll cut you, woman. Give me your coin now or I'll slit your
eyeballs."

"No," I said. "Go away. I don't want to hurt you."

He laughed drunkenly. "Hurt me? Aren't you the saucy one? Maybe I'll have you, after all."

"Go ahead," I replied, "if you think you can do it." And because I wanted him angry, I added, "Except your blade's not stiff enough for the work, is it? You're a harbor bum-boy, aren't you?"

He cursed and hurled himself at me, knife sweeping toward my belly. I danced aside, grabbed his wrist, and with two quick twists I broke it. He screamed as the knife fell, and tried to grab my hair with his good hand.

He missed. I jabbed him under the breastbone with my stiffened fingers, but darkness spoiled my aim. He only grunted, and suddenly he had me by the forearm and was trying to slam me against a wall. I pulled him forward as hard as I could, bent double, and rammed my hip into his belly. He let go of my arm and hurtled over my shoulder. I heard a *crack* as his head struck stone and the thud of his body hitting the pavement, and then he was only a huddled shape at my feet, a shadow among shadows.

It had all happened so quickly. I stared down at him, quivering with reaction. Had I killed him?

Hinges creaked above me and a shutter banged open. A man called, "Get away from my door, you. I know you're there, so try your mischief somewhere else."

If people found me with a corpse, I'd have some explaining to do. I drew back into the shadows and waited until the man grunted and the shutter banged shut. As soon as the street was quiet I hurried away, keeping out of the moonlight and walking as softly as I knew how.

But nobody else bothered me, and I found my way to the prefecture where the porter let me in. My compatriots returned shortly afterward, having searched fruitlessly for me. They'd intended to get reinforcements and go out again, and there was much relief when they discovered they didn't have to.

By that time I'd recovered my poise, and made little of getting lost. But I was almost sure I'd killed a man, and it made me feel very different, as if I'd changed into somebody else. I went to bed and tried to sleep, but a long time passed before I drifted off.

The next day I was tired and distracted, and botched a rehearsal. I wasn't afraid of being caught and accused of murder, for nobody had seen me strike the man down, and anyway, he might not be dead. Even if he were, he'd been trying to kill me, and neither gods nor men could condemn my act of self-defense.

What did trouble me was this: Had I gone too far? Nilang and Master Aa had drummed into me that fighting was a last resort, to be undertaken only when concealment and avoidance had failed. Had I violated this precept in accepting battle with my attacker, whether I'd killed him or not?

It was no defense to tell myself that I was so well trained I'd acted without thinking. I was *supposed* to think, even in the tightest situation. I was fast on my feet and he was drunk, and I might have been able to escape him by running away. But I hadn't even thought of running, and my instructors wouldn't approve of that at all—not so much because I'd fought him but because I hadn't looked for alternatives.

I finally had to face the truth of it: I hadn't thought about running away because I'd wanted to try out my skills, not against a partner in the exercise yard, but against a real attacker. Contrary to all the training of my instructors, I had allowed impulse and desire to rule me. I had failed my first real test.

I spent a full day simmering in a mixture of shame and chagrin. Then, because brooding over my ineptitude was ultimately useless, I resolved that next time I would do better, and tried to put the matter out of my mind. Still, I couldn't help wondering whether I had, indeed, killed the man.

Some three days later, I found out. My fellow student Simi gave me the news; she'd gone to the fish shop around the corner for something to eat and had heard the story. Her eyes glowed with excitement as she told me how everybody in the shop had been talking about it.

"Talking about what?" I asked. We were on the prefecture's garden veranda, where I'd been memorizing lines.

"The Moonlight Girl. A man saw her."

"Bad luck for him," I said. Nobody wanted to see the Moonlight Girl. It meant that the Moon Lady was very displeased with you and that your life was going to be either very short or very unpleasant, or more probably both.

"Well, yes, it was his bad luck because he's dead. But he said the Moonlight Girl killed him."

I pricked up my ears at that. "What are you talking about? You mean she killed him and then his ghost told a spirit summoner about it?"

Simi frowned. "No, he said it before he died. She didn't kill him outright. He died after he met her."

"And does anybody," I asked as indifferently as I could, "know why she was annoyed with him?"

"Oh, yes. It was because he killed his wife. Nobody found her for two days—it was in that next village up the canal. When they did, they started looking for him and somebody came across him lying in a street here, the night you got lost. They thought he'd fallen off a roof and hit his head, and they took him to Our Lady's hospice by the harbor. He was unconscious till last night, and then he woke up and told the priestess the Moonlight Girl had broken his wrist and then felled him with her silver axe, and it was because he'd killed his wife. He asked for cleansing and died a bit later." Her eyes shone. "But isn't it *weird*? You might have been close by when it happened. Didn't you *see* anything?"

"No," I answered. I'd killed him, then. I might have been a little bit sorry about it, except that he'd murdered his wife. "That was all he said? That he met the Moonlight Girl?"

"As far as I know." She shuddered dramatically. "Isn't it scary?"

"Indeed," I said. I felt, however, a certain relief. I'd served justice without knowing it, and perhaps that was the reason I hadn't thought to run away—perhaps the Moonlight Girl really had been after the man and had used me as her instrument. That was far preferable to a failure to live up to my training, and I felt much better after I decided that she must have been with me that night, and that I hadn't been so inept after all.

But whatever the truth of it, I had changed. I now knew that the world was divided into two kinds of people, those who had taken a human life and those who had not, and I'd crossed from one to the other and could never get back. I'd wondered more than once if I could kill, and now I knew; I just hoped I wouldn't ever need to do it again.

Thirteen

❧

*A*s the month of Ripe Grain ended, Master Luasin's Elder Company returned from its tour in Bethiya. The Elder Company was his original troupe, the one I'd seen in Repose, and I was looking forward to meeting Perin again, since she'd encouraged my dramatic ambitions during that long-ago visit.

We ran into each other the day after her return, in the gallery outside the students' stage, as I was heading for the women's costumery after a full-dress rehearsal. On seeing her I said, "Good morning, Lady Mistress Varvasi," and bowed.

Perin didn't answer. She had stopped short, wide-eyed.

I smiled. I assumed she was astonished at seeing me here, and was gratified that she remembered me, since it meant my early acting must have impressed her. Also, I was wearing the costume of an emperor's daughter, which made me look quite regal. Still, her reaction seemed overly dramatic.

A moment passed as she examined my face; she herself had aged a bit but remained very lovely. Finally she said, "And who on earth are you?"

I stiffened. So much for being memorable. "I'm Lale Navari," I said coldly. "We met in Chiran some years ago. I was in a student play you saw there." And I added pointedly, "I'm the daughter of the Despotana of Tamurin."

"Oh, yes," she said, "I remember meeting you." Then she laughed, a sweet honeyed sound. "But you've grown up, and of course people look so different in paint and costume. And you startled me."

"I'm sorry. I didn't think I was so alarming."

"Oh, not at all. You wouldn't have any way of knowing this, but you very much resemble the Surina, especially with what you're wearing."

Here, if I had but known it, was the reason I was in Istana. And here was the reason, too, why Master Lim came looking for me so long ago, and the reason I met Mother on the road from Riversong. But I felt no premonition at Perin's words, nor did I glimpse the faintest shadow of the web in which I was caught, and which I had helped weave by my very existence. Instead, I gaped at her and stammered, "I do?" I had no idea what the Sun Lord's consort looked like. None of the Young Company had ever performed in Kurjain, so they couldn't have told me either.

"I've met her, so I know," Perin assured me. "Your voice is like hers, too. Speaking of voice, was that you singing the Dawn Moon Canto?"

"That was me," I said.

"You're quite good, did you know that? You held your character's grief in, which is the key to moving the audience. She will not weep, so they must do so on her behalf."

I was both abashed and delighted at this, but determined not to show it. "Thank you," I said coolly. "I appreciate your praise."

"I'm sure it's more than you get from Mourken," she said, which was true. Master Luasin's deputy was very sparing of compliments, judging correctly that they would go to our heads if we heard too many of them.

"Do I *really* look like her?" I asked.

Perin regarded me. "Not so much in profile. But straight on, quite noticeably."

I opened my mouth, then closed it. When I wondered about my real family, it was usually about my mother and father, but I'd also imagined siblings. I'd always looked for resemblances in the new girls Mother brought into the school, just in case one of them might be a long-lost sister, but I had never found a likeness that would suggest common blood. Such a likeness would not have meant much, anyway—a washerwoman at Repose had looked just like our Tradition Tutoress, but the two women were quite unrelated.

Also, I knew where the Surina came from. We'd discussed the Sun Lord's marriage at the Midnight School, because it was an important dynastic one. She was of the Aviya bloodline, an old family from the Bethiyan city of Gultekin. Two of her ancestors had been imperial prefects, and one had risen to head the Board of Chancellors in Seyhan, before the Era of the Warring Emperors. She was an only child, her name was Merihan, and she and the Sun Lord had been betrothed when they were children. It was said that after their marriage they quickly became devoted companions, and that the Sun Lord now loved her passionately.

"Anyway," Perin went on, sounding amused, "resembling her is nothing to be worried about. The Surina's very pretty, just as you are."

"You praise me too much," I said.

"We'll see. If your other work is as fine as your voice, you'll go far."

I thanked her again, took my leave of her, and went on to the costumery. She told the rest of the Elder Company about me that morning; they'd all met the Surina, and as soon as they saw me they agreed that I resembled her. But looking like someone famous is tiresome if people keep remarking on it, so I was glad that they soon lost interest in the coincidence.

I did wonder if I'd meet the Surina someday, for I was convinced that Master Luasin would eventually take me to Kurjain with the Elder Company, where I'd appear before the court. But this idle fancy didn't last long, because a boat from Bethiya docked at Istana's waterfront only a few days later, with startling news.

The Surina was dead.

We didn't find out the details until a few days later. Apparently she had caught a chill on the river during the Ripe Grain Festival, and it turned to a fever. After a few days, she appeared to be on the mend, and her physicians were cautiously optimistic. But then, on the fifth morning after she fell ill, her maidservants tried to rouse her, and were horrified to discover that she had died while she slept. The Sun Lord, it was said, was inconsolable.

The first thought was poison, although she had no known enemies and all her food was tasted. In case something had been slipped into her medicines, condemned criminals were forced to consume the leftover drugs, but even the sleeping draft did no more than put them into a doze. Then malign sorcery was suspected, but the spirit summoners and priests who specialized in detecting such emanations could find no trace of them. Later it was decided that she must have had a hidden weakness of the heart; it was known that such infirmities, coupled with fever, could kill.

I gave the affair my professional interest, wondering if the Sun Lord might not have secretly arranged the Surina's death, for after nearly three years of marriage she'd not conceived a child, and he needed an heir. But she could easily have been put aside for another wife, since her family wasn't powerful enough to make trouble over it, so I eventually dismissed the idea—reluctantly, since it fit well with the behavior I expected of him.

Winter arrived. Winter in Istana was warmer than in Chiran, and we never saw any snow, except a few flakes just after the Solstice Festival. With both the Elder and Young Companies presenting entertainments for Yazar every two or three hands, we were very

busy; oration and singing resounded without letup from the rehearsal stages and from the theater. Master Luasin was everywhere, cajoling, encouraging, berating, fuming, persuading,
admonishing. It was five years since I'd last seen him, and he'd
gone very gray—little wonder, given that he dealt daily with the ir-
ritable and touchy race of actors, and was an actor himself. His
nose was more beaky, he was a little more stooped, and he still had
the awkward gait I remembered. Perin told me it was because he
had broken both ankles in a fall some fifteen years ago, and they
hadn't mended as they should.

We students all worked very hard. I gleaned some grudging
praise from Master Mourken, which actually meant I was doing
very well indeed. I also became a sort of protégé of Perin, and by
now had two good friends in Simi and in Eshin, who was the
leather merchant's son. Simi had a lover, one of the actors of the
Younger Company, and among the male students there were a few
who would have liked to share my bed. I found none of them al-
luring, however, and so wasn't tempted. I might have considered
Eshin a candidate, but he had the same inclinations as the Despot
and wasn't interested in girls.

So my spirits were high; I was young and attractive, fascinated
by my vocation and very good at it, and I lived with like-minded
companions in a cultured and elegant city. Few people are so favored, and I often wished it could last forever.

I knew it couldn't. While I wasn't sure what purposes Mother
had for me, once I completed my drama training, I knew they
would include more than being a High Theater performer. But I
was troubled to realize that I had slightly mixed feelings about my
future. My dedication to Mother hadn't wavered, but occasionally
I found myself thinking that it would be pleasant to keep life simple and just be an actress. But then I'd remember what Dilara had
said about the world changing, and us being at the center of it, and
my fleeting uncertainty would vanish. Still, I wished Mother
would let me know what was in store, so I could prepare myself
for it.

In the outside world, not much changed, although Ardavan was proving to be an Exile King in the pattern of earlier times. He cherished his people's ancestral ways, punished Exile nobles who strayed too far from them, and rooted out corruption in his government through a flurry of executions. And sadly, he doubled the hearth tax on all Durdana households under his rule, which caused great hunger and hardship that winter.

However, he assured his western neighbor, King Garhang of Lindu, that he had no warlike intentions now that he had taken Jouhar. I didn't believe this, and probably Garhang didn't, either, but nobody could start fighting until winter passed. I judged that the Sun Lord would be watching Ardavan very carefully, since only Lindu now separated Bethiya from the King's newly expanded realm.

Just after the New Year Festival, there was a brief interruption in the quiet. Word came up the river that three whole counties of overtaxed farmers and townspeople in Guidarat had rebelled, along with a militia battalion, and that Guidarat's Despot was having to fight hard to suppress the insurrection. I wasn't surprised, since he was the kind of man who would skin a sheep for its wool rather than shear it.

But it was the sort of news that made all Despots nervous, since a popular uprising in one realm could encourage malcontents in others. Despots would fight each other for advantage, but instantly closed ranks against trouble from below. So, to help her fellow ruler, Mother sent a couple of infantry battalions by sea, despite the winter gales, and Yazar lent him a cavalry unit that was shipped down the Pearl aboard a fleet of lorchas. With this help, he crushed the rising, and the punishments that followed were savage.

Despite my usual interest in politics, I paid little attention to this upheaval, being too busy to think about anything other than work. This was because Master Luasin had announced that he would select a male and a female student to join the Elder Company on its next tour to Kurjain. The lucky pair would be considered apprentices, but would occasionally get to act in major parts, perhaps even in front of the Sun Lord himself.

This was the first time Master Luasin had done such a thing, and all of us were frantic to be chosen. I had a pretty shrewd idea, though, that the idea wasn't his but Mother's, and because of this I reckoned that I was the woman who would be going to Kurjain— my male counterpart would be along merely for appearance's sake. However, I also knew that Mother would be very angry if I got overconfident and didn't work hard enough to deserve the prize, because it would look suspicious if Master Luasin chose me when I didn't merit it. I knew she had great confidence in me, so I was determined not to disappoint her and kept my shoulder to the wheel.

At the beginning of the month of Rain, Master Mourken uncharacteristically gave us a day off. The others trooped away to the Stoat, where they'd become obsessed with playing a new game that had recently come down the Pearl with the rivermen. You played it with forty-six stiff paper cards that had designs or numbers painted on them; it was called Six Roosters and was a gambling game. It was supposed to have come out of Abaris, and the designs looked Abarite, so this may have been true. The great advantage to these cards was that you could play all sorts of games with them; another was called Lords and Ladies and a third, Simpleton.

I was fond of Six Roosters, but I wanted some time alone to finish a book Perin had lent me, *The Jealous Mistress*. We'd had a typical spring downpour at dawn, but by the time I settled myself on the veranda, the day had turned warm and sunny, with fat white clouds gliding slowly from west to east. A pair of crested ducks paddled about in the reflecting pool in the courtyard garden, bobbing for weed and snails.

I'd just found my place in the book when the porter's boy appeared. "What is it?" I asked, as he fidgeted in front of me.

"Mistress Navari, it's two ladies to see you. They say they're your sisters, Tossi and Dilara."

I closed the book. My first thought was: *Something's happened to Mother.* I managed to swallow, though my mouth had gone dry, and said, "Bring them here. No, wait, I'll come myself."

My heart pounded as I entered the outer courtyard. And there was Tossi, wearing a red skirt and a blue jacket, and Dilara, who was dressed in traveling clothes. They didn't look at all upset, which reassured me, and then I thought: *If it's not about Mother, are they here with an assignment for me? But what can be so important that Tossi left Three Springs? She was never away from it once, in all the time I was there.*

They saw me. Dilara's face lit up and then it was embraces and laughter and *What are you doing here* and *Are you well*, all mixed up together.

Finally I said, "It's such a wonderful surprise to see you both! How did you get here? Wayfarers' Guard? Where's your escort and baggage? Do you want to stay in the prefecture with me? I'm sure Master Luasin wouldn't mind. Do you want me to ask him?"

Tossi raised her hands in mock self-defense. "You haven't changed a bit, Lale—still the chatterbox! But one thing at a time, for pity's sake!"

I subsided. "We're staying at the Wayfarers' hostel in Ropewalk Street," she said. "The Despotana has sent a shipment of tin, and she wanted me to negotiate the letters of credit with the buyer. Dilara came along to keep me company and to see you."

"But I can't stay long," Dilara put in. "I've got a passage on a lorcha, and it sails at noon."

"Oh, no!" I'd been looking forward to a few days with her. "Do you *have* to go?"

"Yes," she said, and then, very quietly, "Orders."

There was no use protesting orders. "Oh, that's too bad. But I'm so glad to see you anyway. . . . Do you need breakfast?"

"We ate at the hostel," Tossi said. "But is there somewhere we can all go and talk?"

I knew the very place, and led them to the gate that connected the prefecture compound to the gardens of Yazar's palace. The gate guard knew me, and once I'd vouched for my two companions, he let us pass. We chattered about nothing in particular as we walked beneath the budding trees, and at length emerged onto the lawn where Yazar's flower-viewing pavilion stood. I'd chosen this because no one could approach within earshot without being seen, and while we could be observed from the upper windows of the palace, nobody could hear us from that distance.

The pavilion contained cushioned benches. Dilara sat down and said, "The Despot does well for himself."

"He does, doesn't he? The food's very good, too . . . but I must say, I'm surprised to see you both. There's no risk, is there?" I asked this because I didn't think for an instant that Tossi was really here to sell tin, although I was sure the shipment existed—there was always a plausible reason for Mother's girls to be wherever they were.

"No risk at all," Tossi said, and added dryly, "Anyway, what could be more natural than for Mother's former students to visit each other? We're sisters, after all."

"Exactly," Dilara said. "Now, Lale, tell me everything you've been doing here. Is it fun? Does Master Luasin treat you well? What's the Despot like?"

I did my best to answer her, and discovered that she herself was working as a public scribe. I tried to imagine Dilara sitting at a folding table with ink stone, paper, and pen, writing people's love notes and business letters for them, and found it difficult. But she made no complaint, and we nattered happily on while the morning passed. Tossi said little as we talked, apparently more interested in Yazar's prize irises, which decked the gardens in great swaths of purple and gold. Eventually she asked if she might look more closely at them, and I told her Yazar wouldn't mind, as long as she didn't go near the palace itself. She agreed, and wandered out into the garden.

This pleased me, for as glad as I was to see her again, her presence had constrained our gossip. Now I could say, "I know you can't tell me exactly what you've been doing, but has it gone well?"

"I had a very important assignment," she said, glancing in Tossi's direction. "It went well. Tossi says Mother is very pleased with me."

"I'm so glad! Will you be going home now?"

"I don't think so."

I studied her narrow face. All morning I'd sensed that she wasn't quite the same old Dilara, and now, in this unguarded moment of hers, I glimpsed the change. She'd hardened in some deep place, had become colder and more secretive. Even as she giggled over my accounts of Master Mourken's artistic tantrums, there was a watchfulness about her that never flagged. She held herself back, in some obscure manner, and I could not help but feel that a little of the old intimacy had ebbed from our friendship. It saddened me.

"How is it really, being a scribe?" I asked. "It's hardly the weaving you hoped for."

She shrugged. "It's what Mother wants, and my clients don't complain. But you know why she did it. It's a portable profession—I can go anywhere and not be noticed much."

"True." I sighed. "You can't drag a loom around on your back."

"No, unfortunately. It's a terrible living, though, being a scribe. It's not hard to do, but if I had to depend on it I'd starve. But Mother sends me money, so I get along."

Tossi was well out of earshot. "Dilara," I said, "I killed a man."

For an instant, that watchful reserve evaporated. Her eyes widened and she exclaimed softly, "You *did*?"

"Yes. But it was an accident. Sort of." I told her what had happened. When I finished, she emitted a soft whistle and said, "Good for you. I'd have made sure of him after he hit the ground, though. Suppose he'd identified you later?"

"It was dark. He never got a good look at me."

Dilara laughed. "Well, he certainly never will now. And here I find myself with the Moonlight Girl. But see how brave I am? I'm not afraid of you in the least."

I laughed, and as I laughed, the palace bell sounded the fifth hour of the morning watch. Moments later the city's timekeeper drums took their cue from the bell, and a low rumble, like that of a distant army, quivered in the soft spring air.

"An hour till midday," Dilara said. "I guess I'd better go. If I'm not on that lorcha when it sails, Tossi will box my ears."

"I suppose you must." I felt very downcast, for our time together had sped so swiftly. My best friend was leaving me, and I didn't know when or where I'd see her again. "Can you find your way? Shall we come with you to the port?"

She grinned, a flash of the old Dilara. "I can find my way from anywhere to anywhere. I just have to get my things from the hostel, and I'm off. Travel light and fast, that's me."

She kissed me on both cheeks and went across the lawn to Tossi. They embraced, Dilara turned on her heel, and vanished among the budding cherry trees. Tossi rejoined me in the pavilion.

"I'm sorry she had to leave so soon," she said.

"So am I. I'm very glad you brought her with you. But you're not in Istana about tin shipments."

"No, I'm not. By the way, Mother's extremely pleased with your work here. She's had reports from Master Luasin, and commends you for your talent and for your diligence."

"I'm very gratified. Please tell her so, and give her my thanks." After a pause I said, "Perin says I look a lot like the Surina. The one who just died."

"Yes, Mother told me that, too, before I left. She noticed it herself a few years ago, she said. It's a very useful resemblance." She smiled. "You'll be sure to catch the Sun Lord's eye because of it."

Excitement vibrated through me. "You mean—"

"Yes, I do. You'll be going to Kurjain with the Elder Company this season."

Even though I'd expected this, it was still a shock to hear it. "You're *sure*? Mother said so?"

"Yes. I brought her dispatch with me. Master Luasin has it by now."

"Well, I do think I earned it," I said. "So I'm to go to Kurjain. What then?"

She told me. It took a while. When she finished, I stared for a long time at the gardens.

"Lale?" Tossi murmured after a while. "Say something."

A ringed pigeon was waddling around on the grass, pecking. I said, "I see now why she couldn't trust anybody but you to come. I'm just trying to grasp it. I never imagined anything so . . ."

I found myself at a loss for words, an unfamiliar sensation. Tossi said, "Audacious?"

"That, yes." I wondered if I ought to be frightened. I'd always known my work could be dangerous and that I might die in Mother's service. But I wasn't afraid; what I felt was nervousness mixed with excited anticipation. I owed Mother everything, and now I could begin to repay her for what she'd given me. And as Dilara had said, I'd be at the center of *everything*.

"You'll do very well, Lale." She took my hands and looked into my face. "You're a fine actress. This is the greatest role you'll ever play."

I laughed. "A secret one. No applause from my audience."

"Except from Mother. And from me. But, perhaps, if it all goes as it should, the world can someday know what you've done."

"Maybe," I said modestly. "I guess we'll see, won't we?"

She had to go soon after that, to attend to the tin business. I would not, she said, see her again before she left Istana. So I accompanied her to the prefecture's main gate and we made our farewells, as would sisters who were fond of each other but now must go their separate ways.

After she left I returned to the veranda and my book, but although I stared at its pages I did not see them. Visions of a glorious future danced before my eyes, for I was profoundly excited at what lay before me. When younger, I'd imagined being written down in the histories, like Maylane, and now it might actually happen. And perhaps I'd appear not only in the histories. Great poets might write about me, and High Theater dramatists portray my triumphs. It was one of the things I'd longed for, this fame, and now Mother had put it within my reach. Once I was in Kurjain I had merely to grasp it, and I had every intention of doing exactly that.

Fourteen

❧

The Elder Company and I reached Kurjain early in the month of New Leaf, after a journey of four days. Including Master Luasin, there were thirteen of us: Perin and Radam the male and female leads, plus the two second leads and the pair of supporting actors. Filling out the company were the musicians Guyal and Yoshin, and the married couple who worked as stagers. And finally there were Eshin and I, the two lucky students who had won apprenticeships in the Elder Company.

We loaded the wagons onto river lorchas at Istana, but we took no horses with us, since we were to remain in Kurjain all summer and wouldn't need them. Then we set out on the first leg of our journey, gliding with sail and current down the Pearl to the city of Sutkagin, where we would take the Short Canal toward Kurjain.

Soon after we set out, I asked Perin the question that had been on my mind for days. We were leaning on the rail, watching the river fishermen bob about in their skaffies. Along the shore, herons and yellow stilts stalked among the reeds.

"What's he like?" I asked. "The Sun Lord, I mean. You've met him."

"Ah." Her face grew thoughtful. "You could certainly say he's well-favored. A strong face, straight back, broad shoulders. He'd make a good lead actor, especially in paint. But he's not as tall as I thought he'd be. In fact, I don't think he's much taller than you. Maybe a thumb's breadth, if that. But . . ."

"But what?" I prompted.

"It's odd, but even when he's in a throng, where the men are taller than he is, he still stands out. It's almost as if as if he's the only one you can see. I'm not sure why that is. You know how a compass needle moves, always pointing south? It's like that. As though he's the south, and everybody else is a needle."

"Really?" I said, startled at her fervor. Perin's observations on men were normally flippant, sardonic, or disillusioned. I'd never heard her speak of one this way, and I decided that she'd been beguiled by the Sun Lord; perhaps she was even infatuated. Powerful men had that effect on many women, and I was a little disappointed to find Perin among them. I had imagined she'd be more clearheaded. Of course, I told myself smugly, *I* was in no danger of having my head turned. *My* eyes were wide open, and I'd keep them that way. Terem Rathai would never make *me* turn pink, as Perin had just done.

"It's hard to describe," she said weakly, and we left it at that.

From Sutkagin we were to follow the Short Canal north to Kurjain. I had missed seeing Sutkagin on my previous river journey, but I now discovered that I'd missed little, for the city was no more interesting than Dirun, except for a vast pink rock rising out of the earth, with the ruins of an enormous shrine to the Bee Goddess on its summit. In the old days the shrine had been a great attraction; people came from all over Durdane to see it and to visit the humming bee caves in the rose-tinted cliffs below.

However, Exile raiders had destroyed both shrine and city during the Year of the Five Emperors; they also burned out the bee caves and killed or drove away all the bees. The city was later rebuilt, but it was thought that the shrine could not be restored until bees returned to the caves. Sadly, they never did, so the shrine remained a ruin. I wanted to see it anyway, but moving wagons around by boat is expensive, and Master Luasin wouldn't allow any time for sightseeing. He had everything transshipped from the lorchas onto five canal slippers as soon as we arrived in Sutkagin, and before I knew it we were on our way to Kurjain.

He had assigned me to the women's bunk wagon with Perin, Imela, and Harekin, who were the second female lead and the supporting actress, respectively. (The lady stager and her husband bunked in with the musicians.) Imela was the oldest of us, quite plain, and usually played dowager roles. I liked her, but I didn't care much for Harekin. She was a fine talent, but she had a supercilious streak and paid as little attention to me as she could. Also, she snored.

Our wagon was chained down in the slipper's midships, and for convenience we slept in it. During the day we sat on the forward hatch in the sunshine and watched the landscapes of Bethiya glide by. This was the south of the Sun Lord's realm, rolling green farmland broken by conical hills, with the canal winding among them like a blue and silver road. The hills had been terraced long ago, and on these were emerald lines of young wheat and barley. Down on the flatland lay more grain fields, as well as vineyards and orchards of peach, plum, cherry, and pear. These were in full bloom, so that we traveled between banks of pink and white clouds, as if the sky had descended to earth. Their fragrances vied with the weedy damp scents of the canal and of the marsh marigolds and purple mud roses that grew along its banks.

Our slippers each had a pair of masts, so that the crew could use the wind if they were out on a big river like the Pearl. But on the narrow waters of a canal, the boats were hauled by enormous horses that lumbered along a towpath. The tow master rode on his beast's back to guide it, but he never had much to do, the animals being so placid. Where there was no towpath, as when the canal went through a town or village, the tow master unhitched the horse and took it on ahead. Then the slipper's crew put their long sculling sweeps over the stern and worked the vessel along until we came up with the towpath again.

This happened several times, since there were four sizable market towns on the canal between Sutkagin and Kurjain, and as many villages. All were in better repair than any I'd seen elsewhere, except in Chiran and Istana, and I noticed few of the walled manors that betrayed the holdings of rich magnates. This puzzled me. We'd studied Bethiya at school, but it was mostly the dynastic history of the Sun Lords, and I'd assumed that there were great landowners in his realm, just as there were everywhere else. I asked Perin about it, since she'd spent a lot of time in Bethiya over the past seven years.

"Well," she said, "it's like this. In the Despotates, the rich magnates have been gobbling up the farmers' lands since the days of the Warring Emperors, because there's nobody to stop them, except rival magnates and perhaps their Despot. But even a Despot can't always curb them. You have to remember that the great lords have armed retainers—a lot of them sometimes—and if enough of them combine against a Despot, they can give him no end of trouble. So he has to be careful about giving them offense."

"I see," I said politely, though I already knew this. "But why aren't there more of the big manors here?"

"Because the Sun Lords have been powerful enough to hold on to some of the old ways," she said. "Bethiya has its magnates, but they're fewer and weaker than in the south, so more farmers still own their land. But I don't think the Sun Lords have done this because they love the farmers. They've done it to keep the magnates down, so as to secure their place as rulers. Also because free farmers make better soldiers, or so I've been told."

This I understood. For about a day I'd been wondering if the Sun Lords, and this Sun Lord in particular, were more concerned for their people's welfare than I'd been led to believe. But Perin's words told me that Terem Rathai and his predecessors thought only of their own power, just as Mother had taught us.

Still, as we made our way up the canal, I didn't see any abandoned villages. Nor was there any sign of banditry, because each market town had a castella garrisoned by a detachment of the Sun Lord's cavalry. At two of these towns we went ashore to eat in a chophouse that catered to canal travelers, and I noted that the local people appeared well fed and clothed and that there were few beggars. Bethiya, at least this part of it, looked better than I had expected.

It wasn't only the towns that were in good condition. At a place called Three Rise Locks, our boats descended to the level of the canal's northern leg, and as the crews maneuvered us through the lock gates, I thought of Riversong and the silted-up canal near it. And later that evening, while we were on our way back to the boats after eating supper, a cavalry squad from the castella clattered past. I knew from the Heron Guard what quality fighting men looked like, and these were as good as any I'd seen.

The next morning we set out on the final stretch of our journey. I sat with the other women on the foredeck as the slipper glided through the thin pearly mist that hung over the water, and thought about what lay before me. My task had been much on my mind ever since Tossi told me about it, although nobody could have guessed this from my behavior. But even if my fellow students had noticed my occasional preoccupation, how could they have imagined what lay behind it—that by autumn I must be the Sun Lord's lover, to live under his roof and know his every thought?

As for me, I am no longer sure how I felt about being the principal character in Mother's great drama. So many terrible things happened because of it that an abyss gapes between my present self and the girl I then was. Indeed, I do not know if the feelings I now recollect are really the ones I experienced on that spring morning, although I can see myself clearly enough, that young woman sitting on the slipper's foredeck, floating along the canal toward her future. But as for how I felt about it . . .

Was I repelled at becoming the intimate companion of a man I considered a tyrant? I don't remember any deep revulsion. But all that turned out so differently from what I expected that I may have been more repelled than I now believe I was. Not that such reluctance would have affected my ability to play the part; I could simulate any emotion I needed to, regardless of my real inclinations. I suppose I thought it would be no worse than an arranged marriage. Those were common enough, and women survived them.

But was I fearful at the risk I was running? I was a spy, and if I were found out, the Sun Lord's inquisitors would torment me until I revealed all I knew. If I were taken, therefore, I must find a way to kill myself. I'd asked Tossi if I could carry poison, but she'd said I should not, that for my security I must possess absolutely nothing incriminating. So I would be left to choose among several less dignified and more painful means of doing away with myself.

But I don't remember being afraid. I'd never scared easily, and I'd never let uncertainty keep me from doing something I felt I should do. If I were that sort of person, I'd never have walked out of Riversong. I knew my fate if I were exposed, but I was utterly confident that my enemies wouldn't detect me. How could they, since I'd been trained by Nilang and Master Aa, the world's best teachers of the spy's art?

But most of all, Mother had set me a great challenge, and I wanted to meet it. I suppose I imagined my future as a vast stage production, a high drama of adventure and heroism. If I were ultimately caught and had to kill myself, the audience would weep or applaud, but then they would all go home, and we actors would take off our costumes and paint and repair to the nearest wine shop. I didn't actually believe the play could end with a real death—mine—and so, as the final day of our journey passed, I did as Mistress Ipip had taught me, and composed myself to ignore such forebodings.

North of Three Rise Locks, the canal wound among hills covered with woodlots, orchards, vineyards, and pastures dotted with sheep and cattle. There were also many plantations of clover for the Bee Goddess's special bees, the ones that weave the soft nests from which gossamin is made. The big domed hives where the bees worked speckled the landscapes for miles.

It was not until the fourth hour of the sun watch that we finally left the rolling country behind. The canal abruptly curved around the flank of a hill, and there, a mile away across the green coastal lowlands, lay the sea's warm blue glimmer and the domes and roofs of Kurjain. Above them rose the slender shafts of firewatch towers, topped by steep conical roofs. I counted ten of them; I'd never seen a place that needed so many.

Perin had tried to describe the city to me, but that first sight of it left me speechless, for the Sun Lord's capital was unlike any other city in Durdane and perhaps in the world. It stood where the Jacinth River met the sea in a myriad of channels and lagoons, and it was on the banks of these waterways that Kurjain was built. Thus its thoroughfares were canals instead of streets, and people and goods got around in boats.

I watched in fascination as we approached. Though three of the islands rose higher than the others, and were crowned by fortifications, it had no walls. I asked one of the slipper's crewmen why not, and he told me it was because Kurjain didn't need any. The harbors could be closed against an enemy fleet by vast iron chains and timber booms, and land attackers would first have to fight their way across the broad outer canals, and then cope with the maze of waterways inside the city.

That made it a tough nut to crack, which was why Kurjain had suffered so little damage during the wars that led up to the Partition. Because it had remained almost untouched, and because it was not only the Sun Lords' capital but also boasted the finest harbor on the northwest coast, it had become the richest and greatest city in Bethiya. Its wealth was built on trade; the Jacinth River connected it to the most populous inland regions of the

realm, and the Short Canal could carry all manner of goods between its deep-sea port and the river ports of the Pearl. The Sun
Lord's census takers counted some two hundred thousand people within its boundaries, but there may have been even more
than that.

The Short Canal ended in Feather Lagoon, beneath the ramparts of one of the fortifications I'd seen from afar. The slipper cap-
tains paid off the tow masters, the crew unshipped their sweeps,
and we sculled along the quays until we found a mooring place
near the customs house, a yellow brick building jutting from the
fortification walls. There were small craft everywhere, not only
slippers but waterspoons, long-necked periangs, the many-oared
dispatch boats called gallopers, and other types I didn't recognize.
At the seaward end of the lagoon ran an esplanade with stone and
brick buildings. Rising on the far side of their roofs were the mast-
heads of many big ships, moored in the deep-sea harbor of Salt Lagoon. The tide was out, but at Kurjain it varied merely by two feet,
so the only sign of low water was a band of soggy weed and bar-
nacles along the faces of the piers.

Feather Lagoon was the second largest of the four main lagoons
of Kurjain, and was easily big enough to accommodate hundreds
of slippers at once. The ramparts above us belonged to the Jacinth
Fortress, which protected the river approach to the city. It was
built of large amber-colored bricks, finely mortared, with a parapet
of red stone. The gate was in good repair, reinforced by iron, and
the sentries looked alert.

A port officer came out of the customs house to inspect the
slippers and their cargo, which consisted solely of our wagons and
gear. The officer knew of both Master Luasin's reputation and his
patrons, so he was very respectful, and the inspection was cursory.
In short order the slippers sculled out of the lagoon, swung around
the west flank of the fortress, and started down a broad canal leading toward the heart of Kurjain.

It was early evening and the city's colors were radiant in the
westering sun. I say radiant, because its builders had used not only

the amber brick I'd seen at the fortress but stone of many hues of yellow and orange, so that the air itself seemed to glow with the colors of a ripe peach. Sunlight danced across the canals, touching the ripples with gold and glimmering on the walls of the buildings, many of which rose straight from the water. They were of three and four stories, with curving roofs of red tile or dark blue slate; the upper floors had tall windows that opened onto iron balconies. The Kurjainese seemed very partial to flowers, for these balconies brimmed with cascades of them, and their fragrances sweetened the damp watery smell of the canal. Other, smaller canals sprouted off the one we were on. Some were so narrow a slipper couldn't enter, and at high tide even the tall stems of the periangs would just slide under the arched bridges that spanned them.

"This is Red Willow Canal," Perin told me. She and I were side by side in the bow with Imela and Harekin; ahead, Master Luasin's slipper wafted over gilded ripples. "It's one of the main ones. The villas on each side belong to well-off families. See the periangs by the water steps? The designs and colors on the hulls tell what bloodline the owners are."

"Which is that one?" I asked. "The purple and yellow, with the . . . it looks like shells."

"Oh, I don't know all of them. It's not one of the great houses, or they'd have something better than a periang. Almost all the magnates live on Plum Flower Canal. I do know those." She laughed. "It pays to."

"You said 'almost all.' What about the others?"

"Ah. Those live near the Sun Lord's palace in Jade Lagoon. They're very haughty indeed."

"I see." The idea of such people didn't alarm me; I was a Despotana's daughter and could be haughty with the best of them. "There *are* streets here, though," I added. "It's not all water." By now I'd seen two or three narrow avenues leading back between the high walls of the canalside villas. At the canal they descended in steps to little stone quays with black iron mooring posts shaped like leaping fish, sea birds, and lions. Periangs bobbed at the quays, their sculls-men chewing on rounds of flatbread as they waited for customers.

"There are streets, yes, just not as many as in normal cities. Some islands are big enough to have squares, though you can't see them from the canal. Many of the villas even have gardens inside their walls. Ours does."

"Oh, good."

"And wait till you see the Round Market," Perin added happily. "You'll love it. *I* certainly do."

We were to live in a villa on Chain Canal, about half a mile from the Sun Lord's palace. The house had belonged to one of the Tanyeli clan, the bitter rival of the Danjian bloodline that had included Mother's husband. After the extermination of both fami-lies, the ownerless place was confiscated for the use of the Sun Lord. He didn't need it, having plenty of accommodations of his own, and had instructed his Ministry of Personnel to let the Elder Company live there during its annual visit to Kurjain. We were for-tunate to get our quarters this way, as Kurjain was a very expen-sive city, and the inns charged what they liked. While we stayed there the ministry furnished a domestic staff; the cook was very good and could do marvelous things with fish, which were deliv-ered fresh to the villa's water steps every day, along with vegeta-bles and bread.

The villa's original furnishings had remained, and the building itself was unaltered except by time. It still had glass in most of its windows, of the fine colorless grade that only the very rich can af-ford. When I first entered the family quarters I received an im-pression of antique opulence, which made me I exclaim in delight, much to Perin's amusement.

But a second look revealed that the opulence had much faded. The furnishings were very old and dark, like the villa itself, so that everything had an oppressive air of age, accentuated by the flaking frescoes and cracked mosaic floors. The two upper stories were fresh enough once we aired them out, but the ground floor always smelled of mildew and canal water.

Inexplicably the villa had no ghosts, or no obvious ones. Given the murderous deeds and the ultimate bloody extinction of the Tanyeli clan, I thought it should have at least a dozen, but the villa's atmosphere was merely gloomy, not malicious. Still, I liked only parts of it: the sunny stone terrace overlooking the canal, the outer courtyard with its fish pool, and the garden of the inner courtyard. The balcony outside my bedroom window was also pleasant, and I liked sitting there when I was reviewing lines or eating my breakfast of fresh bread and grilled silverfin. The villa was so big that each of us had our own sleeping chamber, a luxury I'd never before experienced.

Master Luasin, the musicians, and the stagers spent the next two days going out early and returning late. The latter were unpacking our stage gear at the theater where we were to give our public performances, and Master Luasin was with the officials at the Bureau of Arts, arranging our schedule for the palace theater. We performed whatever works the bureau told us the Sun Lord wanted to see, and since it sometimes changed this at the last moment, we had to be ready with almost anything in the classical repertoire.

The company's first performance of the season, which was always for the Sun Lord, normally occurred a couple of days after reaching Kurjain. But to Master Luasin's disgust, the Bureau of Arts had neglected to inform him that the Sun Lord would not be in the city when we arrived, because he'd gone to the eastern frontier to inspect the border armies.

We couldn't begin our performances until he returned. To do so would have been a grave insult, possibly leading to the loss of his patronage, and Master Luasin would have boiled his own grandmother for glue before taking such a risk. Of course, the Sun Lord wasn't our only audience in Kurjain, although he was our chief and most generous patron. We presented dramas for him every five to ten days, but the rest of the time we performed for paying audiences in Kurjain's largest public theater. We always played to full houses, too, for the High Theater was greatly esteemed by people of elegance and refined taste, and there were plenty of such people in Kurjain. But protocol kept us from declaiming so much as a line in public until we had played before the Sun Lord.

Thus we had time on our hands that couldn't be completely filled by rehearsals. Always curious, I nagged Perin to show me the city, which she good-naturedly did. As we went about, I wondered if anybody would remark on my likeness to the dead Surina. I did receive a few puzzled glances, but that was all. This wasn't really surprising, since few commoners, even in Kurjain, had seen the Sun Lord's consort from close enough to detect how much I resembled her.

As for the Elder Company, Harekin had snidely suggested that the Kurjainese might think I was the ghost of the dead lady and try to exorcise me, but everybody else had lost interest in the coincidence. Master Luasin no doubt had received instructions from Mother to place me in the Sun Lord's view, but he said nothing about it because of the odd relationship into which we had settled. He knew I was more than I seemed, and I knew he worked for Mother, and you'd think we'd have exchanged occasional whispered confidences. But we never acknowledged it, not by so much as a glance. For my part, it was because I preferred to keep my own counsel, and as for Master Luasin, I think he was too afraid of Mother to speak to me without her permission. Or maybe Nilang had shown him her wraiths; I never knew, for he was dead before I had a chance to ask him.

Perin had promised to take me to the Round Market, and about a hand after settling into the villa, we went. The excursion was as much for her as for me, because she liked searching out knickknacks and small articles of adornment—she had a special weakness for gossamin scarves and bracelets carved from opalescent chank shells. So we furnished ourselves with a couple of hemp bags and set out, but we didn't go there directly; she told the periang's scullsman to take us past the Sun Lord's palace first.

The palace stood in Jade Lagoon on Stone Bar Island, one of the largest of the islands that made up Kurjain. On the island's east side ran the Honor Canal, and on the west lay the lagoon's glittering breadth, with the opulent villas of Bethiya's greatest magnates basking beside its esplanades, like frogs around a pond.

Every inch of Stone Bar Island was covered by the palace, whose amber brick walls stood with their feet in the lagoon. Its only land gate was on the Honor Canal side; this was the ceremonial entrance of Dry Gate, connected to the rest of the city by a bridge. There were three water gates, the main one being the suitably named Wet Gate, which opened onto the canal a hundred yards from the bridge.

Our scullsman rowed us along the Honor Canal beside the palace walls. They rose so high above us I couldn't see much of the interior, except some beautifully upswept roofs of blue tile, edged by bright, gilded carvings, and a tall tower with round windows. Dry Gate was closed, but the iron portcullis of Wet Gate stood open, and inside I could see a walled basin containing brightly painted watercraft. Just by the gateway was a guard boat, with two soldiers in it. They watched us as we passed, but it was only because we were women and they liked the look of us.

"It's so big," I said, as the island drew away astern and we emerged into the lagoon. I was impressed, even though I'd known that Terem Rathai wouldn't be living in a prefectural residence left over from the old days. This was because Kurjain, for all its size and importance, had never been the prefectural capital of Bethiya; that distinction had belonged to the city of Tanay. However, Tanay was on Bethiya's eastern border and too close to the Exiles for safety, and it had also been badly damaged in the wars. So the first Sun Lord took himself and his government to Kurjain, and there he built his palace. He'd had a taste for grandeur and pomp, not surprising in someone who claimed to be the successor of the Emperors of Durdane, and if his creation was not as vast as the old imperial palace in Seyhan, it was nevertheless immense. Its name was Jade Lagoon Palace, but everybody in Kurjain simply called it Jade Lagoon.

"It's at least four times bigger than Yazar's," Perin told me. "I've been inside, but I've only seen a tiny bit of it—one of the small banquet halls, and the lesser audience hall. Oh, and the Porcelain Pavilion, because that's where the theater is."

I pondered those golden ramparts, knowing that somewhere behind them was the Water Terrace, where Mother's baby son had died. I grimaced at the thought, but Perin didn't see.

We swung out of the lagoon into Copper Bell Canal. At intervals there were gaps between the buildings, where a street or alley met the water in a flight of steps, with a stone landing at the foot. Once in a while an esplanade ran alongside the water; here the landings were larger, so that a dozen or more craft could moor at their iron posts.

And everywhere was the bustle and hum of Kurjainese life. At the major canal intersections you could hardly see the water for boats: periangs with their passengers; waterspoons carrying white radishes, lettuces, early melons, leeks, strings of dried mushrooms, ducks and geese in cages; fishermen's skaffies piled with the silvery mounds of their morning's catch; slippers in from the Short Canal, deep in the water with timber, stone, hides, grain, wine, and the gods knew what else. Among these humble craft, like swans among ducks, rowed the ornate sequinas of the rich. Their hulls were vividly painted and their upperworks were a riot of gilt, silvering, and gossamin awnings striped like rainbows; Perin said the size of the sequina and the number of its oarsmen denoted its owner's wealth, with six rowers indicating moderate riches and twenty, opulent.

How all these scullsmen and rowers managed to avoid collision, capsizing, and sinking was beyond me, yet they did. But they all yelled good-natured abuse at each other, and to add to this the merchants on their waterspoons and skaffies shouted their prices and stock, calling people to come alongside to haggle and buy. The high walls beside the canal bounced the racket back and forth, and in some places you could hardly hear yourself think for the din.

Copper Bell Canal led straight to the Round Market in White Crane Pool. Kurjain had a score of these circular basins, of which White Crane was the largest. The basins were landmarks; in another city you might send someone to Pear Orchard Square, but in Kurjain you'd tell him to go to Pear Orchard Pool.

I'd expected an impressive market, but the Round surpassed all my expectations, for it was enormous, and almost all of it was on the water. Every kind of merchant boat I'd seen was gathered here in a vast raft of commerce.

Each boat was a floating shop. To do your marketing, you either sculled up and down the lanes that meandered among them, or hopped from boat to boat, using planks laid for that purpose. People rarely fell into the water, but when they did, there was great hilarity as the dripping, grumbling shopper was hauled out, mopped off, and offered a cup of wine to settle the stomach—a necessity, since the canals were very dirty. Kurjain got its water from island wells, but these were not trustworthy, so nobody drank water unless it was boiled or mixed with vinegar or wine. Small beer was the most common drink; it was brewed in huge quantities upriver where the water was clean and shipped to Kurjain in enormous casks. Even so, there were many fevers and bowel complaints during the hot months, and people died of them. Kurjain, for all its opulence, could be an unhealthy city.

But sickness was very far from my thoughts on that bright spring morning. Perin paid off the scullsman, we climbed the steps from the boat landing, and I found myself in the biggest market in Kurjain.

Not quite all of it was on the water. An esplanade ran around the circle and there, facing the great raft of boats, was a many-arched arcade with a shop tucked under each arch. Most of the crowd was Durdana, but there were others, too, both buying and selling. I'd seen lots of foreigners in Istana, but in Kurjain there were half the races of the world: Erallu, Ris Rua, Daisa, Yellow

Smoke Islanders, Avashan, Khalaka, Abarite, and others I couldn't name. Two of these were weirdly painted men with amber eyes, dressed in outlandish garb of fringed deerskin despite the morning's warmth. Perin told me they were Chechesh, from the islands behind the north wind.

We sauntered along the arcade, inspecting the shops. These were of the better sort and it wasn't long before Perin decided she must have a pair of ivory earrings, and set to bargaining for them. Being uninterested in baubles, I wandered a little way on and discovered a bookseller's stall.

To my delight, it had plenty of new books. Istana's single printer had stuck to popular classical texts, most of which I already knew, and its market had offered mostly old discarded volumes of the sort nobody wants to read. But here I found not only secondhand books but mint-new ones, smelling of ink and glue, with titles I'd never seen: *Lives of Famous Immortals, The Ten Thousand Infallible Arts, Records of the Unworldly and Strange, Mysteries of Nature, Dreaming of the Good Old Days*. There were books of stories as well, equally unknown to me: *The Seven Beauties, The Game of Love and Chance, The Journey of Sisima, The Horn of Gold*.

The middle-aged woman in the shop was cheerful, and we fell into conversation. I was pleased to realize that she took me for a native of Kurjain; I'd been in the city only a little while but had already picked up the accent. It turned out that her husband was the printer.

"I've never heard of some of these," I said, setting down *Mysteries of Nature*.

"Oh, those would be the new ones." She showed me *The Game of Love and Chance*. "This just came off the press. The author lives here in Kurjain."

"What's his name?"

"Hm, well, that's between him and my husband. You see, the book's a bit rowdy and adventuresome, not serious stuff, and when a scholar writes such a book, he needs to keep it quiet." She snickered. "Such a man has passed the Universal Examination. He doesn't want his literary reputation to suffer."

"Why does he write it, then?"

"For the money, what else? This fellow is as poor as a road-mender's widow, so my husband says."

"Your husband must have an army of page carvers working for him," I said, examining *The Game of Love and Chance*. Every letter was beautifully executed, without a single burr or splinter mark. "So many pages to cut. And so well cut, too."

She laughed delightedly. "Everybody says that who doesn't know. But he has no carvers at all."

I looked up at her. "He doesn't? Then how does he—"

"It's a new thing. There's two or three printers doing it now. You don't carve a whole page at once, you see, and you don't use wood. Instead you have every letter cut on the end of a little bar of metal, lots of bars for each letter. You might have ten bars with mishan and twelve with sessan, for example. Then you clamp the little bars together in rows, as many as you need to make all the words on a page, and you print from that."

It seemed clumsy to me. "But then you have to keep making more little bars when you want to print a different book."

"No, no. When you've printed all the copies you want of one book, you take the rows apart and rearrange the bars to make a new one."

"I see," I said politely. It sounded clever, but I didn't think it would catch on. You'd need so many of the bars, and every time you wanted another copy of, say, *The Seven Beauties*, you'd have to reassemble them. But with carved pages, all you had to do was put the block in the press and start printing. The man's wife was so enthusiastic about it, though, that I agreed with her that it was a wonderful idea.

That settled, I decided to buy *The Game of Love and Chance*, and we haggled amiably over the price. Eventually we agreed on a fair one, and I got some coins out of my belt pouch.

As I held them in my palm, about to count out the money, my

lips went numb and the back of my neck tingled. On a silver dram, the Sun Lord's embossed profile shivered and dissolved, to be replaced by Nilang's visage in miniature, staring up at me. A voice in my head whispered:

Drum Street, Fat Duck Canal, the blue door.

The face vanished. As always, the sending seemed to last much longer than the heartbeat it actually required. The printer's wife had noticed nothing. I gave her the money, tucked the book into my bag, and slung it over my shoulder.

"Where," I asked, "might I find Drum Street and the Fat Duck Canal? Are they nearby?"

They were very near, in fact, and she gave me directions. A quick glance showed that Perin was still haggling. She liked a bargain well enough to keep at it for a long time, so I decided to slip around the corner and at least look for the blue door.

I went a little way along the esplanade and found Drum Street, then walked along its short length to the canal. This was a narrow waterway; houses rose high on both its banks, shutting out the sun and casting everything into shadow. A stone bridge, balustrades carved with shells and flowers, carried the street over the dark green water. It wasn't a shopping area, but there were still lots of people going to and from the Round with their bundles. Above, laundry sagged from cords strung between balconies. Two women were gossiping across the narrow gap of the street.

A house rose three stories on the canal's far side; the door on its water landing was painted light blue. I crossed the bridge and found the street doorway, whose iron grill stood half open. Behind it, an archway opened into a small garden, into which fell a blade of brilliant sunlight. An old woman, shrunken with age, was standing in the light, looking very happy.

She wasn't Nilang, and I hesitated. But then she bowed as if to someone unseen, turned, and hurried toward me. As I stepped aside to let her pass into the street, she paused and whispered: "Ah, dearie, *she'll* set you right. Nobody could do anything, but *she* did.

I can sleep now, thank the Gentle Goddess. But you must be good, you hear? You must be good."

She tottered away and I went through the gate into the garden. A red willow grew against one wall. Nilang, wearing a green and silver robe, sat on a wooden bench. She was feeding a white pigeon that bobbed in the grass at her feet; unalarmed at my approach, it continued to pluck fragments of nut from her slender fingertips.

"Mistress Nilang," I said.

She glanced up at me. "Ah, Lale. You came quickly."

"I was in the Round," I said. I hadn't seen her for a long time, but she had aged not at all. And to my annoyance, I was no less nervous in her presence than I'd ever been.

Scrutinizing me, she said, "You were surprised at my summons?"

"I didn't think to see you in Kurjain, mistress."

She looked sardonic. "Which is a polite way of saying: 'What are you doing here?' However, you ask a reasonable question. Briefly, I am in Kurjain on your account." She fed the last nut fragment to the pigeon, which fluffed out its feathers as if annoyed, then flew off to perch in the red willow.

I looked over my shoulder at the gate, then up at the windows above us. Nilang said, "No one is listening."

"You said you were here on my account?" I prompted.

"Indeed. I am in the city to transmit your dispatches to the one we both serve. When you have information, come to me."

So this was how I was to communicate with Mother. Tossi hadn't told me, back in Istana, and perhaps she hadn't known. She'd assured me I'd find out when I reached Kurjain, but I'd started wondering when that might be. Now I knew.

"You're surprised that I was sent to you," Nilang went on. "You expected anyone but me. So you ask yourself: How can a certain person dispense with Nilang's skills, even for the highest of purposes?"

"Yes," I agreed, "I was wondering that."

"She can manage without me, though she doesn't enjoy doing

so. Thus you see, Lale, how important you are to her, that I have been sent to Kurjain on your account."

I was honored, and said so.

"My presence will serve other purposes, too," Nilang went on, as if I hadn't spoken. "You will eventually require substances against impregnation. I'll supply them as necessary. You still have the ones I sent you away with?"

"I do. I haven't needed them."

"No lovers?"

"No, Mistress Nilang."

"Good. The Sun Lord will no doubt appreciate your intact state, men being what they are. . . . Another thing. Forget the name you just spoke. Here I have a Taweret name, which is Dasetmeryj Netihur. And I have never set foot in Tamurin. You have never seen me before today."

"Yes, Mistress Netihur," I answered. Then, because the question had been much on my mind of late, I asked, "Everything hinges on whether he'll make a companion of me. If he doesn't, how am I to proceed?"

"By some other means," Nilang said. (I would never think of her as anything but Nilang.) "But that won't be necessary. He will fix on you as the wife he's lost."

I had a question, one that Tossi had not been able to answer. "How long," I asked, "has Mother known I looked like the Surina? She never mentioned it to me."

"What does it matter?"

"Nevertheless, I would like to know."

Nilang shrugged. "Since you were fifteen. That fortunate happenstance, and your acting skill, are the reasons she sent you to Istana. You are now prepared for your work."

It was the truth, yet it was a falsehood in that it concealed a greater truth. I had not asked exactly the right question; although, if I had done so, Nilang would not have answered it. Not then.

"But I'm not her," I pointed out. "Why would he accept me in her place?"

"Because he's human. He will try to recover her by any means, because that's the nature of loss. Even knowing that the presence of his beloved in you is only a phantasm, he will still want you to be her. If you encourage his delusion and cooperate with his longing— but without seeming to—you will own him utterly." She smiled, a rare and unnerving expression on that doll's face. "In short, you must play a role. You must become the woman who was the Surina."

"This assumes he loved her enough to want her back." The idea of the Sun Lord harboring the softer emotions still seemed bizarre to me.

"Oh, he wants her back," Nilang said. "He loves her still. Oh, yes."

I was in no position to argue this. "I'll have to give you reports," I said. "Where and how are we to meet?"

"Here, for the time being, when I send for you. No one in your household will think it odd if you consult a spirit summoner from time to time—everyone does it, after all. If the others want to see me also, bring them, but as far as they're concerned, you and I never met before Kurjain."

"They came to Chiran a few years ago," I pointed out.

"They never saw me, because I was at Three Springs then. Now, as for your reports, you will not write them down. Speak them to me and I will deal with them."

"Yes, Mistress Netihur."

She rose to her feet. "And for the time being, don't exert yourself to see me. You can accomplish nothing of consequence until the Sun Lord takes you up. But you are to prepare the ground, are you not?"

"Yes, mistress," I said. "I am to acquire friends in places of influence, and make myself known as a person of interest and merit."

"Exactly. Placed as you are in the Elder Company, there will be an abundance of such opportunities. Waste none of them."

"Yes, mistress. But unless you need me further, I should go. I came to the Round with someone today. She'll be wondering where I am."

"Be off with you, then."

I left her in her garden and hurried along Drum Street. When I got back to the Round, Perin was bargaining vigorously with a scent dealer, not far from where I'd left her. I had my new book to explain my absence, but I'm not sure she'd even noticed how long I'd been gone.

I'd felt carefree when we arrived at the market, but the mood had fled. Nilang's summons had reminded me all too sharply that I was not in Kurjain to enjoy myself. I was here to carry Mother's war to the stronghold of the enemy, and I would be wise to remember that if I wanted to survive.

Fifteen

By month's end the Elder Company should have put on several dramas, at least two in the palace and the rest for the public. But because we had to wait for the Sun Lord to return, we lost money every day. Master Luasin was angry enough over this to chew swords and spit daggers; his agreement with the Bureau of Arts specified compensation in such a case, but the bureau was reluctant to pay. He managed to remain polite to its officials, but in the privacy of our villa he fumed and fussed, and swore he'd never set foot in Kurjain again, which we all knew was nonsense.

We weren't idle, however. We now knew which plays we were to act for the Sun Lord's pleasure, and to tune our performances we rehearsed them in the villa's inner courtyard. I had already learned all the female roles of the essential High Theater repertoire, which luckily happened to cover the works the Sun Lord wanted to see; otherwise I would have been scrambling to absorb several new parts. Eshin had done the same for the male characters, and we were both polished enough to earn a tentative acceptance from the others. Perin, who was a generous soul as long as you acknowledged her genius, gave me bits of useful theatrical advice, as would an older sister. One was how to avoid being up-staged by another actress, which she said Imela was prone to doing. Perin wasn't above it herself, though, and she and Imela got into quarrels over it. No wonder Master Luasin had gone gray.

The Sun Lord returned to Kurjain near the beginning of Early Blossom, during the Torch Festival. He'd come down the Jacinth River by boat and was arriving at Feather Lagoon, so the Elder Company all went down to the quays, along with most of Kur-jain's population, to see his flotilla arrive. There were a dozen craft, all bedecked with pennants and banners—troop transports carrying his escort of marines; a clutch of dispatch gallopers; and leading them all, the big sequina that carried the man himself. The vessel was painted in his colors of scarlet and copper, with the running stag of his bloodline at the bow, and gleamed with prodigal amounts of gilt and silvering. Her bulk dwarfed any se-quina I'd seen in Kurjain's canals: I counted fifty oars, all swing-ing in perfect unison, a drum thumping the rowing-beat like a bronze heart. That was how I saw Terem Rathai for the first time: as the Sun Lord, standing on the sequina's raised stern deck, wearing a long crimson cloak over his parade armor, waving at the vast and thunderous crowd. He was bareheaded, helmet under his arm, but I could not see his face clearly, for he was too far away.

Nevertheless my heart missed a beat. Until this moment, I'd been able to think of my mission as no more than a play in which I was to perform. But there he was, the very flesh and bone of him, and now suddenly it was altogether real. I was to make a confidant and lover of that man on the sequina's deck; I was to make him rely un-questioningly on my faithfulness and loyalty; and then I was to be-tray him.

We watched the sequina pass. Perin was pink with excitement. I remembered how warmly she'd spoken of him, so I studied the Sun Lord as well as I could from a distance, to try to understand what stirred her. I couldn't detect it, although I noticed that he was slim even with the armor and moved very gracefully. And he was young, having just turned twenty-six when I first saw him.

The sequina passed from the lagoon into Red Willow Canal, and carried my lover-to-be out of sight. I thought, *Well, in a few days it's down to business*, and felt a flutter of anticipation under my breastbone.

It was down to business for the Elder Company even sooner than that, although the Torch Festival was giving most of Kurjain a holiday. The next morning, a message came from the Bureau of Arts: We were to perform for the Sun Lord on the following day, but before that we must present a sample of our work to the Magister of Diversions, so he could be sure we were up to the mark. Master Luasin grumbled at the implied insult, which he endured every year, and that afternoon a bureau official arrived in a palace sequina to take us to Jade Lagoon.

We entered the palace by the Wet Gate and found ourselves in the mooring basin, where the sequina deposited us onto a stone quay. Later I came to know the palace well, but as the official led us into the grounds I had only a confused impression of blue roofs and vermilion pillars, clipped hedges, flagstone paths, ornamental pools, and tall buildings among groves of crab apple and cherry trees.

The official conducted us toward one such building, which Imela whispered to me was the Porcelain Pavilion, where the palace theater was. It was a large structure of two stories, with an unbroken row of big windows under its swooping eaves and a rank of smaller windows below. The window's white stone frames had lattices picked out in red and white. It gained its name, I realized, from the lovely sea-blue tiles that sheathed it from ground to eaves.

Bronze doors opened directly into the theater. Within, the stage and the musicians' gallery were at the far end, and running along each side were three stepped rows of benches. On my right was a gilded doorway, and from this a broad stair descended to the theater's center floor. This floor was called the valley, and in a public theater was for people who couldn't afford bench seats. But in the Porcelain Pavilion, the Sun Lord's dais occupied the valley's center, and on the dais were two chairs of state, one for him, one for his Surina. Over hers lay a gray cloth of mourning, and as I passed it I imagined a chill, as if the woman whose place I was to assume might be watching me with unseen eyes.

Standing near the stage was Tijurian, the Magister of Diversions, a senior official of the Bureau of Arts. He was a stringy, birdlike person with a gloomy voice and a face to match, and appeared to find the Sun Lord's entertainments a very serious business indeed.

We were to present him with the fourth canto of *The Omen from the North*, which has everyone onstage and is very difficult, what with the mixed narrative and declamation, and singing in three modes. Being a meticulous sort, Tijurian also wanted it with the music and the movable backdrop paintings, which belonged to the palace theater and were of the quality you'd expect in such a place. But this was nothing new to my companions, for the Elder Company endured this official examination every year, and they treated it merely as an extra rehearsal.

We weren't introduced to the magister. In fact, Tijurian didn't even glance at me or the other actors—my first example of the haughtiness of many of the Sun Lord's senior officials. He held a quick conference with Master Luasin, they both bowed to the Sun Goddess's cabinet shrine, and then we got started. Eshin and I, being understudies, had little to do except keep out of the way, so we slipped into the wings to watch. I didn't know about the spy holes in the wings then, or I could have peeked out into the theater to see how the magister was responding.

But everything went perfectly, and when the piece ended, a brief silence ensued. Then I heard Magister Tijurian say, in a tone of deepest respect tinged with agitation, "My lord, I beg you accept my worthless apologies. I did not see you enter."

At the same instant, the entire Elder Company knelt on the stage, heads bowed. I'd never seen Master Luasin do this for anybody except Yazar, and Eshin whispered, "Father Heaven, it must be the Sun Lord!"

I suddenly couldn't get my breath, and a wave of vexation swept through me. I was utterly unprepared. I wasn't wearing anything special, and although my hair was clean I hadn't done much with it. And now here he was. I cursed myself for being so careless, though obviously I wasn't the only one to be surprised.

A flat, dry voice said, "Get up, Master Luasin. The rest of you, too. Well, such a pleasure to see you again. I was passing and heard the music. Admirable, flawless as always."

The Sun Lord certainly didn't have an appealing voice. Hearing *that* from the pillow next to mine wasn't something to look forward to. I shrugged off my distaste and listened carefully.

"Thank you, my lord," Master Luasin was saying. "Your praise far exceeds our merits, but your generosity is known to all."

"So I hear," the dry voice answered. It had a faint whistle, as if its owner breathed with difficulty. "I also hear that you have a pair of students with you. Are they here?"

"Yes, my lord."

"Permit me to see them."

Master Luasin turned to peer into the wings. "Lale! Eshin! Come out, if you please!"

This was the moment. I took a deep breath, stood up straight, put my shoulders back, and walked onto the stage.

Tijurian was in the valley, facing the man who stood by the Sun Lord's dais. I almost stopped in my tracks. Whoever that man was, he wasn't the Sun Lord. He was old, withered, plainly dressed, and leaned on a stick. There was nothing memorable about him; he looked like the gaunt old men you see anywhere, all wrinkled neck and spotted hands, sitting in the sun by a cottage door.

I knelt and so did Eshin, and we waited.

"Up you get," the man said. "I don't suppose you know who I

am, do you? No, of course not. Tell them, Master Luasin, and tell me their full names."

We rose, and Master Luasin said, "This is the Lord Halis Geray, the Chancellor of Bethiya. My lord, the student actress is Lale Navari and the student actor is Eshin Dareh."

I noticed that Tijurian had at last taken a good look at my face and was gaping in surprise. But Tijurian didn't matter; only the man by the dais mattered, for this was the monster himself: Halis Geray, architect of the usurper's reign, the butcher of Mother's family and child. He looked so harmless, just an old man with a wispy yellow-gray beard, pointed like that of a scholar of ancient times. But his gaze was hard and perceptive, and fixed on me. I stared into his eyes, then looked away, not because I had to, I told myself, but because he would expect it.

"You, Lale," he said, still with that faint whistle. "Come here."

I went down the stage steps to the valley and walked up to the Chancellor. The hall was silent, as if no one were there but the two of us. I bowed, fingertips to throat.

"Yes," he said at last. "I didn't think my eyes were that bad. Do you know who you look like, Lale?"

"My lord," I said meekly, "the actress Perin, who once met the Surina, says I much resemble her."

Halis Geray pursed his lips. "So you do. A remarkable coincidence."

I smiled winsomely. "My lord Chancellor, one of my teachers exactly resembled a local washerwoman. It was a source of great annoyance to both."

Behind me, the magister emitted a grunt of outrage at my presumption. The Chancellor's eyes narrowed, but the corner of his mouth twitched, and I knew I'd amused him. He said, "Indeed, it must have been vexatious. Magister Tijurian, were you aware of this oddity of Lale's?"

Tijurian said, "No, my lord, it's a surprise to me also. But as for the girl, she's a foundling. Raised in that school of Makina Seval's, out in Chiran."

He would have discovered this from Master Luasin; no one of uncertain background would be allowed near the Sun Lord. But I disliked the way he blurted it in front of everybody and the disdainful way he said *foundling*, as if I were an inconvenience whom my mother had cast off as soon as she bore me. I was nothing of the kind; I was the daughter of a Despotana, and he had no business speaking of me in that tone. I marked him down for future attention.

"Yes, I know where she came from," the Chancellor said. For a horrible moment I imagined he might know much more than that, and might in the next breath say: *And I know what you learned at Three Springs and why you're here.*

But he didn't. My alarm passed, and I waited while he thoughtfully rubbed his chin. "Will we see you in some of the performances?" he asked.

"That's for Master Luasin to decide, my lord."

"Of course. And are you being well treated by the bureau? Is there anything you need that you don't have?"

I was certainly not the person to whom he should put this question—it was Master Luasin's to answer. But I later discovered that the Chancellor liked to make such queries to inappropriate people, to see what might wriggle out from between the tiles. His unpredictability was one reason why so many people were afraid of him; you never knew what question he might ask next, or of whom he might ask it. But he was utterly predictable in one respect: his loyalty to the Sun Lord.

I should have answered, *Yes, my lord, everything is perfect,* but I didn't. I'm still not sure what came over me; no one in her right mind would dare complain to the Chancellor about one of his bureaus, much less in front of a senior official from that very bureau.

But I said, "Well . . ."

Behind me there was an agonized silence. I could almost hear Master Luasin's silent bellow of *Hold your tongue, you stupid girl.*

"Well?" Halis Geray prompted me, with a glint in his sharp green eyes.

"Lord, forgive me, no doubt this is merely an oversight and easily corrected, but since we arrived here we have been unable to perform in front of an audience, for reasons you know. As a result, our income has been nonexistent. The agreement between our Elder Company and the bureau specifies compensation in such a case, but the bureau has been tardy in issuing this compensation. However, I am sure this is merely a misunderstanding that could be wafted away by the proper word in the proper ear."

In a strangled voice, Tijurian said, "You impudent—"

Halis Geray raised a hand, and Tijurian instantly fell silent. The Chancellor looked me up and down with an interest he hadn't displayed before. I stood very still, cursing my runaway tongue, and waited for the sky to tumble down and crush me.

The corner of the Chancellor's mouth again rose slightly. "A misunderstanding," he said in his whistling voice. "Yes. I will look into it. Now, forgive me, honored guests, but I must be on my way."

We all bowed, and he turned and strolled from the theater in a silence thick with the smell of burned bridges. The instant the bronze door boomed shut, Tijurian fell on me in a tirade almost incoherent with outrage. I stood with my head bowed and let his deluge of invective roll over my head, though occasionally I peeked sideways at Master Luasin and the rest of the company. Master Luasin looked furious, but a couple of the others were trying to suppress grins, and I thought I saw Perin wink. Eshin stared at me in astonished awe.

At length Master Luasin ventured to intervene. "My lord magister," he said in respectful tones, "I humbly wish to note that the girl isn't used to palace protocol, and it is clear that I have been very remiss in not instructing her suitably. She isn't worth your attention. Leave her to me, I beg you."

"Remiss!" Tijurian screeched. "Incompetent, more like. Yes. Do that, discipline her, so I won't have to. And keep her out of my sight henceforth. The performance—" He paused, and we all held our breath. He wanted to cancel us, but I knew as clear as day that he was remembering the Chancellor's praise of our work. If we did not appear, there would be questions.

"The performance will proceed as scheduled," he said. "You may go." He turned on his heel and stalked out of the theater.

The stagers raised the backdrops while everybody but me stood around and muttered about the canto we'd presented, but they kept casting sidelong glances in my direction. I remained by the dais, wondering wretchedly how to undo the catastrophe I'd caused. When we left the theater no one spoke to me, except for Perin who gave my hand a secretive squeeze and whispered, "Good luck." Master Luasin wouldn't even look in my direction.

Eventually we were aboard the sequina that was to return us to our villa. I sat next to Perin, worrying fruitlessly. I had no idea what my rash act would cost us. Apparently I'd learned nothing, despite all my teachers' admonitions. My tongue still wagged as loosely as it had in Riversong.

"Lale."

I looked around. Master Luasin was at my elbow.

"Yes, Master Luasin."

"You were educated in a Despotana's court. You know protocol better than your behavior suggests, don't you?"

"Yes, Master Luasin, I do."

"Did you think to help us by speaking out so . . . improperly?"

Did I? There could be no other explanation . . . *Unless,* whispered a small voice at the back of my mind, *you reckoned to make an impression on the Chancellor, who would then recount the amusing incident to the Sun Lord, who would find his interest piqued. Very clever.*

But I didn't see how I could be that clever on the spur of the moment. More likely I'd simply been stupid and thoughtless.

"Yes," I said. "I'm very much at fault. I only wanted to help."

"Never mind," he said wearily. "You've damaged us somewhat with the magister, but he's a rancid swine and I don't mind seeing him vexed, especially since the Chancellor didn't seem troubled about the incident. And now we'll probably get paid, so in the long run perhaps we'll profit more than we lose. But I think I'd better appear to punish you, because the magister will ask." He paused, thought about it, and then said, "So when we open for the Sun Lord tomorrow, you won't be with us."

It was such a ghastly disappointment that I wanted to complain at the top of my voice. Instead I mumbled, "Yes, Master Luasin. I'm sure I deserve much worse."

"But," Perin said in an alarmed voice, "you won't keep her away *all* the time we're here? What good will that do her?"

"She can come with us the second night at the palace. But, Lale, when you *are* in the theater, just stay out of Tijurian's sight, will you? Keep to the wings while he's around."

I nodded. It was settled, and I knew better than to protest. But even in my disappointment and chagrin I knew it could have been much worse. So when we got home, I went to the shrine next door and burned a stick of incense to Our Lady of Mercy, and felt somewhat better afterward.

Nevertheless, I felt very hard done by when they went off to the palace the next afternoon, and for consolation I decided to go and see the theater we were to use for our public performances. This stood in the famous Kurjain pleasure gardens, so I'd be able to look around there as well. As it was the third day of the Torch Festival, I reckoned that lots of interesting things would be going on.

The gardens, which were called the Mirror of Celestial Delight, spanned several of Kurjain's smaller islands. Chiran and Istana had once boasted such places of amusement, but little of them remained in either city, and the Mirror was the first real pleasure garden I'd set foot in. Some of it was parkland, with shade trees and little footbridges over the narrow canals that threaded the grounds. Families went there for picnics and to fly kites in the brisk breezes off the sea, and children sailed toy boats on the ornamental ponds. And on warm evenings the unmarried youth of the city would promenade along the gravel paths, the girls meandering in shoals like daintily colored fish, while the young men tried to attract their interest without risking rejection or, worse, giggles.

The rest of the Mirror was dedicated to more elaborate pastimes. On its east side was the pleasure district proper, where you could find music and dancing, puppet shows, conjurers, acrobats, tightrope walkers, contortionists, sketch artists, and games of skill and chance. If you were thirsty or hungry, you could slip into a grill shop, punch house, wine shop, or buy fried fish at any of the scores of outdoor stalls. If you were a man and wished to meet a lady of negotiable affection, there were two or three discreet brothels. And of course there were the better type of freelance women, as well dressed as any upper-class lady and with some pretension to manners, plying the same ancient trade in the avenues.

Most of the Mirror was safe, even at night, because it was patrolled by a detachment of the city garrison. Crime was bad for trade, and since the Sun Lord owned the Mirror and collected hefty rents and taxes from its tradesmen, all was made to run smoothly. You could be robbed by a pouch cutter or a dip, but the penalties for thieving on the Sun Lord's property were harsh. Lifting somebody's valuables elsewhere in the city would earn you penal servitude in a government quarry, but if you did the same in the Mirror you'd also get a flogging. This kept most thieves away from the place. Even the gambling games were as honest as one could reasonably expect.

I reached the Mirror about the third hour of the sun watch. It was thronged because of the holiday, the air redolent with grilled fish and fried onions, and alive with the cries of the performers and their audiences. I made my way through the crowds, eventually finding my way to the public theater. It was called the Rainbow, and stood where the pleasure district gave way to parkland. It resembled the Sun Lord's theater but was both larger and plainer, being constructed of brick and wood rather than stone and tile. Yoshin, our flute and drum player, had told me it could hold two thousand people, making it the biggest theater I'd ever seen. The

Elder Company had the use of it twice a hand, and we stored our backdrops and other paraphernalia there between our performances. Most of the time it was used for musical recitals and popular drama; one such play was going on now, because I could hear voices raised in declamation from the interior, followed by a loud rumble of applause. I wandered up to the entrance and saw from the chalked notice board that the play was *The Palace of Crimson Mist,* of which I'd never heard: admission a silver dram for the valley, two drams for bench seats.

I decided to take a professional look at the inside. As I did, the audience began to stream out of the building, suggesting that what I'd overheard were the closing speeches. There was nobody taking money at the entrance so I went in, struggling against the flow of the crowd till I got into the valley, and then worked my way toward the front. None of the actors was visible, but as I neared the stage a woman came out of the wings and climbed down into the musicians' gallery. I went over to the gallery and said "Hello."

She'd been looking for her chimang, whose strings jangled softly as she picked it up. I judged her as between my age and Perin's, twenty-four perhaps. She was a little on the plump side, with a pleasing if unmemorable face and curly brown hair cut to shoulder length.

"Hello," she said guardedly, the usual reaction of a player accosted by a member of the audience. "Can I help you?"

I told her who I was, found out that her name was Tsusane, and that she was one of the musicians with the Amber Troupe. She knew about the Elder Company—everybody in the profession did—and had already heard that Master Luasin was back in Kurjain for the season. But she showed no sign of being impressed by my High Theater status, not that I'd expected it. People in the common drama generally felt, with justification, that classical actors were disdainful, arrogant, and narrow-minded, and had altogether too high an opinion of themselves.

Knowing this, I respectfully asked her to show me the Rainbow's backstage, and as she did, I let her know that I was very fond of the common drama. This warmed her up, and we fell into conversation about acting in general, and the vagaries of audiences in particular. When I saw that the others of her troupe had all vanished—after the play's done, no one leaves a theater faster than the performers—I asked if she'd like to join me for a meal.

I did this for two reasons. One was that I still felt out of sorts at missing our opening, and Tsusane seemed good company—she had a tart sense of humor, and liked the same popular songs I did. But the second was that I had work to do. As Nilang had reminded me, I needed a web of unwitting informants in Kurjain, and actors were an excellent place to start. Their profession attracted many enthusiasts and hangers-on, from dockworkers to senior ministers, and they heard things that the common run of people did not. Between the Elder Company's contacts and Tsusane's, I would surely be able to listen at many doors.

No sensible entertainer ever turns down free food, and my dinner invitation delighted Tsusane. She made sure the theater watchman had arrived and wasn't drunk, whereupon we went over to the pleasure avenues and found a chophouse. While we ate, she told me about the common theater in Kurjain. As I'd hoped, the Amber Troupe was very popular. Its members had many admirers, and Tsusane told me, in deepest confidence, that one of its actresses had recently become the lover of the head of the Armaments Bureau, which was a division of the War Ministry. I was covertly delighted at this, and put that woman on my list of people to meet.

Eventually Tsusane wanted to know if I'd met the Sun Lord. "No," I said, pushing a lamb bone to the side of my wooden platter, "but I probably will soon. Our second performance for him will be in a few days."

"Second?" she said. "When was the first? He only got back the day before yesterday."

"It's today," I said. "They'll be finishing up about now."

"And you didn't bother to *go?*"

"I couldn't. I annoyed the Magister of Diversions. Master Luasin had to punish me, and that was the punishment—missing our opening."

She set her beer tankard down. "What in the Merciful Lady's name did you do?"

I told her. As I did, her eyes got bigger and bigger. "The *Chancellor?*" she finally managed to say. "Oh, dear. No wonder the magister was furious. Will you ever be able to perform in the palace?"

"I hope so," I said ruefully.

"It will be all right," she assured me. "Look, we've eaten everything. Do you want to see some more of the Mirror? I'd be glad to show you everything."

I agreed, and we wandered around till early evening. Tsusane liked gambling, and we passed some time in the cheaper gaming pavilions, eventually losing a few spades each. Finally it started to get dark and we left, Tsusane by the bridges—she and another girl shared rooms in a villa on Lantern Market Canal—and I by a periang. As my boat slid along the darkening canals, the festival flambeaux were being lit everywhere in the city, their orange and yellow plumes reflected in the indigo waters like so many drifting stars.

I was well satisfied with my day's work. Tsusane would tell everybody in the Amber Troupe how I'd complained to the Chancellor that we hadn't been paid, and how furious that had made the Magister of Diversions. Those people would tell others, probably with dramatic elaborations, and it wouldn't be long before every actor in Kurjain knew about me. They might not all be impressed by High Theater people, but they'd be impressed by my audacity, and doors would open when I tapped at them.

I smiled to myself in the gathering dusk. My blunder was turning out to be surprising useful; perhaps, I reflected, it would eventually prove to be no blunder at all.

And better still, when I got home, I found Master Luasin in a state of deep satisfaction, because the bureau had paid up at last.

He was graceful enough to credit my sauciness for this, but begged me not to take such drastic measures again. I said I wouldn't, but I knew I lied. Sometimes it took sheer nerve to get things done, and I reckoned that if such forwardness were needed, I was just the girl to supply it.

Sixteen

❦

Five days later, I stood in the wings of the Porcelain Pavilion's theater, in the full makeup and costume of Jian, the doomed younger sister in *Maylane Unyielding.* It was Harekin's usual part, but for this performance it was to be mine.

The message had arrived at the villa the morning after I'd met Tsusane. It was very much to the point, and came from the Chancellor himself:

To the Most Honorable and Accomplished Master Luasin of Istana, Greetings:

It is the Sun Lord's pleasure that the actress Lale Navari shall appear in the Elder Company's next performance, on the afternoon of 13 Early Blossom, Year of the City 1315. The Magister of Diversions is informed of this and will be pleased to approve it.

Halis Geray
Chancellor and Chief Magistrate of Bethiya

That set the wolf among the sheep, let me tell you, for when Master Luasin assigned me the part of Jian, Harekin went to her room and didn't come out all day. Everybody knew what was behind the summons—I looked like the dead Surina and so the Sun Lord wanted to see me, no doubt for morbid reasons. I took pains to appear troubled by this, but inwardly I felt a deep professional satisfaction. Mother's game board was now arranged exactly as it should be.

So here I stood in the theater wing, waiting for the play to begin. I'd now discovered the spy holes, placed so the actors could gauge the audience without being seen, and I peeped through one for my first glimpse of Kurjainese high society.

I'd never seen such a spectacle, even in Istana. Both men and women were luminous in every hue of gossamin; gems glittered at throats and wrists and bodices, dangled at earlobes, sparkled on pale soft fingers. And the hats! Women's hats were not in fashion in Tamurin, but Kurjain was different: here all the women wore them, broad-brimmed floppy things with plumes and pearls and feathers, set on hair coiled into elaborate mazes and sparkling with jeweled pins. The men accompanying these women—most of whom were their wives, but not all—were the great and powerful of the court and government: first rank officials of the Six Ministries; the heads of bureaus; high magistrates of the Superior Judiciary, senior bureaucrats from the Inspectorate. Only in Kurjain, I thought, could there be a gathering like this; it was like stepping back two centuries into the Theater of the Emperors at Seyhan.

Tijurian stood by the Sun Lord's dais. There was a cushioned stool there for him to sit on and a small gong he would sound to begin the performance. He'd already lit the incense cones at the Sun Goddess's shrine, and now he waited for Terem's entrance, looking simultaneously glum and annoyed. I hoped his stool was uncomfortable. I was sure he wasn't at all pleased about my appearance today, but it served him right for insulting my background.

Suddenly the rustle and the murmur diminished, the way it

does when the audience knows the play is about to begin. But this abrupt silence wasn't for us. The gilded door at the side of the theater opened, and the audience with a soft rumble rose as one. They all turned to face the doorway and bowed, fingertips to throat, like a field of bright flowers leaning to a wind.

The Sun Lord entered, striding through the light that fell through the high windows.

He was close enough for me to see him well. As Perin had said, he was a well-favored man, clean shaven with a strong jaw and a pleasing mouth. His hair was very dark auburn, and worn longer than was usual for men, so that it curled about the embroidered collar of his state robe. And at this distance I could see clearly his lack of height; the three dignitaries who accompanied him were all a good two hand spans taller.

But his presence diminished them. I think it was partly the way he moved, for he was the most graceful of men, and partly it was his eyes, which were large and very dark green, like the deep ocean. As I would later learn, when that clear gaze held yours, you knew you mattered to him, even though you might live in a hut and live on ditch water and stale bread. It was profoundly flattering but in a strange way also disturbing: you felt that he perceived hidden excellence in you, and you desperately wanted to prove him right.

The effect seemed uncalculated, and in fact it was part of his nature, not something he'd learned. At the same time, he was acutely aware of this peculiar power of his and knew how to use it to his best advantage. It helped make him a leader of genius, gifted by the gods in a way the world rarely sees—which is probably for the best, since the evil side of that gift is very evil indeed.

But all I saw then was that this man made other men seem smaller. No wonder, I thought, that Perin fairly glowed when she spoke of him. But unlike her, I told myself sternly, I would keep my head. For if I didn't, I might very well lose it, literally.

But I was not quite as cool as I told myself I was. My chest felt as if a small, soft bird were loose in it, fluttering its wingtips against my heart. For a few moments I became quite light-headed, and had to remind myself to breathe.

By now he had reached the theater valley and was climbing the steps to his dais. At the top he halted and bowed to his subjects; they all bowed again in response. Then he sat down, and I thought I saw his fingers make a tiny motion toward the Surina's empty chair, as if to touch an absent hand. But once seated, he sat as still as a block of granite, his face without expression. He seemed to be gazing directly at me, even though he couldn't have known I was watching him.

After a moment, he spoke. He'd had orator's training, because his voice was resonant and pitched to carry, and far more agreeable than Halis Geray's dry monotone. He said, "Honored Magister, be so good as to proceed."

The audience sat down. When the rustling stopped, the Magister struck the gong lightly with an ivory hammer and the play began.

I wasn't onstage immediately, since Jian doesn't appear until the fourth canto, although the audience twice hears her singing offstage. I put my heart into those two songs, keenly aware of who heard me. Then I listened through the third canto, the one where Maylane sets off for the islands to rescue her husband.

And then came the fourth canto, in which Jian discovers the treachery that awaits her sister and seeks to warn her of it. I was on.

Jian must declaim as she walks onto the stage, because she holds the letter from which she reads the enigmatic warning message. The declamation is emphatic, yet even so I heard the spectators' soft gasp as I stepped into view. But I'd prepared myself for such a reaction and didn't miss a beat, continuing with Jian's plea for the Sun Goddess to aid her.

> To you, most gracious deity of summer light,
> My heart sends up these frightened words in hope
> That 'gainst this fearful treachery I may prevail,
> And bring my sister safely home.

There's a counterpoint lyric with the second male lead soon after that, and as I sang I was able to look into the theater. Everybody's attention was fixed on me, but I barely noticed this. It was Terem I wanted to gauge.

His gaze never left me, but he had no more expression than before. I was busy singing, but still I felt a fleeting annoyance that his eyes weren't wide with surprise. It never occurred to me how much pain might lie beneath his impassivity, as he watched a living, breathing woman who was almost the image of his dead beloved.

The canto ended and I went offstage. In the seventh canto I returned, to die as I tried to tell Maylane of the traitors around her. The death scene with the two sisters is very poignant, among the best in the High Theater, and Perin and I played it for all it was worth. By the time I expired in her arms I was hearing muffled sobs from the audience and knew that the Elder Company was living up to its reputation. But when I looked at Terem from beneath my almost-closed eyelids, I saw that his face was as stony as ever.

I was then carried off as a corpse, my part in the drama completed. I'd done my best and could only hope that Terem's love for his dead wife would induce him to look for her in me. Nilang had seemed certain he'd do so, but the Sun Lord was nobody's fool. Would his sorrow and yearning overrule his judgment and ultimately bring him into the arms of an illusion? Until now I hadn't doubted it, but after seeing that cold and indifferent visage, I wasn't so sure.

I was still wrapped in these musings as the play ended. We all came onstage during the applause, and knelt to the Sun Lord, who rose and bowed to us to demonstrate his appreciation. I peeked to see if he was looking at me, but he wasn't. Then he went down from the dais, up the stairs to the gilded door, and vanished.

I suddenly felt very let down. But what had I expected? That he'd call me up to the dais and congratulate me on my work? That we'd all be invited to leave with him, so he could spend some time in my company? Such ideas were ludicrous, as I'd have realized if

I'd known him at all. For I'd been wrong about every eye in the theater being fixed on me; half were, but the rest were on Terem, and he knew it. Any reaction to me would cause gossip, and he hated having people chatter about his behavior and the motives it suggested. So he gave no sign that my presence had affected him; not that he'd have done so, even if we'd been the only two people in the theater—he usually kept his deeper feelings to himself, as much as he could.

I slipped into the wings to avoid the curious stares of the departing audience. Harekin was there, and she embraced me. "It *is* my part," she said, "but you did well with it. A little tight in the high registers, perhaps, but a good first try."

It was a peace offering, so I accepted it in spite of the dig. Then everybody else congratulated me, too. There was general amusement at how astonished the spectators were when I went onstage, as if I'd played a mild practical joke on them. Nobody seemed inclined to see more in it than that, which suited me perfectly.

But as we sculled away from Wet Gate in the early summer evening, Perin leaned over and whispered to me, "He *was* watching you, you know. Remember what men are like, especially the powerful ones. Be careful."

"I will," I whispered back, although she would never know just how careful I would need to be, nor why.

Nothing happened immediately. The next day we performed at the Rainbow. I didn't act, but Eshin substituted once for Kalaj the support actor, who put up with it cheerfully enough. But word had gotten around about the actress who looked like the Surina, and on our second day in the Rainbow we could have filled the theater twice. People wanted me and would not be denied, so I had to come on stage after the play and sing a couple of solo lyrics. I don't know how many of them had ever actually laid eyes on the Surina, but they wanted to see me anyway.

The same thing happened after the third public performance. I didn't like being a curiosity and complained about it to Master Lu-asin. He said I should be patient, that they'd lose interest soon enough, and in the meantime I was helping the receipts. He was right, although a month passed before my novelty wore off.

Tsusane also came to watch me. She brought Yerana, the girl she lived with, and we went to a punch house after the per-formance, where I told them about appearing before the Sun Lord. They were impressed, Tsusane even seeming a little bit in awe of me.

On the day after that, we were supposed to have some time to ourselves, and Perin was taking me to meet some literary friends of hers. But by now I was starting to worry. Several days had passed since my debut before Terem, and I'd expected some re-sponse from him by now. Would he be content with merely watching me onstage? I couldn't do much for Mother if he settled for that.

But moments before Perin and I went downstairs to depart, I heard Master Luasin shouting through the villa for me. We met on the staircase. "Sir?" I asked.

He looked agitated. "Thank the Sun Goddess you're still here. A sequina's come from the palace. The Chancellor wants to see you by midday. He says you may bring one woman with you for propriety. I suggest Perin, if she can spare the time."

She could, and we were off to the palace before the midmorn-ing bell, in a sequina of four oars and a steersman. Harekin came out on the landing to watch us depart, with a knowing look on her face. I knew what she was thinking: that it wasn't the Chancellor who wanted to see me, and that the man who did wasn't looking for musical entertainment.

Perin was thinking this, too, although she didn't speak until we reached Jade Lagoon. Then she said in a low voice, "Lale, this in-terest may seem like an honor, and it is. But you *must* be careful. If he wants what most men do, try to put him off as long as you can. He'll value you all the more for it."

Her assumption that I couldn't control events annoyed me.

"Well," I said with some asperity, "I may put him off for good, if I feel like it, no matter what he wants."

"But, Lale, he's the—" She remembered the steersman a few feet away and lowered her voice again. "He's who he is. You *can't* refuse him. If you do refuse and he lets you get away with it, it's only because he's decided to indulge your whim."

"He'll have to go on indulging it, then." At that moment I realized I had a delicious new role to play: the plucky young heroine who is not to be trifled with, even by the powerful and great. "I'm not a ripe plum," I went on, getting into the spirit of it, "to fall into the lap of a man just because he shakes the tree. Anyway, why do you think he wants *that*? He can have his pick of a myriad women, each one prettier than I am. Maybe he's just curious."

Perin shook her head wearily. "Lale, Lale. Of course he's curious, just now. But you're . . . so like her. What will you do if he keeps seeing you? Falls in love with you? Because if he does, it won't last. Eventually he'll realize you're *not* her. Who knows what he'll do then? What will you do if it all goes wrong?"

If it went *really* wrong, I'd be over the palace wall and running away from Kurjain as fast as I could. But I only said, "I'll have to take my chances, and so will he."

She regarded me with exasperation. "You're an odd one. Doesn't anything scare you? Or anybody? Not even him?"

"Not even him," I said, staying in character, and then we were gliding under the arch of Wet Gate. As we emerged into the palace's mooring basin, the sun slid behind a bank of cloud and stayed there. The breeze was warm and damp, smelling of rain to come.

We disembarked and waited on the quay until an official from the palace administration came to collect us. He was a young man and very conscious of his dignity, although he wore only the white sash of an Eighth Rank official, and the lower degree at that. Still, the sash meant he'd passed the Universal Examination, and his air said that he thought himself a very fine fellow indeed. On his head was the soft black cap of a government official, with a gilt badge on it.

"Put these around your necks," he said, handing us each a bronze chain with a red-and-white pendant to it. The Sun Lord's emblem of a running deer was molded into the glossy ceramic surface.

"Why?" I asked.

His face took on the expression of one who must deal politely with imbeciles. "It means you're here by leave of the Chancellor. You can't go most places in the palace without one, even if you're with me."

"You're not wearing one," I pointed out, "and you haven't introduced yourself."

"I have this," he said tersely, indicating his cap badge. "It means I work in the Chancellery. You may call me Associate Clerk Kirkin. Now come, we must be brisk or be guilty of effrontery through tardiness."

We set off toward our destination. At the back of the quay was a high brick wall with a big double gate, which stood open. The gate had guards in silver-washed armor, who saluted Associate Clerk Kirkin as he led us past. Once though the gate, we were in the main palace grounds, and Kirkin took it upon himself to reveal their mysteries.

"Jade Lagoon is not like the old Imperial Palace in Seyhan," he said. "You would not be aware of this, doubtless, but that was one very large building spread over many acres of land. Jade Lagoon, on the other hand, is many buildings set among gardens. It is thus much more healthful."

"What's behind that wall on our left?" I asked.

"That is called the Lesser Quarter. The palace domestics live there, and it has guard barracks, stables, bakeries, and facilities of that lower sort. I myself spend very little time there, so I cannot really enlighten you further."

Kirkin's superior air was beginning to grate, but I wanted to know as much about the palace as he'd tell me. I went all wide-eyed and kept asking him questions, which he answered in an affected drawl.

"Over there is the Great Audience Pavilion—that's where the senior ministers have their offices. . . . There, with the green roof, that's the Lesser Banqueting Hall, behind that is the Porcelain Pavilion."

"We've been there," I said. "What's the tower I see from the canal, the one with the round windows?"

"It's the Arsenal Tower. It's for the palace fire watch. There's an alarm bell that rings if the sentry sees smoke."

"Oh. Do you ever have fires?"

He disregarded my question and went on. "Ahead on our left, although it's hidden by trees, is the library and the records archive. And now, directly before us, is our Chancellery."

He said it as if he'd constructed the place himself. It was a severe building, as if to emphasize the nature of the activities within: three stories of white stone, with guards at its entrance. Kirkin conducted us past them into an inner courtyard, still nattering away. He was now larding his speech with classical aphorisms, the better to show off his erudition. Perin tried to look properly humble, although she was having trouble keeping a straight face.

But by now I was becoming very annoyed, and finally he went too far. We were hurrying toward a large vermilion and gold door on the courtyard's far side when he said, "Before you is the seat of the Inner Chancellery, where Lord Geray will speak with you. Be careful not to give offense, for as Master Tolan writes in his *Golden Discourse on Manners and Customs*, 'If you do not observe the canons of good behavior, your character cannot be established.' "

His insolence in suggesting I had poor manners was not to be borne. "Indeed," I said in an acid tone, "Master Tolan does write to that effect. But elsewhere he also says: 'Beware of that apparent civility that is a mask for corruption, for debased practices, and for moral deficiencies.' "

Kirkin turned pink and opened his mouth for a rejoinder. I ignored him and continued, "In the light of this second aphorism, there is scholarly debate as to whether your quotation is indeed by Master Tolan, or attributable to an interpolation from the hand of his disciple Adjel. The question has yet to be resolved, although Master Hanay proposes in his *Discourses Weighed in the Balance* that Adjel is the true author. But of course you know all this, and my observations merely inflict tedium upon you."

Kirkin had become bright crimson but managed to say, "Such is the case. You are quite right to point out the complexity of the matter."

Perin was trying desperately not to giggle. Still flushed, Kirkin rang a gong fixed to the doorpost and a whistling voice from within said, "Who?"

"Associate Clerk Kirkin, my lord, with the actresses Lale Navari and Perin Varvasi."

"Admit them."

He turned the door handle and in we went. The door closed softly behind us, and we were in the presence of Halis Geray. The room wasn't large, but it was high ceilinged and lit by clerestory windows; ahead of us, more windows looked into another courtyard with a circular pavilion in its center.

I'd expected guards but saw no one except the Chancellor. He was sitting at a table that must, from its intricate wood and its mother-of-pearl inlay, date from long before the Partition. Its surface was piled with books and papers. We bowed.

Halis Geray leaned back in his chair and contemplated us .Then he said in his whistling voice, "Perin Varvasi, you are as lovely as ever."

Perin bowed again. "The Chancellor flatters me with his recollection."

"You're very hard to forget, dear lady. I've delighted in your genius these last seven years. It is luminous."

"Thank you, my lord."

"And Lale Navari." The Chancellor regarded me as he twisted the tip of his beard into a thread. It was a mannerism I came to know well, and meant he was arranging his thoughts. He never spoke without thinking first, so that a conversation with him was punctuated by moments of silence. It made him sound hesitant and indecisive. He was neither.

"My lord," I answered, standing demurely with my gaze lowered, so that I could look at the papers on his table. At Three Springs I'd learned to read upside down, but unfortunately I was too far away to make out the words.

"I heard that exchange outside my door," he said. "Where did you learn about the Tolan-Adjel controversy?"

"At school in Chiran, sir. I passed the Universal Examination when I was seventeen." At this Perin looked sideways at me, her eyes wide. I'd never told her about taking the Examination.

"Did you, now?" the Chancellor asked, new interest in his voice. "Who graded you?"

"The Examiners' Board of Tamurin, sir. Under the direction of Master Shahen, the Despotana's Principal Magistrate."

"I know of him. He's a scholar of merit. Your grade?"

"Meritorious Distinction, my lord. Though no doubt I was unworthy of it, and Master Shahen was merely being indulgent."

"Hm." He fiddled again with his beard. "I never knew Master Shahen to be indulgent. It is an unusual achievement for anyone of seventeen, especially a woman. You have my congratulations."

"Thank you, sir."

"Do you know why you're here?"

"My lord, it's not my place to assume a reason."

He snorted. "But you suspect what it is, and you're correct. The Sun Lord wants to see you in private. Your resemblance to the lamented Merihan Aviya intrigues him."

"I don't know what to say, my lord."

"To judge by my experience of you so far, I'm sure you'll find something." He stood up. "By the way, do you know what has happened to the Magister of Diversions as a result of that incident in the Porcelain Pavilion?"

"No, lord."

"The Inspectorate has examined the delays in payment, and discovered that there was corruption in the Bureau of Arts, involving the Magister and others. He has now been assigned to duties on the northeast frontier. Some five officials have suffered similar discipline. This correction is to your credit, as the defective behavior had escaped notice until you spoke up."

"I'm gratified to have been of service, sir, even if by accident," I said, and mentally removed the Magister of Diversions from my list of targets.

"Yes, I'm sure you are. Come with me, both of you."

We followed him into a long corridor with many doors. Officials wearing every kind of rank sash and cap badge hurried up and down, carrying sheaves of documents and the flat polished boxes I later learned were official dispatch cases. In the rooms to which the doors led, more officials and clerks hunched over desks piled with papers and thick ledgers bound in wooden covers. Tall document chests stood against the walls, and the air smelled of ink and melted sealing wax. This was where the major business of the realm was conducted, and I realized that just about everything Mother could want to know about the Sun Lord's business was here somewhere. Until now I'd thought of the Chancellery in terms of the Despotate Office in Repose, not realizing how tiny Mother's government was in comparison to this vast bureaucracy. Even if I had free rein of this huge building, which I never would, I'd need years to find everything that would interest her. The thought sobered me, as did being in the presence of Halis Geray. He was affable enough, but I would be very foolish if I deluded myself as to how dangerous he was. If he ever found me out, my fate would be dreadful indeed.

Eventually we reached a door. This opened onto a veranda that ran around the courtyard I'd seen through the Chancellor's office windows. The little pavilion stood in its center, surrounded by shrubbery, gravel paths, and stone flowerpots. The pots held purple ladybells and white hyssop. The lattices of the courtyard windows were closed, but I saw movement behind one; somebody was watching us. A few raindrops pattered on the veranda roof, then ceased.

The Chancellor directed Perin to a bench on the veranda, where a jug, a wine cup, and a plate of cakes was laid out. Then he led me into the pavilion. Inside was a round table of the wood called feather-grain, and two chairs. He took one and pointed at the other. I sat down. On the table were three lovely ceramic pitchers and cups as thin as eggshells, all glazed with serpentine labyrinths of red and gold.

"I do not approve of this," he said. "The Surina is gone and will not come back. But he cannot help himself."

"He loved her, my lord," I said, with exactly the right measures of sorrow and sympathy.

"He still does. But he does not love you. Do you see this as an opportunity to make your fortune?"

He was trying to disconcert me. "No, I don't, my lord Chancellor. I have no desire to . . . to be taken for someone else. It would be like turning into a ghost."

"Yes, I should think so. But hasn't it crossed your mind that you could do very well out of this?"

"It would cross any woman's mind, sir. But as it says in the *Discourse on the Cultivation of the Spirit*, 'He who sacrifices his conscience to ambition, burns a picture to obtain the ashes.' I am determined to resist any such temptation."

"You are very self-possessed, as well as erudite."

"I was raised as a Despotana's daughter, sir. I did my best to learn all she wished to teach me."

"Hm. You don't appear to have missed much. You know of Makina Seval's unfortunate history here?"

"Yes, sir. But she never spoke ill of either you or the Sun Lord. I believe she prefers to put aside those sorrows and rule quietly in Tamurin."

"A wise ambition. And as long the Sun Lord's armies stand between her and the fury of the Exiles, a realistic one. Do you know why I'm talking to you like this?"

"I think, sir, to decide whether the Sun Lord should meet me or not."

"Close, but not the mark, because he'll do as he wishes. I can only make my concerns known. But for the moment, I withdraw them." He clapped, and a middle-aged woman appeared on the far veranda and came toward us. "You must be searched for weapons."

He politely turned his back while she ran her hands over me. I had nothing but the small eating knife everyone carries, and he let me keep that. When the woman went away he said, "I'm going back to work. You will stay here, and Perin will remain on the veranda for propriety's sake. After he leaves, ring the gong by the door where we came out."

"Yes, lord."

He stalked away and vanished into the Chancellery. Perin raised a tentative hand to me. I waved back but neither of us spoke. I heard rain tap the shingles above me, a few drops and then a few more.

A door opened on the other veranda, and the Sun Lord strode into the courtyard. He wore a tunic of white gossamin and deep blue trousers. Around his narrow waist was the black sash with the gold edging that signified the highest magisterial rank; for he was, among other things, the supreme lawgiver of his realm.

I rose, clasped my hands before me, and lowered my gaze to the earth. As he reached the pavilion, I knelt.

He halted at the top of the steps and said, "That's not necessary. Please get up."

I obeyed. Our eyes were almost on a level. I looked into his, into their dark green depths, where a woman might drown. My clasped hands trembled and my mouth went dry. I could not speak. I was in the presence of my enemy. I could kill him between one breath and the next.

He said, "So you're Mistress Lale Navari."

I found my tongue. What to do with it? I must amuse him, or try to. "I can hardly deny it, my lord," I murmured.

He tipped his head to one side. "Do you usually respond to social pleasantries with a literal answer? I didn't *expect* you to deny it."

From this close he was very attractive indeed, so much so that I again felt that breathlessness I'd experienced when I'd seen him in the theater. And I realized suddenly that if I were not so well trained, and so acutely aware of the danger he represented, I might well be susceptible to him. Those eyes drew the gaze, even mine that had so much to hide.

"I apologize for my impudence, my lord. Sometimes my tongue runs away with me, to my great mortification."

"My Chancellor has said much the same thing. And you may leave off saying 'my lord' every time you speak."

This was a surprise. I hadn't thought he'd wear his rank so lightly. "All right," I answered.

"Good. Please sit down."

I did. He joined me at the table and gestured at the ceramic jugs. "We have wine and two kinds of fruit drink: citrine and apple. Which would you prefer?"

I asked for apple. He took the same and poured for both of us with his own hands. Despite his courtesy, or rather because of it, I was very much on my guard. I knew he was intelligent, ruthless, and brutal, for Mother had taught us this, but I also knew that no man or woman is all of a piece. Terem would show me his best side, expecting to deceive me about the rest.

He'd also expect me to be awed by his presence. He was the Sun Lord, after all, and I merely the adoptive daughter of a minor ruler, with no real ancestry to call my own. But I couldn't appear to be too awed, because his Surina wouldn't have acted that way. She'd been his wife, and even wives who respect their husbands don't usually go in awe of them; at least not after a year or two of marriage.

He drank, regarding me over the rim of his cup. I met his gaze and said quietly, "Do I look so much like her, then?"

It made him choke a little. He put the cup down, coughed into his fist—he wore a ruby signet ring that would have bought ten Riversongs—and answered, "You're very forthright."

"I thought it best to clear the air. That's why I'm here, isn't it?"

He frowned. Had I already managed to unsettle him? If so, I was doing better than I'd hoped. The rain had begun in earnest now, light but steady, pattering on the roof above us.

"Yes, that's the reason. And, yes, you do look much like her." His counterstroke was swift. "And you're tired of hearing people say so."

I parried it easily. "Yes, I am. If people always think of how much I'm like somebody else, they can't see me clearly. I prefer to be seen clearly, as I truly am." Of all the lies I'd told in my life, I reflected, this must be among the most extravagant.

He said, "Do you think I see you clearly?"

"No. I think you see her. And that you hope I'll be even more like her than I appear."

He stiffened almost imperceptibly. "You presume to know a great deal about me."

Perhaps I'd gone too far, but I'd set my bridges alight and couldn't go back. In a sympathetic voice—the one I used for the mistress's part in *The Well*—I said, "I know a good deal about human nature. You're wounded in the heart. Who wouldn't seek a balm for such a wound?"

"Ah. Do you think I seek that balm in you?"

"I don't know," I said. "Do you?"

"It would be foolish. You're not her."

"No," I told him softly, "I'm not."

The Sun Lord looked away across the courtyard. Beyond him I saw Perin watching us. But the sound of the rain would hide our voices, and she wouldn't know what passed between us.

"I have very little time," he said. "Will you come here another day?"

"You know I can't refuse such a request."

"You can refuse this one. Say so, and we'll never speak like this again. Nothing awkward will happen if you decline." He essayed a smile, not a very broad one. "I'll still come and watch you onstage. Even though I don't much care for the High Theater."

I'd been about to sip my juice, but at this I set my cup down. "You don't?"

"No. But don't tell anybody, please. Even Halis doesn't know. You see, it's expected that the Sun Lord will patronize the most worthy of the arts. It's also expected that he'll like them. Not to do so would reveal deficiencies of character. But I am very deficient in my character, it seems, and the High Theater bores me into a stupor. I've seen all the classics, I don't know how many times. But for me, twice is enough for any of them."

I'd expected nothing like this . . . this what? This secret confidence? Did he want to be *friends*?

"Then what do you like, for entertainment?" I asked.

He looked almost guilty. "The popular drama. The plays the High Theater sniffs at so scornfully."

I'd have warmed to him if he hadn't been so dangerous. "Well, I rather like those, myself. But do you ever have a chance to see one?"

He nodded. "A year ago I arranged for some performances in the palace, very unofficially. We had several comedies."

I knew whom he meant by that *we*, and I knew infallibly that the Surina had liked the plays, too, and that he'd arranged them for her. I imagined the two of them in the Porcelain Pavilion, side by side in their chairs on the dais, laughing till their ribs hurt.

"The Magister of Protocol must have sent me a dozen memoranda of protest," he went on. "But he's happy now, because I haven't seen one since last summer. But you say you like the common theater?"

"A great deal. The Rainbow's playing *The Tale of the Glass Mountain* soon. I'm going to go, if I can find the time."

"I haven't seen that one. It must be new. But you have very cleverly evaded my question. So I ask it again: Are you willing to come to see me again?"

I ran my fingertip around the cool rim of my cup. Then I said, "Yes, I am. But I can't come when the company's performing, even if I'm not onstage. Master Luasin is very strict."

My effrontery appalled even me. The Sun Lord himself, the absolute ruler of great Bethiya, had asked me to visit him. And what did I answer? That I might find time to do so, provided I didn't have something more important at hand.

To my relief, Terem chuckled. "Indeed, both duty and propriety must be acknowledged at all times. But perhaps Master Luasin might be willing to make an occasional exception."

We both knew he would, without hesitating for an instant. I said, in my politest voice, "Perhaps he might."

"Good. I'll send word in a few days. Refuse me if you must, and I'll try again."

"All right," I said, and he stood up. I rose and touched my throat. "Good-bye, my lord."

"Good-bye, Mistress Lale Navari."

I watched him go, and then he was gone, and our first meeting was over. But to this day I remember every word that passed between us, as if we'd spoken them no more than an hour ago.

And I remember the rain. Was it an omen? I don't think so. I don't believe in omens like that. But it remains forever in my memory, that sound of soft, cool rain falling on the pavilion roof, like tears.

Seventeen

❦

(M)y life had been simple until that meeting. I merely had to convince people that I was Lale the aspiring actress, while concealing the secret self that was Lale the spy. Trained to duplicity, I accomplished this with ease; just as naturally as I painted my face for the stage, I painted my nature as other than it was.

But by the time the month of Early Blossom slid into Hot Sky, I realized that I was changing. It was as if the paint were sinking imperceptibly through my skin, so that sometimes I really was the Lale of the Elder Company, as well as the Lale of Three Springs. Occasionally, especially when I was with Terem, I would pass a whole day without thinking of myself as a spy. I wondered uneasily about this at first, fearing that such forgetfulness might lead to self-betrayal. But then I realized that I should welcome it, for when I *was* only Lale the actress, I was playing my role to perfection. I'd heard older actors say that to actually become their character was the highest achievement of their art, and I was proud that I'd already learned to do it—especially since my life might depend on the quality of my performance.

But even when I was most completely Lale of the Elder Company, I was always faintly aware of that other Lale's unwavering scrutiny. Her presence was a comfort, because I knew that if I needed her she'd be there, capable and merciless. It never occurred to me that I might someday be uncertain about which of these two women, if either, I truly was.

Terem didn't fall easily into my arms, for Merihan had been in her grave less than a year; her tomb stood in the palace necropolis called the Garden of the Ancestors. Despite this he didn't quite feel that she was dead, and when he was with me he could sometimes let himself believe that he'd got her back.

But to do him justice, he was perfectly aware that he wanted me near him because I sometimes seemed to be Merihan. Yet he also rather liked me, simply as me, which unsettled him. Though he never said so, I suspect he sometimes half wished I'd never crossed his path, because I complicated his emotions so much. But as long as his heart could not let Merihan go, he could not let me go, either.

For my part, I knew that Mother would care little how I snared him, as long as I did. But I knew better than to throw myself at him. Instead I held myself slightly aloof, forcing him to come to me. Neither did I try to act as I imagined Merihan might have, because he'd have seen through that in an eye-blink. Instead, I played the role of the scrupulous and clear-sighted woman, modeling my part somewhat on that of the general's sister in The Omens of Dawn. I reckoned this would impress him with my virtue, which it seemed to do.

As the summer days drifted past, my visits to Jade Lagoon became ever more frequent. Each time I arrived, I was met at the Wet Gate by Kirkin. Because he was a clerk in the Chancellery and knew things Mother might find useful, I tried to charm him into talking about his work, and before long I succeeded. In his eagerness to impress me, he sometimes dropped nuggets of information I would otherwise never have learned.

Kirkin conducted me each time to the Reed Pavilion, where Terem and I always met. The pavilion was very private, nestled in an angle of the outer palace walls and screened by a tall boxwood hedge. A pond sprinkled with blue water lilies lay alongside the pavilion, and in its shallows grew the fronded reeds that gave the pavilion its name. Around the pond were thickets of flowers: sea lavender, basket-of-gold, and orange torch lilies, all chosen for their colors and their fragrances. The veranda where we sat was built out over the water, so that you could look down and see rainbow carp shimmering in the cool depths.

In the beginning, Terem and I talked a great deal. I told him about my childhood in Riversong, which interested him because, he said, he knew little of how the poor of Durdane lived and what they suffered. I, of course, assumed that he merely feigned his concern, in order to impress me with his virtue. For he was courting me, there was no doubt of it.

He was also curious about my life at Repose. Here I needed to be careful, although I had carefully rehearsed a version of it that did not betray its central fact—that Mother had taught her daughters to regard the Sun Lord as their deadly enemy. I gave a fine performance, and deceived him without any trouble at all.

It was during this time that I discovered something quite unusual about him, something that was to have the most profound consequences: he was a very good listener. Most people are not; they hear you with half an ear, while thinking about what they are going to say when you've finished. But when I spoke, Terem gave me and my words his full attention, and it pleased me.

That pleasure was the first hairline crack in the protective shell of loyalty I'd forged, over so many years, at Mother's direction. It was so subtle a thing that I felt no alarm, and why should I? The flustered sensations I'd experienced at our first meeting no longer assaulted me, and only occasionally did I feel a curious weakness in my knees when I looked at him.

Not that he didn't attract me; I or any other woman would need to be dead not to feel his allure. But the attraction didn't trouble me, for it would make my eventual role as his mistress all the easier to play—and that prospect, I had to admit, became more pleasing as time passed.

So, because I thought I was keeping such a level head, I failed to see the danger in which I stood. That danger was not that I might lose my judgment to passion; I'd been trained too carefully for that, and besides, I had Nilang's wraiths to keep me loyal. The real peril was a more subtle one: its portent was the happiness I felt when we did no more than talk. *That* was the danger: not lust, who rules the body like a conqueror, but rather love, the thief in the night who comes to steal the heart.

As we grew more familiar with each other, we discovered that we both liked games. Often we played Twelve Lines, though I was no match for him and usually lost. Occasionally we played Over the River, or Odds and Evens, with pebbles for stakes. Eventually I acquired a pack of cards and taught him Six Roosters, which he enjoyed enormously. I was good at gambling and won more often than he did, but he lost cheerfully, something I hadn't expected in a man so accustomed to taking precedence.

Occasionally we tried poetry competitions, a then-fashionable pursuit in which you had to compose a lyric on the spot, and your opponent must respond with a poem of the same form, mood, and imagery. To my surprise, although Terem was a brilliant and polished orator, poetry completely escaped his grasp. I was a dismal poet, but he was even worse. In desperation he resorted to such ludicrous images and language that our contests were never completed but were invariably cut short by peals of helpless laughter.

At other times, we walked in the secluded garden behind the Hall of Records, a quiet place reserved for the Sun Lord's privacy. Terem was a fine archer, and that was where he liked to practice. When I discovered this, I asked if he would lend me a bow, and thereafter we passed many happy hours shooting at straw targets. In those days, upper-class women often played at archery, so he found nothing odd in my interest—I merely had to pretend to be much less skilled than I was.

Perin had warned me to expect his erotic approaches almost as soon as we met, but she misjudged him. Despite all the time we passed together, we didn't exchange even a touch of the hand, much less become intimate. In fact, gossip had given him very few lovers even before his marriage, and after he and Merihan were wed there had been none at all. In this he was quite unlike his predecessors, who were notorious for the number and expense of their mistresses.

There was calculation in this. Halis Geray had put Terem on the dais with the intent that he would behave according to the precept of the *Golden Discourses*, which goes: "If a ruler cannot rule his own conduct, how can he rule the conduct of others?" The decorum that now reigned in Jade Lagoon suggested that the promise had been kept, which helped obscure the brutal slaughter and infanticide by which Terem had ascended the dais.

Meanwhile, outside the palace walls, the world went on. Terem's War Ministry continued to strengthen the army and the defenses of Bethiya's border with Lindu, and the Ministry of Supply searched high and low for good cavalry mounts and recruits. Ardavan sent emissaries and gifts to Terem, as well as to every other ruler who might conceivably become an enemy or an ally. These were accompanied by effusive assurances of Ardavan's desire for peace.

Nobody believed him, and his multiplying armies and ambiguous intentions unsettled the sleep not only of Garhang, Lindu's king, and Terem's military officials, but also that of the Despots of Anshi and Panarik. These two men remembered all too well how Ardavan had built troop barges before he turned west and overran Jouhar. If he ever made good his earlier threat and got his Exile horsemen across the river, he would make short work of both Anshi's and Panarik's infantry brigades. And nobody except Ardavan knew what he would do then.

By the middle of Hot Sky, I was visiting Jade Lagoon as much as one day in three, not including the days of the Elder Company's performances in the Porcelain Pavilion. Master Luasin, having done his part in getting me into Terem's company, no longer risked the ire of the other actresses by substituting me for them. Consequently I only performed twice more in the palace, both times because Imela had a cough.

Even by this time, surprisingly few people knew about Terem and me. I came and went at Jade Lagoon very quietly, by hired periang and not by a palace sequina, and Kirkin never identified me to anyone we encountered. I also wore my hair pulled straight back and fastened with a silver clip, which changed the shape of my eyes and cheekbones so that I looked much less like the Surina. Moreover, I was only one person among the many who had business at the palace: magistrates, bureaucrats, messengers, officers of the army and the fleet, tradesmen and tradeswomen went in and out at all hours. With so many other minnows in the stream, I passed almost unnoticed.

But I was watched as I went about the city. I'd expected this and would have been very surprised if Halis Geray had ignored me, given my budding affair with the Sun Lord. Four of the Chancellor's people followed me, working in shifts of two. They were fairly good at their trade, and an untrained person would not have detected them. I never tried to shake them off, not even when I went to Nilang's, because giving them the slip would be a clear signal that I was more than I appeared to be.

As for actively seeking out military and diplomatic secrets, Nilang had forbidden me to do this, for I was far too precious an instrument to risk in humdrum spying. However, I did have to report on my conversations with Terem, and on anything else interesting I might observe in Jade Lagoon. I never wrote any of this down, not even in the poem code we'd learned at Three Springs—the domestics at the Chain Canal villa might be working for the Chancellor, and scribbling such stuff would be unforgivably stupid. I gave my reports orally to Nilang, who encoded them onto slips of paper that resembled the jottings of a very mediocre poet; if necessary, she added further information using invisible ink. The paper became packing for small items that she sent by Wayfarers' Guard to a trading company Mother owned in Sutkagin. From there the package went by courier to Repose. Mother reversed the method to communicate with Nilang.

I sometimes wished Nilang's sendings could be used to transmit such complicated messages, for the discovery of even one would be enough to hang us both. Still, we were reasonably safe from detection. To catch us, Halis Geray would have to intercept a package, realize that the packing paper was more than it seemed, decipher the code somehow, and finally trace it to Nilang—not easy, for she never sent a dispatch unless she knew she was free of watchers, and nothing in the package indicated its origin. And to muddy the waters further, I took to visiting two or three other spirit summoners, so Nilang wouldn't stand out. The Chancellor's men did watch her house for a while, but she never did anything suspicious, so eventually they left her alone.

Nevertheless we had to be careful. Halis Geray's men were skilled enough to be dangerous, and Mother had a healthy respect for his deviousness. Much depended on hiding her activities from his searching eyes, and to this end she had steered clear of Kurjain until I was ready to go there. I suppose if he'd suspected the existence of her web, and bent all his energies to uncovering it, he might have had some success. But to him, the greatest threat was the Exile Kingdoms and especially Ardavan, and that was where he spent most of his money and directed most of his agents. The others he devoted to watching those citizens of Kurjain whom he suspected of disliking the Sun Lord's rule.

I was soon sure I was not among these latter, if only because Terem was, or seemed to be, very open with me. Just as I recounted my years in Riversong, Repose, and Istana, he told me about his early childhood in the coastal city of Jilmain. He also told me about his adolescence at Jade Lagoon, as he came to manhood under Halis Geray's tutelage. But what he never mentioned, until one sultry afternoon in Hot Sky, was how the Chancellor put him on the dais of Bethiya.

I'd brought a copy of a new comedy, *The Scandalous Mother-in-Law*, and we'd just finished reading it to each other. On the table were a plate of honey cakes and a pitcher of white wine diluted with the juice of blackberries. Terem picked a cake and ate half in a single bite.

"You're very fond of those, aren't you?" I said.

"Yes. Gluttonous. My mother used to make them." His face took on a distant expression. "I was seven when we came to Kurjain. She'd baked us some for the journey. I was eating one when the sequina carried us through Wet Gate. I still remember that."

"Oh," I said, wondering what was to come next.

"I didn't understand clearly what was going on," he continued. "Neither did my mother—if I was puzzled, she was astounded at what Halis planned for me. And not much wonder. My father's bloodline was very old, but it was also very minor, with no important connections. In fact, we'd almost died out—he was a regimental commander in the Red Stag Brigade, but he was lost in a shipwreck when I was three, and my mother had been very ill ever since. The only other relatives I had were an aunt and uncle."

He flicked a crumb of honey cake into the water and watched a carp rise to take it. "It was a month after the Water Terrace massacre, and there still wasn't a Sun Lord. A few Tanyelis and Danjians were left, children and remote branches of the two bloodlines—but nobody wanted them on the dais, and the Council of Ministers was still wrangling over who should sit there. Everybody thought they'd eventually pick a man from one of the old magnate lines."

"But they didn't."

"No. They would have, except for Halis. But he persuaded them that it was warring bloodline interests that had nearly wrecked Bethiya and it would be better if the new Sun Lord didn't have a big family that would cause trouble. He'd known my father and thought well of him, and I certainly didn't have many relatives. So in the end he induced the Council of Ministers to choose me." He smiled sardonically. "They weren't inclined to argue, because Halis already had the support of the army. He'd promised most of the confiscated Tanyeli and Danjian estates to the senior officers, to get them on his side. So I mounted the dais, and the Council named Halis regent as well as Chancellor. One condition he made was that my aunt and uncle couldn't reside within a hundred miles of Kurjain—his worries about relatives abusing their position, again. He was even reluctant to let my mother come to Kurjain with me, but he did because she was so ill. She died here when I was ten. My aunt and uncle are still alive, but I rarely see them."

"But why didn't Lord Geray . . ."

"Ascend the dais himself? There were some who wanted him to. But Halis didn't *want* to be Sun Lord. Also, he knew that the officers who supported him wouldn't like a scholar-magistrate, which he is, as ruler. But they could abide him as regent, as long as the new ruler was of a soldierly bent. Mine was an old military family, so I was deemed suitable."

"But why did he choose a child instead of an adult?"

"Ah. He said it was because a child wouldn't be corrupt, and as my regent he could correct my moral shortcomings as I grew."

We had gotten to the stage where I could tease him a little. "How well did he succeed in this?" I asked.

"Alas," Terem replied in a mournful voice, "even now, my shortcomings outweigh my virtues as the sea outweighs a raindrop."

I gave him the disbelieving smile he expected and said, "You quote from the *Moral Discourses of Master Kostan*. Nevertheless, you see yourself as a person of high character. You invoke Master Kostan only for the sake of modesty."

"Indeed?" He smiled. "Perhaps I do. And you? Are you as exemplary as you seem to be?"

"Not at all. I'm an actress. Everyone knows that actresses have very bad characters indeed."

His eyebrows rose. "Not High Theater actresses. And anyway, you're a Despotana's adopted daughter. You're more than an actress."

This was certainly true, although not quite in the manner that

Terem imagined. "I suppose I am. But as for that, perhaps I'm really the daughter of some terribly rich and virtuous family in . . . I don't know, in Panarik or somewhere, and they've been grieving over my loss for twenty years."

His face turned somber, and without any warning at all he said, "Would you like me to look for them?"

I wasn't sure I'd understood him. "Look for who?"

"Your parents."

I felt as if somebody had knocked my breath out of me; my throat closed up and for a dreadful moment I thought I might burst into tears. I controlled myself, although I don't know how. Perhaps it was because I knew I had to think, for if anybody had the power to find my mother and father, this man did.

But what was I to answer? I could cry *Yes, oh please, find them.* But suppose he succeeded? What would I do then, faced with parents and possibly siblings? There would be filial demands on me, and everybody would expect me to meet them. I might have to leave Kurjain, and if that happened, everything Mother and I had worked for would be at risk. And suppose my parents were of truly low station? Terem knew me as a Despotana's adopted daughter, as fit company for his rank. But suppose he discovered that I had sprung from a family of gravediggers or porters of night soil? What would he do then, despite his protestations of regard for me?

I couldn't let him look. But I couldn't simply refuse. No normal foundling would reject his offer.

Watching me carefully, he said, "You don't have to answer now, Lale. But didn't you ever ask the Despotana to do this for you?"

"No," I said, "I didn't." But I remembered how, a very long time ago, I had thought about asking.

"She gave me everything," I said slowly. "She lay beside me when I was sick, and she risked dying of the sickness herself, in doing that. How could I not consider her my true mother?"

"Ah. You mean you didn't want to seem disrespectful to her?"

He'd thrown me a lifeline without realizing it. "Exactly so," I said. "To ask the Despotana to find my real family would suggest

she'd failed me somehow. It would have been exceedingly disrespectful."

Terem considered this. "But perhaps she wouldn't feel that way,
now that you're grown."

"But *I'd* feel that way," I said fervently. "Of course I want to
know what my bloodline is. But not if it means showing contempt
for the Despotana and all she's done for me."

I saw that I'd risen in his estimation; his gaze was admiring.
"You're sure of this?"

"Yes, I'm sure." I looked down into the pool, where the carp
shimmered like rainbows undersea. Claws of grief tore at my in-
sides. But there was nothing I could do.

"Very well, I'll make no inquiries," he said.

At those words I had to fight back a sob, because a tiny part of
me was hoping that he'd insist on the search anyway, no matter
what the cost to Mother and her plots. And then I thought: *How
much must I give up for her? Does it have to be everything, forever?*

I'd never had such a dreadful thought before, and it frightened
me badly. I thrust it from my mind in an instant and tried to forget it had ever been there.

Unaware of my turmoil, Terem was still talking. "In fact," he
said, sounding as if he were proud of me, "you've just proven that
you *do* have an exemplary character. Not everyone would show
such regard for an adoptive bloodline."

"You flatter me too much," I said dully, as I struggled to regain
my composure. I was not disloyal, I told myself, I was *not*.

"No flattery at all, only the truth. Halis will be pleased to hear this."

"He will? Why?"

From beyond the palace walls came a distant slow clanging: the
bell in the Round Market sounding mid-afternoon. Terem picked
up a cake and nibbled at it. "He's had doubts about my . . . connection with you. This will help assure him that it's good, not bad."

Despite my pain and distress, I realized that this was turning
out better than I'd hoped. I'd not only wriggled out of a tight spot
but also seemed to have turned it to my advantage.

"But what doesn't he like about our connection?" I asked. "Surely I'm no threat to you or anybody else."

"Well . . . all right, here's what bother him. When the mourning period for Merihan is over, I have to consider finding a consort. I must have a son, to secure the succession." He looked grim and sad, then rubbed his face as if to remove the expression. "In other words, I'm eventually going to marry again. Halis was worried that I might choose you as my wife."

"Your wife?" He'd managed to startle me, for Mother's schemes assumed that at best he'd make me his Inamorata. This was a peculiarly Bethiyan court title that formally recognized a woman as the Sun Lord's consort, although she was not married to him. An Inamorata was more than a mistress, although rather less than a wife.

"Correct me if I'm wrong," I went on, "but I didn't think a Sun Lord could marry a woman of an unknown bloodline. Mine could be full of village imbeciles. Being Makina Seval's adopted daughter isn't nearly enough."

"That's what concerned Halis. Do you want more wine?"

I held out my goblet. It was part of the set we used on these occasions, with tiny gold flowers and birds fired into the deep blue glaze. "But if I'm right," I said as he poured the pale lavender liquid, "why did the Chancellor think you might be so rash as to marry me?"

"Because in one way you fit the need. You see, Halis picked Merihan for me because she came from a family like mine. Old and respectable, that is, but not wealthy or well connected. With us as a couple, the powerful bloodlines would be kept out of the palace for a generation, so we wouldn't have another disaster like the Tanyeli-Danjian struggle. If that had become a civil war—and it might have—we'd be so weak by now that Ardavan's horsemen could romp all the way to the sea."

"So, since I don't have any bloodline baggage, Lord Geray thought you might consider me as a wife."

"That's what he thought."

"And did you also think it?"

Terem got up from his chair and went to lean on the veranda rail. He stared down at the clear green water, where the carp swam. "It's impossible anyway, because your bloodline is unknown. But that's not why I offered to look for your kin. I mean, it's not to let Halis sleep easier of nights."

"Why, then?"

"Because I wanted to reunite you with your family and make you happy."

Again he'd surprised me, and for an instant I lay utterly open to that strange allure that hung about him; the allure that said: *Follow me and you can do anything. All is possible with me. I am the path to your dreams.*

I set my goblet down very carefully because my hand shook. But he was still looking down into the pool and didn't notice.

"I'm perfectly happy right now," I said, as much the liar as ever.

"Perfectly?" He laughed. "The gods will be jealous."

"Then whom will you marry?" Of course it didn't matter to me what woman shared his bed, as long as she didn't keep him out of mine. But Mother would need to know his plans. His marriage would have consequences.

"I don't know yet. Halis is mulling over several prospects."

"I presume none of these prospects has too many relatives?"

"That was our intent. But Ardavan's rise has changed matters. He's very dangerous, and now I could use some allies."

"I see. So you may marry outside Bethiya, for an alliance against Ardavan?"

"It's possible." He grimaced. "It's too bad Yazar never gave up his preferences long enough to make a daughter or two."

All this would be interesting information for Mother, coming as it did from the Sun Lord himself. It would be even better if he'd name some of the women, but I didn't dare press him. Perhaps he'd go on by himself.

Unfortunately, he didn't. Turning from the pool to me he said, "I thought it better that you know how things stand between us. I hope you're not disappointed."

"I am not in the least disappointed," I said sharply. "Let me remind you that I didn't seek you out; you sought me out. I never came here hoping to climb onto the dais with you, and it does not disappoint me that I can't." Then I couldn't resist adding, "Even if I had the best bloodline in Durdane, I still wouldn't be your wife."

No man likes to hear such a thing from a woman, even if he has absolutely no intention of marrying her. Terem was no exception. "Why not?" he demanded.

"You love Merihan. You'll take your next consort for state reasons, and she'll have to live with your memories. But I don't."

He frowned. "I don't see Merihan in you, not now."

"So you've told me. I still don't believe you."

"Oh, very well, I do, but not as much as before. You're more . . ."

"Difficult than she was?"

He laughed, but without much humor. "That would be a word for it."

"If I were not difficult, would you enjoy my company as much?"

"No, I suppose I wouldn't." He glanced up at the sun. "But that was the third hour bell a little while ago, and now I must go and see Halis, and you must go home. Without being difficult."

"Very well," I said, rising. He often broke off our meetings this way, abruptly. He was annoyed with me, too; I could tell from the set of his mouth. But he'd get over it, and my departure now would be convenient—I could stop at Nilang's on my way back to the villa and tell her what I'd learned. So far I'd had little useful information to give her about Terem's intentions, but at last I was making progress.

Eighteen

❧

*A*fter we left the Reed Pavilion, Terem and I parted in the court-yard behind the Chancellery, where I would remain until Kirkin arrived to escort me back to Wet Gate. I waited patiently for some time, but Kirkin didn't appear and I began to get restless. We were performing in the Rainbow that evening, and if I didn't see Nilang in the afternoon I'd have to go to her tomorrow morning. That would interfere with the picnic in the Mirror that Perin and I had planned. We were supposed to meet several of her friends there, as well as Tsusane, and go gambling afterward.

More time passed, but still Kirkin didn't arrive. I now had a choice. I could either return to Wet Gate without him, which would allow me to go to Nilang's, or I could seize this chance to reconnoiter the palace and its grounds. I'd been hoping for an opportunity to do the latter, and here it was. The pendant Kirkin always gave me on my arrival at Jade Lagoon was a high-ranking one, so I reckoned I could go most places without interference. If anyone questioned me, I'd say I'd gotten lost; and given the labyrinth of gardens, covered walks, galleries, pavilions, and other buildings that made up Jade Lagoon, that was plausible enough.

Feeling as if dozens of eyes were watching from the Chancellery's upper windows, I left the pavilion and slipped out of the courtyard by way of the gallery on its west side. The gallery ended in a glade among a stand of laurels; here I should have turned left, to take the gravel path toward the Wet Gate. Instead I turned right, to cross in front of the rambling House of Felicity, the Sun Lord's personal residence. Beyond this was a region of the palace where I'd never been, and I set off to explore it.

I wasn't alone among its glades and shaded avenues and pavilions. The day had turned very sultry and most people who could stay indoors were doing so, but inclination or duty had brought others outside. Men wearing multicolored rank sashes strolled along the avenues, some accompanied by their wives, for many senior officials and their families lived in the residential pavilions of Jade Lagoon's northeast quarter. There were also a few unescorted ladies, wearing pendants that denoted various kinds of high status.

I received some curious glances, but no one questioned my right to be where I was. Soon I came to a big round shrine with a dome; it was for the Beneficent Ones, and I slipped inside to see what it was like. It was very richly appointed, the interior all gold leaf and vermilion and blue paint, with a floor of polished white stone. Under the dome, the Seven stood in a half circle, gazing down at me with varying degrees of benignity. I knelt before them to send up a general prayer for mercy, success, protection from enemies, good luck, riches, beauty, and health: in other words, what I saw as the essentials of a complete life. When I was finished, I added a silver dram to the flowers and coins already in the offering tray, and slipped back out into the sunlight.

Shortly after that I came across a second shrine, this one standing within a grove of dark cypress trees. The trees told me whose place it was, but I went inside anyway. Standing over the offering tray was the Lord of the Dead, his robes carved from black pitch-wood, his haunting visage cut in ivory to show the pallor of death. His face was turned down and aside, in the classic pose. The artist who made him had a fine hand, for he'd caught perfectly the mingled sternness and sorrow of the one who takes our lives, not because he is our enemy, but because it is the way it must be. He reminded of me of my brief and unpleasant sickbed encounter with the Quiet World, so I quickly left him some silver and went on my way.

Eventually I emerged into a glade bordered by lime trees. To my right, a stone wall rose above the treetops, its height pierced by arrow slits and crowned by battlements. That, and the tower rising from one corner, told me it was the Arsenal; the Treasury would be adjacent, and the Mint behind. It was a well-guarded area, and as I was leaving the glade a half-dozen soldiers tramped past me, going off watch under the command of a bored-looking troop captain.

After they went by, I walked for a long time but saw no one else. Cicadas buzzed, grasshoppers sang, bees hummed, the breeze was warm and smelled of the sea and flowers. It was such a lazy summer afternoon that I almost forgot why I was here and imagined how nice it would be to find a secluded bench where I might take a little nap.

Eventually I came to a wall, which angled out of the bushes ahead of me. It was half again my height and, like so much of the palace, built of amber brick. An open archway pierced it, and beyond the arch there was a big rhododendron bush that concealed whatever stood within.

I walked under the arch, around the rhododendrons, and stepped into a place of tombs. I'd discovered the necropolis of Jade Lagoon, the Garden of the Ancestors. All the Sun Lords of Bethiya would be here.

And their Surinas. That thought bothered me. I wanted to leave, but there crept over me a peculiar notion that I ought to find her grave, and . . . what? What should I do there, I who was the enemy of the man she'd loved? I should go nowhere near her. There was a whiff of sacrilege about it, as if I exulted over the death that had brought me such good fortune.

But I didn't turn back. Impelled by a need I did not understand, I went looking for her.

She wasn't hard to find, since her grave was the newest in the garden. It was set among willows and cypresses; marigolds had been planted around it, bright as gold and copper coins. The tomb was of northern design, like a little house with a peaked roof and swept-up eaves, the walls painted white and blue and the roof tiles glazed yellow. Where the windows and doors would be, in a real house, were tinted carvings of the dead woman's life: Merihan as a child, Merihan at her wedding, Merihan enthroned next to the Sun Lord, sitting straight and proud, her hands resting serenely on the arms of her state chair.

I stared at her various faces. She did look like me, although she was prettier, or the sculptor had flattered her memory. I was sorry in a way that she was dead, for by all reports she'd been a sweet-natured and gentle woman, which I certainly wasn't. But now I wasn't sure why I'd come looking for her. I really had nothing to say to the Surina, being who I was.

With that, it occurred to me that hanging around her tomb might not be wise. She'd certainly have had the proper rituals at her death, so her idu-spirit presumably wouldn't trouble anybody, but I wasn't exactly her friend and it might be foolish to risk drawing attention to myself. I bowed respectfully to her largest image, the one with her and Terem together, and departed. But as I left I saw a cleared place among the trees next to her tomb and I thought: *That's his, he's keeping that so he can lie next to her some-day.*

It was a thought tinged with sadness, so I brushed it off and went looking for the arch by which I had entered. But I'd got turned around somehow, and instead I found myself in front of a different stretch of the necropolis wall.

This part had a slatted wooden gate between blue pillars. Discreetly, I opened it a hand's breadth and peeked through the gap.

Beyond it, another garden awaited me, but it didn't appear to have any tombs in it, so it wasn't part of the necropolis. I put my head around the gatepost for a better look, saw that it was deserted, and slipped through.

It was a larger garden than my first glimpse had suggested, rising away from me in three shallow terraces to end at a high wall; above the wall, on its far side, rose the roof of a pavilion.

And filling the air was the sound of running water. In fact, water was everywhere: in streams, in miniature cascades, in tiny waterfalls, in brooks and rivulets, in pools and fountains. The vegetation beneath my feet was not grass, but a springy green carpet bearing tiny flowers with orange petals. Here and there stood wooden benches, and almost at my feet was an oval pool, containing red and blue fish whose fins waved like gossamin veils in the slow current.

It was quite the most wonderful place I had seen in the palace. I could imagine spending a whole summer here, with books and conversation, surrounded by the murmur of bees and the splash of water. But today I couldn't linger, because Kirkin, assuming he'd missed me by now, would be beside himself with anxiety. Spotting a gate in the far wall, which would lead in approximately the right direction, I started across the garden.

I was halfway to the gate when I realized where I was.

I stopped in my tracks and looked all around, but there was no doubt about it: I had wandered into the Water Terrace. Men and women and children had died here, hacked to ribbons by swords and axes, impaled on spears, screaming as they died. I might be standing in the very place where Mother's baby was murdered.

Every trace of loveliness fled. The scent of flowers turned to the sickly reek of blood, the springy turf felt like a corpse underfoot. Sickened and disgusted, I ran to the gate, wrenched it open, and hurried through.

I found myself in a covered walkway, one of the open-air galleries that connected several of the palace buildings. After closing the gate firmly behind me, I stood still for a bit, catching my breath and swearing to myself that I'd never go this way again. Then I tried to work out where I was.

The walkway resembled a very long curved veranda, but open on both sides. Because of the curve I couldn't see all the way along its length, but a glance outside showed me that it led to a large building. From the roofline and the colors of its shutters, this was the House of Felicity, where Terem lived. Now knowing where I was, I started along the gallery's curve, intending to cut around the back of the residence and head for Wet Gate.

I was a quarter of the way along the gallery when the woman came into sight. She was proceeding slowly away from me, with such a graceful gliding walk that she seemed to float over the ground. Her clothes were very rich: white shoes, a skirt of gleaming silver gossamin with a water design at the hem, and a high-collared silver jacket embroidered with blue and red swordtail butterflies. On her head was a hat with a broad floppy brim, not quite in the newest fashion, with an amethyst ribbon and a white plume.

Not wanting to overtake her—with those clothes she must be of very high rank and might ask questions I'd have to answer—I slowed my steps. I expected her to draw away from me then and vanish around the curve, but she also seemed to have altered her pace, for she remained in view. I slowed even more, but still she didn't vanish. Now there was something vaguely familiar in her aspect. Had I seen her in the Porcelain Pavilion, among the audience? That hat, those butterflies . . .

No, I'd seen them just a little while ago. They were very like the ones Merihan worn in her tomb carvings. Indignation rose in me. It was truly tasteless for a court lady to wear clothing so much like the Surina's, less than a year after her death. It bordered on inso-lence, and at the very least was highly disrespectful. Who did this woman think she was?

Or was she up to the same game as I? Did I have a rival? Had Terem really been going to see the Chancellor, as he'd told me, or was it this woman he went to meet? The possibility of competition hadn't occurred to me. There had been no gossip to suggest a rival, and if Terem were sharing his bed, I was sure I'd have sensed it. But still—

I was now annoyed enough to disregard caution; I wanted a look at her face, so I'd know her again. I picked up my pace, intending to overtake her before we reached the gallery's end.

Then, as I was catching up, I began to notice that the clothes and hat weren't just good copies of Merihan's grave dress. They were *exactly alike*. And the figure before me carried itself like a young woman, as if Merihan herself glided along the gallery . . .

Years before, on the foggy walls of Repose, I'd been badly frightened by the ghost of the magistrate's wife. But that was nothing to what I felt now. Such an unreasoning dread seized me that my steps faltered and I could suddenly not put one foot ahead of the other. I stopped short, and to my greater horror the woman stopped short, too. She knew I was behind her. She would turn around in the next instant, and she'd look at me.

The thought almost unhinged my knees. I didn't want to see her face. I didn't need to. I knew who stood there before me. She'd come out of her tomb because of me. She knew who I was. She knew *what* I was.

She began to turn around.

"No," I screamed, but my tongue was like wood in my mouth and my scream became a croak. I wanted to run, but the thought of having her behind me froze my heart. Helplessly, I closed my eyes and waited for I knew not what. I tried to pray to the ancestor who'd saved me in the Quiet World, but even these words failed me.

How long I stood there, like a trapped thrush who had given herself up for lost, I have no idea. It wasn't really a day and a night, but it seemed as if it were. And with every instant, I imagined, the specter approached. I could *feel* it, the cold radiance shriveling my flesh.

Suddenly, a frightened and angry voice said, "*Mistress Navari!* What in the gods' name are you doing here?"

My eyes flew open. Merihan was nowhere to be seen, but Kirkin was hurrying around the gallery's curve toward me, looking distraught. My savior. I could have kissed him.

He halted before me, pale and sweating from heat and distress. "Where have you been?" he demanded. "I've looked everywhere for you." He was so upset that he forgot his usual deference.

"Did you see her?" I asked, still befuddled.

"What?" He glanced into the gardens. "See who?"

"The woman. She was—she was looking at me."

He looked at me, too, and realized that something had just frightened me very badly. His gaze flickered uneasily around the gallery. "I didn't see anybody. You were just standing here. Alone, with your eyes closed."

"She had a hat on," I told him. "With a plume in it. There were butterflies on her jacket."

He'd started to regain his color, but at this he suddenly lost it again. "Butterflies?"

"Yes. Her shoes were white. She had a silver skirt on."

His throat moved as he swallowed. "Did you see her face?"

"No. Have you—"

"Don't speak of it," he said hurriedly. He took my elbow, began to pull me along the gallery, then disobeyed his own order by muttering, "But she's never appeared *here* before."

I halted, making him stop, too. "It's a ghost, isn't it? The Surina's."

"Be quiet." He sounded angry. "We're not supposed to talk about it. The Chancellor forbade us."

"But it *is* her, isn't it?"

"Yes. She's walking. Nobody knows why. Three people have seen her in the last two months. You're the fourth."

Kirkin was very upset. I could tell because he was talking like a normal person, without his usual pomposity. But at his words I felt an enormous relief. I'd been frightened that the Surina's ghost had come out of its tomb because of me. But if she had appeared to other people as well, that told me that I was nothing special in its sight, which meant I wouldn't likely wake up tonight and see her staring at me from the foot of my bed.

"Does the Sun Lord know?" I asked.

He shook his head. "Maybe, maybe not—he doesn't talk to *me*. All I know is, we're not supposed to mention it to anybody. It's a very bad sign."

This was true; an unquiet ghost often presaged misfortune for the household in which it walked. "Has anyone tried to ease her?"

"Yes, the best spirit summoner in Kurjain, a month ago. The Chancellor thought he'd done it, but now you've seen the thing, too, so it didn't work."

He'd got me moving by this time, and we were nearing the end of the gallery. "She hasn't hurt anyone, has she?" I asked.

"No, just frightened them badly. Like you."

This annoyed me; he didn't have to make such a point of it. "So I can't say anything about her? Not even to the Sun Lord?"

"I wouldn't, if I were you," Kirkin said. "If he knows and wants to talk about it, I'm sure he'll say so."

It occurred to me that I'd be better off not mentioning the ghost to Terem, anyway. Merihan was rival enough, lying quiet. She'd be more a distraction if Terem knew she was still wandering around the palace.

"I think I'd better go home," I told him.

On the way to the Wet Gate, Kirkin again asked what I'd been doing, and being in no mood for meekness I berated him for having left me waiting. Then I told him I'd gone for a walk and gotten lost. He was in no position to castigate me for my wanderings, for he'd failed to attend me when he should have and would have been blamed if I'd suffered harm. He was aware of this, and almost begged me not to say anything about his tardiness. I promised, and left him standing on the quay looking both relieved and annoyed.

As it turned out, I did have time to go to Nilang's on the way home. I told her what Terem had said about marriage and alliances, and when I finished she said I was doing well, and that his interest in Yazar was important. And was there anything else?

"There is," I answered. I described my reconnaissance in the gardens and my encounter with the Surina, and passed on what Kirkin had said about the other sightings.

Nilang studied me with her enormous blue eyes. "And why do you think she walks?"

I shrugged, to show how nonchalant I was about seeing ghosts. I'd glossed over the terror the apparition had raised in me, but I don't think Nilang was fooled. She knew a lot more about spirits than I did.

"I don't know," I admitted. "Is it important?"

"If it affects your hold on the man. Not otherwise."

"It won't," I told her. "I'll see to it that it doesn't."

Still she studied me. I got the most uncomfortable feeling that she was trying to perceive my thoughts. What for? She could have no doubts about my loyalty. My reports were all Mother could wish. I never stinted my efforts on her behalf, and I always did as I was told. And I did it willingly.

"You may go," Nilang said. She closed her eyes as if releasing me, and waved in dismissal. I got out of her presence as fast as I could and went home to Chain Canal, where I worried all evening over what she might be thinking about me. But finally I told myself that my loyalty to Mother was just as perfect as Nilang's, which meant I had nothing to fear. And with that I put the matter out of my mind.

Nineteen

❧

Summer's end drew near and I began to wonder whether Terem was as taken with me as Mother's grand design required. The Elder Company would return to Istana in little more than a month, and he seemed pleased to go on as we were. This was most unsatisfactory. He had to ask me to stay in Kurjain, either because he'd already become my lover or because he intended to.

But what would I do if he didn't ask? I couldn't go back to Istana. I'd have to manufacture some excuse to remain, although I felt it was poor tactics. He'd assume it was because I couldn't bear to leave him, and that would remove some of the challenge my aloofness represented. His interest in me might then diminish, a result I was very unwilling to risk.

Nilang was no help. She merely frowned at me when I expressed my concerns and said, "This is your responsibility. See that you fulfill it."

Perin was more useful. She'd had a lover in the city last year and had taken up with him again; he was a poet of independent means and a formidable reputation among the aesthetes of the capital.

However, she needed occasional respites from his intensity, and on these occasions we went to the luxury shops in the various markets or made an excursion to the Mirror.

Perin knew I was seeing Terem every few days, as did the whole of the Elder Company. Everybody except her thought I'd become his mistress by now, and I didn't bother to correct them. But with the exception of Harekin, who was beside herself with envy, the troupe saw a good thing in my meteoric rise, for it never hurts to be a colleague of someone close to the mighty of the realm, or in this case, to the mightiest. Only Master Luasin, who alone had an inkling of what I was up to, kept his opinions to himself.

Perin approved of the way I was making Terem dance to my tune. His very reticence, she assured me, proved that I was no passing fancy. She had even begun to hope that he would make me his Inamorata, rather than a mere unofficial mistress. I certainly hoped he would, too, because as Inamorata I would be socially recognized, so that I could not only appear in public with Terem but also attend state occasions at his side. And while being the Inamorata would not give me the rank or power of a Surina, I would still be a very important woman indeed—even if I had little formal authority, I'd have the Sun Lord's ear beside me on the pillow. That was no minor thing; every magistrate, military officer, government minister, and magnate in Kurjain would tread carefully in my presence. More to the point, I'd be much better placed to influence Terem's actions and to know and hear things that Mother could use against the power of Bethiya.

But as time passed and Terem still didn't declare himself, Perin began to fret. One day at the end of Hot Sky, as we were on our way home from a poetry recital at her lover's villa, she took it on herself to question me.

"What are you going to do about him?" she asked. "It's not all that long till we leave for Istana."

"I don't know." Our periang was gliding along Copper Bell Canal. Beneath the eternal watery odor of the city the scents of late summer drifted in the air: flowers a little past prime, fading leaves, dry moss. And the sunlight fell differently, with a tint of rusty gold.

We were on facing seats and she leaned toward me, eyes worried. "Lale," she said, "do you love him?"

This was a part I knew how to play. "I think so," I answered with just the right touch of tremulousness and a perfect quiver of the lower lip.

"Oh, dear Lady of Mercy," she said, sighing, "that's too bad. Look here, can't you keep your head a little better than this? You won't know *what* you're doing if you let your heart rule you. It gives him all the advantages. And if he's besotted, too, it just makes everything worse. Neither of you will know hand from foot."

"I can't help it. Hasn't it ever happened to you?"

She looked sour. "Once, and I'll never let it happen again. But this isn't the Lale I know. I thought you were very levelheaded. What will you do if he doesn't ask you to stay? "

"I don't want to think about that," I said piteously. "Maybe he will."

She sighed again. "Well, if it's really what you want, don't give in to him till he does ask, and—this is *very* important—not until he's established a household for you. Not a place inside the palace, if you can manage it. Nothing's worse than having a lover under the same roof. Also, the domestic staff always knows everything you do, so remember you won't have any secrets *at all*."

"I'll be extremely careful," I said. "But maybe he's waiting till his official year of mourning for the Surina is almost over. That's not till the end of Ripe Grain."

"But surely he could give you a hint."

"Maybe he will. I don't want to press him."

"Well, if he does ask, he must agree to let you keep acting, because you may need an income of your own for when he gets tired of you—he might cut off your allowance, no matter what he promises. The High Theater troupes here aren't very good, so they'll be glad to have someone with your training. I'll have a word around."

"Thank you, Perin. You're very kind to me."

"If I were truly kind to you," she said gloomily, "I'd tie you hand and foot and take you back to Istana with us." Then she brightened. "But look, if you do this right and you have enough time, you can be set for life. Get a fat allowance out of him, make sure he pays it regularly, and invest it well. Don't spend it all, which is probably what I'd do. Then, when it's over, you've got your independence. Look at Alidz Ayraman. She was Minister Dermenj's friend, and now she owns land everywhere and has literary parties every month."

All this was good advice, and if I'd been what Perin thought I was, I'd have been wise to take it. Not every girl in that position did; the last two Sun Lords had maintained mistresses by the shipload, but most of these finished their days in impoverished obscurity. I wasn't concerned about that, though, because no matter what Terem did, I could always depend on Mother.

But as the events of the next day informed me, even Mother could not protect her daughters from everything.

Tsusane had invited me to visit her in the villa on Lantern Market Canal, where she rented rooms with the scenery painter Yerana. I'd diligently cultivated Tsusane's friendship and by now we'd spent a fair amount of time together, often at the game pavilions in the Mirror. I'd asked her to dine at Chain Canal, but she was uncomfortable with High Theater people—except me—and had declined. She was usually good company, although over the past couple of hands she'd occasionally seemed worried and morose. I'd asked her what the trouble was, but she said it was merely her temperament.

Along the way she'd introduced me to others of the Amber Troupe, who in turn had introduced me to more people. I thus had a widening circle of acquaintances in the city, through both her and Perin—I knew writers, artists, some junior officials of the Bureau of Arts, a handful of well-to-do merchants with aspirations to culture, and even a brigadier of the city garrison who wrote very presentable poetry. Consequently I was becoming quite the social flutterer, a role I enjoyed immensely, although it cost me a good deal of sleep.

So on that afternoon I went off to see Tsusane, intending to cheer her up, if need be, with an excursion to the Mirror. I checked for followers as usual, and noticed, as my periang sculled along Lantern Market Canal, that I again had only one minder instead of two. This had been happening frequently of late, and on three occasions they'd left me entirely alone. I reckoned they were getting tired of watching someone so patently harmless as I and had agreed that one would follow me while the other found more congenial pursuits. This time my minder was the freckled one, who was following along in a skaffie. When I disembarked at Tsusane's villa, he stopped a few landings away under a wine shop sign, and as I told my scullsman to wait for me, I saw him slip inside. I was, apparently, to be on my own today.

Theater musicians weren't lavishly paid, and Tsusane's villa was a slightly seedy one that stood across the canal from the Ten Thousand Hues Dye Works. The two rooms she shared with Yerana were on the fourth, topmost floor, up a rickety outside staircase from a dark courtyard that smelled of the nearby public latrine. But the rooms were more pleasant than the building's appearance would suggest, for Yerana had painted them with irises, mountain landscapes, and fanciful plumed birds in cages. Across the door to the sleeping chamber she had hung a curtain with a good imitation of Shiran's *Girl Gazing at the Moon in Water*.

Yerana wasn't there when I arrived. She'd gone to visit her mother, Tsusane said, in a village upriver, and she wouldn't be back for a few days. I thought Tsusane seemed nervous and unhappy, and I suggested that we go over to the Mirror for our evening meal.

She demurred. And then, to my surprise, she went and closed the shutters of both the balcony door and the window, leaving the room in ocher dimness. The shouts of the canal boatmen and the clatter of tubs from the dye works diminished along with the light.

I suddenly realized she didn't want to be overheard, and alarm swept through me. "What's that for?" I asked, as lightly as I could. "Are you trying to hide from an angry lover?" Though I knew she didn't have one, angry or otherwise.

"Please." She sounded distraught and frightened, and my heart sank. She gestured at the table and I sat down across from her. "Lale," she said, "can I trust you?"

"What is it?" I asked, thinking that it was a stupid question to ask someone you'd known less than two months. "What's got you so upset?"

"Please," she repeated. "Can I trust you?"

"Completely." I spoke the lie without an instant's hesitation. Even then I hoped it was something to do with the theater. I knew she'd had a fight with the sivara player two days ago, and he could be very unpleasant.

"It's about the Sun Lord." She could barely get the words out, her voice shook so. "It's said you know him."

"Only a little," I said. She wanted something. A chance to play at the Porcelain Pavilion? I might be able to arrange that. But why was she so frightened?

"Some . . . people," she said, "some people want to know how he's going to celebrate the Ripe Grain Festival. Is he going to Profound Tranquility Square?"

This square was the largest public plaza in city; at its center stood the double shrine of the Bee Goddess and Father Heaven. In imperial times a festival ceremony had been held there, but it had fallen into abeyance long ago. Terem had revived the ritual last year, to the delight of the population.

"I don't know," I said. A cold premonition stole over me. "Why?"

She wouldn't meet my gaze. "They want to know, that's all. They want you to tell them . . . through me, they want you to tell them what his plans are. They'll pay you well. You'll never be in any danger. They'll make sure you stay safe. It's nothing, really. Just a word or two, that's all."

An abyss opened at my feet. My word or two would tell them

where to be waiting. In the dense crowds, assassins could vanish. They were planning his murder, and they needed me to help them.

I was appalled. What were they thinking of, to approach me in this clumsy, horribly dangerous way? Didn't they know *anything* about conspiracy? And why did they think I could be so easily bought? Was it because I was an actress, no better than a whore with a second profession, happy to fatten my purse if it involved little risk? If I hadn't been so alarmed, I'd have been very, very angry.

But no matter how inept they were, they'd have taken precautions. Yerana's curtain hid the sleeping chamber, but I'd wager my life that at least one of them was in there listening. If I refused Tsusane's offer, they'd have to kill me. That would explain her fear. So I had to pretend to be as stupid and venal as they thought I was and get out of here as fast as I could.

But what if she's working for the Chancellor, and the Chancellor suspects Mother, and he's trying to trap me?

The thought was an icy deluge. If this was so, then with a single wrong word I might condemn myself.

But what to do? If Tsusane's offer was real, then enemies lurked behind the painted curtain, waiting to hear my answer, which must be *yes* if I wanted to leave here safely. But if she spoke with the Chancellor's mouth, my answer must be *no*, or it was the Arsenal dungeons for sure.

So I didn't say either. Instead I rose very deliberately from my bench, as if pondering what she'd asked. Tsusane watched me, agony in her gaze, and I knew that this wasn't her idea. Someone had forced her to approach me.

"I have to think about this," I said. "Are you *sure* it isn't dangerous?" I kept one eye on the curtain, which was three paces away, immediately beside the door to the outside staircase. Had it moved very slightly? A breeze through the shutter slats? Or someone's breath coming faster as he listened?

"No, not dangerous." She attempted a reassuring smile. It was ghastly. "Just promise me. That's all."

"What will happen if I don't?"

Her eyes moved very slightly toward the sleeping chamber, which told me everything. She said, hopelessly now, "They'll hurt me. Oh, please, Lale. *Please*."

I sprinted for the door. The man must have been watching through a slit in the curtain, because he came through it like a marsh ox through a reed fence. The drapery tangled him for an instant and I had time to wrench the door open, but he got me by the arm as I hurled myself onto the outside landing.

He was a big man and he tried to pin my arms against my sides, but he was off balance. I dragged him onto the landing, got my left arm free, and jabbed him, stiff-fingered, under his rib cage. He gasped and let go of me, doubled over, then fell heavily against the rickety landing rail. It gave way with a *crack* and he pitched out into space, four stories above the courtyard paving. I'd paralyzed his breathing and he couldn't scream, but he did make a frantic grab for the edge of the landing. He might have saved himself, except that I kicked his hand away from the boards so that he went straight down, silently, onto the stones. Inside, Tsusane had begun to sob, although she hadn't put her nose out the door. Maybe she thought I was already dead.

I wasn't, but two men were standing at the foot of the staircase, and from their expressions they intended me no good. I debated running back inside and jumping from the balcony into the canal, but four stories was a long way down, and if there were boats below me I'd be killed.

The staircase was almost as dangerous. The men stared up at me, perplexed and alarmed, their dead colleague almost at their feet. They probably thought he'd fallen by accident. They were a few years older than I, heavy jawed and sallow; they might have been brothers. Both were well dressed, one in green and one in yellow, and had neatly trimmed hair. They were no doubt armed, although I couldn't see a blade.

The one in yellow said, "Come down, lady mistress. We won't hurt you."

Not very likely. They'd seen that I was trying to get away, so they knew I'd refused to work for them. But I'd bluff as long as I could.

"Please," I quavered, "he slipped. I don't know what happened. It wasn't my fault." I knelt, as though to look over the landing's edge at my handiwork, and surreptitiously removed my sandals. If you're trained, you can do a lot more damage with bare feet than with shod ones.

"It's all right," Green assured me. "Just come down. We only want to talk to you. It was an accident. We'll tell the magistrates so."

Yellow knelt by the body, nodded, and stood up. "He'll be fine, mistress. Just knocked out. Come down, there's a sweet girl."

I'd heard the noise when he struck the ground, and he was never going to be fine again. But they were trying to reassure me, so I took the bait and descended, apparently hesitantly, to the landing above them. All the while I was considering what to do. I was at a disadvantage, because I had to get away without betraying my fighting skills. I could explain one corpse as a lucky accident, but three might raise eyebrows, especially Halis Geray's.

"Come down, girlie," Yellow coaxed. Up in her rooms, Tsusane was still weeping. Three or four heads had popped out of windows above the courtyard to see what was happening. My attackers-to-be noticed this and became more agitated. Neither had realized that I was now barefoot, not that it would have meant anything to them.

"Promise you won't do anything to me?" I asked tremulously. A distant part of me *was* frightened, and also very angry, but otherwise I had become what Master Aa had taught me to be—a fine needle's point of will and concentration. It made my acting even better than usual. And this time, unlike that night in Istana, I was thinking ahead.

"Of course not," said Green. "You must have misunderstood what Tsusane said. Come with us and we'll explain."

They'd explain me into the depths of a lagoon, they would, with iron lashed to my ankles. I could scream for help as I stood here, but that probably wouldn't put them off. Where were the Chancellor's minders when I needed them?

Green lost patience and started up the stairs. I waited until he was just below me, then kicked him in the mouth. The ball of my foot connected solidly. Teeth shattered, blood spurted, and his head snapped back. I'd withheld some of my strength so as not to break his neck, but the blow still threw him off the stairs and practically into his comrade's arms. They both fell in a heap; I swung myself over the landing rail, hit the pavement running, and raced for the courtyard's street gate. My foot was stinging, a hazard of that technique; I'd cut it on a tooth.

I heard Yellow running in pursuit. He must think I'd felled his friend with a lucky kick, or he wouldn't be so foolhardy. I'd chosen the street because a periang wouldn't move fast enough to get me out of his reach, but this was little better, because he was catching up. My foot hurt badly now; I'd got grit in the cut, and it was slowing me down. I might have to fight him after all, in front of more witnesses, curse him.

There might be another way. Ahead was an alley. I flew into it and saw ahead the blue-green glitter of Lantern Market Canal. Close behind me I heard his laboring breath, and wondered vaguely if he had a knife.

The alley stopped at the water's edge. I hit the end of the paving and jumped. A periang flashed past beneath me, a rush of wind blew my skirts up, and I plummeted into the canal. I let myself sink. Green water frothed past my face like splintered emeralds, turned immediately to dark jade, then indigo. The canal was thick with sediments, the runoff from the dye works, and pitch black only an arm's length down.

To my water-deadened ears came the thump and rush of a body hitting the canal. He'd come in after me. Good.

I struck out for the surface. My skirts trailed around my legs but, being gossamin, absorbed little water and didn't trouble me. Turning in the direction from which the splash had come, I broke into the sunlight, blinking.

People in boats pointed at me and gesticulated. Yellow had seen me rise to the surface and was only five paces away, swimming strongly. Probably he intended my drowning to look like a failed rescue, ending with the loss of my corpse in the murk of the canal.

I let him almost catch up with me, then took a huge breath and slid under the surface. He followed, the fool, and tried to get his hands around my throat. I brought my knee into his groin. The water cushioned the blow, but it was hard enough to double him up. We were now sinking slowly into darkness; I twisted, got my legs around his waist, and clamped myself there. He was struggling now, not fighting. My fingers found the numbing place in the hollow of his neck; his back arched as he lost control of his lungs and tried to breathe the canal. His struggles grew feeble, but I was running out of air myself, so I let go of him and swam toward the faint light above.

I broke surface in a rush, breathing hard, and trod water as I looked around. Yellow didn't reappear. Thirty paces away, the scullsman who had brought me to the villa watched me openmouthed. I waved violently at him. A couple of skaffies came up, both loaded with crates of geese that honked and flapped in excitement. The woman in one cried, "Where is he? Where is he?"

"I tried to help him," I gasped. "I tried, but he just slipped away."

"Oh, the poor man," she wailed. "And you risking your own pretty self. Come aboard here, mistress, let me help—"

My scullsman was approaching with the periang. "It's all right," I said to the woman, supporting myself on the wale of her craft. "There's my boat." I glanced along the canal toward the wine shop, but there was no sign of my minder. He and his colleague didn't know it, but they had just ended their careers in the Chancellor's service, and serve them right.

The periang glided up to me. The scullsman helped me aboard and I said, "Take me to Jade Lagoon."

I was still dripping when we reached the palace mooring basin; I was also shoeless, my right foot still bled, and I was filthy from the canal. A less impressive specimen you could not have met, and

I had to speak firmly to the guard captain before he agreed to summon a very alarmed Kirkin, who took me to the Chancellery. It happened that both Terem and Halis Geray were there, and after some difficulty with the underlings I got in to see them.

"Lale, what's happened?" Terem asked. The Chancellor watched me without expression. I could hear the faint whistle of his breath going in and out, in and out.

I hesitated, just for a moment, or I would prefer to think I did. For I'd liked Tsusane, and she was the first friend I'd made in the city. But now my words would be her death, for it was clear that there was a plot against the Sun Lord, and she was in it. I tried to make myself feel better with the thought that a genuine friend wouldn't have put me in such terrible danger, which was true; but I didn't think she'd done it willingly.

"My lord, I think someone means you harm during the Ripe Grain Festival," I said, and then I told them everything, except the part about my killing two people. I said the man upstairs had fallen, that I'd made a lucky kick with the second, and that the third one must have been a poor swimmer, while I was a good one.

When I finished, Terem's face was cold and white. I'd never seen him look like that. He said, "Lale, you might have been killed."

This had been very unlikely, but I realized I was a little too calm for a girl who had just escaped murder. So, with a tremble in my voice and a frightened look on my face, I answered, "I know. I'm just starting to realize it."

He hurriedly poured me a cup of unwatered wine and held my hand while I drank some. His touch was pleasantly reassuring, for he was right—I *might* just possibly have been killed. It was three against one, after all.

I set the cup down and murmured, "Thank you, my lord."

Still looking distressed, he kept my hand in his. "This girl Tsusane—she told you no details. Why do you think there's a plot to assassinate me?"

"Sir," I said with some asperity, "if they were planning something joyful, they wouldn't have attacked me to conceal it."

The Chancellor asked, "Did you recognize any of the three men?"

"No, lord. I have no idea who they were."

"But I do," Halis Geray said, which made me very glad indeed that I'd reacted as I had to Tsusane's proposal. He and Terem scrutinized me for several moments, and I began to wonder a little nervously what the Chancellor was thinking. At length he said, "You keep your head in a crisis, don't you?"

I bowed slightly. "I do my best, Lord Chancellor."

"Also you're very resourceful. Unusually so."

That was an avenue best left unexplored. "Sir, I think I'm very lucky. By rights they should have killed me twice over. But they were so, well, inept."

"Inept is the word for it," Geray said dryly, and turned to Terem. "I think we've let them run long enough. They've tried to reach inside these walls through her, and that we shouldn't permit. Also, we didn't know about the musician girl until now, and that bothers me."

Terem nodded. "Bring them in," he said.

Afterward, people called it the Hot Sky Plot. At its center was a man named Laykan. It so happened that his family had, for almost a century, managed the government salt monopoly at the coastal city of Gao. However, Laykan had skimmed most of the profits during the past twenty years, and when the Inspectorate discovered this, the monopoly was taken away and Laykan had to pay a ruinous fine. Angry over this perceived injustice and his family's resulting impoverishment, he began to think treasonous thoughts. He moved to Kurjain and began to look for people with grievances of their own, and in such a large city he soon found them. Among his recent recruits was Tsusane's younger brother, a rancorous youth who had failed the Universal Examination twice, blamed the government examiners, and wanted revenge. Through him, Laykan discovered Tsusane's connection to me, and the assassination plot flowered.

Unfortunately, poor Tsusane was blind to her brother's defective character and believed the lie—which he himself concocted—that he'd be killed if she didn't persuade me to join the conspiracy. As if that weren't enough, they'd threatened her life as well.

Laykan was a much better embezzler than a conspirator, and his incompetence had doomed the plot from the beginning. He was so maladroit that Halis Geray had known about his machinations since early summer, but the Chancellor had merely watched the conspirators to see how far the contagion would spread. It was fortunate for me that he didn't discover Tsusane's involvement until I revealed it; otherwise I might have been under deep suspicion as well.

Tsusane tried to flee the city, but they caught her just a few miles upriver. The rest, a round dozen excluding the two I'd already done for, never got out of Kurjain. The speed of the arrests shook me, and I realized that I'd been entirely too indifferent to the danger the Chancellor represented; he was not an enemy to be trifled with. My minders were promptly changed, too, though Terem never let on to me that I'd had any.

My connection to the affair inevitably got out, and to my gratification it turned me into a popular heroine. I became the brave young woman who risked her life to warn her noble sovereign of treachery, just like Jian in *Maylane Unyielding*. I pointed this out to Master Luasin, and he immediately ran four special performances of the play in the Rainbow, with me as Jian—over Harekin's furious protests—and we packed the theater each time. Rumors began to fly as well that Terem was my lover, but even though his mourning year wasn't quite finished, nobody thought the worse of us for it. We were being somewhat improper, but he was well liked and I was brave, beautiful, and loyal, so the people of Kurjain were happy to forgive us.

I didn't give evidence during the treason trials, since most of the conspirators confessed in the hope of obtaining mercy. This speeded everything up, and all the trials were over by the middle of Ripe Grain. By that point the mood in the city was vengeful,

Terem being so admired, and the magistrates were not inclined to mercy despite the confessions. They condemned all the convicted to execution by slicing, the hideous and prolonged death reserved in those days for traitors. The sentences went to Terem for confirmation and he, in the name of compassion, commuted most of them to hanging. Only Laykan and two others suffered the full penalty.

Tsusane was among those to hang. I hadn't seen her since that dreadful afternoon, and didn't really want to. She could have gotten me killed, and her disregard for my health still annoyed me. But I didn't think she should die, since she was in the plot under duress. I put this to Terem on the day before the executions.

"I understand why you're sympathetic," he said. "She was your friend. But she should have reported the threats to the magistrates. You know what the law is, and so did she. To be aware of a conspiracy against the sovereign, and not reveal it, is a capital offense."

"I know she *deserves* to die," I answered. "All I'm saying is that mercy wouldn't be amiss. She's hardly a threat to you now."

"I've shown enough as it is. Halis wanted to arrest the plotters' families as well, just in case we'd missed some people, and I wouldn't let him. Anyway, you might have died because of her. I can't forgive that."

"But that's the point," I said. "If I can still want her pardoned after what she did to me, why shouldn't you consider it?" I touched his hand. "Please, Terem."

It was a kind of test. He'd already thanked me profusely for my courage and loyalty and given me a very fine emerald necklace to show his appreciation. But would he free Tsusane for me, when his inclinations were so much toward executing her? If he would, I could be much more confident that we had a future together. In the uproar of the past half month I'd hardly thought about the Elder Company's impending departure, but now that things were settling down I had to attend to my task again.

"Is this what you truly want me to do?" he asked.

"Yes. Please. Give Tsusane her life, for me."

He sighed. "I'm very unwilling, but for you I'll do it."

I felt a flush of gratification, some of it on Tsusane's behalf. "Thank you," I murmured. "When will she know?"

"I'll sign the commutation this afternoon. She is to be exiled from Bethiya. Do you want to tell her?"

"Yes."

I went to the Arsenal later in the morning. Tsusane showed the usual marks of imprisonment; although these were mostly pallor, gauntness, and dirt, for her confession had spared her judicial torture. She wept when I told her she was to be pardoned and exiled, and I left some money with the Arsenal's governor to help her on her way. The next day she was gone. I heard later that she went to Istana to look for work, but Yazar's lovely city was burned and pillaged a few months later, and I never found out what became of her after that. I suppose she cursed the day she met me; I would have, if I'd been her.

Twenty

❧

$\mathcal{A}$ few days after the executions, I received one of my usual summonses to the palace. That particular day marked the beginning of the Ripe Grain Festival, and as the periang bore me toward Jade Lagoon I saw preparations everywhere. Windows were wreathed with autumn flowers, bridges bore garlands of plaited grain stalks, and people had taken their little plaster statues of the Bee Goddess and Father Heaven out of storage and put them in the niches over their doorways. There were extra flambeaux ready along the canals, and the bakers were making the traditional festival cakes, heavy with raisins and almonds. Street jugglers and mimes were already out, although the festivities didn't formally begin till sundown. Only in the palace were the preparations subdued, because the official mourning for the Surina was still in effect.

I observed Terem carefully as we settled into our accustomed seats on the Reed Pavilion's veranda. He seemed very preoccupied, but I wasn't sure why. We avoided any talk of the conspiracy and instead chatted desultorily about the festival. But after a while he fell silent. Around the margins of the pool, the reeds whispered to each other; the torch lilies were fading and their fallen petals drifted on the water like ships with orange sails.

He said, "You visit spirit summoners from time to time, particularly a Taweret summoner. But you've never mentioned this to me. Why?"

A tremor of fear ran through me. Why did he mention this now, with so little warning? Had Halis Geray, in rooting out the conspirators, dug too deeply for my safety?

If so, I could only play the innocent. I stared at Terem as if in disbelief and said, "How did you know?" Then, as if light dawned, I went on, "You mean you've had me *watched*? Whatever for?"

"Lale," he said, "you recently stumbled into a plot against me. Halis watches people to forestall exactly such things."

This didn't sound like an accusation, so I maintained my tone of vexed surprise. "All right, but why should he watch me? I'm no conspirator, as I must have proven even to the Chancellor's satisfaction. Are his minions still peeking at me from around every corner or is he satisfied now that I can be trusted?"

"I was satisfied about that almost from the beginning. And it's been for your protection as much as mine. You insist on going alone about the city, and Kurjain is not the safest of places, as you've discovered."

Much relieved to be under no suspicion, I allowed myself to appear mollified. "Yes, I can see that. Perhaps I'll forgive you. . . . What was it you wanted to know about the summoners?"

"You've never told me you visited them."

I looked away as if abashed. "I was embarrassed to admit what I was doing. I know you don't keep a court sorcerer because you think they're charlatans. I suppose a lot of them are. Yazar has one, and the man's a fraud."

"Some are less fraudulent than others. Is—" he stumbled over Nilang's tongue-wrenching name—"Dasetmeryj Netihur an adept?"

"I'm not sure. I only go because I sometimes have bad dreams, and because I . . . well, sometimes I ask her who I'll marry."

His eyebrows rose. "And does she tell you?"

"Not exactly. She says there is uncertainty around my future, but she thinks he'll be a rich foreigner and very tall and handsome."

He laughed. "No summoner forecasts an ugly spouse and poverty, not if they want to keep their customers. Have you ever asked her to try raising one of your ancestors?"

"No, I haven't. I suppose she might get *something*, but who knows if it would be an ancestor or something nasty? Or she might be making it up as she went along. Anyway, since I don't know when I was born or where my ancestors' tombs are—or if they've even got tombs—there's not much point. I did try a calling ritual when I was at school, but it didn't work, and I've never bothered since."

He knit his fingers together and appeared to study the reeds. "I've sometimes done callings on my birthday," he said, so quietly I could barely hear him, "at the family graves. My father came and spoke to me once. He said he was proud of me. My mother has never appeared."

"I saw it done in the village where I grew up," I told him. "A woman managed to get some ancestor or other to come. I don't think she liked it. I'm not sure I'd try it myself, even if I did know my birthday and my bloodline. But you were lucky to see your father. It doesn't work for a lot of people."

"No, it doesn't." He slumped wearily in his chair, an uncharacteristic posture. Only when truly despondent—which happened very rarely—did he lose his physical grace. "I went to Merihan's tomb and tried. But nothing happened. We weren't of the same blood, so how could it?"

I'd realized some time ago that he knew nothing of Merihan's ghost. "Terem," I said, "She's gone. Let her lie in peace. If she needs to speak to you, she'll find a way."

At my words he roused himself and sat up. "Yes, you're right. I must stop this. My mourning will be over soon, and people will expect the palace to come back to life." He cleared his throat. "Lale . . . I've been thinking of having popular dramas in the Porcelain Pavilion again. Would you like that? I haven't seen *Robbers of the Marsh*, and I hear it's very good."

He was on the edge of declaring himself. I knew it, I knew it. And so I said, "Terem, you've given me an idea. Would you like to hear what it is?"

That evening at dusk, my skaffie approached the water steps at the west postern of the palace. I could dimly see the two sentries in the shadows of the gate alcove and near them a third figure, not tall, in dark clothing.

I sculled the boat alongside the quay, and as Terem climbed aboard I said, "Does anyone know you're here?"

He gestured at the sentries. "Only them. They won't speak of it. Where did you get the boat?"

"It came with the villa." I was pleased to see his clothes wouldn't attract attention; they were fancy dark green ones embroidered with silver, but everybody wore their best finery at festival and he wouldn't stand out.

"Do you want me to scull?" he asked, still on his feet amidships.

"No, I'll do it. I've been practicing since I got to Kurjain. But sit down and be still, unless you want a bellyful of canal. Are the Chancellor's men still following me?" Actually, I'd checked for minders on my way from the villa and knew I had none, but a true innocent would ask.

"No, I told Halis it wasn't necessary."

"Even for my protection? Or yours?"

"Not tonight." He saw the hempen bag in the bottom of the boat. "What's in there?"

"You'll see." I pointed the skaffie toward Pearl Shrine Canal. There was no wind and the fading sunset had turned the lagoon to a sheet of lilac glass. Terem asked, "Will we be in time for the opening?"

"There's a second performance, because of the festival. We'll make that easily."

Neither of us spoke much as we glided across the water. There were many boats on the lagoon besides ours, drifting through the dusk. On the esplanades the flambeaux were springing to life, flaring in gold and amber and multiplying their flames in the lagoon's darkening mirror. On many of the boats, people lit torches in answer, colored festival torches that burned with tongues of shimmering green and blue.

The light on Terem's face became brighter as we approached the flambeau-lit esplanade and the entrance to the canal. When I judged I had enough illumination to work with, I shipped the sculling oar and sat down on the thwart in front of him. He watched in perplexity as I opened the bag and took out some little pots of face paint.

"What are you up to, Lale?"

"You don't want to be recognized, do you? It would spoil the fun."

"You can change me that much?"

"Of course. But I can't do it properly unless you keep still."

He composed his features and I went to work. I didn't give him a full stage treatment, just enough to put five years on him and change the positioning of his cheekbones and the fullness of his nose. In daylight you'd see the paint, but in the flickering torchlight of the festival nobody would be likely to notice it.

I'd never touched his face until now. In fact I'd hardly ever touched a man's face at all, except once in a while to help Eshin put on his stage makeup. But that had been merely helping out. This was different. I hadn't imagined that the act of disguising Terem would feel so deeply intimate.

I started to notice sensations that flustered me. They were like the ones I'd had when I first met him, only more intense. He kept his face perfectly still but I sensed a change in his breathing. Mine wasn't as regular as it should have been, either.

"You'll do," I said tersely, finishing the job a little more quickly than I'd intended. I stowed the paints, took up my scull, and started us toward the canal. A musical troupe with flutes and drums was playing on the esplanade, an old harvest song called "The Barley Reaper." Three women were dancing under a flambeau, in full festival dress, all flounced skirts and gauzy flowing sleeves. Mixed with the odors of the canals were the fragrances of incense and almond cakes and stewed plums, all the smells of the festival.

"Who do I look like?" he asked, touching his cheekbone hesitantly.

"Be careful you don't smear it. Well, you're a bit like Lord Kazaz in *Three Brothers*."

"Oh, him. Well, it could be worse. I suppose I can smile now?"

"Certainly."

He was looking very pleased with himself. "I can't remember the last time I was in the city without a retinue."

"So you've done this before?" I was slightly disappointed, having imagined myself the only instigator of such excursions.

"Assuredly. I used to slip out of the palace and wander around the city alone. I'd talk to people in the wine shops and the markets, to find out what they thought about things. But they sometimes recognized me and that took the fun out of it. I was spotted more and more often after a while, so I stopped."

"You made yourself an easy target. Suppose somebody like Laykan had been after you?"

He shrugged. "That's what Halis used to say. It drove him wild that I'd go around without protection. But nothing ever happened to me."

Nothing would happen to him tonight, either, for he had better protection than he knew. I concentrated on sculling us along the canal without collisions, for it was crammed with boats, many bedecked with garlands and effigies of the Bee Goddess woven from wheat straw. Music and laughter drifted across the lagoon. In Kurjain you wouldn't get much sleep on the first night of the Ripe Grain Festival, even if you were inclined to try.

Eventually we reached the quays of the Mirror. So many boats were already there we could hardly find a place to moor. Terem looked annoyed at this, being so used to having his way cleared for him, until I said, "Remember you're just another citizen."

He laughed and said he'd try. I slung the makeup bag over my shoulder and we began to make our way through the crowds. It was easy to see where we were going, for so many bonfires were burning that the night turned almost into day. Open-air stages had been erected among the pavilions, and on them dancers strutted and swayed to the jangle of sivaras and the twitter of flutes. The yeasty scent of festival beer hung in the air, mixed with the smell of burning pitch from the flambeaux.

There were shooting galleries, too, where young men fired arrows at straw targets decked out to look like Exile warriors. Seeing this, Terem decided he must try his hand at it. We found a gallery near the Rainbow and he paid five copper spades for three shots. The bows weren't particularly good, but he picked out the best, a stiff hunting weapon that was somewhat oversize for his small stature. The proprietor handed him the arrows with a sardonic smile, and there were snickers among the more knowledgeable onlookers; a man who over-bows himself is an object of derision. But I'd seen him at archery, and knew what was about to happen.

He nocked the first arrow and drew the bow with ease. An instant later, without apparently aiming at all, he made his shot. The arrow flashed down the gallery's length, hit the straw Exile in the left eye, and stood there quivering.

The snickering stopped. The proprietor looked worried, as if already counting the spades he'd lost. Somebody muttered, "Luck," and Terem loosed the second arrow.

It planted itself in the target's other eye. It had barely struck when the third shaft nailed the Exile's mouth shut. Terem lowered the bow and said, "That's what Kurjainese archers do to Exiles."

They cheered him then, and even the gallery owner looked a little less sour. We collected his winnings and I hurried him through the applauding crowd in the direction of the theater—his makeup was good, but somebody might see through it if they paid attention long enough.

We reached the Rainbow to find it already emptying from the previous performance. I'd bought our admission tokens that afternoon, the silver-washed bronze tags for the expensive seats, and we went straight in. Clusters of lamps hung near the ceiling, throwing a dim orange illumination over the vast interior. Although the upper lattices allowed the entry of the sea breeze, the theater was very warm and smelled of sweat, lamp oil, stale food, and face paint. It was full, too, a packed audience despite the hour.

Someone came out and lit the stage lanterns, the onlookers settled down, and the play began. I'd seen *Robbers of the Marsh* before, but it was worth seeing again, being very exciting with lots of love triangles and mistaken identities and sword fights. Still, by the time it ended, I thought I'd melt from the heat, and I wasted no time getting us into the fresh air. Terem was grinning hugely and chuckling.

"I see you enjoyed yourself," I said. Torchlight gleamed on his moist forehead; Sun Lord he might be, but he could sweat just like anybody else.

"I did. It was excellent. Shall we find something to drink? I'm parched and hungry, too."

We went to a grill shop nearby, where we drank small beer flavored with mint. Terem ate steamed crab with chestnut paste, and I had a generous portion of grilled eel. As soon as we'd finished, he decided we must try the gambling pavilions. The card games I'd learned in Istana had already made their way to Kurjain, so we spent a long time at the tables in the Hall of Munificent Destiny. Terem didn't do well, losing some fifteen drams, but I won six, to his simulated chagrin.

By the time we left Munificent Destiny, dawn was not far off and the Mirror was emptying as the night's revels tapered off. I was growing anxious, for I still hadn't found the right moment to remind Terem of my impending departure, and no suitable occasion presented itself as we headed to the quays with the rest of the stragglers, homeward bound.

This time he insisted on handling the skaffie, and we proceeded smoothly along Pearl Shrine Canal until we reached the lagoon. Only a few boats wandered its dark waters now, with an occasional voice raised in drunken song. The crescent moon had sunk long ago, and on the esplanades all but a few of the flambeaux had gone dark. Instead of torch flames, stars glittered in the lagoon's rippling black mirror.

Like the flambeaux, our conversation slowly guttered out. A dance drum sounded faintly from the direction of the Mirror and distant voices drifted through the night, but the only sounds nearby were the chuckle of water around the skaffie's bow; then, distant and somber, the bell in the Round tolled the fourth hour of the night watch. Ahead of us, the palace floated on the lagoon, its walls a soft gray in the starlight, the Arsenal tower rising ghostly above them.

The rustle of water faded. He'd stopped sculling and the boat glided on in silence. I looked down at the water, black with stars in it. We could have been drifting across a night sky, and I felt a moment of eerie vertigo.

"What are you thinking about?" I asked.

"The future," he said, and I felt a thrill of anticipation. Was it to be now?

"Whose future?" I asked, keeping my tone light.

"Yours. Mine. Everybody's."

I had no idea what he was talking about. "Everybody's?"

"I mean the future of the Durdana."

"Oh, that future. What of it?"

"Let me ask you a question, Lale. You grew up in a ruling household, and you're very well educated. You've traveled. You've seen Tamurin, Guidarat, Brind, Bethiya. What do you think is happening to us?"

He was after a real answer, not an amusing one. "I think we're fading," I said, "except perhaps here in Bethiya. Nothing is as it was. In Riversong . . . there was a castella there a hundred years ago, and a canal. There were merchants and warehouses and cargo boats. But it's all gone now, all rotted away. Most of the places I've been are like that, or becoming so. Chiran isn't what it once was, neither is Dirun. Istana's still lovely, some of it anyway, but it's so much smaller than it was before the Partition." I wrapped my arms around myself; the breeze off the sea was cool. "And I think most people are poorer than their grandparents were, at least in the Despotates. Only a few are better off—the ones who are very rich, like the families in Guidarat, with their big manors and their tenant laborers."

"And Bethiya?"

"I've only seen the part along the Short Canal and Kurjain. But here it's better, I think."

"It is, for the moment. But compared to what Bethiya and Kurjain were before the Partition . . . even here we have declined sadly, Lale."

"But you have new things," I reminded him, "ones the empire didn't know about. The special clear glass the artisans make, so people with bad eyes can read. That new way of printing books. The timekeeping bell in the Round, that doesn't need anybody to strike it."

"True. But, Lale, it's not enough. The Exiles rule the richest of our old lands, and the Despotates become poorer and weaker by the year. Someday they'll be no better than the Chechesh chiefdoms, all ignorance and squalor and a darkness of mind and spirit. The lamps will burn longer here in Kurjain, but for how long? Suppose another cavalry horde comes out of the steppes, the way the Exiles did? We only just held the barbarians the last time. What hope will we have if it happens again?"

I thought about a world without the High Theater or the Ripe Grain Festival, a world without books or the music of sivaras, a world without cities like Kurjain, and I said, "If that happened, what would be the use of living?"

"Exactly. So do you know what I dream of?"

It clearly wasn't me, at least not at the moment. "What?"

"I want to bring the old world back to life, the way it used to be. I want to free the conquered lands. Bring all Durdane together, as it once was."

"How?" I asked in reluctant fascination. I felt it again, that fervor in his spirit that could stir the heart and make one believe that anything was possible. It even affected me, I who had been so carefully schooled against it. If I'd been an ordinary person I'd have been willing to lay my life at his feet.

"We must destroy the Exiles," he said. "Root, branch, twig, and leaf."

Such talk was cheap and it irritated me. Every Sun Lord since the Partition had promised to free our enslaved kindred in the east and drive the Exiles back through the Juren Gap. None had.

"Who is 'we'?" I asked. "Surely you don't mean an alliance of Bethiya and the Despotates against the Exiles? It's been tried time and again, and nothing's come of it. You'd have more luck herding snakes than persuading the Despots to agree on anything."

"Assembling an alliance would be very difficult," he admitted. "Still, it's worth trying. But I may have to fight the Exiles alone, at least in the beginning."

"Forgive me for saying so, but you're not the first Sun Lord with such ambitions. Why do you think you can do this?"

"Because I *know* I can. I've known it for as long as I can remember."

"You mean it's your destiny?" I tried to keep disbelief out of my voice and succeeded, I think.

He laughed. "What's destiny? It's what men say was ordained after it's happened. No, I simply believe I can do it."

"Suppose you succeed. When you've destroyed the Exiles, what then?"

"I'll move my capital to Seyhan. And after that, we'll see what we shall see."

His face was shadowed and I could not read his expression. I said, "You'll proclaim yourself Emperor, won't you?"

"Will I?"

Of course he would. While he'd never openly admitted such imperial ambitions, it was widely suspected that he harbored them. Why else would he be arming Bethiya as he was?

"And then you'll call for the Despotates to submit, whether they want to or not. Am I right?"

"Not necessarily. There are any number of reasons why I wouldn't."

I didn't believe him. Beneath his affability and charm the tyrant lurked, avid for power, just as Mother had always told us. Worse, he was that rare kind of leader for whose dreams men will agree to die. But those dreams were Mother's nightmares, and my sisters', too.

Should I stop him now, before he'd fairly begun? It would be so easy: a blow to the throat and then into the lagoon with him, everything very quiet and quick. I could be out of the city before dawn, looking like anyone but Lale the actress. Terem would soon be missed and so would I, but his body might not be found for a day or two. Until then, they'd assume that whatever had happened to him had also happened to me, and it would be some time before I became a suspect. By then I'd be so long gone they'd never catch me.

But I couldn't do it without orders. Furthermore, I felt an unexpected revulsion at the idea of killing a man I knew so well, and who trusted me. Such scruples wouldn't have troubled Dilara, and I berated myself for my weakness, but there it was.

He was again sculling us toward the gray bulk of the palace. I said, "But I think you *will* try to make them submit, and then it's war again. But haven't we had enough fighting and misery over the past hundred years? Drive out the Exiles if you like, but why ruin the Despotates even more, in the name of a new empire?"

He made an exasperated noise. "The Despots fight each other

at the least excuse. When they do help each other, it's only to crush rebellions. You know that as well as I do. If we can get our empire back, such things will end."

I remembered my childhood, the armored men from Kayan rampaging through Riversong. "I suppose so," I agreed unwillingly, "but there hasn't been a Despotate war for years."

"Only because everybody wore themselves out in the last round. Even wolves have to rest. But Panarik and Dossala are getting ready to fight again."

"Yes," I admitted. Two magnate clans, one on each side of the Panarik-Dossala border, had come to blows, and each had enough influence to drag their respective Despots toward war. A war would be lunacy for Panarik, situated as it was opposite Ardavan's domains, and extremely vulnerable if its army were tied down in fighting Dossala.

"And it will go on," Terem added, "until the Exiles destroy the Despotates one by one, or until the Despotates destroy themselves, or until somebody forces them to behave."

"And that somebody would be you."

"If not me, then who else?"

He had me there. I knew of no one but Terem who might actually realize the old dream of restoration. But that didn't mean he should try it. What if his attempt forced the Exile Kings to unite under Ardavan, and together they defeated and overran Bethiya? Then Ardavan could turn on the Despotates, and thanks to Terem's ambitions, the horsemen would rule from the Juren Gap to the sea.

I was about to tell him this when I thought: *Use your head, you stupid girl. He's a man. He doesn't want an argument—he wants you to say he's right. He wants you to tell him how much you admire his daring and his resolution. Argue with him, and you may argue yourself right out of his life.*

"You're right," I said. "I can't think of anybody to do it but you. It's just that I never knew you dreamed with such boldness. No other Durdana ruler these days has the courage to face the Exiles."

"You flatter me," he said dryly, and I wondered if I'd gone too far. But apparently not, for he added, "I'm glad you approve. Not everyone will."

"The Exiles certainly won't."

He laughed into the darkness. "Indeed they will not. So, Lale, will you join me in this wild pursuit of the dream?"

Twenty-one

෨

At first I didn't comprehend him, and several moments passed before I found my tongue. When I did, all I could say was, "I don't know exactly what you mean."

"It's simple enough," he told me. "You and I have become very close. I don't want to lose you when the Elder Company leaves."

Here it was, all unlooked-for. "You want me to stay in Kurjain with you?"

"Yes. In the palace, if you will."

I tried to collect myself. Negotiations had begun. "This is very sudden."

"It's been in my mind for longer than you might think. But now it's possible, because I know I can trust you utterly."

"Ah. Because of the Hot Sky Plot."

"That's right. You fought your way out of a trap, at the risk of your life, to tell me I was in danger."

This was not exactly true. I'd fought my way out of the trap because *I* was in danger. I'd been worried mostly about me, not him, but if that was what he wanted to believe, let him.

"So," he said, "will you come and live with me?"

I trailed my fingers in the cold lagoon, remembered how dirty the water was, and hastily withdrew them. Then I said, "This is not quite the declaration of passion that one sees in the drama."

I was, in fact, rather disappointed at his lack of ardor. I felt that a well-wrought, declaration-of-love scene should have some emotional color to it and that he was depriving us both of a memorable performance. But it was more than that. I wanted him to say he loved me.

"Look," he said, with a note of desperation in his voice, "I can write a classical love lyric as well as most of the poets in Kurjain—"

"No, you can't," I said, irritated at this oblique approach. "Your poetry's even worse than mine."

"Well, yes, you're right. But even if it *was* any good, you've never invited that sort of thing. You give me the sense that if I acted the lover in the way the poets portray it, you'd think me foolish. So I've not been sure what to do. You're always just a little out of my reach, just beyond the touch of my fingertips."

I was sure it was still his dead Surina he wanted, and I felt an unexpected and senseless stab of jealousy. "How did you woo Merihan, then?" I demanded. "With talk of empires, as you've done with me tonight?"

He must have thought I actually wanted to know, for he said, "Not entirely. Merihan was less interested in such things than you." I thought I heard him sigh. "Perhaps this is the wrong time to tell you my plans. But I did so because you're a very intelligent and perceptive woman. And I know you can be trusted. I wish I could say as much for some of my officials."

"Do you want me, then," I asked, "as a counselor or a lover?"

After a silence he said, "Both."

I glanced toward the palace. Its walls loomed close in the starlit darkness, cliffs of gray pearl. Ahead lay the landing stage and the black blot of the postern gate.

"Do you love me, Terem?" I asked.

He didn't answer for two or three strokes of the scull. Then he said, "I wasn't sure until tonight. You didn't notice, but I was watching you during the play. When Minaj discovered his lost son living with the robbers, your face lit up with joy, but then you suddenly looked so desolate I wanted to weep. And I realized I loved you."

I was nonplussed. Had my face really worn such expressions? I couldn't remember being aware of them. I remembered being happy at the dramatic moment of the discovery but not especially joyful, or desolate afterward for that matter—it wasn't *that* good a play. Still, if the illusions Terem had manufactured from my countenance had made him fall in love with me, so much the better. I suspected that what he really felt for me was pity and sympathy, (neither of which I wanted or deserved) laced with physical desire. He also might have calculated that I could be a useful connection to the Despotana of Tamurin, despite being only her adopted daughter, and one among many at that.

But none of this mattered as long as he believed he was in love with me. That belief was all I needed.

I was thinking this when he asked, "And how do you feel about me, Lale?"

I should have said, *Of course I love you, truly, passionately.* That was what he wanted to hear. But what came from my lips was, "I have very deep feelings for you, Terem."

"But do you love me?"

"How could I not love the Sun Lord?"

"In the name of Father Heaven, stop being so awkward!" He sounded exasperated. "Not the Sun Lord. Me, a man. Do you or don't you love me?"

"Terem, please listen," I said earnestly. "You're the Sun Lord, and I'm only an actress of uncertain birth, and beside you I'm powerless. If I leave my profession to follow you, and you someday tire of my presence, what will become of me? You know what happened to the lovers of the last two Sun Lords. I don't want to end that way, drowning myself in the Honor Canal or begging on the Salt Lagoon docks. And remember, the

Chancellor wants you to marry someone of proper rank and bloodline, which certainly excludes me. I do love you, Terem, but what will you do with me when you bring the new Surina to Jade Lagoon?"

He stopped sculling. "You *do* love me?"

A suitable line from *The Game of Love and Chance* suggested itself. "Why do you think I put up with you, you impossible man?"

I thought he was going to scramble along from the stern for our first kiss, because the boat rocked alarmingly. "Steady," I said, holding onto the thwart. "I won't go away."

"I hope not," he said, staying put. But there was great relief and a kind of bubbling happiness in his voice. "Not ever, I hope."

"Until you find a wife."

"Please stop worrying about that. I've no intention of marrying this year or next. There's too much to do, and I'm not satisfied with any of the possibilities Halis has brought me."

Mother would be pleased to hear this. Better yet, if I kept him happy, he might be less inclined to replace me through a dynastic marriage, and my work could go on.

"But you *will* marry, Terem." I let sorrow seep into my voice. "You'll have to, someday. What will become of me then?"

"I've already thought about it. If you come and live in the Reed Pavilion, I'll give you title to a villa in the city on one of the best canals. I'll also settle a life income on you, so you'll have your upkeep if you decide to go and live there. All this will be legally set out and sealed under my hand and paid from my estates as long as you live."

And then he added what I'd dared not hope for. "Along with that," he said, "I'll make it as formal as I can, short of marriage. I want you as my Inamorata."

I was glad the darkness hid my expression, for I was trying to suppress a delighted smile. Perin could hardly have asked for more. More to the point, Mother would be very, very happy. Even Nilang might sniff her approval.

And me? Was my delight only in my success at getting Mother

what she wanted? I thought it was, but I had so perfected the art of lies that I could conceal the most obvious truth from anyone, including myself. And this truth was that I stood on the brink of falling in love with my enemy, and didn't know it.

"All right," I said softly. "I'll come to the Reed Pavilion, Terem, and be your Inamorata."

The palace walls suddenly loomed above us; the skaffie was almost at the postern's water steps. I seized a mooring ring, drew us alongside the quay, and Terem shipped his scull and climbed ashore. I stood up and he helped me onto the stone beside him.

The guards were nearby, in the shadows of the narrow gate. He kissed me anyway. I'd had an idea of what to expect but I was still astonished at how strongly I responded. As the kiss deepened, I felt the same disturbing sensations that had troubled me when I was applying his disguise, but this time they were much more heated and showed powerful signs of becoming warmer still. He was holding me tightly, and I felt profoundly safe and protected. An illusion, for I'd die the slicing death if he ever found out what I was.

I managed to draw back and whisper, "Terem, I have to go home. Perin will be wondering where I am. And your mourning for the Surina isn't over. We must observe custom, or people will speak badly of you."

He released me. We were both breathless, as if we'd run a long distance. "You're right," he said in a hot voice that warmed me even more. "But as soon as the palace is out of mourning, you'll join me?"

"Yes," I murmured, "I said I will. But . . . Terem, may I send word to Mother? She'll approve, I know, but it's best I tell her soon."

He stepped back, still holding me by the shoulders. "You can tell her in person, if you like."

"I can? What are you taking about?"

"She'll be here soon after the end of the month, with four other

Despots. They're coming to discuss an alliance. I've kept it quiet so far, but I'll be announcing the state visit in a couple of days."

I could hardly believe it. I'd see Mother again, after almost two years. But my delight was tempered by a sudden worry that it might be a trap for her, if not for all the visiting Despots. The Chancellor had a hand in this, after all.

I gave several exclamations of delight and thanked him for telling me, although I was quite chagrined that I hadn't found this out before he told me. "But how," I went on, "did you persuade them all to come? Despots don't like straying far from their capitals, and they're putting themselves in your hands."

"I promised them help if they returned home and found trouble, and I swore on my honor that they would have safe conduct everywhere in Bethiya. Also, they know I'm their strongest support against Ardavan. Altogether it was enough to get them here, although it may not be enough to persuade them to an alliance."

I relaxed. Mother was safe, for I knew that Terem would always stand by his personal oath. "You can persuade them if anyone can," I told him. The eastern sky was no longer perfectly black, and I heard a gull cry plaintively from the lagoon. "But look, dawn's coming. Really, I have to go. But I'm so glad you told me . . . May I tell Master Luasin that I won't be going back to Istana? And Perin? She's such a good friend to me."

"You can tell the whole Elder Company, if you like, but caution them to keep it quiet until the mourning period ends. That's just a few days from now."

"All right," I agreed. He helped me back into the skaffie and I put my face up to his. He kissed me again, and then I sculled away from the quay. I was weary but exhilarated. The first game of the match was over and I'd won. Or I thought I had.

Propriety demanded that we tell Mother of my new status before she arrived, so Terem and I wrote a letter asking her blessing and sent it off by government courier. I dispatched my own account of the event by way of Nilang, including all that Terem had told me of his intentions to restore the empire.

He also announced the Despots' state visit. Preparations for it began immediately, causing sleepless nights among the protocol officials at Jade Lagoon but excitement in the rest of city, for we Durdana delight in spectacles. In such feverish activities the end of Ripe Grain slipped by, and White Dew began. The official mourning period for Merihan ended on the second of the month, and three days after that, I became Terem's Inamorata.

I was not to be his wife, so the occasion did not have the spectacle and opulence of a state marriage. I was just as glad of this, because the ritual of a Surina's elevation took two days and required a month of rehearsals beforehand, and I had better things to do with my time. But to be installed as Inamorata took less than an afternoon; it was a simple ceremony, in which Terem pledged to provide for me while I was his consort and decreed that this provision would continue even if he should set me aside. For my part, I agreed not to do anything that would disgrace him or his station and that if I did, he need no longer support me.

I was, I confess, a little disappointed that the ceremony didn't have more passion to it—when our witnesses were announcing the terms, it sounded more like a commercial arrangement than a love affair. On the other hand, I didn't have to swear fidelity to Terem in the name of Father Heaven and the Bee Goddess, as a bride would. Consequently, I reckoned, I was in no danger of divine retribution for spying on him.

After the pledges, an honor guard conducted Terem, me, and the witnesses to the Lesser Banquet Hall, where we ate the celebratory meal. With us were some fifty guests, including the Elder Company, the Chancellor, Terem's chief ministers and their wives, and assorted hangers-on. Compared to the vast festivities of a Bethiyan dynastic marriage, it was tiny, but I didn't care. Terem and I sat side by side, and it seemed I could feel the warmth of him even through my court robes.

By the time we'd eaten and the speeches had finished, night had fallen and it was time for us to go. An honor guard and a torchlight procession escorted us to the Reed Pavilion, which would be my residence in the palace. The soldiers took up station around the building, and the guests, except for Perin, dispersed.

Tradition dictated that a woman of rank should prepare the Inamorata for the Sun Lord's bed, but I'd chosen Perin instead, to her incandescent joy. So while Terem went to the salon, where his body servants would help him change, I retired with Perin to the attiring room that adjoined the bedchamber.

The servants had already been in to light the lamps and lay out my night clothes, which the palace seamstresses had produced under the fastidious eye of the palace's Wardrobe Mistress. My robe was of layered blue gossamin, translucent and embroidered with white and gold roses, with a cloud design behind them. Its sleeves hung gracefully in the latest fashion, and over it I wore a mantle dyed the priceless scarlet hue called heaven's dawn.

Emitting exclamations of delight, Perin helped me undress and put on the robe and mantle. When we were finished, I stood before the tall silver mirror and considered the results. This, I decided, was clearly what I'd been born for; I'd never looked so marvelous in my life.

"What do you think?" I asked Perin.

"I mustn't say, or the Moon Lady will be jealous of you." She laughed. "But I think the Sun Lord will approve most heartily."

She helped me adjust my hair and fixed some slight imperfections in my makeup. "There, you're ready for anything," she said. "Are you nervous?"

"A little," I confessed. "I hope I please him."

"Oh, you will. He's your first, for one thing. That always pleases a man. However, just in case . . ."

Perin whispered several suggestions into my ear. I giggled, but they sounded interesting.

"I'll be sure to try them," I said, when she finished.

"Merciful heaven, but not all at once! You want things to last, not finish in a dozen heartbeats!"

"I'll be careful, then."

She accompanied me into the bedchamber, where a dozen bronze lamps bathed the carved paneling and the ceiling frescoes in a rich soft glow. Underfoot, the floor was laid with cream-glazed tiles and scattered with gossamin rugs. The high bed occupied the center of the room; near it were a couch and two chairs, as well as a low table set with wine and water jugs, and several dishes of sweetmeats. We were, apparently, expected to keep our strength up.

Perin kissed me on both cheeks and said, "It's time. Be happy, Lale."

Ever the actress, I answered, "I'm sure I will."

She slipped from the room. I composed myself demurely on the couch, hands clasped in my lap, and waited. Nothing happened. I was more nervous than I'd let Perin know; I poured myself a little wine, without much water, and drank it.

Soft footsteps. Terem entered the room, stopped short, and stood gazing at me. I would have risen, but I was abruptly unsure whether my knees would work as they should.

"Lale," he said.

"My lord," I answered. "Terem."

He cleared his throat as if unsure of himself. "I've never seen you more lovely."

"Thank you." He was no less a delight to me: his robes, trimmed with red badger fur, shimmered in russet and gold, and on it were running deer whose eyes and hooves were rubies. And oh, he was a handsome man, and those green eyes . . .

"Come sit with me," I said. My throat was dry. "Wine?"

"A little, please."

He joined me on the couch. For all my usual glibness, I could find nothing to say, and I didn't understand why I suddenly felt so awkward. Why wasn't he helping me with this?

But I wasn't sure, now, what I expected of him. It wasn't that he'd stride into the chamber, carry me off to the bed, and immediately make love to me—I wanted a more tantalizing approach. Besides, he wasn't much bigger than I was, so being lugged around the room, however romantic that might be, was probably not in my future.

I poured wine for him and had some more myself. I'd drunk only a small amount at dinner, but now I was beginning to feel a pleasant mellowness.

"Do you," I asked as I gazed thoughtfully into my cup, "regret finding an actress in your bedchamber?" I didn't realize until I'd spoken that I was quoting the heroine of *The Butterfly Dream*, a book I'd borrowed from Imela. I could only hope Terem hadn't read it.

He regarded me as if I'd grown a second head. "Of course not. But you're teasing, aren't you?"

"Yes." I drank a little more wine and put down the empty cup. I was more relaxed now, even though Terem kept looking at me in a particularly intent way, which made me feel as if my bones were beginning to melt. But I didn't quite know what to do next. Why in the name of Our Lady of Mercy didn't he just kiss me?

Instead he took both my hands in his and said, "For that matter, do you regret finding *me* in your bedchamber?"

Another phrase from *The Butterfly Dream* leaped into my head and popped out of my mouth before I could stop it. "On the contrary," I answered, "I think I am the most favored woman under the sun, or under the moon, too, to have you love me."

Terem looked pleased, if a little mystified. But my performance still wasn't moving him in the right direction, so I cast around in my memory for other lines that might do the trick. Among them I found the courtesan's advice from *The Three Beauties of Golden Mountain*, wherein she says to her sister, "A man's ear may attend to a woman's speech, but what seizes his eye is the sway of her bottom."

"Terem," I blurted, "have you ever seen the tassel dance?"

His eyebrows rose. "No, I've never heard of it. But it sounds interesting. Will you show me?"

When Kidrin taught it to me years before, I'd had only an inkling of what its movements represented. But as a grown woman I knew very well what the gyrations meant, and if I hadn't been reckless from the wine, and from certain other sensations as well, I'd have blushed to the roots of my hair.

Even so, I tried to wriggle out of it by saying "Oh, but I haven't any tassels."

Terem leaned closer. "Well, maybe you can pretend you do. Where is it from?"

"The south, I think," I answered weakly, wondering if I remembered the steps. "I learned it from another student at school. She came from Guidarat."

"I'd be delighted to see it. Please show me."

I'd got myself well into the soup kettle now, so there was nothing to do but cast caution to the winds and oblige him. I stood up and pushed a rug out of my way, and as I did, the steps of the dance came back to me, along with the song Kidrin had used for it: "Stepping Down the Mountain."

I hummed several notes to get my rhythm, sang the first line, and then, chanting, swept into the dance. After a dozen steps I realized that my robe's hanging sleeves would do nicely for tassels, so I sinuously removed my mantle and let it float to the floor. Terem watched me, wide-eyed, and his face told me *exactly* what he was thinking about.

Encouraged at this, I let myself go shamelessly, my hips swaying, my hair flying in fluid arcs. It really *was* a lovely dance, and showed a woman's form to her best advantage; no man with a pulse could watch it unmoved. Terem was very far from cold-blooded, as I well knew, and I reckoned we were soon for the bed. This thought heated me so much that I gave an extra-lavish gyration.

If I hadn't drunk just a little too much wine, I might have gotten away with it. But my left hand swept from my hip just a little too far, my sleeve flew wide, and the hem snagged a lamp in a wall niche. The vessel toppled, clanged to the tiled floor, and spilled a puddle of oil, which instantly began to burn with a clear yellow flame. I shrieked, tripped over my own feet, and fell flat on my behind.

Terem yelled, jumped up, then roared with laughter. He kept laughing as he grabbed a cushion and started to beat out the flames. My cheeks burning with mortification, I seized a bolster from the couch and helped him. Moments later we'd extinguished the fire, but by that time he'd infected me with his mirth, and I was starting to giggle. He managed to blurt, "You looked so—surprised!" and then I was laughing as hard as he was, and we clung to each other, tears streaming down our cheeks, cackling like lunatics.

"That's not how it's supposed to end," I finally informed him in a strangled voice.

"I didn't think so," Terem answered, and then his arms were around me and suddenly we weren't laughing anymore. Moments later I discovered that he was much stronger than I'd thought, for I abruptly found myself lifted off my feet and carried lightly across the room. It felt perfectly marvelous, and I wrapped my arms around his neck and kissed him.

He put me on the bed and we sank into its downy billows. I reached up for him and he came down to me, and somehow my robe vanished and so did Terem's, and his touch was on my skin, everywhere, and mine on his, and at last he held my face in his hands and looked into my eyes as if he found the goddess there. And then everything happened just as I'd hoped it would, but in ways I'd never felt or imagined, and to my deepest astonishment and joy I forgot who I was and what I was, and gave myself to him utterly.

And as I did, and because I did, the tiny fissures that had so subtly undermined my loyalty joined into a single, ruinous crack. But, like a flaw deep in the marble a sculptor intends for his masterpiece, it lay as yet hidden from my awareness; only when the chisel struck the marble's grain in just one way, and in no other, would the stone split into ruin and reveal the fatal imperfection, love, within.

In the morning I had a slight headache from the wine, although the rest of me felt very agreeable indeed. I'd have happily remained in bed with Terem all day, but the realm demanded his attention for a few hours; also, I had to go to Chain Canal to say good-bye to the Elder Company, which was leaving for Istana at noon.

A ten-oared sequina took me to the villa, and I arrived just as the troupe was about to board a periang for Feather Lagoon and the cargo slippers. The sequina ran alongside the villa's water steps and I hopped ashore as Perin came out onto the landing.

We hugged each other. "How are you, little sister?" she asked, holding me at arm's length to look into my face.

"I'm very well, Perin," I said. "Oh, very well indeed."

She squeezed my hands. "I'm so glad. He has such a treasure in you. Oh, look, I think they know who you are."

I turned. Out on the canal was a cluster of a dozen periangs and skaffies; in one was Perin's lover, looking wan and woeful, and in another slumped one of Eshin's friends, who appeared the worse for drink. But everyone in the other boats was watching me. They'd obviously spotted the sequina's palace insignia and had realized who it carried, for a woman called, "Perfect happiness to the Inamorata!" and several others applauded. It was all I could do not to give them a stage bow with extra flourishes, but that would have been beneath my new dignity, so I waved politely instead.

I kissed everyone in the company good-bye, including Master Luasin. Last aboard the boat was Perin. She leaned over the periang's side, her bracelets jingling, and we embraced again. "Good-bye," I said. Suddenly I felt quite weepy.

She gave me one of her brilliant smiles. "Don't cry, little sister. We'll be back in the spring. Keep well."

"I'll do my best," I told her, and then the scullsmen leaned to their oars and the periang bore her away. Just before it swung into Red Willow Canal, she waved furiously and cried, "Good-bye, Lale!"

"Only till spring!" I called, but I'm not sure she heard me, and I never saw her again.

Twenty-two

❧

The Despots reached Kurjain on 15 White Dew, some two hands after I became Terem's Inamorata. Mother was not among them, but a dispatch arrived to inform us that she would arrive on the sixteenth.

The four who first arrived ruled the Despotates of Guidarat, Brind, Jegal, and Anshi. What they had in common was that their northern borders all lay on the Pearl River, facing either Bethiya, the Exile kingdom of Lindu, or Ardavan's domains of Jouhar and Seyhan. The ruler of Panarik, the fifth of the river Despotates, had declined the invitation; threatened by the Despot of Dossala to his south and Ardavan to his north, he dared not leave his capital.

Terem and his chief ministers welcomed the visitors with a procession of honor from Feather Lagoon to the palace. He'd declared a public holiday, and the crowds were vast; the very rooftops rippled and swayed, such banners they had, and you could hardly see the canal for boats. People threw late roses down from the balconies, and the breeze swirled with petals of white, gold, and crimson.

I was with Terem on the foredeck of the *Auspicious Moon*, the fifty-oared state sequina that led the procession of gilded and garlanded vessels. It was my first appearance in public with him and I was a little nervous, for this vast gathering was the most enormous audience I'd ever had. And I wasn't sure how they'd respond to me. They'd liked me well enough at the Rainbow, but I worried that they might see me as the Surina's usurper and make their displeasure known.

But I needn't have worried. We'd just set out from Feather Lagoon when Terem said to me, "Wave, and see what happens."

I did. They'd been cheering their throats sore, but when I raised my hand to them the thunder of their delight shook the roof tiles. It was exhilarating beyond anything I'd ever experienced, and I thought: *When I walked out of Riversong, this is what I wanted. And now I have it.*

The uproar lasted all the way to Jade Lagoon, and I was almost dizzy with bliss by the time we reached Wet Gate. I savored my new status even more at the palace's Pavilion of Illustrious Audience, where Terem welcomed each Despot formally to Kurjain. I stood beside him, and each ruler returned my bow of respect as if I were an equal. Yazar did more; he remembered me from Istana and gave me a wink, as if he applauded me for my enterprise. In response I smiled sideways at him in the pert way he'd always found amusing.

After the reception, the four Despots and their entourages dispersed to the Pavilions of Welcome, which stood in a compound in the northeast of the palace grounds. Now all Terem had to do was wait until Mother arrived, and then the discussions, for which he had such ambitious hopes, could begin.

That evening, he and I went to the gardens behind the Hall of Records, where we sat on the bank of the reflecting pool. A place god shrine stood on the bank opposite us; a frog had taken up residence on the mossy offering tray under the god's stone chin, and watched us with golden eyes. We were talking about Terem's plans for an imperial restoration. There seemed to be little he hid from me now, and I would have plenty to tell Mother when she arrived.

"But," I asked, "will you admit to the Despots that you want a new Empire of Durdane, once you've driven the Exiles out?"

"Why not? They already suspect me of harboring such ambitions. Every Sun Lord has done so. To deny it would be pointless."

"You may not be able to persuade them to join you, then," I told him. "Why would they want a new Emperor telling them what to do?"

"They wouldn't, so I won't ask them to accept it. Instead, in return for their help in destroying the Exiles, I'll swear that the empire's mandate will run only north of the Pearl. I'll leave the Despotates, including Tamurin, to themselves."

"They won't believe you. Anyway, what does it profit them if you do smash the Exiles and restore imperial rule?"

Terem selected a pebble from the pool's bank and tossed it at the frog, who paid no attention. "For one thing, the river Despotates will be free of the Exile threat. For another, the conquered lands will be open to trade again, which will please everybody. Yazar, for example, will have more places to send the goods that come up the Long Canal. Finally, I'll make treaties to guarantee the sovereignty of each Despotate. If Guidarat attacked Kayan, for example, the empire would help Kayan's Despot."

I mused on this. An appeal to greed and fear might move them. And then there was the fact that all Durdana, from rulers to gravediggers, hated the Exiles. Even hard-faced Despots might be moved to fight the barbarians, provided they risked nothing by it. But I still wasn't optimistic.

"And how do you think the Despotana of Tamurin will answer my proposals?" he asked.

Terem had never asked me about Mother's policies, because he knew of and respected my filial loyalty to her. While I thought about how to answer, I studied the place god. He was a sardonic-looking fellow, with a sharp chin under a pale beard of lichen.

"I don't know what Tamurin can offer you," I said. "You need the other four Despots because their brigades can support your forces in the field, or at the least they can threaten to outflank Ardavan from the south. But Mother has no common border with Bethiya or the Six Kingdoms, and her army isn't among the larger ones."

"True, but those mountain pikemen of hers are exceptional. Even a brigade, if she could spare it, would stiffen my infantry more than two of Guidarat's. Also, Tamurine ships could endanger the sailing routes to Kurjain, if the Despotana were hostile to me. She's never attempted to interfere with Bethiyan sea trade, but an alliance would ensure against it."

"Well," I said, "she hates the Exiles as much as anyone. She might agree to help you, especially if you add the guarantees."

"Talk to her quietly on my behalf, then. Tell her how much she's needed."

"I'll try."

He touched my chin to turn my face to his. "Lale, this has to be said, especially now that the Despotana is coming to Kurjain. You know how I came to sit on the dais of Bethiya. I was a child then, and I had no hand in it, but if what happened to your adoptive mother could affect the trust I put in you, tell me now."

You had no hand in it, I thought, *but the Chancellor did.*

That was what I told myself, to quiet the twinge of discomfort that lying to Terem now aroused in me. These twinges had troubled me more frequently of late; in fact, although I was loath to admit it, the deceits that had earlier flowed so sweetly off my tongue now left a faintly bitter taste. Only when I reminded myself that I lied to protect those I loved did the savor become palatable.

So I said, "It's true I owe her my filial regard, but I belong to you now, Terem, not to her, and she would never want me to deny my bond to you. And to the best of my knowledge, she wants only to rule quietly in Tamurin, keep her school for her daughters, and have nobody trouble her."

"I have no intention of troubling her." Terem said. "But when you speak to her, tell her how much I'd value her help. And assure her that she's under no threat from Bethiya."

"I will," I answered, and we left it at that.

Mother arrived late the following afternoon, but with much less ceremony than the other Despots had enjoyed. Even her escort was half the size of those the other Despots had dragged in their wake. Had I been more astute, I might have realized that this betrayed her obsession with concealment and secrecy. But seeing that I shared a little of that obsession myself, perhaps I would have found nothing odd about it.

Like the other Despots, she and her entourage had come up the Short Canal aboard several passenger slippers. Terem and I—on this occasion without the government ministers—went in the *Auspicious Moon* to greet her as she disembarked at the Jacinth Fortress. I hoped she'd received the letter concerning my new status, and I was waiting with delicious anticipation for her to see me beside the Sun Lord, in my rich new clothes and my fashionable plumed hat with a big drooping brim.

I wasn't disappointed. Mother spotted me on the sequina's deck as she disembarked from the slipper. A smile of delight and recognition spread over her face, and I knew the courier had found her.

The official greetings had to be dealt with before we talked, but during the ceremony I hardly took my eyes from her. She'd outwardly changed very little, and was still a short, dumpy woman of indeterminate age with a plain round face. She had violated Kurjain fashion by not wearing an elaborate hat, and her clothing did not draw the eye, either. But none of this mattered to me, because I was so happy to see her again and hear her lovely melodious voice.

With all the bustle, it was not until we were aboard the sequina that Terem could turn to her and say, "My Lady Despotana, Lale and I have written to tell you that she has consented to be my Inamorata. I gather from your demeanor that you have received this letter, and I earnestly entreat you to approve the match we have made."

Mother put her hand on my arm—we were seated on benches on the *Auspicious Moon*'s afterdeck—and leaned toward him. "My joy in comparison with yours," she said, "is as a dewdrop beside the Great Green, but it is still great. You have my blessings, and I implore the Beneficent Ones to forever give you the greatest delight in each other."

She kissed me on both cheeks, and then she and Terem also exchanged kisses. For her it must have been like kissing a serpent, but she showed no distaste. I marveled at her poise and resolved that mine would always equal it.

But what with getting her installed in her quarters and then attending the evening banquet, we found no time to talk. After the meal we exchanged a few words, and she promised we'd meet privately as soon as she could arrange it. But much of the next day she spent with the other rulers, listening to Terem argue for his scheme of alliance, so it was not until late in the afternoon that she came alone to the Reed Pavilion. She found me waiting on the veranda. I'd already dismissed my domestics to spend the night in the servants' compound, and the house was empty.

I sank to my knees and bowed my head as she approached. She took my hands in hers and raised me up, and in that warm sweet voice she said, "Lale, how beautiful you've become. It would seem that palace life suits you."

I bowed modestly. "My honored mother is gracious to praise the undistinguished features of her worthless daughter. And it is only through her ceaseless labors that I have reached a station so far above my scanty merit."

She burst out laughing and so, after a moment, did I. "Lale," she said, "you've become a *very* good actress. You have never for a moment believed yourself to be of scanty merit, but you sounded most convincing."

"I do my best to be convincing," I told her. "So far, apparently, I have succeeded."

"Indeed," she answered in a suddenly serious voice. "And a very good thing that is, too. Your servants?"

"Dismissed."

"Even so, we shall talk in a more out-of-the-way place. Come."

I was about to say I'd take her wherever she wanted to go. But then I remembered that she knew Jade Lagoon long before I did, and I obediently followed her along the path beside the outer fortification wall. I asked her lots of innocuous questions about Repose and the school, wondering all the while if she found her memories of the palace distressing. But I saw no sign of it.

I didn't realize, until we had reached the place, where she was leading me. We stopped; I looked at the carved wooden gate, and at the wall in which it stood, and I heard the sound of running water.

"Mother?" I ventured. "This goes to—"

"I know where it goes," she said. "Open it."

I obeyed. The door swung silently on greased hinges. Beyond lay the Water Terrace, where her son had died so cruelly.

I watched Mother with worry in my heart. I knew she was in terrible pain, and I hated the brutal men who had inflicted it on her. For a moment it sickened me that Terem, even though he had had no hand in the killings, was my lover.

"Must you go in?" I asked.

She nodded and went through the gate. I followed. We walked along the path that led across the lower terrace to a wooden bench and the plum tree that shaded it. A little waterfall tumbled over red-veined gray rocks nearby and splashed into a pebbled channel that meandered through the greenery. The ground cover's flowers had become tiny seed pods since I'd last been here, the crimson specks sprinkled thickly among its leaves.

Mother sat on the bench and gestured for me to join her. When

I'd settled myself she said, "No one will hear us over the sound of the water. What do you know of the usurper's plans for these Despotate alliances?"

I told her everything he'd told me, none of which was very alarming. "But I think he sees Yazar as the best prospect for an ally," I ended. "Yazar's the richest of all the river Despots, even if he spends every spade that comes into his hands. I wrote to you that the Sun Lord once told me he wished Yazar had a daughter for him to marry."

"So you did." She touched my hand. "In fact, Lale, you've exceeded my greatest expectations of you. I thought at the best that you'd become his mistress. I never hoped you'd captivate him enough to be his Inamorata."

My cheeks grew warm with pleasure. She had never praised me so highly. "I did my best," I mumbled.

"I knew you would. But what you did with that Hot Sky conspiracy—that was brilliant. You could have found no better way to gain his trust."

"It was luck," I pointed out. "I didn't arrange for it to happen."

"But you saw the chance, seized it, and turned it to your advantage. That's the mark of an adept. Even Nilang could have done no better."

"You honor me too much," I said, although I was feeling very pleased with myself.

"Do you feel he trusts you now?"

"Very much so. Since I came to live in the palace, we've been eating most of our morning and evening meals together. He talks freely about the Chancellery's doings and about the War Ministry. He's very proud of the new cavalry brigades and tells me a lot about them." I went on at some length about troop dispositions, supply arrangements, cavalry remount tallies, and the like.

When I finished she asked, "And he doesn't worry that you'll pass such information to me?"

"No. He thinks my loyalty is to him alone, and anyway he doesn't consider you a threat. Neither does Halis Geray."

"And why should they?" she said softly, as if to herself. "How could Tamurin and poor Makina Seval threaten mighty Bethiya? Me with my meager four brigades against the Sun Lord's myriads? What use would such information be to me, the usurper thinks, even if I had it? What *contempt* I suffer."

"There's more," I said. I told her about the army engineers Terem had recently sent east, and the strengthening of the Jacinth and Pearl river flotillas that Kirkin, in a fit of self-importance because he was drafting the orders, had told me about.

"What sort of craft?" Mother asked.

"Troop carriers and rams. Also artillery boats—catapults, mostly, but stone kickers as well."

"Hm. What else?"

"The Chancellery has been exchanging messages with King Garhang of Lindu. Terem told me the King wants Bethiya's support against Ardavan, but Garhang doesn't want to give anything in exchange. Terem has asked him to allow free movement of the Durdana out of Lindu, but Garhang balks."

Mother snorted. "Of course he does. If Garhang opened the border, every Durdana in his kingdom would run away. This Sun Lord is making conditions he knows the Exile won't accept. But would Bethiya give Lindu aid under any circumstances, do you think?"

"Terem's extremely uneasy about that. He says the people would be very angry if he helped an Exile King, unless he got a something very important in exchange. It goes much against his grain, too."

"So he won't likely ally Bethiya to Lindu, no matter how threatening Ardavan seems, even if these talks with the Despots fail?"

"I don't think so."

"Very well. This is a situation I want you to watch carefully. Now, is there anything else?"

"I'm ashamed to say there is not."

She patted my hand. "What you've given me is excellent. And so much of it revealed over dinner . . . but the pillow talk? Men are apt to gossip after the woman has sated them, assuming they don't turn over and go to sleep."

I felt myself turning pink, which was silly, because she'd asked a professional question, not a personal one. I said, "He doesn't do either. He prefers to talk about lesser matters. Things from his childhood, places in Bethiya he thinks I might want to see. I don't think it's wise to prompt him in other directions. It would be out of character for me, and he might wonder."

"Yes, one must be patient in these things. . . . Does he please you as a man?"

I had hoped she wouldn't ask this. The truth was that the excitement Terem aroused in me was both profound and intense, and I had been participating in our nightly intimacies with a shameless lack of reserve.

But I couldn't prevaricate with her. "He does please me that way," I admitted. "I can't seem to help it." Would she order me to stop experiencing these new pleasures? It would be like trying not to taste wine while it sloshed around in my mouth.

But Mother didn't seem perturbed. "Such feelings are natural," she assured me. "The usurper is not without allure, and his power adds to the erotic aura. However, I must warn you against a possible risk in such gratification. While the pleasure is purely of an animal nature, in a woman it can eventually arouse tender emotions toward the man, even if these were absent in the beginning. So I caution you, Lale—remember always whose daughter you are, and never let this person's outward nature blind you to his inward one. He would slaughter you in an instant, and me with you, if he knew the truth about us. A tenth of what you've just told me would be sufficient to condemn us both."

"I'll be very careful," I said humbly. I was grateful that she understood and hadn't rebuked me.

"And you must be careful not to get with child," she went on. "It would hamper your activities. Nilang is seeing to that?"

"Yes. I use the preparations she gives me."

"Good. Now, to other practical matters. How much freedom of

movement do you have? How do you spend your days? Do you have trouble seeing Nilang, now that you live in the palace?"

I described my routine at Reed Pavilion, which began with a dawn breakfast before Terem he went off to his labors. Usually I had a nap after he left, to recover from the night's pleasures. On rising, I might read for a while or stroll about the palace grounds. I avoided the covered walk where I'd seen Merihan's ghost; one encounter with that unhappy spirit was more than enough. I had very few domestic staff by palace standards: two older women to keep the pavilion clean and tidy, and a girl from Sutkagin who saw to my personal needs and served Terem and me our meals.

In the afternoons I often went into the city, sometimes to visit friends. Many doors had opened to me in the aftermath of the Hot Sky Plot, and I could have spent every waking moment being entertained. But most often I went to oversee the furnishing and decorating of the villa Terem had given me. It wasn't a big place, but it was very elegant and comfortable, with a courtyard garden and three balconies overlooking the glittering band of Cloud Mirror Canal. Even though I'd spent little time there as yet, I loved it. It was the first home I'd ever owned, and every time I stepped onto its boat landing I thought of the hovels of Riversong and smiled.

As for getting around, Terem had put a sequina at my disposal, but I preferred to use the common periangs licensed for the palace mooring basin. "And an escort?" Mother asked, when I told her this. "He doesn't let you go about Kurjain without protection, surely?"

That question, in fact, had brought Terem and me close to our first real quarrel. I'd said I didn't want palace guardsmen tramping behind me everywhere I went, especially when I was with friends. He said it was imperative. I was too well known and not everyone loved him—the Hot Sky Plot proved that—and I should be more careful. I told him the conspirators were all dead and nobody would hurt me. Then I said I simply wouldn't stand for it and that I hadn't agreed to be his Inamorata to lose my freedom, and did he now want a different Lale from the one he'd fallen in love with, a Lale who wouldn't put her nose out of doors unless she had a clutch of sweaty soldiers to protect her?

He still protested vehemently but stopped short of making it an injunction from the Sun Lord, which I could not have disobeyed. Finally we compromised: If I went out by myself I'd wear a wig and some subtle face paint. For fun, I got several wigs from the Porcelain Pavilion stage stocks and tried to look a little different every time I slipped out of the palace. My friends thought it was hilarious.

What I'd been worried about, of course, was having my escort interfere with my visits to Nilang. No doubt I could have dragged the men to her house and made them wait outside—not even the Chancellor questioned my apparent penchant for spirit summoners, especially since he'd investigated them all and discovered nothing. But doing so would have increased my risk of detection slightly, and this way was better.

I told Mother how I'd managed the problem. She nodded in approval but said, "Nevertheless, don't ever assume the Chancellor isn't suspicious of you. He's suspicious of everyone. You may never know if, or when, he's decided to watch you again."

I said I'd be very careful and then told her about the ghost of the Surina. Mother frowned, pondering the matter. Then she said, "Has anyone else seen it?"

"Yes, several times. But not Terem, and nobody's told him."

"Don't you tell him, then. Its nothing for you to worry about, especially since other people saw it before you did. She'll stop walking as time goes by."

I agreed, and then asked a question that had puzzled me for some time: How was Mother managing without Nilang? The sorceress had been in Kurjain as long as I had, after all.

"Nilang is more valuable here with you," she told me. "You, of all my daughters, need her most."

"But what about Three Springs?"

"It's no longer the Midnight School, as you girls used to call it.

The instructors are still there, for when I need it again, but I've decided I have a sufficiency of my special daughters for the moment. So I've closed it, and Tossi has come back to Repose to help me. So Nilang is perfectly free to be here."

"I see. Is Dilara well?"

"She's very well. After you, she is the prize of the Midnight School."

I was very pleased that Mother regarded my old friend almost as highly as she did me. "I'd like to see her again," I suggested hopefully.

"Perhaps you will, when the time's right. Just now, it isn't."

That was clearly the end of that subject, so I said, "Another thing. Terem has asked me to persuade you to support him during these negotiations with the Despots."

"Naturally he would do that. Very well, tell him you've tried, and that while I would not commit myself, I did not dismiss such a possibility."

"All right . . . Mother?"

"What is it, child?"

"I don't understand how you can . . . how you can sit in the same room as the Chancellor. I worry about how much it must hurt you. And he must suspect how you feel."

She touched her fingers to her lips in the old pensive gesture. "Oh, yes, it hurts, and he knows it. But he thinks I care as little for my murdered ones as he does, and that I can forget them for necessities of state. So I grind my teeth and listen to him, and remind myself that his days are numbered. There is nothing, Lale, like the presence of one's enemies to refine one's resolve. Not that mine has ever faltered."

"Nor has mine," I said.

We sat without speaking for a long time. Late afternoon sunlight lay across the Water Terrace. A flock of blue-and-white thrushes were bathing in a pool on the far side of the terrace; in a month they'd be down south, for I remembered seeing them in Riversong at the beginning of the wet season.

"It happened on a day like this," Mother said at last. "The

ninth of this very month. I wasn't here, but I know where everything happened. My son died in that pool where the thrushes
are, do you see? My brother was murdered on the second terrace
there, and my sister, too. She was with child. And there were
many others."

I stared down at the turf. I was afraid that if I looked up, I might
see what she was seeing.

"That was how it ended. But the feud was years old even then.
It wiped out my husband's bloodline and the Tanyelis, but it destroyed mine, too, because of our alliance with the Danjians. My
father was poisoned and my mother died of grief. My uncles were
murdered, my cousins slaughtered, my friends strangled and
thrown into the canals at night. But we gave as good as we got,
right until the end. Even then we might have won, if Halis Geray
hadn't betrayed us."

I made not a sound. I wasn't even sure if she spoke to me or to
the bitter ghosts that must throng this garden.

"He promised us refuge here, then let the Tanyelis and their
men in through the Dry Gate and the posterns. He intended us to
destroy each other, but we didn't see it in time. At the end there
were two grown Tanyelis and three of their whelps left and a
cousin of mine, but Halis Geray hanged all the adults at the Jacinth
Fortress for being conspirators at insurrection. The Tanyeli brats he
disinherited by decree and sent them to live with peasant families
on the northern frontier. They all died of one thing or another, perhaps with his help. Me he left alone, because I was out of his reach
in Istana and because with my little boy dead, I was no threat. And
he wanted to seem a little merciful, though there was no more
mercy in him then than there is now."

She took a long, shaking breath. "But did the Ministry of Rewards and Punishments arrest him for his murders? Did the generals at the War Ministry rebel? Did the other great bloodlines rise
in protest against what he had done? No. They knew where their
bread was baked. . . . How many of them had sworn friendship and
support to the Danjian clan when we were powerful and rich?

Many. How many helped us when we were dying on the Water Terrace? None. Everyone betrayed us."

I heard her sigh, and I hoped desperately that she was finished. I wanted to comfort her with an embrace, but I dared not touch her.

She pointed to the pool where the thrushes twittered and splashed. "Did my little boy die quickly when the blade pierced him? I don't know. Perhaps he drowned. He was too little for such deep water. He had just begun to walk."

"Mother," I whispered, "please don't."

"And who murdered him?" she asked, though not of me. "Everyone did. The Tanyeli, yes, they held the steel. But it was those others, too, the ministers, the generals, the magnates, the great bloodlines. Oh, they had rich pickings afterward, they knew they'd get their rewards. They slaughtered my child for them. His blood is on all of it."

I now wanted above all else to get Mother out of the Water Terrace. I'd never seen her face so white and stark, as if an angry ghost had drained the lifeblood from her.

"Mother," I pleaded, taking her limp fingers and kneading them, "we shouldn't be here. Please come away. We'll go to the pavilion and have some wine. Please. Your hands are so cold."

She turned her gaze to mine and to my shock she didn't seem to recognize me. "I'm here to be near my son," she said. "I came to tell him what I'm going to do. So close your driveling mouth, you stupid girl."

It was as if she had slashed me across the face with a whip. Her words took everything she'd ever given me and tossed it rotting into a cesspit. It turned me from the Inamorata of the Sun Lord into Lale of Riversong, the wretched, scrawny child cast up like stinking fish on the banks of the Wing, motherless, fatherless, worthless.

Worthless? I had always been worthless. I was nobody's daughter. I didn't belong to her, after all. I didn't belong to anyone.

I released her hand and wept silently while she stared across the

Water Terrace. And as I wept, thoughts crept through the veils of my grief. Thoughts about Mother and her slaughtered family. Thoughts about Terem and his dreams. And about how, through me, his dreams would fail.

And then I thought: *But it isn't his fault they're dead. Why should he be punished for it? And might it not be better if he won and made his dreams come true, so that such things would never happen again?*

Fear struck through my grief, like lightning through a cloud. Such thoughts were treachery, disobedience, disloyalty, ingratitude. But surely I didn't mean them? Surely I wasn't losing my faith? I must never lose my faith. Mother had given me everything I'd ever longed for. If I lost my trust in her, if she lost her trust in me, it would all drift from my hands like ashes.

And then I thought: *But if she trusts her daughters so completely, why does she bind us with Nilang's wraiths? Are we all Adrine to her?*

Instead of an answer, I heard Mother's whispers. She spoke to her child, I knew, although her words were so soft I could make nothing of them; she was like a woman speaking in her sleep. But in this place of ghosts the Quiet World felt very near, and with growing dread I sensed it draw nearer still, as if the fury of her grief had roused the spirits that lingered here.

It was a hairsbreadth away, then less, then less. And then a crack opened between the worlds, and something came through it. To my sight it was only a wavering blur, like the heated air above a fire, but to my inner vision it had shape and nature. Its form seemed that of a child, but within it burned a seething malevolence that almost stopped my heart. Above all else I wanted to flee, but I could not leave Mother alone with a thing so dreadful. I could only listen as she whispered to it, ceaselessly, on and on and on.

How much time passed as she communed with the thing she'd summoned, I don't know. Perhaps not long, for the sun had hardly moved when she fell silent. And as her whispers ceased, the shapeless thing I thought to be her son screamed a silent, frenzied scream, and vanished. On the instant, I bust into uncontrollable sobs.

"Lale?" Mother exclaimed, "Lale, my dear, what is it? What's the matter? Why are you crying?"

"You were—" I blurted, and then I saw her face, worried and loving, and I realized: *She doesn't remember what she called me. She didn't mean it. It was her grief that spoke. I'm still her daughter. I still belong to her.*

My relief was so profound that I blubbered anew. She put an arm around me and asked again, "What is it?"

I couldn't hurt her by repeating what she'd said. Finally I snuffled, "I saw him. I saw your little boy. He came."

"Yes," Mother whispered, smoothing my hair. "Yes, he did. Nilang taught me how, the Taweret way. I call him every year on his birthday, and often he comes to me. I hoped I could find him here, too, because this is where he died, but I didn't expect him to come so easily. And I didn't expect you to see him, my dear. Is he not a lovely, sweet child?"

I blinked at her though my tears. That was not what I'd seen at all. But perhaps, I thought desperately, what I'd seen was something else, something that had slipped through with the little boy's spirit. That made more sense. Mother's child wouldn't likely appear to me, who was not his blood kin, but a spectral predator from the Quiet World had sniffed me out once before.

"He's sweet indeed," I answered tremulously. I was so glad that she was no longer the woman who didn't know who I was. She was Mother again. Yet beneath my gladness lay disquiet. How could the woman I knew so well become that *other*, a woman I didn't recognize, a woman with such a savage and bitter tongue?

And then, surfacing from the past like a bloated corpse rising through black water, came the memory of Tossi standing at Adrine's prison door and saying to me: *Do you mean to suggest that Mother's mad?*

But not even now could I bring myself to think that she was, or might be. For if I did, I must acknowledge that everything that mattered to me, the very weave of my life, indeed the whole purpose of my being, was the design of a madwoman. How could I allow myself to accept such a hideous truth? The world and all in it would turn to dust and ashes.

Yet even had I faced that nothingness, I could not have imagined what she whispered to the thing from the Quiet World. How could I, who still loved her in spite of everything, have suspected what she planned for us all? Not even Halis Geray, in the blackest forebodings of a sleepless night, would have believed her capable of such atrocity. It truly was madness. Yet if the aim of her grand design was demented, her execution of it was not; in that regard, she was as lucid and cunning as the great Chancellor himself.

"I'm sorry," I said. "I'm all right now."

Her arm tightened around my shoulders. "It shows how much you care for me, daughter," she said. "As I care for you. And remember, someday all our work will be finished. We'll have won, Lale, and the tyrant won't threaten us any more. What would you like to do, my dear, when peace comes?"

I realized I had no idea. My part in our struggle had so consumed me that I'd never imagined an end to it or what might become of me afterward. "I'm not sure," I answered hesitantly.

"You told me a long time ago you'd like to be a printer. Is that still what you want?"

"Well," I said, "I don't think so, not anymore. I like acting. What I'd love to do would be to run a theater somewhere. Maybe I'd even write some plays myself and have them performed." But as I spoke, I remembered that there would be no Terem in my audience, and my heart sank.

Mother looked into my eyes. "Something troubles you, Lale?"

Long ago she'd warned me never to lie to her. But now I did, and she'd taught me well, because she thought I told her the truth. "It's not every day one sees a ghost," I said. "It scared me."

"They can be troublesome company, I admit. But not my son's, he's a sweet boy. . . . As for the theater, Lale, someday you'll have one, I promise. But come now, we've spent enough time here. We'll go back the pavilion, and I'll tell you more about what's been happening at home."

Together we left the Water Terrace. She never gave it a backward glance, and neither did I.

Twenty-three

&ℯ

Terem's negotiations for his Despotate alliances failed, as every such attempt had failed since the Partition, and for the same reasons: distrust, avarice, fear, pride, and envy. I'd expected it, even if Terem hadn't.

Mother and her fellow rulers had been gone for a couple of days before we found some time together. We were spending it in the Hall of the Thousand Manifestations of Loveliness, where the Sun Lords displayed the best of their art collection. Most of the paintings, sculptures, and ceramics predated the Partition and were the finest Durdana masterpieces in the world, barring those in Seyhan that the Exiles had stolen from us.

The hall was in the House of Felicity, a place I disliked. This wasn't because Felicity was oppressive—it was surpassingly beautiful—but because everything Terem did within its lovely walls was governed by custom and ceremony. Bethiya had preserved more of our imperial traditions than any other Durdana realm, and the daily life of the Sun Lord reflected this. Part of the protocol was that we must be surrounded by a cloud of household domestics, like gnats that don't bite but still get into your eyes and ears. Had I been the Surina, who customarily lived in the House of Felicity, I'd have had to endure this as well as the ceremonial, and I wondered how Merihan had put up with it. No wonder Terem escaped to the simplicity of the Reed Pavilion, and me, whenever he could.

"I'm sorry I wasn't able to persuade the Despotana," I told him as I gazed at the painted screen before us. It was Sudai's most famous work, *Doves Resting on a Peach Branch*. I'd heard of it in school but until recently hadn't known it was right here in Kurjain. It was an astonishing achievement. You'd swear that if you offered seeds to the three plump birds, they'd lean from their branch to pluck the morsels from your fingers.

"Your adoptive mother and Yazar were the least difficult of the whole crew," Terem said grumpily. He was very disappointed, not least because his usual ability to inspire devotion and allegiance had failed to shift the Despots' obstinacy. He was accustomed to getting his own way, and was deeply annoyed when he didn't.

"She's having trouble with Khalaka sea raiders," I reminded him. "She needs her troops. Also, she doesn't trust Guidarat's Despot."

"Who would?" Terem snorted. "Somebody wrote, 'What will be said of the ruler who lets his people starve?' It could have been written about him."

"Indeed. What are you going to do now?"

He looked around. A male domestic stood motionless near the hall's door and there were probably three others just out of sight beyond it. In a low voice he said, "We're going to war with Lindu."

I pricked up my ears. "We are? Why?"

"Because a victory over an Exile Kingdom is the only way to convince the Despots to join an alliance. And the time's ripe. Garhang's becoming more and more frightened of Ardavan, and he's ready to talk about opening the border. So I've encouraged more discussion with him."

"But you just said we're going to attack Lindu."

"Of course we are. But if he thinks I'm contemplating some

kind of defensive agreement, he may relax his guard against us. Halis and I are hoping he'll shift part of his cavalry from our border to his frontier with Jouhar."

"You wouldn't *really* make an ally of him, would you?"

He laughed. "There's no chance of that. Can you see me helping an Exile King keep his throne, so he can go on oppressing his Durdana slaves? People would call me traitor."

"Garhang must be singularly inept if he doesn't know you're playing him like a fish."

"He is not completely inept, but his judgment is made defective by his fear of Ardavan. My guess is that Ardavan intends to gobble up Lindu next spring, as soon as the weather's good enough for fighting. Then we'll have him glowering at us across the Savath. I don't want him that close."

"So we strike first?"

"Exactly. I'm leading twenty infantry and ten cavalry brigades into Lindu before this year's campaigning season ends, and I'll have Garhang's neck under my heel before winter."

He smiled, and in that grim hard smile I saw an aspect of him I'd suspected but never witnessed. I knew many sides of him now, among them the boyish companion of our night in the Mirror, the passionate lover of the Reed Pavilion, and the grave and thoughtful sovereign of Bethiya. But in that moment I perceived the essence of him, the true nature that underlay the faces he presented to the world. Beneath them all he was a brilliant, ruthless visionary, whose dreams were glittering and dangerous.

"Can we beat them?" I asked.

"Yes. We can beat them."

He never doubted it, then or later, even when catastrophe loomed over him like a mountain. That perfect certainty could, and did, inspire men and women to follow him to the death. For he appeared to know, as if a god had told him, that our victory was ordained, and how could anyone imagine defeat when he did not? Hardly anybody around him *did* imagine it, except me, and that was because I was in a position to make it happen.

"When will you attack?" I asked, as I calculated how soon I might get this news to Nilang.

"We'll march into Lindu at the middle of the month." he said. "There will be no announcement of the invasion until after it's under way. I want to catch Garhang by surprise."

"I'm looking forward to this," I told him. "I've never seen an Exile Kingdom or a war."

He frowned at me. "Lale, this is an army on the march into enemy territory, with a battle at the end of it. It's no place for a woman of rank. You'll stay here."

"No, I won't," I retorted. "I'm coming with you. I've never seen a war, and I want to. Besides, there are lots of women camp followers. Who else does the laundry? I could do yours, if I had to. I learned how at school."

Terem sighed. "You will not do laundry or anything else. I give way to you in most things, dearest, but not in this. You are to stay in Kurjain. I want you safe."

"Is that the Sun Lord's injunction?" I hoped he'd back away from a direct order.

"It is. I'm sorry."

"No, you're not."

"Be that as it may, you must remain here until I return. It shouldn't take long. Garhang's realm is a house of sticks. One good kick and the whole ramshackle pile will come crashing down."

"And suppose Ardavan doesn't wait for spring and marches over the border at you instead?"

"A risk I must accept. But I expect to crush Garhang and seize Bara, his capital, before month's end. By then it'll be too late in the season for Ardavan to mount a serious attack against us, so we'll have the winter to build up our strength in Lindu. Next spring he and I will try conclusions in earnest, but it will be on his territory, not ours."

"But I'll miss you!" It was the expected thing to say, but as I said it, I realized that it was true—and that I'd miss him a great deal. But at the same time I was worried about being left in Kurjain, not knowing what he was up to. I was just as much a soldier as he was, and I had my orders. If I failed to obey them by letting him get out of my sight, Mother wouldn't like it at all.

He took my arm and led me to a wooden pedestal on which was a little stone sculpture. "I'll miss you, too. But it's how it must be. Look, I had these brought out of storage. They're said to be from the late Commonwealth, two ladies in white jade. Perfection."

"Yes," I agreed, "perfection." The argument was finished, he'd made up his mind, and there was no more to be said.

Terem left for the east on 28 White Dew, traveling by boat up the Jacinth River. The attack on Lindu was still a deep secret, so it was given out that the Sun Lord was inspecting the border fortresses. His strategy was not as secure as he imagined, though; I had sent the news to Mother the day after he told me about it.

A few hours after Terem's departure, I left the palace for my villa on Cloud Mirror Canal. Before I went, I informed the Chancellery that I would reside there until the Sun Lord came back to Kurjain. I spent the night at the villa and then, very early the next morning, I told my domestics that I was returning to Jade Lagoon. Since I came and went at odd intervals, they saw nothing peculiar in this; nor would they have seen anything peculiar in the plump-cheeked young matron with braided hair who, about an hour later, boarded an eastbound river lorcha in Feather Lagoon. She carried a journey-bag over her shoulder, and wore unmemorable traveling clothes and a pair of sensible weatherproof boots.

What wasn't visible was the fighting knife beneath my jacket and my well-packed money belt. The garments and bag I'd bought in the Round, while the braided wig and the wax cheek pads were from the theater stocks at the Porcelain Pavilion. The knife came from Nilang. We reckoned that I had several days before people at Jade Lagoon and the villa compared notes and realized I was at neither place. By that time I would be far from Kurjain. Mother already knew I was on the road, for Nilang had transmitted a sending to Tossi back in Chiran that said: *Lale follows sun eastward.*

The lorcha took me as far as the city of Gultekin, six days' travel up the Jacinth; there I intended to transfer to a smaller waterspoon for the rest of the journey. As soon as I got ashore, I found an alley and discarded the cheek pads and the wig; Gultekin was a middling-sized city and I thought it unlikely that I'd be recognized so far from Kurjain.

Despite the urgency of following Terem, I was curious to see Gultekin because it was Merihan's home, and as far as I knew her parents still lived here. I might even have time, I reflected as I sauntered out of the alley, to see the house where she grew up.

This idea, once it came to me, took on an oddly compelling force. Instead of following my original plan, which was to proceed upriver without an overnight stop, I found the best inn Gultekin had to offer, and took a private room overlooking the garden. I then determined the whereabouts of the Aviya residence from the landlady, and in the early afternoon went out and found it.

The house stood where Nine Grasshoppers Street opened onto the round plaza called Gold Sand Circle. This was a well-to-do quarter of Gultekin, and only the dry, crumbling fountain in the plaza's center suggested that it had decayed from a more opulent state. The Aviya villa—a small mansion, really—stood on the east side, surrounded by a brick wall pierced with a single carriage gate. Next to that was a smaller entry for pedestrians, with the Aviya bloodline emblem of a white hare painted on it. Rising above the wall were the green-tiled roofs of the various wings of the mansion, which was of two stories.

Having found the house, I wasn't sure what to do next. I wasn't even certain why I'd come here. As I stood a few paces from its entrance and puzzled over this, a heavyset street peddler came around the corner and banged on the pedestrian gate. Judging by the reed cages he carried, he was an itinerant toad seller; householders bought the little creatures to eat garden slugs and other pests. Soon a snub-nosed young man opened the gate and the peddler lumbered through it.

In the madness of the next instant I utterly forgot myself. I called, "Please wait," and hurried after the peddler. The young porter looked startled but said, "Yes, mistress?" as I slipped past him into the courtyard.

I stopped and looked around. Through an archway to my left I glimpsed a garden, with tall autumn sunflowers and an old apple tree in full fruit. At any instant I expected the porter to express astonishment at my resemblance to the daughter of the house, but he didn't—he must be a recent addition to the household, one who had never seen Merihan.

At that moment I might have turned and fled, and much that followed would have been very different. But instead I took further leave of my senses and asked, "Is your master or mistress at home?"

"Honored lady, they're in the garden." He frowned. "Did you have an engagement to see them today? I was not informed."

"I'm from Kurjain," I said. "We have . . . acquaintances in common."

"May I tell them who calls?" He already didn't think much of me, turning up unannounced and without attendants. I hesitated, trying to think of who I might pretend to be. Saying I was the Sun Lord's Inamorata would merely convince him that I was demented.

I was spared answering by a woman who came through the arch. She was about Mother's age but slender, with a small oval face and gray hair cut short. She must have been gardening, because plant stems and sunflower petals clung to her skirt, and she held a small pruning knife. But she was no servant; her clothes and her smooth skin told me that. I wanted to flee but stood as if rooted to the earth.

She said to the toad seller, "I'll need five of them." And then she saw me. She stopped in her tracks and the knife tumbled from her fingers onto the courtyard stones. It made a soft *ting*, like the chime of a tiny bell.

There was a long silence.

"Ilishan," Merihan's mother called in a trembling voice. "Oh, Ilishan. Look."

"What is it, Nirar?" A man appeared in the archway. It was Merihan's father, silver haired and sharp nosed, with the bearing of an officer and the heavily muscled arms of a man trained to weapons. At the sight of me he went white and put his hand on the wall for support.

"*Merihan?*" he said, and the pain in his voice seared my heart.

I didn't know what to do. I cursed myself for having come anywhere near this place. What had I hoped to accomplish with my morbid curiosity? All I could do was hurt them.

"My lord Aviya," I blurted, "I'm not her. I grew up in Chiran, in Tamurin. I'm Lale Navari. I've come from Kurjain."

"*You!*" Merihan's mother said. But of course they would know my name. How could they not have heard that the Sun Lord had an Inamorata called Lale and that he'd taken her the instant his mourning for Merihan was finished?

"Why have you come here?" her father demanded. "The Sun Lord passed through Gultekin days ago." He was still staring at me, as if he could scarcely believe the evidence of his eyes.

"I—I know he did," I stammered. "He doesn't know I'm here. I just wanted to see where . . . where she grew up."

"She's so like her," Nirar whispered. "And yet . . . not."

"How could you do this to us?" Ilishan burst out. An angry flush had replaced his pallor. "Do you think we don't know how you snared him, you with your look of her, and Merihan not a year in her tomb? Have you no pity, to come here and throw yourself in our faces? No respect?"

"I'm sorry," I answered, my gaze cast down, my face burning with shame. "I meant no harm. I didn't think."

"I don't care if you're his Inamorata or not," he went on, as if I hadn't spoken. "Nor that you can dispossess us with a word to him. Do that if you will. But get out of our house. You're not welcome."

His wife put a hand on his arm. "Ilishan, wait, perhaps—"

"No. I don't want her here. She'll bring us nothing but suffering." To me he said, "I don't care if you have a dozen guardsmen outside my house. Get away with you, or I'll have you thrown into the street. Veraj!"

The porter took a tentative step. Eyes brimming with tears, shaking with humiliation, I stumbled through the gate and heard it slam behind me. A woman carrying a basket of squash glanced at my face as she passed, then hurried on.

I could do nothing more. I'd already done too much. I walked back to the inn, paid for the room I'd never used, and collected my few belongings. Then I trudged down to the river docks, and before the supper hour came I was aboard a waterspoon heading east.

I caught up with Terem at Tanay, which in imperial times was Bethiya's prefectural capital. It stood on the shores of Blue Sea Lake, which was the source of the Jacinth. Twenty miles east of Tanay, over a range of low hills, was the River Savath and the border with Lindu.

In the years since the Partition, Tanay had become a fortress city, guarding Bethiya's eastern frontier against the Exile Kings. Terem had strengthened its already tremendous walls, and adjoining them built a huge, fortified compound that could accommodate a dozen infantry brigades and three of cavalry. But the multitude overflowed even this; when I arrived, the lakeshore beyond the compound was dark with leather tents and smoking from a myriad field kitchens. It was the greatest Durdana force gathered since the end of the empire: ninety thousand men, the Army of the East.

Terem was ensconced in Tanay's citadel, which towered over the lakeshore gate. The sentries at the citadel entrance didn't want to let me in, but while I was arguing with them, a brigadier who knew me from Jade Lagoon came along. After some exclamations of disbelief he took me to the map room on the uppermost floor of the keep. Terem was there, reviewing the army's marching orders with his senior commanders.

He wasn't pleased to see me, although he didn't say so in front of his men. The officers had no idea what to make of my escapade, and gawked at me until Terem sent me to wait in an adjoining chamber, which proved to be his private quarters. He joined me there a short while later.

He was infuriated, but at the same time I sensed that he was secretly happy that I'd showed up and also that he had a sneaking regard for what I'd done—he had plenty of audacity himself and admired it in others. So we had it out, Terem fuming about the risk I'd taken in traveling alone and how I'd disobeyed his instructions. I countered that I had arrived intact and that all he had to do now was let me tag along with his escort. In response he said I wasn't going farther than Tanay, and I told him I'd slip away and join the laundrywomen then, and was he going to lock me up to prevent it? Then I told him I could ride as well as he could, and if he gave me a good horse I'd be just as safe as he was. And finally, I said, if he really wanted the troops to see how confident he was of our victory, what better way than to let his Inamorata come along?

I got away with it. He finally threw his hands up in exasperated capitulation, and I ran forward and kissed him. We hadn't seen each other for almost three hands; one thing led to another, and there was a camp bed in the corner of the room. After that I was in no danger of being sent anywhere I didn't want to go.

The Army of the East marched from Tanay two days later, on 14 Cold Dew. The cavalry screen set out at first light, and as the sun rose over the hills the infantry vanguard followed. On its heels came Terem and me with our escort, and finally endless columns of foot soldiers flanked by masses of horsemen. Farther back lumbered the supply column and the siege train, then the rear guard, and at last the disorganized throng of camp followers that follow any army.

The city had turned out to see us off, and enormous crowds jammed the ramparts. As Terem and I rode from the main gate, they saw his golden helmet and crimson cloak, and cheered until I thought the stones of the walls would crack. Behind us swayed the standards of the army, flowing banners on tall gilded staffs, and among them was one that signified Terem's great dream. He'd kept it secret even from me, and I didn't recognize it at once. But when I did, my breath caught in my throat, for high above the helmet crests of our bodyguard blazed the three golden roses of the empire. The crowds saw it and like me they gasped; and then the roar came like thunder, for the Rose Standard had not gleamed over a Durdana army for a hundred years. A chill ran down my spine, and I must say that even Master Luasin could not have staged a better spectacle. So I have to give credit where it's due: Terem certainly knew how to manage an audience, including me.

It was profoundly, grandly, gloriously impressive. The grumble of drums, the metal-tongued boom of signal horns, the rumble of marching men and cantering horses, armor and weapons jangling, morning sunlight gleaming on steel and bronze, and all the brave banners . . . it is as vivid to me as if I were again in the midst of it. I'd never ridden with an army, let alone one of this size and strength, and it made my blood sing.

For a while, in spite of my exhilaration, I tried to remember that this tide might someday roll over Tamurin, and reminded myself that I was among the enemy. But the splendor of it soon drove such thoughts from my mind, and I found myself longing for Terem's victory.

The first day's march took us to the village of Bittersweet, on the west bank of the Savath. A cavalry brigade had already crossed upstream at Black Carp Ford and had driven off the Exile pickets on the far shore, thus clearing the way for our engineers to span the river. This was made easier by the ruins of an old bridge that had been broken long ago in the civil wars. Its piers remained, and the engineers were already fixing timbers to the masonry to form a crossing. A castella stood just outside the village, where a border garrison was stationed; Terem set up his headquarters there.

By now I was wondering which of my Three Springs sisters my clandestine contact might be and when she'd show herself. I knew there hadn't been enough time for Mother to both receive my message and get an agent as far as the Savath. However, Nilang seemed able to act without Mother's direct instructions, and before I left Kurjain she'd promised that someone would find me before we left Bethiya. But the frontier was now at hand and I was becoming concerned.

The answer came as I was washing the journey's dust from my hands and face in the room Terem and I were to share. I felt the numbness and the tingling, the water in the basin puckered and rose in a thin stalk, then flattened into a disk at the tip. The disk grew a face like Master Luasin's, which leered at me disgustingly. Then Nilang's voice in my head whispered, *Dilara, camp followers,* and the water collapsed into the basin, splashing me.

Dilara! I was so happy I did a little dance. Months had passed since we'd last seen each other, and so much had happened to me since then. I could hardly wait to tell her about it.

As it turned out, though, I had to wait until evening, when Terem finally went into an orders council with his officers. As soon as he left me to myself, I slipped out of the castella—in the bustle of soldiers dashing to and fro, nobody took much notice of me— and hurried into the city of tents that surrounded it. Sunset was near as I walked along the riverbank, watching the last of the camp followers straggle in: the laundrywomen I'd threatened to join, kitchen girls, trinket hawkers, spirits-of-wine peddlers, women with lovers in the ranks, seamstresses, horse dealers, and the inevitable contingent of strumpets. They were a cheerful, rowdy crew, squabbling over the best campsites like a flock of finches over spilled grain. Excitement hung in the air, sharpened by tension: tomorrow we would be across the Savath, where no Durdana army had trod since the Partition. It wasn't exactly hostile territory, for over there the common people were our kin. But looming beyond them were the Exiles, who would kill us all if they could.

In my travel clothes I didn't stand out in the mob, and nobody recognized me. But nobody approached me, either, and I found no sign of Dilara. Dusk drew on; I knew I'd have to return to the castella soon. With growing alarm I began to imagine all sorts of nasty things that might have befallen her.

As I went around the corner of a tent a voice at my elbow said,

"And would the noble lady need her skirt or jacket mended? No expense at all, the best work you could ask, only a copper spade or two, thanking the lady's generosity."

"No, I— *Dilara!*"

"None other," said my old friend, grinning. On her face was the same infectious, impudent grin I'd missed for so long. She fingered my jacket's weave. "Very fine cloth, the honored lady is clearly well-to-do."

I wanted to hug her but dared not. All we could to was exchange a warm touch of the fingertips as she examined my jacket. I said, "I got the sending a few hours ago. I didn't dare hope it would be you. Where have you come from?"

When she answered, I caught the odor of wine on her breath; unusual, because she'd never been a drinker. "Gultekin. I've been there for a while. I've got a public scribe's booth in the Miscellaneous Market. Then a sending came from Nilang, ordering me to join the army at Tanay and stay with it until you found me."

"I'm so glad to see you! I came through Gultekin six days ago. If I'd only known you were there . . ."

"I left some time before that. But you'd better not stay here long or he'll start wondering where you are. What were your orders?"

"Nilang said to tell you if he'd changed his plans, but he hasn't. He's going straight for the throat, straight to Bara. He hopes to draw Garhang's forces on him in dribs and drabs, so he can defeat them as they come. If Garhang hangs back, he'll take the city by storm."

"Good. Nothing for me to do, then, but tag along. If you need to talk to me, find some mending to be done."

"I will. What were you supposed to do if he'd changed things?"

Dilara shrugged. "Go down the Savath to Konghai and leave a message with one of our sisters. Then I would have come back and tried to catch up with the army, and you."

I frowned. "We're a lot closer to Lindu than Tamurin. If Terem changes his plans, the news won't get from us to Mother in time for her to do anything about it. What good is that to her?"

Again the shrug, a reminder that unlike me, Dilara never puzzled over Mother's intentions. She was too single-minded; she followed instructions with perfect fidelity but remained indifferent to the reasons behind them.

"I don't know," she said. "But listen, we've got at least one battle ahead of us. If things go badly, find me. We can probably fight our way out together, if we have to."

I'd tried not to think about being on the losing end of a battle, but she had a point. "I'll bear it in mind. But now I'd better go back where I belong. Keep yourself safe."

"And you. But try to find some mending from time to time."

"I will," I said, and after a surreptitious squeeze of her hand, I hurried away to the castella. Terem never noticed I'd been gone.

Twenty-four

❧

The next morning the main body of the army crossed the Savath. I rode with Terem just behind the three thousand men of the Iron Shield Brigade who had the honor of being the first infantry unit to enter Lindu. Ahead of us lay the conquered lands we had come to free.

I'd heard about the misery of the Durdana under Exile rule, but nothing had prepared me for the reality. Because only Exile settlements were allowed within ten miles of the Savath, these were all we saw at first. They were rough, wattle-built farmsteads with thatched byres and outbuildings, and each had a good-sized horse corral, fenced with thornbushes or palisades. Before the Partition there had been Durdana villages here, but all that remained were green mounds with the stubs of walls here and there. Nor were there any crops waiting to be harvested, for the Exiles had turned all the land over to pasture for their horse herds.

But for many miles we saw no barbarians, for they'd taken their families, horses, and possessions and fled before our advance. Some had burned their farmsteads to deprive us of shelter, or so they thought, although none of us would have willingly entered such stinking places. Sometimes we saw their roughly constructed tower tombs, dark stone fingers poking nastily into the sky, but their only decent buildings were the wooden temples they built to their bizarre single god, who condemned our Beneficent Ones as demons. Terem had forbidden looting or wanton destruction—because it encouraged indiscipline, not out of any regard for Exile sentiments—but whenever we came across one of these temples, he ordered it burned. So the army's path was marked by rising columns of black smoke, and I began to perceive the desolation that lies beneath war's glitter, its brave music, and its rattle of drums. But the desolation was happening to the enemy, so it seemed very good to me.

Later that morning I saw my first Exiles. Our patrols brought in a pair of stragglers, who were hauled before Terem and our interpreters. I'd always had a vague idea of the Exiles' appearance, but the reality took me aback even so. They weren't the giants their fearsome reputation suggested, being of common height, although they were very burly. Their hair was straw yellow, like that of the Daisa, worn in thin braids that swung at neck and cheeks, and their eyes were so dark they were nearly black. They had fair skin, much of it covered by swirling multicolored tattoos. Exile women are not allowed these designs, but any barbarian could tell a man's station by the hues and patterns he wore. I'd never seen anything so alien, and winced at the thought of such creatures enslaving my people.

The men were interrogated but knew nothing useful. I expected them to be executed, but Terem said through the interpreter, "Go and tell your kin that I will spare those of you who leave our soil. The rest I will kill, without exception." Then he pointed east and they fled across the meadows, followed by hoots, jeers, and flung stones. He was very clever in this, for by making them run away he turned the Exiles into cowards and objects of derision, and thus strengthened our soldiers' confidence.

In early afternoon we reached territory where Durdana were al-

lowed to live, and then I wished that we'd burned everything the
Exiles had built, not just the temples. After the conquest, their
Kings had given estates to all their soldiers, so that even the low-
est cavalry trooper had a good acreage, tilled for him by the local
Durdana, who became his serfs. Exile nobles got bigger estates,
which included villages and towns, and many of the Durdana citizens were forced into serfdom, along with the farmers who had already been on the land. This ruined the trade of all but the largest
cities, and even these decreased in size by more than half. In the
cities, Exile officers took over the best residences and the most
profitable businesses, and disposed of the former owners as they
pleased.

The Exile word for Durdana was *fath*, which could mean either
"farmer" or "worm." This was how they saw us: as worms squirm-
ing in the mud, but they treated worms less harshly. During the
early years after the Partition, many Durdana in the subjugated
lands killed themselves to escape their misery; to halt this loss of
their serfs, the Exiles decreed that the suicide's immediate family
must all die by slow disembowelment. Many others tried to escape
to the free lands, whereupon the Exiles applied the disembowelment penalty not only to the fugitive's parents, spouse, and children but also to his relatives of the first and second degree. Given
our tradition of filial loyalty, this slowed the escapes to a trickle.

I cannot begin to describe all the misery I saw between the Savath River and the walls of Bara, so I shall let the city of Sila stand
for all. The main column of the army marched around it, but
Terem and I and the Iron Shield Brigade went through by way of
the central street.

The Exiles had allowed only a few cities in the conquered lands
to keep their walls, and those of Sila lay in broken heaps where the
barbarians had pulled them down. Where the main gate once
stood was a wide gallows, with a dozen bodies hanging by the
heels; all had been flayed and gutted. Within the town, pavements
had disappeared beneath a century of filth, the arcades of the mu-
nicipal market were ruinous, and the roofs of the public baths had

fallen in. From the shrines of the Beneficent Ones, the images were long gone, and the shrine to the Lord of Starlight was now the garrison's stables. A handful of the best old residences had escaped only because the local Exile lords lived in them. Every other building, be it of stone, wood, or brick, was decayed to the point of collapse.

And the inhabitants? The Exile overlords and their households had decamped, no doubt expecting to return once Garhang had disposed of us. As for our fellow Durdana, I'd expected them to flood into the streets, shouting in rapture at their deliverance, but they didn't. Instead, they crept from rotting doorways and stood blinking at us, like ragged prisoners too long from the sun. All looked wasted and drawn. Not one had ever had enough to eat, and through the rents in their rags I saw, on many, the marks of whips.

A few raised tentative cheers, but these were not taken up by the others. "What's the matter with them?" I asked Terem, who looked grim.

"They don't believe it yet," he said. "When they do, they'll kill any Exile they can lay hands on. And they'll look for Durdana traitors who worked for the overlords. I'd rather fall into a fire than be one of those."

A temple to the Exile god stood on the central square. We didn't burn it because the rest of the city might take fire—which might have been the best thing to do with it—but Terem ordered the pottery image taken out and smashed. I'd never seen one before. It was a nasty combination of man and some kind of bird, glazed a poisonous green. A crowd had gathered in the square by then, and when the hammers came down on the image the townspeople finally awakened and spoke—not with a cheer but with a snarl. I'd never heard anything like it, and it chilled my blood: a sound of fury and hatred, swelling with every stroke of the hammer.

When the hammers fell silent, so did the mob, and Terem spoke.

"People of Durdane! Brothers and sisters! I am Terem Rathai, Sun Lord of Bethiya, and here with me is the Army of the East. For a hundred years the Exiles have enslaved and oppressed you, but the justice of Durdane is now upon them, and you are free. We are the doom of the barbarians, and I swear to you by the Beneficent Ones, and by the Lord of the Dead, that I will not rest until the last invader is driven from the sacred earth of Durdane."

I watched them as he spoke, and I saw the light of faith awaken in their faces. It was a kind of sorcery he had, to banish doubt and fear by his mere presence, and those who heard him speak of our future believed in it utterly, because he believed so utterly in it himself.

And his words moved me as well, for as I listened to them I thought: *Isn't this what we truly need? Someone to lead us out of this wretched world of Despotates and Kingdoms, someone to restore to us our stolen inheritance?*

Where these musings might have led me I don't know, for the crowd roared as he ended his speech, and somebody screamed about Exile riches. Then the mob was streaming out of the square toward the nobles' quarter.

"Perhaps, for once, they'll find enough to fill their bellies," Terem said. And then to his second in command, General Ajirian: "That's all here, get the men moving."

So we left Sila and marched on toward Bara. During the next several days there were more scenes like that, but to describe one is to have described all. Suffice it to say that by the time we were a day from Garhang's capital, we'd acquired another thousand camp followers from Lindu, mostly young men, and also a few young women, eager for revenge and loot. Thousands of others, released from bondage but unwilling to believe that the Exiles wouldn't come back, were streaming west toward the Savath. The army was moving so fast in the other direction that I hardly had a chance to speak to Dilara. Twice I managed to slip away and find her, but there were too many people around for us to talk much.

By the time we were a day from Bara, Terem was becoming annoyed. Garhang had not offered battle, thus depriving us of the chance to defeat him a slice at a time. Terem was sure the King was in his capital, though, and a captured enemy officer confirmed this. He also boasted that no matter how enormous our host, Garhang's horsemen would finish us off in a day. Terem sent the man back to Garhang with a message: If all Exiles left Bara by the following evening, they could do so unmolested; if they remained, he would give them no quarter. The answer, predictably, was silence.

Terem next decided on a stratagem. The Army of the East had trained in night marches, and there was a full moon, so we set out for Bara after dusk, and were very near it by the middle of the night watch. Then we rested until daybreak, whereupon we made our final approach to the city. This took Garhang by surprise, and he didn't get his men into the field until we were less than two miles from Bara's walls.

I could easily make out the city's ramparts across the plain that lay at the bottom of a large oval valley. The heights around the valley were thickly forested, and Terem sent out cavalry patrols to make sure that no enemy lurked in ambush. The rest of us marched in from the northwest, and even now I wonder what Garhang and his men thought when they saw us pouring down upon them: our infantry deploying into massed squares of pikes and crossbowmen, with hordes of cavalry trotting on the wings. I like to think they felt a cold premonition, for Garhang had sent half his forces east to watch Ardavan, and we outnumbered them three to one. However, they'd beaten us at worse odds in the old days, when they fought under Pakur One-Eyed, so they probably thought they still could.

But despite their confidence, they weren't the warriors their great-grandfathers had been. Their nobles had become soft, and half the warriors they commanded were no longer cavalry. Their ancestors of those had so looted and ruined their stolen estates that their descendants couldn't afford the expense of horses and harness and went to war on foot. Yet even in their decline, no Despotate army would have been a match for them. Only the Army of the East was their equal, or so Terem believed and the rest of us hoped.

A ruined stone barn stood on a knoll near the center of our infantry line, and we established our headquarters in the grass-grown barnyard. Dispatch riders came and went; Terem and his officers issued orders. It takes time to put a large army into battle formation, and the sun was well up before all the brigades were in place, with the baggage train and the camp followers a quarter mile behind the lines. It was a cool bright day, the air smelling of autumn leaves and dry grass, with a breeze from the northwest; above the helmets of Terem and his officers the Rose Standard glittered in the sunlight. Half a mile to our front, Garhang had settled his troops into their ranks. His line was as long as ours but thinner. And we had a lot more horsemen.

At length Terem left his officers and came over to me. "If anything goes wrong," he said, "stay with Captain Sholaj. I've ordered him to get you out of here if he has to."

I glanced toward the captain, a long-jawed young man who was watching the Exile lines with blood in his eye. "I'll be all right by myself, Terem. It's not fair to make him my nursemaid."

"He'll follow orders, like everyone else, and so will you. Do as he says until I come back."

This wasn't the time or place to argue, so I said, "All right."

"Now we start," he said. "Wish us luck. You'll be able to see most of it from up here."

He returned to the standards and gave an order. Soon a signal horn blared, and the brigade signalers repeated the notes along the battle line. Pike heads glittered. The horns blared again and our line began to move.

Few events are as confusing as a big battle, although historians talk of them as if they were as easy to follow as a game of Twelve Lines. But nobody involved in one, including the commanders, can tell much about what's going on once the fighting starts. As for me,

I've never been much interested in how a battle worked, only in who held the field at the end of it.

A light drizzle had fallen before dawn, just enough to lay the dust that can obscure a battlefield, so I had a fine view. The fighting began as Garhang, in foolish overconfidence, ordered his infantry to charge. His foot soldiers quickly became disorganized, and our crossbowmen maneuvered out of their protecting pike squares and felled hundreds of them. When the Exile cavalry tried to break our squares, they met a steel thicket of pikes, and the crossbows shot down their mounts by the score. And then, at the moment of their greatest disorder, our horsemen charged their wavering ranks and cut them down like grain; the remnants fled in terror for the shelter of the city. Unsupported and outflanked, with our cavalry in their rear, the enemy foot was lost; perhaps one in five reached Bara's gates and safety.

Garhang's army had collapsed so quickly that the sun seemed barely to have climbed in the sky. Our joy and exhilaration can scarcely be imagined; even Dirayr, the most dour and crusty of Terem's staff, was jumping up and down in excitement. Never before had Durdana soldiers destroyed the army of an Exile King. We knew now that the conquerors could be conquered.

But our elation lasted only a little while. We saw a rider come racing toward us along the valley, and behind him, up on the valley's forested brim, there was a small clot of cavalry. I thought at first that it was one of our patrols. But as I watched, the horsemen turned and vanished into the woods.

Terem and his officers stopped talking. In growing apprehension, we watched the lone rider approach. Soon he was a bowshot from our knoll, his horse at full stretch, sweat gleaming on its flanks. He had lost his helmet, and when he was fifty yards away I saw blood on his armor; his shield arm dangled uselessly.

He reached us and dragged his exhausted mount to a halt. Captain Sholaj grabbed the horse's reins, and the young trooper leaned over his saddlebow, breathing in great gulps and dripping blood from a slash along his jaw.

"What is it?" Terem asked, perfectly unruffled.

"Exiles," the trooper gasped. "Coming from the south, through the woods. Thousands of them, foot and horse. They had screening riders. Killed everybody but me."

"What standards? Garhang's?"

"No, lord." He swayed and almost fell from the saddle. "Their shields had the red scorpion."

A silence. Terem's face became very thoughtful and his eyes narrowed. Finally he said, "It's Ardavan, then. Very well, trooper, you've done fine work. Go to the baggage train and have your wounds seen to."

"Yes, lord." The young man pulled his wheezing mount around and trotted away.

"Now we have some busy hours at hand," Terem said, sounding almost jaunty. He began to issue a stream of orders, messenger after messenger galloping away to deliver them. I didn't pay much attention, because I was watching the south rim of the valley. After a short interval the horsemen reappeared from the trees. More followed. And then, like waves breaking over a sea wall, came Ardavan's Exile battalions.

There seemed no end to them. Hordes of infantry and horse moved steadily down the slope, and still they came. I hadn't imagined, when they first appeared, that we might be outnumbered, but after a while I began to worry. Terem seemed unperturbed; he'd sent off all his orders now and watched intently as our Army of the East turned to meet its new foe.

In that hour, had it not been for the relentless training of our men, we would have been staring into the maw of disaster. But when Garhang's army broke, our infantry squares had remained in place instead of dissolving into a raggle-taggle pursuit of the vanquished. Thus our line was intact, and, once it turned south, was capable of facing the enemy. Our cavalry was in disarray, unfortunately, but the troop commanders had seen what was approaching us. They had been trained to use their heads and they did so; I could see hurrying bands of horsemen re-forming into larger masses and streaming toward their positions on the wings.

But we would still need all the luck we could get. Ardavan's force had completely emerged from the woodland now, and it was at least as numerous as ours. It proceeded remorselessly down the valley toward us, rank on rank, column on column, with clouds of horsemen roiling excitedly around it. The barbarians' drums thumped and thudded, and with them came a droning bray like that of some weird and furious ghost. It was the wail of Exile war pipes, so alien that I shuddered to hear them.

It crossed my mind then that we might lose. I wasn't exactly frightened at this prospect, but I certainly felt very apprehensive. I wondered if Terem and I would get away if the battle went against us and what would become of Dilara.

And then I thought: *How did Ardavan happen to be here?*

Cold suspicion invaded me. Was this unexpected collision not chance at all, but ambush? Had Ardavan known that Terem was marching on Bara? And if he did, *who told him?*

Not Mother, I thought, surely not Mother. Surely she would not have ordered Nilang to betray Terem's intentions to Ardavan, so that he might trap and destroy us here. She might hate Terem, but it was unthinkable that any Durdana ruler would help an Exile King. What must have happened, I told myself, was that Ardavan had decided not to attack Garhang next spring, as Terem had expected, but to strike at him before winter's onset. So now here he was at Bara, and so were we.

I watched the gap between the battle lines diminish. When it was down to a quarter mile, Terem turned to me and said, "I'm going to see to the cavalry reserve. Get on your horse, be sure you stay with Captain Sholaj, and do what he tells you."

He took me by the shoulders and kissed me gently. And suddenly I realized that this might be the last time I'd ever touch him, and that he might die on the bloody, torn earth of the battlefield, and instantly I was stricken by such fear that I could scarcely breathe. It shocked me to my marrow. Did it mean I *loved* him?

It was a question I did not want to answer or even think about. All I could do was whisper weakly, "Come back safe, Terem."

He nodded and released me. We mounted our horses and he reminded Sholaj that he was to be my escort, an order the young officer acknowledged with poorly concealed reluctance. Then Terem and his bodyguard, with several dispatch riders and the trooper bearing the Rose Standard, rode down to the reserve cavalry positioned behind our right wing. The rest of the staff and I waited, listening to the howl of the enemy pipes and watching the Exiles advance.

They reached us, and it began.

I'd imagined, because of the speed with which we'd defeated Garhang, that all battles were over swiftly and that either Ardavan or Terem would be the victor before the sun reached its zenith. But time passed, the fighting went on and on, and then went on some more. Crossbow bolts flew in shoals, pike squares clashed with Exile battalions and drew bloodily back; waves of horsemen collided, milled about, and separated. Signal horns boomed; dispatch riders raced up and down. The din was tremendous: metal crashing on metal, the shouts and roars and screams of two hundred thousand men. Over the cacophony I called to Sholaj, "How long can this go on?"

"Until they break—or we do," he said grimly. General Dirayr had ridden off to see to the left wing, and only six of us remained on the knoll. Terem and the imperial roses were still with the cavalry reserve; I could see the sunlight splintering on the gold.

Ardavan had held back a mass of horsemen, and now he unleashed it against our right wing. What he was intending, I'm not sure. But he'd probably noted our mounted reserve there and reckoned that his cavalry could beat ours without working up a sweat, and that once he'd defeated our reserve he could roll up our infantry line as he pleased. So out of the afternoon sunlight came a vast black wedge of horses and warriors, bearing down on our line's extreme right. It swept aside the tired Durdana riders and poured around the end of the infantry wing, heading straight for Terem and the Rose Standard.

Horns brayed. The standard surged forward, Terem beneath it, and our reserves made the trot, then a canter, then thundered into a gallop. The enemy redoubled their pace and the two huge masses slammed into each other like battering rams. My hands clenched painfully on my mount's reins as I waited for disaster to befall us. No Durdana cavalry had ever beaten Exile horsemen in an even match.

Our world hung in the balance in those instants. I believe now that we would have lost the Battle of Bara and all else along with it, if Terem hadn't been there. His men would not give in while he fought stirrup to stirrup with them, and, little by little, they held the Exiles and then began to force them back. The black mass surged and swirled, and suddenly I saw Exile riders at the far edge detach themselves and ride pell-mell for their own lines. Other joined them and then others, and suddenly the whole Exile cavalry force was in flight, the enemy riding for their lives with ours cutting them down as they fled, leaving score upon score of hacked and skewered bodies in their wake. I held my breath, terrified that our men would lose their heads and pursue the Exiles right into their own lines. But Terem halted them in time and pulled them back, still in good order, to re-form on our right wing.

He had saved us for the moment, but still the bloody day went on. I'd never seen a truly savage battle, but even my inexperienced eye could tell that both sides were suffering horribly. Dead and wounded sprawled in windrows between our pike squares and the enemy's triple line; slaughtered or disabled horses lay everywhere, others galloped riderless in terror, and those still bearing riders were so exhausted they could barely trot. But it could not go on forever. By mid-afternoon we and the Exiles had fought each other to a standstill.

What happened next was a most curious thing to see, and almost unknown in the annals of war. The fighting slowly died away, the lines edged apart, and men too exhausted to raise their weapons leaned on their comrades and on their pike shafts, and glowered at the enemy. The clang of iron on iron slowly fell away, to leave only that ghastly song of a battle's aftermath, the shrieks and moans of the mutilated.

Ardavan was no fool. He recognized that his men couldn't fight any longer and that he risked losing everything if he persisted. So did Terem, and soon after the two armies drew apart, an Exile horseman under a blue flag of parley rode toward our lines. Terem sent a herald to meet him. Then messages went back and forth for a considerable time, but by late afternoon we and the Exiles had agreed on a truce until the following dawn. Both sides collected their wounded, pulled back to opposite ends of the valley, and made camp.

But Terem knew the extent of our casualties, and as the dusk thickened he called his brigadiers and senior officers to his tent. Even now I can see him in the rusty firelight, still in half armor, his hair dark with dust and sweat, telling his men they had won.

It sounded true enough as he told it, and also true in itself, I think. We had met the best leader the Exiles had found in a century, engaged him at even numbers, and fought him to a standstill. We had proven that the Army of the East could hold against the best the Exiles could throw at it. Even more important, we had shown that Durdana cavalry could defeat Exile horsemen. Next time, Terem said, we would drive the enemy wailing from the field.

But, he went on, while the enemy had lost many men, so had we. To fight the next day was to risk throwing away our victory, for King Garhang still held Bara, and, given that we'd made war on him, he was very likely to give shelter and support to Ardavan. Moreover, the campaigning season was near its end, and when the rains began we must not be caught in hostile country with no city as a base. So, he concluded, we must be content with this first triumph, and withdraw across the Savath. In the spring we would return with even greater forces, and finish Ardavan for good.

It was a mark of his leadership that he then asked for their opinions. Nobody was eager to withdraw, since we'd marched with every hope of taking Bara and all Lindu, but we invited disaster if we remained in the field. A few cavalrymen—always the most pugnacious of soldiers—said they would gladly fight in the morning, but the consensus was against them. So Terem said we would return to the Savath, and that we would start out that very night.

Few armies could have managed such an orderly retreat, in darkness, after a day of furious combat and a night march before that. The Army of the East did it, which was at least as much of a victory as standing up to Ardavan. We lit hundreds of campfires to make the Exiles think we'd settled in, and then, with infinite labor and weariness, got under way.

We took our less wounded with us in the baggage train, but hundreds were too badly hurt to be moved. These begged to be spared the torments that the Exiles would inflict on them, and we did what we could. I remember one in particular, a young pikeman with a hideous belly wound, who held a comrade's hand as a second friend slid a merciful knife into his heart. There were too many such scenes by far, but there was no help for it.

We were lucky that the moon had waned only a little as our vanguard set out for the Savath. By dawn we were miles from Bara, and when Ardavan looked for us that morning, he found only trampled ground and smoking campfires. Our escape was a victory of sorts, but it was far from the triumph we'd envisioned when we marched out of Tanay, and in the following days I saw the other side of war. We were not a defeated army, cut to ribbons by the enemy and fleeing for our lives, but it was bad enough even so. The wounded slowed us down and many died, to be discarded like rubbish beside the road, with only the briefest of rituals to lay their ghosts. Some camp followers died of exhaustion, or straggled away and were never seen again. And on the third day, to add to our miseries, it began to rain.

Two things saved us from Ardavan. First, we'd hurt his army very badly, and his cavalry was in no condition for a serious pursuit. They did harass us for the first few days, but our horsemen were still their equal and, with their newly minted confidence, drove the enemy off each time.

Second, Ardavan was busy dealing with Garhang. He didn't want to leave an unsubdued Bara in his rear while he chased us, so he spent his remaining energy in the capture of that city and let us get away, damaged and bloody, but far from defeated. By the time he'd taken Bara and cut off Garhang's head, it was too late to catch us.

Still, Terem's grand design of seizing and holding Lindu had failed, which was a bitter disappointment. Nevertheless, he thought, as did everyone else in the army (including me, despite my moment of suspicion) that Ardavan's sudden appearance at Bara was mere unlucky chance. But we were wrong. What had happened was this.

Terem had indeed befuddled Garhang with hopes of a Bethiyan alliance. Consequently the king had sent half his forces to guard his eastern frontier with Ardavan, who was lurking just beyond it with a considerable army. But the general whom Garhang had put over these troops had heard rumors of the alliance and didn't like them, and on his arrival he promptly transferred his allegiance, and that of his men, to Ardavan.

And it was exactly then, only twenty days after I told Nilang about the planned invasion of Lindu, that Ardavan received word of Terem's intentions. That word had come from me by way of Nilang; my suspicion that this might have happened, but which I had so swiftly discarded as unthinkable, had been correct.

But it is no wonder, really, that I did discard the idea. It seemed so unreasonable—what purpose of Mother's would be served, if her plots only replaced Terem's tyranny with that of the Exiles? I might have accepted the truth, if I'd known how much further her plans went, but who could have imagined their reach? Certainly not I, being as much in her grip as I was.

As for Ardavan, his contempt for all Durdana was so great that he could not see Mother as a serious threat, and so did not suspect her ultimate intentions toward him. He was, however, glad enough of the information she'd been sending him since he conquered Jouhar. He didn't trust her, but he'd acted on the news of Terem's advance anyway, since it was exactly what he wanted to hear. It put him in a position to surprise and crush the Army of the East, take Lindu from Garhang, and invade a badly weakened Bethiya in the spring. And so he marched west to Bara, where Terem gave him a drubbing he did not expect.

We were eight days reaching the bridge at Bittersweet. Thousands of Durdana who lived along our line of march followed us west, terrified of the vengeance of the returning Exiles. Many died of cold and hunger on the way, for with the added mouths we were very short of supplies. As we went, I discreetly searched for Dilara, but in the disorder of the retreat I didn't find her until four days had passed. She looked weary but undaunted. I gave her some bread; she soaked it in a little wine she had and ate it hungrily. Being deft at sewing up wounds, she'd been helping with the injured. But there was no time to talk, and I didn't see her again until the night we crossed the Savath.

"I'll be in Tanay while you are," she told me then, her face a white blur in the gloom. "Come to the Serpentine Market and find me there if you have news."

"I have some now," I said. "He's going to put eight brigades into winter quarters in Tanay, and bring them up to strength by taking men from the other ten. Then he's sending the ten depleted units to Gultekin for reinforcement over the winter. Then we're going back to Kurjain, where he intends to raise more men, enough for four more infantry brigades and one of cavalry."

"I'll send it on." She secretively touched my hand. "Take care. I wouldn't want to lose you."

"Nor I you," I said. "When will I see you again?"

"I don't know," she answered, "but you will."

Twenty-five

❧

Terem and I returned to Kurjain on 15 Lesser Frost, two hands after the campaigning season ended. The Chancellery had put it about that the invasion of Lindu was a punitive expedition, intended to warn the Exiles that we Durdana were no longer to be taken lightly. The original intent of freeing Lindu was quietly set aside, and the Battle of Bara was described as a great victory. All Kurjain turned out to welcome us home and you'd have thought, from the celebrations, that we'd slaughtered Ardavan's troops to the last man. But the truth was that Ardavan now ruled in Lindu, with the bulk of his army in winter quarters there. Terem's most dangerous adversary now sat on the east bank of the Savath—the very situation he had wanted to avoid.

I settled into the Reed Pavilion again, with occasional forays to my villa. I apologized to the Chancellor for vanishing as I had, but he appeared to be amused at my audacity and to consider my escapade a sign of my devotion to Terem.

The truth of what I felt for him was far more complicated. My fear for his life at Bara had been real enough, and such feelings had not arisen merely because I so willingly shared his bed, as Mother had suggested they might. They'd also grown because we had so many things in common. Some were small, of course: a taste for sticky almond pastries, for the bird paintings of Master Sudai, and for silly popular comedies about mistaken identities.

But others were not so minor. Terem didn't think great magnates should be allowed to subvert the laws for their own gain, and neither did I. He didn't think people should go hungry and ragged while their Despots gorged themselves on delicacies and dressed in gossamin, and neither did I. And he thought it reprehensible that we Durdana should be as weak and divided as we were. To remedy this, he wanted our empire back, and I was no longer perfectly convinced that this would be the disaster Mother had forecast.

Such speculations defied everything I'd been taught, but they wouldn't go away. Unhappily, I had nobody to talk to about them, and often wished Dilara were nearby. Yet I knew that even if she were, I could never speak to her about my doubts, for she would certainly not share them.

And with this, I became even more acutely aware of how much I had changed since I arrived in Kurjain. I had begun to care for Terem; I had begun to imagine a world free of Exiles, Despots, wars, and injustice; and now I was beginning to be wary of my closest friend.

On many nights now, I slept badly. And in my worst moments, in the hours before the tolling of the dawn watch bell, I acknowledged that Mother intended to kill Terem someday and that I could probably not prevent it. I dealt with this in the only way I could, by telling myself that it was still too far off to worry about. But it was always there, like one of Nilang's wraiths trembling at the edge of vision.

A few days after we got home, Terem told me that the Despot of Brind had sent him a secret proposal. It so happened that the pay of Yazar's army was severely in arrears, and his men were simmering with mutiny. Unfortunately, Yazar had run out of people to lend him money, and he dared not raise taxes further.

Moreover, he noted in his letter, his cousins were of an insubordinate nature and might use the army's discontent to Yazar's great disadvantage. He suggested, therefore, that if Terem would supply money to pay his grumbling troops, he would, in return, name Terem as his heir, both to his estates and to the dais of Brind itself. But until the arrangement was concluded, secrecy was of the essence.

The offer was very attractive, and Terem told me he intended to continue the negotiations. So the next morning, after he left for work, I went to the villa, then to the Round, and then to Nilang.

I had to wait in the garden until she finished with a legitimate client. When the man left, she admitted me to her summoning room, a whitewashed cubicle with Taweret signs painted on the walls. I sat on the stool opposite hers, and as usual she asked, "No one dogs you?"

"No. I'm never followed now."

"He may be waiting for you to grow careless."

"I'm never careless," I said, because I wasn't.

"What news have you brought for the one we serve?"

I told her about Yazar and his secret offer. Nilang looked distant for a few moments, as if digesting its implications. I waited.

Her brilliant blue eyes suddenly focused on me and she said, "You're troubled by something. What?"

I stared at her dumbly, fumbling for an answer. What had she perceived in my face? Or could she actually see into my mind?

I found my tongue, and with an expression of demure embarrassment I said, "Mistress, he keeps me awake much of the night with his erotic appetites. I'm tired, that's all."

Nilang's gaze didn't waver. "I said troubled, not tired. What is it?"

I cast about frantically. "I have bad dreams. From Bara. It was . . . bloody. And we had to kill so many of our wounded, to keep them from the Exiles."

"Ah. Blood and death trouble you, do they?"

"Sometimes. Because there was so much of it." In fact I'd never dreamed about the battle.

"For someone of your training, this seems peculiar. You've killed."

"Yes, but that seemed different." I felt as if I were trying to clamber out of a sand pit, but my struggles only dug it deeper.

Nilang appeared to study the Taweret signs she'd applied to the walls. I'd never been sure if the polychrome patterns were writing or images; perhaps they were both. But when I saw them from the corner of my eye they always seemed to writhe a little, and I never looked at them too closely.

"Proximity to another person," she said softly, "can sometimes bend one's convictions—even if these convictions are strongly held—toward that other person's point of view. Such influences become all the more powerful if one senses an affinity with that individual."

I felt a spasm of fright. Did she suspect my growing uncertainty, or was this merely a general warning? "My convictions are unshaken, mistress. But I will take your words to heart and redouble my guard against improper influences."

Her gaze was still on the wall, but I knew she was observing me. "I wonder if they are as unshaken as you would have me believe. Or as you would have yourself believe."

How could she suspect anything? These must be merely probes, as if she searched for signs of infection in a wound.

"I can only repeat what I've said," I told her. "My convictions are not influenced by his."

She folded her arms and slid her narrow hands into her sleeves. Then she said, "Mothers and daughters arise in several ways. There is the natural way, by which we all enter the world. There is the merciful way, by which a woman cares for the girl of a deceased relative. There is the charitable way, by which foundlings are brought under a mother's care, although there is no conjunction of bloodline."

She paused, leaving me not only uneasy but mystified. "Yes, mistress," I murmured.

"And then," she said, "there are the other ways. I have my daughters, too, Lale. You've met them."

Her gaze slid to mine and held it. I felt the blood drain from my face. This was a warning, and no doubt about it. And in that moment my understanding of my plight crystallized, as swiftly and icily as frost flowers bloom on a winter window.

I was trapped. I had been trapped from the moment I set foot in Three Springs, although only now did I understand the unseen manacles that bound me: my love for Mother, my filial obligation to her, and my duty to my sisters, all stronger than iron links could ever be. But there were other fetters, too: my terror of the wraiths, my fear of Nilang's sinister powers, my dread that the Chancellor would discover me and that I would die the foul death of a traitor. I was chained hand, foot, and neck.

Even so, I thought: *What if I told Terem what I really am? What if I confessed everything?*

Clammy sweat broke out all over me. Adrine's shrieks rang again in my ears as the wraiths made her tear at her flesh. She said they'd begun to go for her eyes. What would it be like, to lose control of my hands, to feel my fingernails ripping at my eyelids, thumbs digging into the sockets, screaming at myself to stop? Bile rose in my throat and I choked it back, barely.

And the wraiths weren't all that awaited me if I confessed. For I was far more a traitor than poor Tsusane had ever been; for me there would be no exile. If the wraiths didn't finish me off, I would die by slicing, unless my confession moved Terem to commute it to an easier end. But my treachery was so profound and complete that perhaps he would not.

As for running away and keeping silent about Mother's secrets,

I remembered what Tossi had told me at Three Springs: Nilang and my erstwhile sisters would hunt me down, and I'd be watching my back for the rest of my life, which would probably be short.

Perhaps I could try to help Terem covertly, by giving Nilang false or inadequate information, but I had no confidence that I could deceive her for long. And when she uncovered my deceit, what would she do to me? What sorcerous punishments could she inflict? The thing that had almost devoured me in the Quiet World, could she give me to *that*?

I didn't want to go into the Quiet World, either by death or sorcery. I had so much: wealth, fame, youth, a measure of power. I wanted to stay alive to enjoy it for as long as I could. But the only hope of that was in perfect, unstinting loyalty to Mother. Every other road led to death, or worse.

All this went through my mind in the space of a few heartbeats. Then, with a dry mouth, I croaked, "Lady mistress, my loyalty is untainted."

She pursed her lips a little as she scrutinized me. Then she said, "There is news from Chiran. The Despotana has adopted a daughter."

I was so relieved at the change of subject that I hardly wondered why Nilang thought this worthy of mention. I said, "The girl is very fortunate. I was destitute and abandoned once, and I know how much better the child's life will now be."

"This is not that kind of adoption. The girl is of the Laloi bloodline. She is no waif."

I said, "Oh." I knew of the Laloi. They were an old, wealthy Tamurin family with roots going back to the empire, in whose magistracies they had been prominent.

"Her name is Ashken," Nilang continued. "The Despotana has made the girl her heir and has also taken her into the Seval bloodline. Ashken Seval, as she now is, will rule Tamurin on the Despotana's death. This news will be in Kurjain soon. The Despotana wished you apprised of it beforehand, as a courtesy."

Incoherent thoughts swirled through my brain. Of course Mother wouldn't live forever; she needed an heir. I'd never given the matter much attention, for it seemed to have little to do with me. Yet now I felt a sharp twinge of jealousy. It wasn't because I'd ever dreamed of being Mother's heir; that could never happen. No, it was because Mother had given some other girl her bloodline name. Now the girl was a Seval, while I was just a Navari. It was silly to feel this way, and I was lucky to have a family name at all. But Mother's act stung my heart nonetheless, though my mind understood the need for it.

"I will write and tell the Despotana how pleased I am for her," I said.

"Do so, but wait until someone at the palace tells you it's happened. Now, is there anything else for our beloved mistress?"

Something peculiar in the way she said *beloved mistress*, and the fact that that she'd never spoken of Mother that way before, gave me pause. There was a hint in the tone of something sardonic, almost of contempt. Yet I wasn't sure I'd really heard it, or if I had, what Nilang meant by it.

But then, if she did suspect that I might contemplate treachery, as I indeed had with my thoughts of confessing all to Terem, would she not try me in just this way? Was her tone a provocation, a test to see if I might respond to hints of disloyalty on her part, and thereby condemn myself? Or was it something else?

I wasn't about to be drawn into whatever lethal games she might be playing. So I merely said, "No, there's nothing."

"Go, then."

I did, and gladly. On the way home, I thought about Terem, the wraiths, and about Mother having a new daughter and a real heir. For no clear reason I became so frightened I started to tremble and didn't stop until after I reached my villa. Usually I felt very snug and secure under its roof, but hours passed before the fear left me, and even then I kept wondering how much Nilang suspected of my disloyal thoughts.

৯৬

Lesser Frost ended. With its end came the New Year's Festival of the five Solstice Days, with lavish celebrations both in the palace and in the city. I made myself appear to enjoy them, but my enjoyment was tainted. I slept badly and twice dreamed of Adrine's death, except that I was Adrine. I woke sweating and shivering and Terem worried that I was sickening with a chill. He was especially concerned because that was how Merihan's fatal illness had begun, so I had to endure the attentions of one of the palace physicians. The woman found nothing wrong with me but asked if I had any signs of quickening. Terem and I had been sleeping together for three months now, so she thought it about time, apparently. I told her I did not, nor did I tell her about the precautions I took against conceiving a child, just as I hadn't told Terem. I saw less of him now, as he was so occupied with preparations for the war that was to begin in the spring, and I occupied myself with reading and visiting friends.

The month of Snow began. Thin sheets of ice, smooth as fine glass, formed at the margins of Reed Pavilion's pond. Terem and I moved to the winter bedchamber and slept on the tiled stove. In the other rooms braziers glowed, and in my villa the servant girls wore leggings under their skirts. The month lived up to its name as snow fell twice, but as usual in Kurjain the blanket was only a finger's thickness and melted by late afternoon. Still, it clung lacily to the trees and was very beautiful while it lasted.

Then, just after the turn of the month, Mother sent word, through Nilang, that she was especially happy with me. This, she indicated, was because she could not allow Terem to inherit Yazar's realm and riches, and my timely warning of the secret negotiations had given her time to forestall it. I was still enough her creature to be pleased by such congratulations, when I might more justly have tied iron weights to my legs, and thrown myself into the nearest canal. But I had no idea, yet, of what I had done.

In early Snow, word came to the Chancellery that Ardavan had concluded an alliance with the three remaining Exile Kings of Suarai, Ishban, and Mirsing. This information was a month old when we got it, and, disturbingly, it also suggested that the three monarchs would provide Ardavan with troops, no doubt in the hope that this might secure their shaky thrones. But unsettling as the report was, it was utterly overshadowed for me by the news from Istana.

This first reached Kurjain around 13 Snow, a day of sleet and freezing fog. But it didn't come in all at once, and several days passed before the details of the revolt against Yazar became common knowledge. They were horrible, but for me, the worst horror of all came from Nilang.

I'd felt a mounting dread as the stories trickled into Kurjain, and finally I slipped away from Jade Lagoon to find her. I knew I didn't look at all well, but she made no comment upon it, merely waited for me to speak.

"What happened?" I asked her. "What did she do?"

Her thin black eyebrows rose. "What would you expect? She informed Yazar's cousins that he intended to bequeath the Despotate to the Sun Lord. They acted."

Nausea surged in my belly. "But I thought . . . Mother has so much money. I thought she'd give Yazar what he needed, so he wouldn't have to go to Terem at all."

"Why would she pay for a result that others will give her for nothing?"

I could barely speak. "So it was me—"

"Yes. You have given her a great victory over the Sun Lord."

My next words were like lye in my mouth, but I uttered them because I had to. "I'm glad. Glad that I served her so well."

"Good," Nilang said. "But I see that you are indisposed. Go home."

I did, and before very long I knew the full, hideous story.

Warned by Mother, Yazar's cousins rebelled before he could conclude his arrangements with Terem. Many of the Despot's unpaid soldiers joined the revolt, but others remained loyal, and fighting broke out in Istana. Soon the people of the city's poor quarters, who had felt the grip of Yazar's tax gatherers most bitterly, boiled out of their warrens and added their fury to that of the rebels. Other troops marched in from garrisons elsewhere, some declaring for Yazar, some against him. A fire started in an oil storehouse by the canal docks, and in the turmoil no one tried to extinguish it. The flames spread rapidly, and by evening almost all Istana was alight, except for Yazar's lovely palace and the prefecture, where Master Luasin and both the theater companies were in residence.

Then Yazar was killed and his last loyal troops gave way, and all that night the mob and the rebels sacked both palace and prefecture. In their fury at Yazar's luxurious ways, they slaughtered every person they caught within the walls, then burned everything to the ground. None of the Younger Company, and only a few of the Elder, escaped the butchery. Master Luasin was not among them. Nor was Perin, my sweet beautiful Perin, my friend. I never found out exactly how she died, but enough stories reached Kurjain for me to know that she'd had no easy death.

When I heard this, I went to my villa on Cloud Mirror Canal and walked its rooms like a weeping ghost. Terem thought it was because my friends were dead. He was right, but what he did not know was that they were dead because I'd killed them.

I didn't sleep for days, nor did I eat; food sickened me. I went nowhere near Nilang, for I feared that she would look past my grief and perceive the remorse beneath it, and the reason for the remorse. Terem wanted me to return to Jade Lagoon Palace but I refused, knowing I couldn't go near him in this state; I didn't know what my grief might cause me to blurt to him. So I remained alone with my pain, in the beautiful villa I had purchased with my iniquities.

I pulled myself together finally. I could do nothing else; to go on as I was would invite more questions than I could afford to answer. Seven days after I had immured myself at Cloud Mirror Canal, I returned to the palace, pale and weary, uncertain what to do next.

I was certain of one thing, however: I should do nothing without plenty of forethought. To act rashly, given the web in which I was ensnared, was to risk disaster. But if I waited . . . one never knew what might turn up. This gave me a little hope, and pretty soon I managed to seem like my old self again, if somewhat subdued. Terem was much relieved, and I felt that in a few more days I could brave Nilang's presence. But sooner or later, I told myself, I'd find some way out of my predicament. I had always been good at getting out of things.

That was at the end of Snow. On 2 Greater Frost, I went with Terem to the army barracks attached to the Jacinth Fortress, to review one of his new brigades. The sun was out and they made a brave sight: thousands of armored men in perfect rank, the officers' parade plumes bobbing above their helmets, the long pikes stabbing toward the blue heaven, the brigade and battalion standards and the company banners aglow in the winter sunlight.

I watched from the portico of the headquarters building as Terem began the final ritual of the review, the sacrifice to Father Heaven and the Lord of the Dead. It had been a long ceremony. My feet were cold, and I wanted to go home.

Terem had just lit the incense when I heard an urgent voice within the headquarters. A rumpled young man with courier insignia appeared beside me in the portico, along with the fortress vice-commandant. The latter was always the epitome of polite behavior, but neither he nor the courier even glanced in my direction, and I realized that they were both extremely agitated. I wanted to ask them what the matter was, but their grim faces silenced me.

I waited uneasily for Terem to finish. At last he did, the horns boomed, and the brigade began to march off the parade field. As soon as they did, the vice-commandant and the courier hurried onto the parade ground. I followed.

"What is it?" Terem asked as we reached him. "News?"

"My lord, yes. The courier has a dispatch from the east. The seals were broken at the Chancellery, and Lord Geray sent it directly here."

Terem took the packet, opened it, and began to read. I watched his face, my alarm increasing as his mouth grew tight.

"He's gulled me, by Father Heaven," he said furiously, rolling up the dispatch. "Well, now we have to set to work. Sooner than I'd expected, curse him. Ah, well, the sooner begun, the sooner ended."

"My lord?" I asked. "What's happened?"

"Ardavan's over the Savath, with more than a hundred thousand men behind him. Came boiling out of his winter quarters eleven days ago. He left twenty thousand to mask Tanay and the border fortresses, but he's got plenty left, and it looks as if they're heading for Gultekin. He means to put an end to us."

"But it's winter!" I exclaimed. "Nobody fights in winter! What will they live on?"

"Plunder and scavenging and speed. He's a gambler, is our Ardavan. Risks all to take me with my trousers around my ankles. But we'll see if he can move fast enough. If he doesn't, I'll give him a trouncing he won't soon forget."

He strode into the headquarters building with me hot on his heels, and in minutes we were on our way to the palace. As the sequina raced through the water, with periangs and smaller craft darting out of our way like frightened water beetles, I asked, "What are you going to do?"

"Fight him. He hopes to defeat me a piece at a time, before I can concentrate my strength, so that he'll outnumber me in every fight. But I've got ten brigades at Gultekin, three here, and demi-brigades at Takrun and Malal. He'll lose men on the march. I may be able to match his numbers by the time he makes Gultekin."

"But our men are in winter quarters. Will they be ready to fight?"

"They'll have to be made so. Unless we want Exile horsemen in Kurjain by the time the month's out."

He sounded calm, but from the set of his mouth I knew he was very, very angry—mostly at himself, because he'd underestimated Ardavan's willingness to gamble his army on a surprise attack. But nobody else had foreseen it, either. In winter, armies belonged in winter quarters. To campaign in bad weather was to invite calamity. Everybody knew that, except, apparently, Ardavan.

To my surprise, Terem suddenly laughed. I said, "What's so funny?" He smiled ruefully. "He has nerve, I'll say that for him. Can you imagine the uproar in the War Ministry if I'd suggested the same thing? He knows how to lead men, no doubt of it. I wish there were two of him, and one was on my side."

"You admire him, don't you?"

"Yes. And I want him dead. There's not room in the world for both of us."

"When you go to Gultekin, I'm coming, too."

He grinned. The sequina's oars swept the canal like flails, hissing. "Could I stop you?"

"No, not unless you lock me up."

"I'd never do that. I'll be happy to have you with me, but we'll have little time together while we're there, and when I tell you that you must leave, you must do so. Is it a bargain?"

"Bargain," I said, and we clasped hands on it. In that moment, inexplicably, I was happy. But then I remembered that I had to tell Nilang what Terem was going to do, or risk terrible consequences. My happiness fled, and I was my gloom-laden self again.

That evening, while I was rummaging through my old traveling chest for clothes for the journey, I came across a packet of papers. They were the love poems poor Adrine had written before she died; I hadn't looked at them for a long time. I leafed through them and one caught my eye.

Dreaming in the cherry orchard, hear my song:
A night without him
    Is ten nights long.

I read it several times, realizing that I understood Adrine at last. Now I knew why she had done what she had, at the cost of every-thing. Now I knew what she had felt for Lahad, because I felt it for Terem. It was a spirit as dangerous as Nilang's daughters, and per-haps more powerful.

It was love, and just as Adrine had been doomed to it, so was I.

Twenty-six

❧

Thus for the second time in a year I came to Gultekin, this time with the Sun Lord and his army, now called the Army of Durdane. Messages carried by the gallopers of the river fleet reported Ardavan's main force as two days' march away, moving relentlessly toward us. He'd captured a lot of shipping and had used it to speed his infantry down the Jacinth alongside his racing cavalry; our river rams sank some of these troop transports but not nearly enough. And while the winter weather and straggling had taken a toll of his numbers, he'd had even more men when he started out than we'd believed—the reports stubbornly kept saying that eighty thousand marched on us. And it appeared, from the presence of the royal standards of Suarai, Mirsing, and Ishban, that the three remaining Exile Kings were with him.

And we Durdana? Terem had pulled together a respectable army, almost as many men as Ardavan supposedly commanded. There were additional brigades in garrison in the northwest, but while they were marching our way, they could not hope to reach Gultekin before Ardavan. Forty thousand more men were in the east, but Ardavan had left enough forces in his wake to keep them from coming quickly to our aid. They'd have to fight their way west, and would never get to us in time to help.

There was one good thing about the decline of our cities over the years: Gultekin had plenty of abandoned buildings to shelter our men from the winter's rigors. The city was also a district government seat and was therefore walled, but these fortifications were of no great strength; if Ardavan defeated us, the city was doomed. Many citizens had fled, and the price of a downriver boat passage had increased tenfold. The district magistrate, however, showed no alarm, and most of his submagistrates and other officials remained at their posts.

The government buildings, while old, were well kept up. They were in a gated compound by the river wall; Terem moved me, himself, and his staff into the villa that was designated for official visitors. The rooms were spacious and the windows all had glass in them, a good thing given the cold winds blowing from the west. In the south wall of our bedchamber was a door that opened onto a small wrought-iron balcony, with a view over the compound wall and the city roofs.

We were blessedly free of the protocol that governed Terem's days at Jade Lagoon; there was no time for it. But there was little time for us, either, for Terem was carrying the whole army on his back. Fortunately our troops were in good spirits, bolstered by the knowledge that at Bara we'd given as good as we got, and they were prepared to repeat the success.

But a draw wouldn't be enough; we had to defeat Ardavan decisively and send him staggering back across the Savath. Terem was certain we'd do it, certain with that conviction that was so much of his strength. I was less sanguine, but of one thing I was sure—no other man could lead us to the victory we so desperately needed.

Nevertheless, the atmosphere in the government compound was tense, and in spite of Terem's relentless optimism I found the place oppressive. Worse, I could not, for the life of me, think of a way to remain loyal to Mother and at the same time serve Terem and his cause. It was, of course, impossible to do both, but I could *not* bring myself to believe that. I consequently spent many hours in feverish speculation about what course I should take, but every solution I devised had at least one fatal flaw. The best I could think of was to play to each side as long as I could, and hope that some miracle might save us all.

Nilang had instructed me to contact Dilara in the Miscellaneous Market. So, late in the afternoon of the day after we arrived, I slipped through the gates of the compound and set off into the city. Because so many people had fled, the streets were almost empty of civilians; nor were many soldiers about, since Terem kept them busy digging field fortifications outside the walls or carrying out combat exercises. The weather added to the sense of desolation: the sky was gray, with low-hung clouds creeping out of the west and a dank gusty wind that threatened freezing rain.

The way to the market took me through Gold Sand Circle, where Merihan's mother and father lived. I passed by on the far side of the plaza but noticed a wisp of smoke from the mansion's gable vent, as if someone in the kitchen were preparing an evening meal. The Aviya family was among the more stouthearted of Gultekin's citizens, if they had remained so long.

I located the Miscellaneous Market in a small plaza near the city's river walls. It was probably a busy place in normal times, but not now. Three shops in four, and all the booths, were shut and deserted. I asked at one of the shops for Asmiri the public scribe, and was directed to a commercial tenement, one of those rattletrap places where the landlord rents out open-fronted shops with a tiny room or two above each, for the shopkeeper to live in.

Dilara, or Asmiri as she now was, had the third one along. But its stout wooden shutters were closed tight. I banged on them, worrying. Had she been called away unexpectedly by some order from Mother?

Suddenly the shutters rattled and a bolt scraped. Dilara put her head out and said, "Ah, you found me."

"I'm a trained finder of things."

She snickered. "Aren't we both? Have you eaten? There's a chophouse around the corner that's still open. I can get some food and bring it up in my rooms. That'll be safe enough."

I looked at the sky. The winter days were short, and dusk would soon be at hand. But Terem would be with his officers for hours yet in the compound's commandery building. And Dilara and I hadn't talked in such a long time. "That's a good idea," I said.

"I'll need my dishes. Come up."

I slipped through the shutters and peered around in the gloom. I was in a tiny scribal shop, with pens, sealing wax, paper, ink stones, all the gear of the scribe's trade. At the rear was a narrow wooden stair, which we climbed.

What I found at the top saddened me. It was a dark little place of two rooms, not even as good as Tsusane's had been, and Dilara's usual indifference to her surroundings didn't help. In one cubicle was a narrow bed, the floor beside it sparsely strewn with her few clothes. In the other was a table and two stools, a smoldering brazier, and a cupboard. The narrow window was sealed with thick paper and admitted a gray, watery light. It was all so poor and mean that I got a lump in my throat and swore to myself that someday I'd make sure that Dilara lived as well as I did.

She asked me to feed the brazier and went away with the dishes. I'd just got the room warmed a little when she returned with vegetables, fish pastries, and a jug of Danshur peach wine. We lit her two little lamps, then sat at the table and ate.

We talked about Repose and my life in Kurjain, but as our meal progressed, I realized that Dilara, beneath her usual veneer of cool detachment, was very excited. She drank more wine than I did, and I wondered, a little uneasily, if she'd become fonder of it than was wise. She'd always been abstemious in the old days, but now I remembered the wine on her breath the night before we invaded Lindu and how she'd had a flask with her even during the retreat.

At length my curiosity made me ask, "Dilara, what's going on? It's something important, isn't it?"

Her eyes gleamed in the lamplight. "I was saving it to tell you later. But now's as good a time . . . Lale, our victory's near. In a couple of days it'll be over, and we'll have won."

"What? How? Are you supposed to be telling me this?"

"Yes, I am. Nilang told me to. She's somewhere here in Gultekin. That's how important this is, that Mother's sent her. And you're part of it."

"I'm part of *what*, Dilara? For pity's sake, tell me!"

"There's going to be a battle, obviously. But the night before it happens, the usurper dies. Remember once I said that somebody should kill him? Well now's the time, and I'm to do it."

She must have taken the shock on my face for delight, because she laughed and said, "You mean you didn't see this coming? Why ever not? When could be a better time?"

When, indeed? I *should* have seen it. But I'd shut the thought of Terem's death from my awareness, telling myself always that it was a long way off.

Now it was here. I had to stop it. If I could just persuade Dilara that I should be the assassin—

"Why has she ordered you to kill him and not me?" I asked. "I can get to him much more easily."

"Because Mother doesn't want any risk to you. You're too valuable—you know a lot of important people, and she knows you'll continue to be useful even after we've won. You're to go back to Kurjain when he's dead and wait for orders."

"What if you can't get to him?"

"I was coming to that. If I miss, Mother says you'll have to take over for me. I have the double poison for you, the same as Adrine took. If he's still alive at dawn on the day of battle, get them into him as quickly as you can, both doses together so it's fast. He can't be left alive long enough to reach the battlefield."

"But," I objected, "with both doses together, it'll be obvious he died of poison. They'll look everywhere for suspects, and I'll be one of them. What does Mother want me to do in that case?"

"Get out as soon as you can, once he's swallowed the stuff. You remember, there's a little delay before it acts. Head for Dirun and take a ship to Tamurin. You should be able to get clear. His officers will be too busy losing the battle to chase you, and the Exiles won't march west till they've occupied Gultekin."

"You're taking your life in your hands, Dilara. He's very well guarded."

She shrugged. "Mother has told me what to do. That's all there is to it."

I didn't want to think of her death, my oldest friend. I wanted her to come to her senses, to go away somewhere and be a weaver. But I knew she never would. She'd carry out her orders or die trying.

"And Ardavan will win," I said, half to myself.

"What of it?" Dilara answered. "The usurper will be gone and his army with him. No Sun Lord will ever threaten Mother again. Don't you *see*, Lale? It's almost over. Soon we can go somewhere and just be ourselves. The way we used to talk about, remember?"

"But can we? What if Kurjain falls and Ardavan conquers Bethiya? What will happen then?"

Again the shrug. "Mother will know how to deal with Ardavan. Anyway, we could go to the Despotates. There's lots of opportunity for clever women in the south."

Her blindness took my breath away. I wanted to scream at her: *Ardavan won't stop at Bethiya—he'll take the Despotates, too, and then where will you run? Everything will go down into the dark. We'll all be slaves. How can you want this?*

But I didn't dare speak. Her eyes glittered and I could see her sharp little teeth, and I knew she'd call me traitor if I did, and I didn't know what might happen after that.

But surely there's a way out, I thought, as I tried to choke down my despair. *If I can keep Terem alive, maybe he'll defeat Ardavan, and then I'll work out what to do next. But how do I stop Dilara?*

I could try to kill her. But she was my best friend, or she once had been, and I couldn't bring myself to do it. Moreover, I wasn't sure I could beat her, and if I were dead she'd get Terem for sure. I was still trapped, and my happiness at being in her company had fled. Now I wanted nothing so much as to get away from her. But I had to play the game out, as if I agreed with it, so I said, "You're right. I guess we could go south, if we had to."

Dilara picked up her wine and gulped it. She'd already consumed well over half the flask, and now she upended it to drain the last drop into her cup. "And do you know something else?" She leaned conspiratorially toward me, her cheekbones stark in the flickering light of the lamps, flushed with drink.

"What?" I asked, making my voice eager.

"Can I trust you, Lale?"

"With anything."

"I shouldn't tell even you this, but you're my sister and we're both from Three Springs. Mother wouldn't mind, now that it's all so nearly over." She paused dramatically and said, "You're the Inamorata because of me."

Fool that I still was, I had no idea what she meant. "I am?" I asked stupidly.

She laughed. "A surprise, isn't it? Everybody thought the Surina died of sickness, even you. Well she did, sort of. I gave it to her."

"*Gave* it to her?"

"That's what I said. Lale, she was my finest work. Even you didn't suspect, did you?"

"No," I whispered. Oh, poor ghost, no wonder you walked. Murdered, and with no justice for your death.

"It took a lot of planning," she said proudly. "I began by getting a place as a cleaning girl at Jade Lagoon. That was the easy part. You know how the menials come and go."

"Yes," I answered dully.

"Then I watched how things worked for a couple of months, but I couldn't find a way to get at her. But finally we were sent to clean the Porcelain Pavilion, and by the time we left, I knew what I'd do. I used her chair, the one on the left of the dais, I'm sure you've seen it. Nilang gave me the poison—it was one she never told us about at Three Springs. I mixed it with a little oil and painted it on the chair arm, where the Surina would rest her left hand."

"But the Pavilion's well guarded," I said. "All the palace buildings are."

Dilara laughed. "You *did* train at Three Springs, didn't you? I got in by the roof and through the upper windows; any of us could have managed it. And they don't guard the inside, only the outside, the fools."

"And the poison worked."

"Perfectly. It's only potent for a day and a half, but I knew there was a performance that night, and I was sure she'd get it on her palm, and she did. It's slow, but it looks like a flux of the lungs, and that was the end of the Surina, and your way was clear." She giggled. "I hope you appreciate my help. You're living in luxury because of me."

All I could say was, "How did you know you wouldn't kill the Sun Lord?"

"It was a possibility. But her death had to look natural, and this was the only way I could find to do it. Nobody else could sit in that chair, and the Sun Lord's was on the opposite side to the poison, so he wasn't likely to touch it. I told Mother, and she decided to take the risk. It worked."

A flood of sorrow swept through me. I hadn't known Merihan. She was nothing to me. She'd been an obstacle and Mother removed her. But still, inexplicably, I grieved for her death.

Dilara was scrutinizing me anxiously. "I did well, don't you think?"

She wanted my praise. Astonished at the warmth and sincerity

I could still put into my voice, I said, "You did brilliantly. Mother must have been very pleased."

"She was. But for this I'm going to need your help. I have to know in advance when he's going to join battle."

"All right. How long do you need?"

"He'll probably strike at the Exiles early in the day. If you tell me the evening before that, it'll be enough. I'll also want to know his movements between then and the next morning, if you can find them out."

"He'll fight soon," I said. "He intends to attack as soon as the Exiles reach Gultekin, to catch them tired." I paused, then asked, "How are you going to kill him?"

"I'll work something out. Better if you don't know."

I wanted to press her to tell me more but dared not. "I'd better be off," I said.

Before I left, she gave me the poison in two small ceramic vials, their stoppers sealed with wax and secured with thin copper wire. I wrapped them in a scrap of paper and put them into my belt pouch. Then she came with me down to the street to say goodbye. Outside, the evening was cold and damp, with an edge of the night's frost to come.

"Until later," Dilara said. I had to embrace her in farewell, although my heart rebelled at it. With deep relief I at last slipped away into the deepening dusk.

Terem and his officers were still conferring when I reached the compound, and I returned to our quarters in the villa without attracting attention. The house was almost deserted, barring the handful of servants the district magistrate had found for us. When I reached our bedchamber I went to the balcony door, undid the latch, and drew it open, admitting a flood of chilly air. Some twenty feet distant was the parapet of the compound wall. Dilara could come over it easily, then reach the bedroom by way of the balcony. Or, if he slept instead at his battle headquarters outside the walls, she'd track him down there. Or she might take him as he mounted his horse or as he walked among his soldiers. He'd be easy enough to find, and she was prepared to buy his death with her own.

I closed the balcony door and examined the latch. It was laughable. If she came this way, she would get past it in an instant.

I had the servants bring food to the bedchamber; there was no point in waiting for Terem, who might be half the night. As I began to eat, the majordomo came to the door and said, apologetically, that a message had come for me that afternoon, but the fool of a gate porter had neglected to bring it to him.

I took it and dismissed the man. The message was a single sheet of good rag paper, not the cheap wheat-straw kind, folded four times and sealed with white wax. The seal emblem was a leaping hare, the same hare I had seen on the gate of the Aviya mansion. Puzzling over this, I broke the seal and unfolded the paper. Inside, I read:

To her Honorable Excellency, the Lady Inamorata Lale Navari, greetings:

It would be our pleasure if the Lady Inamorata might honor us with her presence, at our home in Gold Sand Circle, at some hour before tomorrow morning. Sadly, we intend to remove from Gultekin at that time, owing to the unfortunate events now occurring in the east.

Nirar Aviya her seal
Ilishan Aviya his seal

Before tomorrow morning! I looked at the window, and through the distortion of the glass I saw that full darkness was near. I cursed the slackness of the porter, pulled on my outer clothing, and raced down to the compound gate. I knew Terem would be furious if he discovered I was out at night alone, so I demanded an escort from the guard captain. As soon as I got it I set out for the Aviya mansion, accompanied by two large soldiers carrying flambeaux.

What could Ilishan and his wife want with me? It must be to apologize. No doubt they were worried about how they'd treated me and wanted to mend their bridges—I could cause them trouble, and they would know it. I could think of no other reason for them to be so suddenly polite. In a popular drama I would have had a premonition, but as I hurried through the dark streets I felt nothing of the kind.

We reached the villa and the young porter admitted us. It was a different visit from last time, me with armored men at my back and the flambeaux blazing in the gloom. In the outer courtyard were many bundles, bales, and chests, signs of the family's impending flight. And before the gate had properly closed, there stood Ilishan in the entrance to the inner court, with the torchlight turning his silver hair to copper.

Twenty-seven

❧

He led me into the house. Within, signs of hasty packing disordered what must be, in calmer times, an elegant dwelling. He took me into the second of two reception rooms, this one lit by lamps hanging from bronze chains. A stack of cane packing chests took up one end.

"We have little time," he said, "and I beg you to forgive us for the meager hospitality we offer tonight. But the house is in uproar, as you see."

"It doesn't matter," I told him. "I'm used to uproar."

He looked relieved and said, "Please be comfortable. I'll find Nirar and have wine sent in."

He went away. I could hear thumps and bangs and agitated voices elsewhere in the house, as the servants went at the packing. Then a girl of about sixteen, looking tired and frightened, brought wine and cakes, put them on a table, and scurried away.

Almost immediately, Ilishan returned with Nirar. We greeted each other stiffly. There was an awkward silence, made no less so by the way Nirar kept looking at me, as if she were fixing every detail of my features in her memory. Her eyes were red rimmed and I suspected she'd been weeping.

"Sit, lady mistress," Ilishan said, and we all did. Silently he served our wine, a transparent gold vintage. Then he said, "We are most profoundly sorry for our behavior when you came to us before. We beg that you will accept our apologies. We spoke out of ignorance and distress."

"You have nothing to apologize for," I assured him. "The fault was mine, in descending upon you with such effrontery. I am most deeply mortified at my disrespect and bad manners."

We bowed to each other, the jaggedness of our first meeting a little smoothed. But I sensed already that this was not why I was here.

"Tell her, Ilishan," Nirar murmured.

Her husband cleared his throat. "Very well. There is no way but to say it. Lady mistress, we lied to the Chancellor long ago, when he came looking for a girl of the Aviya bloodline to betroth to the Sun Lord. We lied to everyone. Merihan was not our daughter."

I gazed into my wine cup. On its white interior glaze were yellow butterflies and blue swallows with russet breasts. The golden wine made them look as if they were flying through summer sunlight. I felt suspended in time and space, as in the fleeting moment when one has stepped off a precipice but has not yet begun to fall.

"Not your daughter," I said.

"No. Our marriage was childless, and we were humiliated that we couldn't have an heir. Even so, when we first took her in, we didn't intend the falsehood. But others thought she was ours, and we felt better for it, so we lied." He passed a hand over his brow. "Once we had done that, we were trapped. To admit the truth later would be to admit we had lied earlier. Nirar would have done so, but I couldn't endure the stain on my reputation, so I forbade it. And when we agreed to betroth Merihan to Terem Rathai, there was no going back. The Chancellor wanted the Aviya bloodline, not the bloodline of an adopted child. To confess afterward what we'd done . . . you see?"

"I see," I replied, still feeling suspended. "But *someone* must have known. How could you keep such a thing a secret?"

"Chance. We didn't find her here. We were in Istana, where I was Bethiya's emissary to the old Despot, the one before Yazar. We knew Merihan's blood parents; he was a junior magistrate and she was a composer, and Nirar and she were with child at the same time."

"But you said—"

"Our daughter died as I bore her," Nirar interrupted gently. "I was injured. There would be no more children. It happened the day before Merihan was born."

I nodded; there was really nothing to say.

"And on that day," Ilishan continued, "the old Despot died, and Yazar went after the dais. Merihan's father was of a bloodline that was Yazar's enemy, and everyone knew what would happen if Yazar won. But it was a hard birth, and Merihan's mother was too weak to move, and her husband wouldn't leave her. So they gave Merihan and her sister to the mother's parents to hide."

"Merihan and her *sister*?"

"Yes. There were two daughters, born moments apart."

I stammered something, I don't know what. Ilishan put up a hand. "Wait, listen. The grandparents couldn't manage both girls, and begged us to take Merihan. We agreed. The next day, Yazar took the dais and the executions began. Merihan's parents were among the first to die. Her grandparents fled with the other child, fearing for themselves and for her, too. To protect Merihan from Yazar, we said she was our daughter and concealed the death of our own. The substitution worked, and we left Istana as soon as we could. And having begun with a falsehood that was justified, we went on with it, which was not. But we loved Merihan as if she were our child."

"And the other daughter?" I whispered.

"We don't know. We don't know where the grandparents went, but we think they went south by the Long Canal."

I said, as if in a dream, "And from there to the South Canal, and then to the Wing. And down the Wing to Riversong. That's where the villagers found me, in a boat washed into the shallows. An old man and an old woman were with me, but they were dead. I was just a few months old."

Nirar took a sharp breath and Ilishan looked startled. "An old couple?" he said. "Do you know anything else about them? What they looked like?"

"No. Nothing at all."

"It might have been them," said Nirar. "Oh, the poor souls."

"But it's such a long way," I said, still grappling with the possibilities. "And I was old enough for solid food when the villagers found me."

"True," said Ilishan, "but Merihan's grandparents would have fled as far as they could, and it might have taken them that long. They had to keep running, you see—Yazar was merciless in those days, and he weeded his garden thoroughly." He looked down at his hands. "Very thoroughly indeed. He left none of Merihan's bloodline alive on either side, except for the very distant branches."

"And what does all this make me?" I asked. I suspected, but I had to hear it.

"We think," Nirar said in a trembling voice, "that you are Merihan's twin sister. Not of exactly the same appearance, as most twins are, but near enough. And your voice is almost hers. Hearing you in another room, I'd think she was alive again."

She sobbed and covered her eyes. Ilishan put his hand on her arm.

"But why tell anyone now?" I could barely get the words out. "Why tell *me*?"

"Because it's a terrible thing not to know one's ancestors," Ilishan said. "After you first came here, Nirar and I talked about you for many days. We agreed that for us to suspect so strongly who you were, and then keep it from you would be an even worse dishonor than our earlier lies had been. So we decided to tell you, and when we heard you'd come here with Terem, we grasped at the chance. We can't know for sure that you're Merihan's sister. But the evidence is so compelling that we had to speak. It's even more compelling, knowing now the way you were found on the Wing."

My head was spinning. And then, stark and cold, the thought came to me: *But if this is true, then Dilara murdered my sister. Merihan was my only living kin, and my best friend gave her poison.*

But Dilara did it only because Mother told her to. Dilara couldn't have known who Merihan really was.

And then, like an adder creeping from beneath a stone, a voice said: *But Mother knew. She must have. How could it be an accident, that she adopted a child who fit so well into her plans?*

I remembered Master Lim coming to Riversong, and how interested in me he'd been. And then, when I was running away, how I met him on the road, and how Mother came down it so soon after. I'd always thought it no more than chance. But now I knew, as surely as I breathed, that it was never chance. It was design.

Mother had been looking for me. Even as I rode with her to Tamurin, she knew who my parents were and where I came from, and she knew about Merihan. All this time she knew, and she never told me.

How long had she worked Merihan and me into her plans? I could only guess, but it must have been years; the years of searching for me, the years of building her grand design around the two of us, the years of preparing me to take my sister's place. And never, not once, did I suspect. Everything had conspired to blind me: the apparent legitimacy of Merihan's Aviya parentage; the ludicrousness of any notion that we might be related; but, above all, my love for Mother and my trust in her.

And she had betrayed that love and trust. She hid my origins from me, she who spoke always of faith and devotion. No treason of mine could approach her monstrous treachery. She had murdered Merihan and ruined me.

Nirar watched me anxiously, for I was trembling like a willow leaf. "My dear," she said, "how can we help you?"

I shook my head, unable to speak. There seemed to be two of

me. One self knew beyond doubt that Makina Seval had used me and my sister most evilly, and with that knowledge came a searing resolve to be avenged. But my other self still believed that there must be some explanation, that the woman who had given me a home and a place in the world could surely not be so wicked. Surely she would never have ordered my sister's death if she had *known*. And perhaps, perhaps, perhaps all the evidence was wrong, perhaps Merihan wasn't my sister after all. How could I ever be sure?

Ilishan poured me more wine and I took half of it at a gulp. "What were their names?" I asked, as the drink warmed my icy hands and stilled my shaking. "My . . . our mother and father?"

"She was Galara of the Seyisan bloodline," Nirar told me. "He was Talas Othkun. Both were good families, well respected. Yazar's destruction of them was iniquitous and unnecessary."

It seemed that my past reeked of such evils. Mother, whom I revered, had killed my sister; Yazar, whom I liked, had slaughtered my parents. But I couldn't tell Ilishan and Nirar the truth of how Merihan died. To do so I would have had to reveal my part in it. It would have been not only cruel, but also dangerous and useless.

Exhaustion swept through me. I wanted to know so much more: about my real family, about my parents, about my sister and what she wanted from her life, about the things she liked and disliked, how she spoke, the books she read. But at the same time I wanted to curl up in a warm dark place and sleep and sleep, forgetting everything. I could sustain no more. The day had almost broken me.

"I have to go home," I said. "I need to think. Will you forgive me?"

"Of course," Nirar said, though I could tell she didn't want to let me go. "But there's something else I need to tell you. Tomorrow is your birthday."

"Tomorrow?" Suddenly I had a real birthday, not the false one I'd lived with for so long.

"Yes. We'd hoped to spend it with you, if you wanted to, but now—" She gestured helplessly at the cane chests, packed and ready to go.

"I understand."

"But when you return to Kurjain," she went on hopefully, "will you come and see us? Perhaps we could do it then."

There was a silence as we all remembered Ardavan and the battle that was to come, and that we might lose it. At last I said, "Yes, I will. But in the meantime, I'll say nothing of this to Terem, because the news should come from your lips, not mine. If he asks where I was tonight, I'll merely say that this was a courtesy call."

Ilishan sighed. "For the moment, I agree. But I've had too much of secrets. I'll tell him everything when he comes back to Kurjain. It will be a relief."

"I'll help you with him as much as I can," I said, rising. They took me to the outer court, where my escort waited. In the flickering light of the flambeaux, Nirar embraced me. "It was Our Lady of Compassion who brought you to Terem and to us," she said. "There's no other explanation for it, the way you were lost and the way you've been found. Praise the goddess."

I didn't know whether to laugh or weep. It was by no divinity's hand that I was here; it was by the murderous ambition of a woman in Tamurin. But I said, "Praise the goddess," and kissed her cheek. It was wet and so was mine.

"We've hired a watchman for the house," she told me. "If you want to come back in daylight and see where she grew up, do. We'll tell him you're to be admitted and that he's not to trouble you."

I thanked them and set out for home. I was so weary that I could hardly put one foot ahead of the other. Everything ran around in my head like a whirlpool of filthy water, choked with offal and drowned corpses, the wreckage of my life. I'd have been better off dying on the Wing with my grandparents, if they were my grandparents.

A sleety rain began to fall as I reached the villa. Terem wasn't there. I went to bed and wept and wept, and still I did not know what to do.

❧

In the morning I woke and thought: *Today is my birthday*.

I'd still been awake when Terem came in, but by then I'd finished crying and pretended I was asleep. I was vaguely aware of him rising around dawn, but I drifted off again. Now, full morning sunlight fell through the window and across the bed coverings. The air in the room was cold.

I lay there and thought about all that had happened to me since the last time I awoke. The strangest seemed to be this: that I knew my real birthday and that it was today.

But then doubt crept in. Was this really my birthday? Was it not possible, no matter what Ilishan suspected, that I wasn't Merihan's sister after all? I had to be sure. I had to *know*.

And it came to me suddenly how I might, just possibly, find out.

I rose and rang the gong. A servant brought me hot water to wash my face and something for my breakfast. I made myself eat the bread and honey and drink some small beer, although I had no appetite. Then I went over to the commandery to see what was going on. Hardly anybody was there, and a clerk told me that Ardavan's vanguard had been sighted some ten miles east of the city. He'd be here by mid-afternoon, and the Sun Lord and his staff had gone out to move the army into the positions prepared for it.

I left the compound and walked toward Gold Sand Circle. By now everybody in the city would know that the Exiles were at hand, including Dilara, and she'd expect me to tell her Terem's intentions. I still hadn't decided what to do about that. Indeed, I felt oddly detached from everything, including myself, as if my awareness had become slightly separated from my body. I was still aware of my pain and sorrow, but they were distant, as though they belonged to someone else.

It was a pleasant late winter day, crisp and sunny, the puddles skimmed with ice and crackling under my boots. But the streets were eerily empty. Every window was shuttered, every house gate closed, every market stall barren, every shop sealed tight. Terem had set patrols in the streets to keep order, but they were fewer than yesterday; he'd pulled almost every man into the battle line. A few civilians were about, and some I didn't like the look of— thieves, I suspected, sniffing about for places they could loot when night fell. But they left me alone, luckily for them.

It wasn't long before I was banging on the Aviya gate. After a while the watchman came and peered at me though the spy hole, then let me in. He was a brawny fellow with a short sword at his belt, and greeted me respectfully. I gave him a coin and went on into the inner court, where I entered the house.

It looked different, mainly because it was so much emptier than last night. But as I wandered through its rooms, where some of the furniture still remained, I slowly became more and more aware of how familiar it felt. Behind this door should be a writing room, and here it was. At the end of this passage should be a bed-room, and here it was. This covered walk should lead to the kitchen, and it did.

By now I was eerily certain that this was the house I'd seen in those vivid daydreams when I was a child in Riversong. This door, then, should lead to the secret garden.

I went through it onto a veranda, and found what I'd expected to find. Not so secret a place, really, for it was the garden I'd seen though the courtyard arch, the one with the old apple tree. Had there been such a tree in my long-ago reveries? I couldn't remem-ber. But I knew, somehow, that this was a place Merihan had loved. And today was her birthday, and possibly mine, and one is always closest to one's family dead on that day. And though Merihan's body lay in a tomb in far-off Kurjain, might she still hear her sis-ter's call from the garden that was so dear to her?

I hadn't tried the ritual for years, not since those two failed at-tempts in Repose. I didn't have the incense and the proper sacred objects, and I'd forgotten most of the incantation. All I could do was sit on the bench at the foot of the apple tree and ask her, from the depths of my heart, to come. So I did.

Nothing happened. I was comfortable enough; the day was windless, and the sun was warm in that sheltered place. I'd slept badly and misery had worn me down, but I was alert in a shaky, feverish way.

I leaned my back against the rough comfort of the tree and continued to wait. Still nothing happened, and I grew more and more downhearted. If Merihan didn't appear to me, it would be a strong sign that we weren't of the same blood after all, which would mean that Galara and Talas weren't my parents. I didn't know how I felt about that. It would mean that Mother hadn't murdered my sister, and that she therefore hadn't betrayed me after all. Yet I desperately wanted to believe that I'd discovered my family.

But at last I knew it was useless. There was nothing here for me, after all. Above my head, the apple tree's branches rustled sadly as the wind brushed them.

But there was no wind.

The hair on the back of my neck bristled. I hurriedly stood up and turned around.

A young girl was sitting in the apple tree. She was perhaps eleven, with auburn hair and green eyes. She wore loose summer clothes and her bare feet were dusty.

"Hello," she said. "I'm Merihan. You're my sister, aren't you?"

"Yes," I said, "I am." I knew she was dead, and that she was from the Quiet World, but I was unafraid. I knew, somehow, that nothing would harm me while she was here.

"What's your name?" she asked.

"Lale."

She inspected me up and down. "Am I going to look like you when I grow up?"

"Yes, very like me." She didn't know what was to happen to her. Or perhaps she did, and it no longer mattered.

"That's good, because you're very pretty. Sometimes I dream about living in a village far away. I never have to go to my tutors, and it's always warm, and there's a river and I can swim in it. Is that you I'm dreaming about?"

"I think so. I dream about you, too."

She grimaced, then laughed. "Not about my tutors, I hope?"

"No, not about them." I drank in her features, her expressions, her movements. They were mine, but not altogether. She was Merihan.

"Are you going to stay?" she asked. "I'd like it if you would. I miss you, you know. I've always missed you."

"I've always missed you, too. Are you happy here?"

"Oh, yes. Except sometimes I'm lonely because I know that you and I should be together, and we're not. Do you know I'm to marry the Sun Lord when I grow up? His name's Terem."

I nodded. "Yes, I knew that. Do you like him?"

Her eyes got round. "Very much. He's handsome, you know, and he's very kind to me. I like him a lot, which is a good thing, since I'm to be his Surina and live in the palace with him. Have you ever met him?"

"Yes. I know Terem quite well. I'm very fond of him, as you are."

My sister smiled. I knew that smile, for it was also mine. "You look so happy when you say that. Have you fallen in love with him? I bet you have."

I considered the question, and how she might feel about my answer. Then I said, "Merihan, I love him with all my heart. I hope you don't mind."

"I don't mind at all. Would you die for him, the way people do for each other in the stories?"

Without hesitation I answered, "Yes."

"So would I. But you didn't tell me if you'd stay here. I hope you can. I'd like to talk to you whenever I wanted."

"I'd like it, too. But I can't stay, Merihan. I wish I could, very much. But I can't."

She looked downcast. "I was afraid of that. You're a grown-up, and grown-ups always have so much to do. Is that it?"

"Something like that."

She brightened. "But perhaps you'll come back sometimes, will you? Just once in a while, so we can see each other? We're the closest of kin, after all."

"Yes," I said, "we are, and I'll try. I'm so glad I found you."

"So am I," she answered. "I love you, dearest sister."

"I love you, Merihan."

I blinked because my eyes were full of tears. When I could see again, she was gone.

"Merihan," I whispered, "don't go. Please."

In the garden, all was silent.

"Please," I said. Vertigo swept through me and I leaned against the rough bark of the apple tree. How long had I been here? The sun had passed zenith, and my feet and hands were chilled.

I looked around. All seemed as it had been, but now I had reached another country, on the far side of grief, in a place where all was clear and cold, like this windless afternoon in the depths of winter. I stood under the tree for a while, thinking. I knew everything now. I knew what I had to do.

I rose and left the garden, without once looking back. Poor shade, did she linger there still, waiting for me to rejoin her? She had only to be patient for a little while; I would not be long.

Twenty-eight

❧

I left the garden by the archway. When I came into the outer courtyard, there was Nilang, wearing nondescript traveling clothes. The watchman lay at her feet, his sword still in its scabbard.

I remained in my distant refuge of wintry clarity, where nothing could surprise me. "Why are you here?" I asked.

"I have the same question for you."

I was no longer afraid of her, but I knew I must be careful. "I'm here because I was curious about the Surina."

"Does your curiosity extend to calling her from her rest?"

This penetrated even my cold tranquility. She was a sorceress; had she sensed what had happened in the garden? I shifted my feet very slightly, into the stance of attack. But I didn't want to fight her. I had important things to do, and ridding the world of Nilang, even assuming I could manage it, was not among them.

"How could I summon her?" I asked. "She's not my blood, and she lies in Kurjain."

"Indeed. Yet it has occurred to me that your resemblance might have raised questions in your mind. Of a possible relationship."

I made myself laugh. "Her parentage is established and well known. Mine is not. She's nothing to me."

"Nonetheless, you are here."

I shrugged. "The usurper still dotes on her memory. The more I know of her, the more I can emulate her and thus secure his attachment to me."

Nilang bowed slightly. "Your foresight and resourcefulness commend you. Where are you going now?"

Here was a way to assert the loyalty I suspected she was probing. "Can you find Dilara?"

"Yes."

"Then tell her the usurper will fight in the morning. She must deal with him tonight."

"Very well. And you will complete the task if she fails?"

"I will. How can I help her reach him?" If I knew what Dilara was going to do . . .

Nilang tilted her head to one side. "This isn't a question you should ask."

I looked contrite. "But I want her to succeed."

"She will. Where do you go now?"

"Back to the compound. I'll stay there till it's over." I wondered if she would let me pass.

"Do so. I'll leave here after you've gone."

She stepped aside to let me go. I was very alert, but she made no hostile move, and I found myself outside the gate in the cold sunlight.

It was later than I'd thought, mid-afternoon. I returned to the government compound, neither hurrying nor dawdling, and asked if the Sun Lord had returned. But he hadn't; he was still outside the walls with the army. So I trudged over to the stables and ordered a mount to be saddled, and then I went to the villa and up to our bedchamber. The servants had lit a brazier, and with the sun pouring in as well, the room was pleasantly warm. I got my cosmetic box from my traveling chest, sat on the edge of the bed, and opened the lid. I'd hidden the double poison in plain sight, among my vials of scent.

I knew what I must do and also what must happen to me afterward, unless I took precautions. Nilang's presence at the Aviya mansion had reminded me of that, if I needed a reminder. Her daughters would come for me and I was in no mind to suffer what Adrine had suffered. I would kill myself first.

I had no doubt I could do so, yet I felt that I ought to commit myself, as one commits one's fate to the sea by sailing out of harbor. So I took up one of the vials, broke the seal, and drank the venom. It was oily but almost tasteless, with just a hint of citrine. Nevertheless I choked a little getting it down. My eyes watered and I wiped them on my sleeve, but I was almost sure I wasn't crying.

I reckoned that, to ensure my death, I had to swallow the other dose before the second hour of the dusk watch. That meant I had to keep the second vial with me, and it must therefore seem to be other than it was. Because it already appeared to be scent, I would perfect the illusion; I unsealed it and added a tiny drop of Blue-Tinted Cloud from one of my perfume vials. A sniff told me the method had worked.

I resealed the waxed stopper over the brazier, slipped the vial into my belt pouch, and left the villa. My horse was ready; I mounted, clattered out into the street, and headed for the Gate of Double Happiness. I had never seen a city as deserted as Gultekin, every boulevard and avenue lying empty. Had I been in a normal state of mind it would have been eerie and sinister, but in my present state I thought little of it.

The city gate still stood open. The sentry captain recognized me and asked if I wanted an escort; I told him I didn't and rode through. And there, spread out before me on the gently sloping plain, lay the war camp of the Army of Durdane, all ditches and palisades and spindly wooden watchtowers and tents. The men had been building the camp for days, and now they'd moved in. From this base, tomorrow at dawn, they would move out to fight the Exiles.

I looked into the distance. Some three miles to the east, its crest visible above the palisades, was a low ridge. Lying across this crest was a dark shadow, like the shadows of clouds. But there were no clouds, and I realized it was a vast mass of horsemen. Ardavan had come.

I asked a passing cavalry captain if he'd seen the Sun Lord, and he told me that Terem had gone north toward the river. I followed, riding across the dry brown winter turf and the half-melted mud churned up by tens of thousands of men. Terem wouldn't like this warm weather, and neither would Ardavan. They both needed hard, frozen ground for their horsemen.

I found him by the Jacinth. There was a castella there, and the engineers had roughly repaired its gates and ramparts. Terem was using the topmost floor of the keep as an observation post and headquarters. He wasn't especially surprised to see me, and neither were the other half dozen officers present, even though I'd walked in on a staff conference. During the invasion of Lindu I'd acquired a reputation for audacity and impudence; despite the grimness of the situation, a couple of the younger officers smiled surreptitiously.

"I wondered how long it would be before you turned up," Terem said. Before I could speak, he took my arm and dragged me to the narrow window. "Look there, on the ridge. He's already set up his headquarters. It's right under those banners. The white splash, that'll be his tent."

"I see it," I agreed. "My lord, there's something I have to tell you."

My tone must have struck him, because he released my arm and looked into my eyes. "What's the matter, Lale?"

"May I tell you alone, my lord?"

It was a difficult moment. The enemy was almost at our throats, and here was the Sun Lord's Inamorata asking him for his precious time. The smiles vanished and I saw Terem waver, almost annoyed enough to dismiss me.

I could blurt out everything, but I didn't want to reveal, in front of his men, how utterly he had been duped. "My lord," I whispered, "I beg you."

"Continue without me," he said to the others, and we went through a low doorway onto the castella rampart. I made sure the door was closed behind us. There was nobody on the wall walk, but on the distant ridge the shadows were spreading like spilled oil. There were so many of them.

"Are you ill?" he asked. "You don't look at all well."

"Terem," I said, "a woman my age, named Dilara, is going to try to kill you before morning. Don't sleep at the villa. Keep a ring of guards around you at all times. She won't have to get close to you to do it. She never misses with a throwing knife. All she'll have to do is see you. And the knife will be envenomed."

He stared at me for a long time. Then he said, "Lale, I know you're an actress, but this is too much. What in the name of Father Heaven do you think you're playing at?"

"You know me better than that, Terem."

Alarm awakened in his face, and a terrible apprehension. "How do you know this?" he asked.

"I'm a spy," I said. I felt as if I were speaking lines. "Makina Seval sent me to Kurjain to become your lover. I've been telling her everything you intend to do. I told her you were going to invade Lindu, and I think she told Ardavan, and that's how he stopped you at Bara. And now she's ordered your assassination, so that Ardavan will win tomorrow."

He still couldn't quite believe me. But then his expression changed, and I knew he'd seen that I was neither mad nor deluded and that this horror I spoke was the truth.

"You," he said slowly, "you've been betraying me all this time?"

"Yes. Utterly."

After a long silence, during which I watched Ardavan's host flood slowly across the distant ridge, he said, "So good an actress. I never doubted you for a moment. Not even Halis doubted you."

"I was well trained," I told him. "It took years. The Despotana has been at this for a long time."

"Why? How does an Exile victory benefit her?"

"She hates you," I said, "and the Chancellor, and many others in Bethiya. I don't know why she wants Ardavan to win, unless it's for that. Or maybe it's something else. It could be anything. I think she's mad."

Terem shook himself, as if a nightmare gripped him and he struggled to awaken from it. "Tell me," he rasped, "why I shouldn't kill you where you stand."

"Kill me after I've told you everything I can. It's not just me and Dilara who work for the Despotana, Terem. She has people everywhere."

"And now you've betrayed her, as well as me. Why should I trust you?"

"I've been on the wrong side," I said wearily. I didn't want to explain myself. I couldn't, not in the time we had. "I realized it too late. Please, Terem. Do what you like with me. But protect yourself."

"This Dilara. Why should I fear a woman so much?"

"You don't know what she's capable of. She was trained as an assassin by Taweret fighting adepts. If she stood here instead of me, you'd be dead by now."

His expression, which had already passed from disbelief to shock, was now stark with fury. "You'll tell me everything. And you'll tell Halis, too."

"Halis will have to hear it from you, Terem. There's a curse on me for betraying the Despotana. I won't live long past sunset."

There was another long silence. During it, he somehow mastered his rage, a thing few men could have done after such an injury. At length he said, "Why have you betrayed me, Lale? I thought you were on my side. How did she make you do such things?"

"It was because I loved her. She was my mother. I thought she loved me back. But she doesn't, and she never did. I betrayed you, yes, but she betrayed me. She murdered Merihan. She used Dilara to poison her. Dilara herself told me that."

He passed a hand over his eyes. "Merihan, too?"

"Yes. It was to clear my path to you."

"Did you know my wife was to be killed?"

"I swear I did not. I didn't find out about her murder until yesterday. But you didn't know everything about your Surina." I took a deep breath. I had told Ilishan I wouldn't reveal the truth, but what was one more treachery among so many? "Merihan wasn't of Aviya blood, she was a secret adoption. And she was my sister. The Despotana always knew she was my kin, but she kept it from me. So you see, Makina Seval had Dilara murder my only sibling."

He glowered at me. "You're mistaken. Or you're lying. Merihan was an Aviya."

"Ask Ilishan. He told me she was adopted, and he intends to tell you the same. But think, Terem. Why am I so like Merihan? It's because I'm her twin. The Despotana knew about me a long time ago, and plotted to put me in Merihan's place. She hoped you'd see in me the one you lost. And you did."

He hit me backhanded across my cheek. It was a hard blow, hard enough to make my ears ring, and it hurt. But it was far less than I deserved and far less than I must still suffer.

"And I thought," he said, "that you loved me."

I laughed. It made my face hurt even more. "That's the terrible part, Terem. I do. Why else do you think I've told you all this now? I could have betrayed you and lived. Now I've betrayed *her*, so I'm going to die."

"Ah." His mouth was a cold, disbelieving line. "From this supposed curse the Despotana laid on you?"

I put my hand to my throbbing cheek and rubbed it. "Not *her* curse. The Taweret spirit summoner I go to in Kurjain, remember her? She was the Despotana's house sorceress, and she's no charlatan, she's real. She laid it on me years ago. I once saw a girl die from it. And the Taweret fighting teachers were hers—she helped the Despotana from the beginning. She came to Kurjain when I did, to relay orders to me. We called her Nilang. She's here in Gultekin somewhere, to watch me."

"Describe her and the other one."

I did so. When I fell silent we stood there, three paces apart. His face was that of a soldier who has taken a sword in his belly and thinks he is going to die. I had never seen Terem look like that, not even at Bara. It was more terrible to me than murderous fury.

"I have much to do," he said in a toneless voice. "I'm sending you back to the villa, where you'll be put under guard. While you're there I want you to write everything down. I will send someone for it before midnight. You are not to speak of this to my officers or anyone else."

"I will be dead by midnight," I said.

"No curse works that fast, even a Taweret one. When I've beaten Ardavan, I'll consider what to do with you."

I bowed my head in submission. He was right about the curse; Adrine would have needed days to die from the attentions of the wraiths. But I had my little bottle. I would write as much as I could, then drink from it.

He took my arm in a painfully tight grasp and led me back into the keep. We'd been gone for some time. The officers looked up from their tablets and tallies, expressions of perplexity on their faces at first, then alarm. I bore the mark of his hand on my face, and we could not be mistaken for a happy couple.

"The Inamorata has been threatened with assassination," Terem said. "So have I. Captain Sholaj, find six men and a sub-captain. Have them escort her to the villa and put her into the bedchamber. They are to place a guard at her door and below her window. Clear the building of servants. No one is to go in or out. Tuhan, I need a hundred men to search the city for a pair of women. As soon as you're ready I'll give you particulars. Get to it, both of you."

Thus he dismissed me, and Sholaj took me away and delivered me to the soldiers.

I suspected I had little time before Nilang's daughters came for me, and I was right. As we neared the city gate a subtle unease began to penetrate my strange calm. I took it at first for apprehension about what was to happen to me, but as we passed through the gate I saw the shadows clustering beneath the arch, and I knew.

But it was not as bad as I'd feared, and the soldiers around me noticed nothing. I didn't tear at my face or shriek or throw myself from my horse, although in another hundred yards my heart was pounding with an eerie, unfocused dread. But I mastered it, though my hands shook and I knew my face was white. The subcaptain glanced curiously at me once or twice but said nothing and delivered me as ordered to the compound.

And then, as I dismounted by the villa entrance, the dread left me. I was astonished. Was this what had sent Adrine into paroxysms of terror? If such tremors were all Nilang's wraiths could achieve, perhaps I could manage them. Against my will, a tiny thread of hope began to weave itself through my heart. Perhaps, I thought, time had worn the curse away. Perhaps, with me, Nilang had got it wrong. Perhaps my love for Terem would armor me against the wraiths.

So, as the soldiers escorted me upstairs to the bedchamber, a foolish part of me began to build temples in the air. I would manage Nilang's daughters after all. Then all I'd need was a little time; I'd deal with the guards, slip over the wall and out into the countryside. I'd vanish. I'd be free at last, free of everyone.

And then what? My hopes crashed in ruins. I would have to run forever, with not only Mother, Nilang, Dilara, and all my former sisters on my trail, but also a furious and vengeful Terem. Even with all my skills, I'd never find a place to lay my head. And I would always carry with me my own curse: that I loved Terem, yet had so utterly betrayed him. What good was escape to me now?

The bedchamber door closed behind me and I was alone. Faint heat radiated from the brazier near the balcony shutters. The sun lay close above the western horizon, and the light through the window was tinted with copper. On the table by the window lay reed pens, ink, and a sheaf of the paper Terem used for dispatches.

There was a lot to tell him, and I must get started. I kindled a lamp from the brazier and set it on the table. Then I bowed my head and asked Our Lady of Mercy for her protection, that she might shield me in spite of the evil I had done.

I was still praying when they came for me. It was not like the first time. It began painfully, like a coarse cloth drawn over an exposed nerve. Then the corners of the room darkened and began to writhe. My calm slipped away to be replaced by a clammy sensation of dread, and then, suddenly, everything in the room terrified me. The pen on the table seemed a writhing worm, the window glass was full of malevolent eyes, and I *knew* that the lamp wanted to crawl into my mouth and feed on me.

I looked down at my hands. My fingers had curled into talons. From the corners of my eyes, I saw the shadows flicker and slither toward me. My muscles gave way and I sank to my knees, then to the floor. A paralysis took my limbs. My tongue was frozen in my mouth. I could not even scream.

The shadows touched my face. And then they were inside me.

Nothing could have prepared me for it. I became *inhabited*, unspeakably, disgustingly inhabited. Nameless things squirmed through my flesh, wriggled in my blood. They rose through my throat and invaded my eyes and made me see the living horror I would become. They coiled in my ears and made me listen to my screams, slithered into my nostrils and made me smell the stench of my degradation.

Yet they would not allow me to shriek as Adrine had shrieked, and I could emit only husky grunts, like those of an animal. I don't know how long I lay on the floor, jerking and drooling and making such noises, but the sun was just below the horizon when they left me.

When they were gone, I remained there in stunned, quivering silence. Their departure was no relief, for I knew they would come back, just as they had come back for Adrine. But now I knew what was going to happen to me and how I would feel when they took my mind and body for their pleasure. It was the last refinement of agony, this knowledge of the horrors to come. Now I understood why Adrine had wanted to tear out her eyes.

At that, I felt my hands creeping toward my face, and I sat up with a gasp. My fingers were hooked claws. I straightened them slowly, one by one.

The light in the bedchamber was red, and in its corners lurked rusty clots of shadow. After a while I was able to stand up. Paper and ink beckoned me. I stumbled to the table and stared down at them. How could I write what he wanted to know? My hands trembled in uncontrollable spasms, and I could think of nothing except what was going to happen to me again. My cold serenity had abandoned me. I could barely master my fear.

Something fluttered darkly near the bed. I cringed and it was gone. My imagination. Or perhaps not.

For the first time in my life, my courage failed me. I couldn't face them again. I had done as much as I could; I had confessed to Terem and given him the warning he needed. The rest he must manage for himself. I was past helping him.

I sat on the edge of the bed and fumbled through my pouch until I found the vial. My fingers trembled so badly that I could barely loosen the wires that secured the stopper, but I managed it at last, broke the wax seal, and got the vial open. The scent of Blue-Tinted Cloud drifted from it. I was safe, or soon would be.

I put the vial to my lips and drank. The poison was thin and watery, not like the first I had taken. When the vial was empty, I let it fall to the floor, where it broke.

It seemed very strange to me that this was to be the final hour of my life. I had come to such a sorry end, after all my dreams of glory and triumph. But I felt no dread of death, only a vast relief. I knew dying was going to hurt, because it had hurt Adrine. But it wouldn't go on very long. And compared to the horror of the wraiths, it was nothing.

I lay back on the bed, stared at the ceiling, and waited. The room slowly darkened as the daylight failed. The pains would begin soon, and I awaited them eagerly, as a woman awaits the soft footsteps of her lover on the stair.

Twenty-nine

❧

Outside the window, the murky light of winter dusk dimmed toward blackness. An hour had passed since I emptied the second vial, and still the venom had not touched me.

In growing despair, I lay on the bed until full night had fallen. But at last I accepted that it was useless to wait any longer. The poison had failed. I didn't know why. I had taken it soon enough after the first dose for it to act.

I wept for a while. Then I got up and tore a long strip of gossamin from one of my skirts and twisted it into a thin cord. There was an iron hook in the ceiling beam, from which the hanging lamp was suspended; it looked as if it would bear my weight.

I was braiding the noose when I glimpsed motion from the corner of my eye. They were coming again. Frantically I tried to complete the noose and almost dropped it.

The movement again. It wasn't right. Shaking with fear, I made myself look.

The latch on the balcony door was slowly lifting.

Dilara, it must be Dilara. My fear abated, to be replaced with sudden hope. Perhaps I could save Terem before I died. I had the advantage of surprise, and the cord in my hands would serve as a garrote. I hid it in my sleeve and took a step toward the door.

The door opened. Nilang was there.

Frozen with dread, I stopped in my tracks. I was certain she had come to watch my torment, and that she had brought her daughters with her.

The gossamin cord slipped from its concealment and fell at my feet. "No," I whispered. "Please."

Her gaze went to the broken vial on the floor. In a low voice she said, "Have you taken both, you fool?"

I didn't know what else to do, so I nodded. Then a faint spark of defiance woke in me. "It didn't work. You're not as smart as you think you are." I could call the guards, but I would kill her myself, if the wraiths gave me time.

In two swift steps, watching me all the while, she reached the vial's fragments and picked one up. Sniffed.

"You put perfume in it?" she said in a disgusted tone. "No wonder you're alive. The scent took its power. Did I not instruct you in this?"

I moved a little toward her. "I don't remember. But it doesn't matter, because you'll never reach him now. He knows about you and Dilara and Mother. I told him everything."

"Ah," she said. "So I was right about you, after all. Do you want to live?"

My mouth dropped open but no words came out of it. I had no idea what had come over her.

"Fool of a girl," she snapped. "I can release you, but not here. Come quickly, if you want your freedom."

I can release you. I heard only that and clutched at its forlorn hope. "The guards," I said.

Nilang made a dismissive gesture and blew out the lamp. In the sudden darkness I felt her hand on my sleeve, tugging me onto the balcony. Outside, a quarter moon shed a thin illumination over the city's roofs.

She'd come up by a soot-black rope and a padded grapnel. In moments we were over the rail and on the ground, the rope slithering down after us. At my feet lay the form of the guard who'd been stationed below the balcony. I wondered if he was dead.

Again the tug on my sleeve. We kept to the shadows by the wall, until we were well away from the villa and behind the stables. Up the steps to the wall walk, the rope again, down the other side and we were in a narrow, deserted street.

I felt the tingle along my nerves again, and a stealing sense of horror. "They're coming," I gasped. "Stop them."

"I cannot," Nilang whispered. "I must exorcise them. Just a little farther."

Around a corner, then another. She opened a door in an alcove, pulled me into a narrow courtyard. Another door closed behind us and I stood blinking in a dim yellow light. A lamp burned on a stone floor; near it lay a satchel, a leather bag, a water jug, and a wine flask. We were in a windowless room and I saw shadows moving in its corners.

"Hurry," I croaked. "Please. They're close."

Nilang left me by the lamp, rummaged in the satchel, and drew out a pottery jar. "Put out your tongue," she ordered. I obeyed and she smeared a paste from the jar onto it. It tasted foul and I gagged, but whatever it was, it worked quickly. In moments I felt drugged and stupid, too befuddled even to fear the wraiths. I sank to the floor and tried to keep my eyes open.

Nilang lit something in a shallow bowl and I smelled the scent of burning sweetcup. She inhaled the drug several times, then seized my chin and pulled my head up. Her gaze locked on mine. I tried to look away but could not. She began to whisper to me, murmurs in a language I almost knew. Sometimes her voice deepened as if others spoke through her mouth; then the speakers seemed to converse gravely among themselves at the edge of hearing. I could not tell what they spoke of, but it frightened me.

At length I could see nothing but her eyes, like blue pools in which I softly drowned. I felt her slender dry fingers touch my lips.

I opened my mouth. Nilang's voice hardened and she spoke three harsh words, as if to call something from deep within me.

My sight returned. A cataract of nausea bolted into my throat. With it came a rush of vaporous substance, foul as the exhalation of a charnel house. It poured from my mouth like smoke, clotted in the dim light into a wavering shadow. Nilang spoke to it in that same harsh voice, her face drawn with strain, and I knew it did not want to go. It wanted to live inside me, consuming me from within until I died.

She gestured and spoke again, and it went.

I fell over sideways and vomited onto the stone floor. I had little in my stomach and not much came up, but I retched for a long time. Finally Nilang brought me wine and water in a pottery cup, and made me drink it. There must have been something else in the mixture, too, for my head cleared almost immediately.

We sat on the floor and studied each other. I felt a most peculiar sensation of lightness. I had not realized until now how much a part of my life the wraiths had been. I had never given them much thought, because it was easier not to, but they had always been *there*, like invisible jailers. Now I was free of them.

"Why have you helped me?" I asked. "I betrayed her."

"That betrayal is precisely the reason."

"I don't understand."

"I think you do. Use your wits, girl."

From across the years, Mother's words in the sickroom at Repose returned: *Remember that you are bound to me.* And now I remembered other hints: the taint of contempt I'd once heard in Nilang's voice when she spoke of Mother; the fleeting perplexity I'd felt in Kurjain about her real allegiances; and in the last few months, her ambiguous probes of my loyalty—not, as I'd imagined, on Mother's behalf but rather on her own.

"You don't serve her willingly, do you?" I asked.

"I do not."

Furiously I burst out, "Then why didn't you tell me before? I could have done something. Stopped her somehow."

"Don't be a fool. How could I take that risk unless I were sure you had turned on her? I have tried to sound you for disaffection, the gods know I have—when your friends died in Istana, and you knew their deaths lay at your door, and when I told you that she'd made the girl Ashken her heir. And I did so again today, in the Aviya house, after I sensed the shade of the Surina with you." Her mouth twisted. "But you are a fine actress, I give you that. It wasn't until I saw the soldiers bringing you here, and sensed the wraiths come to you, that I was sure."

I said, "She always knew Merihan was my sister, didn't she?"

"Yes. Or she was almost sure of it, when she brought you to Repose. I probed you soon afterward to be certain."

Memory stirred in me. "It was the first time I saw you. It was in the palace. I fell asleep."

"You did not. There was a drug. With its help I opened the deep levels of your thought, where your awareness of your sister lies hidden."

This startled me. "It does? How?"

"The awareness arises when two minds share the same womb; it persists after birth but is difficult to draw forth. But when I questioned you, you revealed it, and the Despotana knew you were the one. Then I placed an injunction in you to forget my questions."

"But how did she even know I existed? I don't understand why she looked for me in the first place."

"It was through me. When she heard about the Sun Lord's betrothal years ago, she wished to know more about the Aviyas and the Surina-to-be, so she sent me to Gultekin to accomplish this. I established myself as a summoner, then arranged for the child to become ill with a harmless malady. When her parents brought her to me, I perceived a difference in their essential natures."

"In other words, that she wasn't their daughter."

Nilang made a gesture of assent. "More than that, when I secretly probed the girl, I discovered her awareness of a womb sister, although in a place hidden from thought. I told the Despotana of your existence, and she realized that controlling the blood sister of the Surina might bring advantage in her secret wars. So she began the search, and five years later she found you."

"And she intended to substitute me for Merihan, even then?"

"She has always spun many threads; that was only one among them. But when you were fifteen, she sent me to Gultekin, and on my return I told her how closely you resembled Merihan. So she chose that particular strand to weave into her design. . . . How did you find out?"

"Ilishan told me. Then, this morning, I spoke with Merihan in the garden. She appeared in the form of a child, but she was my sister."

Nilang nodded. "I felt her presence from the street. It was why I came into the courtyard—I wanted to know what you might have learned. But as I said, you are a fine actress. I still could not tell for certain if you had turned your coat."

I sat for a while, revolving many thoughts. Then I said, "She's mad, isn't she?"

"As a lunatic babbling in the street? No. But as one driven by a ghost, yes."

"But it's a real ghost," I said. "Not something out of fancy. Am I right?"

Her eyes narrowed. "You know about this?"

"I saw it," I told her. "It came when I was with her on the Water Terrace. She said it was her son and that she called him every year—and that you'd taught her how, in the Taweret manner."

"Oh, I taught her, yes. It would be better for her if I had not, but she would not be denied."

"She thought it was . . . sweet and gentle, but that's not what I saw. What *was* it?"

Nilang's gaze became distant. "There is more than one way to call the dead. The one I taught her is powerful but dangerous. If the passions of the summoner are unbalanced, as hers were and are, they may attract entities of cunning and malevolent character. That is what happened—worse, the creature plucked from her mind the appearance and voice of her child and took on both. It has deceived her for years, and its whispers have nourished her hatred, her grief, and her craving for revenge. Her thirst is now too vast for any vengeance to slake it. In that way, you are right. She is mad."

In that moment, despite all Mother had done, I almost pitied her. "But didn't you *warn* her?" I asked.

"Once. She would not believe me. After that, I kept my silence."

"You hate her," I said. "That's why you helped me, isn't it? You hate her."

"Hatred is not why I helped you," Nilang answered. "I helped you because, in turn, I need your help."

I could not imagine what use I could be to Nilang. "Why?"

"Have you not listened? I am bound to her, and I need you to set me free."

"You? With your powers? How could she bind *you*?"

"She did not. An enemy from my homeland did." A look of irritation crossed her face. "Must you allow your curiosity to run riot in this manner? Your endless questions are vexatious."

"If you want me to help you," I said, "you'd better answer them. I want to know what I might be getting into."

She raised her hands in a gesture of frustration, then let them fall into her lap. "Very well. Years ago, through the machinations of its rivals, my clan fell under accusations of treason and blasphemy. Many were executed. I was among the accused, and with a few of my followers I fled across the sea and came to Chiran. We needed to eat, so I became what you Durdana call a spirit summoner."

"And Mother found you."

"No, my enemies found me. One was named Aquika, who was my equal as an adept. She was to bring me home to hang, and she had men like Master Aa with her to see that I went."

"But you're a sorceress—"

"Pah! Sorcery cannot turn aside a blade or a blow, no matter what the stories say. My people and I fought Aquika's men in Chiran's streets with steel and other devices, until the uproar brought the Heron Guard down on us. They were too many for even Taweret fighters to resist. So we let them take us all to the Despotana."

"I remember," I said. "I heard talk of it when I first came to Repose. She gave you sanctuary, then threw your pursuers out of Tamurin."

"Oh, that was what you heard, was it? There was more to it than that." Her hands clenched. "The Despotana misses no chance for advantage. She brought Aquika and me before her in secret at night, and told Aquika she could take me away to my death. But when I pleaded for sanctuary, the Despotana appeared to reconsider, and she said I might have it, provided I bound myself to her service—which was what she had intended all along. What choice did I have? I agreed."

"What did Aquika do?" I asked. I'd never imagined a drama like this. I saw it in my mind's eye: Mother's gold and green audience hall, shrouded in night, the lamp flames reflecting in the white tiles of the floor, Mother on her dais with the alien sorceresses before her.

Nilang laughed, a low harsh sound. "Aquika did not like it. But she did as much against me as she could, telling the Despotana that I must strengthen my oath of obedience with Taweret magic. That was a circumstance I had hoped to avoid, but what was I to do? It was swear or die, so I swore, and did the ritual and the summoning up of the witnesses, as Aquika demanded."

In spite of the fix I was in, these revelations fascinated me. "And what if you try to escape the binding?"

"It is subtle. If I flee, alone or in company, then within a day I find myself walking in at the same door by which I went out. And if I do not obey the Despotana's instructions, I must suffer visitations from the Quiet World, to remind me of my oath. The reminders are not gentle, and even I cannot endure them for long. As for betraying her outright or trying to kill her, if I did that, I would die by something worse than wraiths. Nor can Master Aa or my other servants remove her, because they are as bound to me as I am to her, and where I lead they must follow. In consequence, I have always served her to the best of my ability."

I frowned. "But telling me all this—isn't that against the binding? Won't you suffer for it?"

"Think harder, girl. How could I teach you at Three Springs if I could not speak freely? How can you and your sisters work to her best advantage, if you may not talk to each other about your tasks? But we *can* talk, because your wraith initiations and my binding are our common bond. They keep us from revealing secrets to those who are not initiates, but they must allow us to converse among ourselves. What use to the Despotana is an army of mutes? She knows better than to bind us as tightly as that."

A haunted expression passed across her face. "Although I dare not speak too directly, even to you, about what I need. Even to go this far may be a risk. But I must accept it, because it is the only road that may one day take me to my home and to my daughter."

I'd thought I was past surprise, but this jolted me. "You have a *child?*" I asked. I had never, ever, imagined that Nilang might be a mother.

"Do you think you are the only one who has suffered kin loss? Yes, I have a child. But I have not seen her for sixteen years." Her face contorted, and for an instant I saw what lay beneath her alien impassiveness: humiliation, sorrow, longing, fury, loneliness.

"It was because of my daughter that I submitted. I wanted to live, because I hoped that some day I might be with her again. Had it not been for my child, I would have died before submitting to the Despotana." Her voice rose. "I, bound to an outlander! I, who was sorceress to Tjekert-Rabaka and spymistress of the clan of the Khepekaremun! To put my neck under the heel of a madwoman!"

She fell silent, and I heard her quick, angry breathing. Then she hissed, "She has stolen my life and kept me from my daughter, and you ask me if I hate her. Can you not determine this for yourself?"

"So," I said, "you want me to kill her for you. *That's* why you saved me."

Nilang leaned forward. "I released you from the wraiths, girl, and for that you owe me a life. I cannot advise you to remove the one we speak of, but if her heart stopped, I would be free."

"And there's no other way for you to escape her?"

"None. I cannot lift my binding as I lifted your wraiths. It is irrevocable while she lives."

I thought about that, and then I thought about Mother. At some moment in the past few hours I had stopped loving her. Now I wanted revenge for her treachery and I wanted justice for my sister's murder. And I knew, too, that Terem and I would never be safe until she was dead.

But I wasn't the only person she had betrayed. "All this time," I said, still hardly believing it, "she's been helping Ardavan, hasn't she? She told him Terem was marching on Lindu, hoping he might catch us at Bara. Then she told him we weren't ready for a surprise attack in winter. Father Heaven only knows what else she's given him. And now she intends to kill Terem and let the Exiles conquer Bethiya. Or am I mistaken in all this?"

"You are not in the least mistaken."

"But why didn't she order Dilara to kill him at Bara? Ardavan could have wiped out the whole Army of the East."

"True. But by the time the news reached the Despotana in Chiran, it was too late to get such an order to Dilara, even by one of my sendings. And I had no authority to order your Sun Lord killed—that, she has always reserved for herself. But if she'd known his intentions sooner, he would have died at Bara. He moved too fast for her, and that saved him."

"How long has she been allied to Ardavan? Does he even know she's helping him?

"He knows. When he overran Jouhar he saw what he might do for her, and she sent me to speak with him in secret. He was suspicious at first. But he knew what had happened to her family. The Exiles are great believers in blood vengeance, so her offer seemed a likely thing to him. Thus I was able to arrange the agreement between them: together they would destroy Bethiya, and thereafter Ardavan would guarantee the Despotana's rule over Tamurin."

"But that makes no sense," I protested. "What does it profit her if Ardavan takes Bethiya? There must be more to it than vengeance for her son's death. And she must know that Ardavan's guarantees are worthless."

Nilang cocked her head. "Ah. Do you remember how I told you she had adopted a formal heir? The girl named Ashken?"

"I remember, but—"

"Be still and listen. Suppose Ardavan, by the end of this year, conquers Bethiya and the remaining Exile Kingdoms. Now he sits in Seyhan, supreme lord of all the lands north of the Pearl, from the Juren Gap to the sea. But the Exiles are few and the Durdana are many, and his power will be more secure if he acquires legitimacy in the eyes of the conquered. How better to do this than take a wife from an ancient Durdana family, a wife descended from a great bloodline of the empire, and found a dynasty with her?"

"Ashken," I said. "He marries her. That's part of the bargain."

"Yes. Then he proclaims his rule in the old style, and an Emperor and Empress sit again in Seyhan."

"But," I objected, "there's still nothing in this for Mother."

"The story proceeds," Nilang said. "Ashken is now with child, and the Despotana dispatches ladies-in-waiting from Tamurin to assist her. The Empress bears a son, and soon afterward, Ardavan dies of an illness and the boy becomes Emperor Minor. The Empress is his Dowager Regent, and governs in his name."

A small cold smile touched her mouth. "And Ashken summons her beloved adoptive mother, the Despotana of Tamurin, to help her manage the realm. What could be more natural? And with the Despotana come more ladies-in-waiting, all trained at Three Springs, and people who object to the regency experience fatal accidents and lingering illnesses."

I closed my mouth, which had fallen open. Then I said, "And Mother rules the empire from behind the dais."

"Your perception is commendable," Nilang said in a sarcastic voice, "if somewhat tardy."

"But what if Ashken has a daughter? The Exiles reckon succession only in the male line."

"A male child will be substituted, if necessary, in the hour of birth. Remember that Ashken will be attended by your sisters of Three Springs."

At first I thought the whole scheme as mad as Mother herself was. But then I thought again, and realized that she could do it. She had achieved so much else, why not this?

"You helped her plan it all," I said accusingly. "That's how you know."

Nilang sighed. "Have you not heard me? I had no choice. But in the matter of which I spoke, what is your answer?"

Even with what I now knew, I hesitated. Old habits are not so easily broken, and I had loved Mother for a long time. But then I remembered Merihan, and Perin, and Adrine, and all the young men who died at Bara, and I thought of how many more would die if Mother lived.

"I'll do it," I said. "We'll get to Chiran, somehow, and I'll do it."

"Chiran? There is no need to go to Chiran. The Despotana is not there. She is in Kurjain."

I gaped at her in astonishment. "What nonsense is this? Why would she gamble with her freedom by going to Kurjain? She puts herself in Terem's grasp."

"Ah, but she thinks no one knows about her plots and that no one would ever connect her to his assassination. Also she thinks that her presence in Kurjain is unlikely to be detected at all, and so believes herself doubly secure."

"But why does she need to be there? Why not stay in Chiran?"

"Because in Kurjain she is some fourteen days closer to the center of things. She missed killing the Sun Lord at Bara, because of that fourteen days' delay, and she does not want to miss him a second time. So she came secretly to Kurjain just before the Sun Lord marched to Gultekin, and gave Dilara and myself our orders—Dilara to kill the Sun Lord, me to tell Ardavan that the assassination is at hand. The Despotana will wait in Kurjain, until she receives my sending to tell her that he is dead and that Ardavan is sweeping across Bethiya. Then she will return to Tamurin, and prepare Ashken to marry the new Exile Emperor."

I thought hard. With my warning, Terem might survive Dilara. But he still might lose tomorrow's battle, and the barbarian darkness would sweep across the world. Killing Mother would not change that.

Suddenly I sat up straight. Her death was only part of the solution. The rest of the answer was right in front of me.

I said, "You're supposed to tell Ardavan that Terem is going to be killed, so he can take better advantage of it in tomorrow's battle?"

"Yes. I am to slip across the lines tonight. He knows me from the earlier negotiations, as I told you. I cannot avoid doing this, if that is your plan. She has ordered me to go, and go I must, or suffer."

"I understand that," I said. "Look, I'll dispose of the Despotana for you, but first you must help me with something else."

"And what might that be?"

"When you go to Ardavan, there's nothing to keep me from going, too, is there?"

"No. But to what purpose?"

"So I can assassinate him," I said.

"*What?* Are you as mad as she is? Suppose you come to grief? Who will dispose of the Despotana then?"

"We can kill him if we act together. You're always telling me to think, Nilang. Now you do the same. If we remove Ardavan, we wreck Mother's plans from end to end."

"Wrecking her plans does not interest me. Her death is enough, so I can go home and find my child."

"But if you help Terem now, perhaps he'll help you later. He's the Sun Lord, Nilang. If any power can reunite you and your daughter, it's his. He could even bring her here to Bethiya, where you'd both be safe."

I had never seen Nilang appear uncertain until now. "But we've been his enemies," she protested. "Once Ardavan is dead, why should he do anything but execute us?"

"I know him, Nilang." Or I hoped I did. I was taking a tremendous gamble by expecting to negotiate with him, but he was already hunting us, and it seemed our best chance of survival. "He's not a tyrant. He's an honorable man. At the least, he'll give us our freedom in return for his victory. And remember, I've already told him about Mother, and he wants her dead as much as we do. If I can't manage to kill her, he will. You'll be free either way."

She chewed her lower lip, frowning. "I am still bound. If I tell him what I have told you, I will die in torment. You will have to speak for me. And I cannot be present. If I am, the binding will make me try to silence you."

"I'll speak for you, Nilang." A thought struck me. "You said she expected a sending as soon as Terem was dead?"

"Yes, I am to speak to her through Tossi."

"Can you send her a false report that will keep her in Kurjain until we reach her?"

"That feels too close to betrayal. The binding might strike me down. I dare not."

"If she hears nothing, how long before she takes alarm and leaves Kurjain?"

"I cannot tell. A few days, perhaps."

"Then we might just have time to get to her, if Terem helps us. But he won't do that unless I assassinate Ardavan. What do you want to do, Nilang?"

After a long silence, she rose to her feet. "Win all or lose all, then," she said. "Come with me to the King."

Thirty

❦

I lay very still in the brittle winter grass and studied the fires of the Exile camp. Sleet pecked at my cheeks; bad weather had moved in on a freezing wind from the west and shut out the starlight. Without the distant glow of the watch fires I could not have seen my hand in front of my face; Nilang, though she was only an arm's length to my right, I could not see at all.

I was lucky to have made her an ally. Out of her satchel had come black clothing—she'd come prepared for anything, it seemed—and charcoal dust to darken our faces and hands. There was also a thin Taweret murder blade for me, like the one she carried. Dressed and armed, I slung her rope over my shoulder and we left.

In the deserted streets we saw none of Terem's searchers, and we got onto Gultekin's southeast rampart without incident. There were sentries, but they were staying close to the meager warmth of their cressets, and didn't see us as we roped down the outer face of the city wall. Getting from the wall to the Durdana camp took little time, but then we had to work our way eastward through our lines without being caught. It was like threading a dangerous maze, for many of the battalions that would fight on the morrow were already in position, and the soldiers had lit fires to keep warm. We had to pass so close to them that we could hear the men's voices as they cursed both the cold and the Exiles and boasted about the enemies they expected to kill. But we moved slowly and carefully, our bellies on the frosty grass, no more than black shadows on the black earth, and no one saw us.

Eventually the firelight and the voices lay behind. Once in the no-man's-land between the armies we moved faster; now, as I lay on my belly in the darkness, only a stone's throw separated us from the Exile pickets. I could see them moving up and down, silhouetted in the glow of their fires. As far as I could judge, it was about midnight.

I slid closer to Nilang and whispered, "What next?"

"We try to get in without being killed as spies. I have a pass token, but they must have a chance to see it. Stay behind me and make no suspicious movements."

We stood up and approached the black silhouettes ahead. Nilang had something in her hand, which she held out in front of her; it gleamed dull gold and ruby in the firelight. Our garb and blackened faces made us hard to see, and the nearest picket still hadn't noticed us when Nilang called to him in the Exile tongue. Even in the bad light I saw him stiffen with surprise, and then the glint of a spear blade as it swept down to threaten us.

"*Lal stepanu!*" he shouted, or something like it. Nilang answered briefly and waved the medallion. We were very close to the man now, and two others had joined him. I could make out their facial tattoos and the pale streaks of their yellow mustaches.

The first speaker noticed the medallion and squinted at it. His eyes widened abruptly and suddenly he looked agitated. "Ardavan *terk malag?*"

"Ardavan," Nilang answered. "*Hagalas.*" I vaguely remembered that *hagalas* was the Exile word for "friend."

They lowered their spears a little and she let the first man examine the medallion. I stood beside her and peered at the thing. It showed a red scorpion on a gold ground, Ardavan's house emblem, with a squiggle of Exile script under it. The Exile soldier deciphered it aloud, haltingly.

"We're lucky," Nilang said from the corner of her mouth. "He has the rank marks of an undersergeant, and he can read the medallion."

"What does it say?"

"That the bearer and companions are in the service of the King and under his protection."

The officer grunted, waved at us to follow, and off we went through the tents of the enemy camp. Much of the Exile soldiery wore Ardavan's scorpion emblem, but I saw a good few with the white snake insignia of Mirsing, others badged with Ishban's black moon, and more with the thunderbolt and ox of Suarai: Ardavan's royal allies were with him. The Exiles were doing the same things that their Durdana counterparts were doing not far away: eating, drinking, sharpening weapons, cursing, gambling, telling jokes, boasting. I now knew enough about armies to sense that these men were tired, although they appeared not at all downcast by being so far into enemy country in the depths of winter. In fact, they looked very confident of their victory, and my heart sank a little.

We reached the royal tent. It was of a good size and made of white leather, the blazon of the red scorpion on the hanging that closed its doorway. Two guards in scale armor stood by the entrance, each with a drawn yataghan, the curved Exile cavalry sword. Like everybody else, they stared at us. Our sergeant spoke to one of them, who then put his head inside for a moment. Then he brought it out and stared at us some more.

At length a man looked out of the tent and waved at us to enter. I found myself with him and Nilang in a sort of cloth anteroom; male voices came from behind a curtain. They sounded cheerful.

"Why are you here?" the man asked in atrocious Durdana. He was in early middle age and wore no armor, but his clothes and bearing marked him as someone of rank. He had begun life uncomely and was little improved by his facial tattoos. Some were disembodied mouths with teeth.

"I have news of the Sun Lord and his army," Nilang said.

He regarded us with his black eyes. "Give it me, then."

"I may tell it only to the King. Tell him the Taweret is here and he will see us."

"Who is this?" Meaning me.

"That is for the King to know."

He looked thoughtful and went into the other room. I heard voices, then a silence. Suddenly several armored officers came out, glowered at us, and left the tent. The ugly man followed them, looking bemused.

"Come," said a deep voice within.

We entered, and for the first time in my life I saw the relentless enemy of my race. He was a tall man, well built, and handsome even with the tattooing. His clothes were simple: a scarlet tunic and black leather trousers and boots, worn beneath a knee-length Exile mantle of some black and gold fur. The gold in the fur was the color of his hair, which hung in the customary slender braids along his lean cheeks. He had a sensitive mouth and his hands were long and graceful. He'd kept two guards by him, who stood with drawn yataghans and watched us carefully. I couldn't have got past them even if I'd been willing to buy his life with my own, which I wasn't.

Rugs covered the tent floor. Nilang prostrated herself on one and so did I. After a moment, the deep voice said, in the Durdana of an educated man, "Ah, the Lady Preherwenemef. Get up, both of you, and tell me why you're here."

We rose, with me wondering how many names Nilang had, and how Ardavan could pronounce this one. He seemed to like rings, for he wore several, among them a thick gold and crimson seal ring on his left thumb.

Nilang bowed and said, "I bring you respectful greetings from my mistress, the one you know of. As we speak, she makes your Empress ready, and to ensure a propitious matrimonial prospect, she has sent this girl and me to lay bare the enemy's plans."

"Leave off the Durdana speeches," Ardavan said. "How many men has he, how good are they, and what is he going to do with them?"

"Before I tell you, dread King, know that your victory is certain. The one I serve has promised that the Sun Lord will be dead by dawn."

"So she's finally decided the time's right, has she? She could have done away with him at Bara and saved us all much inconvenience."

"Circumstances precluded such an act," Nilang replied smoothly, "but this is his last night among the living."

"I hope as much. But his generals may still fight, so answer my questions."

As he spoke, it struck me suddenly how much like Terem he was in his confidence, his ambition, and his genius for leadership. If they fought as allies, between them they might conquer the world. But as Terem had said, the world had room for only one of them.

"This spy has studied his forces closely," Nilang said. "Tell him, girl."

I obeyed. Ardavan was unlikely to be frightened if I told him our men were superbly trained and ready for battle, so I went the other way in the hope of making him overconfident. I minimized our numbers, then said our infantry was dispirited at having to fight in the cold and that most were badly trained and likely to flee at the first opportunity. I said the cavalry mounts were suffering from lack of forage and that they were out of condition from being in winter quarters—which was somewhat true but not nearly as bad as I made it. Finally I said that Terem's senior officers had lost confidence in him since the failure at Bara and were likely to disobey his orders if they disagreed with them.

Ardavan was a brilliant and capable leader, but what I told him was what he wanted to hear, and even the most brilliant man or woman can be ensnared in such a way. In short, he swallowed all of it, and I knew it would soon find its way to his generals and his allied kings. And once that happened, all I had to do was kill him.

As I spoke, I noted an opening in the leather wall behind him, through which I could see another room with a low, fur-draped bed. It was at the back of the tent. No doubt there would be a sentry patrolling outside the tent's rear, and I could only hope Ardavan didn't also post a guard in the sleeping chamber with him.

He questioned us a little more and then dismissed us. Nilang requested shelter until more of the night had passed, so the Sun Lord's men would be sleeping when we slipped back through the lines, whereupon Ardavan ordered an attendant take us to a small oxhide tent near his own. It was full of bundles and bales, and lit only faintly by campfire light seeping through the door slit. The attendant grudgingly brought us a blanket and some hard Exile bread, at which we nibbled. Then, with the smelly brown blanket wrapped around us, we settled down to wait.

Time crawled by. The wind rose, shaking the tent's walls. I peeped outside occasionally; sleet was falling heavily now, forming an icy crust on the trampled ground. The sounds of the camp waned as the fires burned lower and as men sought their tents and sleep. Finally I could hear only the hiss and bluster of the wind and the occasional distant neigh of an uncomfortable horse.

It must now be far past midnight, with the late winter dawn no more than a few hours away. "Now?" I whispered. In the gloom Nilang gave an almost invisible gesture of assent.

We renewed the blacking on our faces and hands; I rolled up the blanket and tucked it under my arm, and then we crept from the tent. Outside it was very dark, the faint glow of banked fires dimmed further by veils of freezing rain. I was very glad of my padded trousers and jacket, and I pulled my hood closer about my hair.

The rear of the royal tent was not far away. Sure enough, silhouetted against its paleness, there was the guard I'd expected. I stood up, trusting the darkness to conceal my movements, then made my way toward him. He saw me coming but didn't speak, frightened perhaps to wake his master on the other side of the tent wall.

I giggled softly in my most girlish voice, and stopped just a foot away from him. He made a noise of surprise and anticipation and reached for me. I backed away.

A shadow rose behind him. He made another faint noise and fell into my arms, though not in the way he had intended. I eased him to the ground and Nilang leaned over him and slit his throat. He gurgled once, but the wind covered the sound. When we covered the body with the blanket, it was almost invisible in the murky darkness.

I squatted by the tent wall, used the Taweret murder knife to make a tiny slit in the hide, and peered through. A hanging lamp burned dimly, revealing the bed with a man lying on his stomach under a heap of furs, his face turned toward me, asleep: Ardavan. No guard stood by him, although one probably lurked beyond the hanging that hid the chamber doorway.

Thanking the Beneficent Ones for the wind's hiss, I carefully made a long slit in the thin leather, just above ground level. Then I checked Ardavan again. He had moved, but only to turn his face away from me. So much the better.

I eased myself through the slit, while Nilang remained outside to guard my avenue of escape. Ardavan didn't stir. I crept to the bed where he slept and went up on my knees, the murder blade in my hand.

The Taweret weapon was thin and narrow, made to slide between bones and reach vitals. His braids had fallen aside, leaving the nape of his neck bare. I studied it, so pale and defenseless, and selected the place where the blade would best sever the cord that enables both movement and breath. Now the steel tip hovered a finger's breadth above his skin.

I hesitated, suddenly repelled by what I was about to do. When I killed the other men, it was because they were trying to kill me. But this strong and vibrant young King was asleep and defenseless, and I was about to dispatch him like an animal. The tip of the knife wavered.

And then I remembered the town of Sila in Lindu, the gallows with its poor flayed corpses, the ragged men and women, the children huge-eyed with hunger, the whip scars and the desecrated shrines, and I remembered that the man under my knife thought that we deserved no better and that all this awaited us under his hand.

I drove the blade deep, and Ardavan died without a sound. There was very little blood, since his heart stopped almost at once.

I waited a few moments to make sure he was dead. Then I pulled his hand from beneath the furs and removed his seal ring. Clutching it tightly, I slid back through the opening in the tent wall. The wind was cold enough to take my breath away. "He's dead," I whispered as I slipped the ring into my pouch. "Let's go."

We hurried toward the perimeter of the camp. My heart was pounding now in fear that someone would find him and sound the alarm, but all remained quiet. The weather was so foul that no one except the sentries were out, and Nilang's medallion got us past them without incident.

Now we were in no-man's-land. As we hurried away from the Exile camp, my apprehension eased. But I was not, oddly enough, thinking about how I had killed the great King Ardavan and thus changed the world, nor of how the historians might write of my courage and resolution, as I'd always dreamed. What I felt was that I had atoned, if only to a tiny degree, for my many treacheries, and that perhaps Terem might now hate me a little less than before.

We stopped at an ice-glazed puddle to scrub the charcoal from our faces, and then went on. Our watch fires and the black wall of our camp palisade drew nearer. I was taking us toward the riverbank and the castella, hoping that was where Terem was passing the night. I was very cold now, for the wind was as keen as my knife; snow had displaced the sleet and was collecting in thin drifts on the frozen earth. As we went, I rehearsed again and again what I would say to Terem, hoping he would believe me, and hoping, too, that what I'd told Nilang was right: that he would at least give us our freedom for what we'd done.

I knew something untoward had happened as soon as we came through the palisade. The campfires were freshly stoked, although it was too early for the men to be at battle preparations. Yet they were awake, standing in knots around their fires, talking and gesticulating.

"What's going on?" I asked the second-captain who was taking us to the castella. I'd expected him to clap manacles onto us both when I identified myself, but although he was beside himself with curiosity about the Inamorata's nocturnal wanderings, he was properly respectful. This suggested either that nobody knew I'd escaped from the villa or that it was known at higher levels but was being kept quiet.

"There's a rumor that somebody tried to kill the Sun Lord a little while ago," he said. "But he's not hurt, they say."

"Thank Father Heaven," I said, relief making me weak in the knees. Even given my warning, I hadn't been sure that Terem would escape Dilara's skill. "Who tried to kill him?"

"It was a woman, or so people are saying, and she's dead."

I blinked hard. Dilara had died trying, then, as I knew she might. I tried to feel satisfaction but could muster only a dull grief. I could no longer bring myself to judge her. She was my sister's murderer, true enough, but how much better was I? I had caused Perin's death, and Master Luasin's, and many more besides.

We reached the castella, where the second-captain turned us over to the officer of the watch, who happened to be Sholaj. He almost lost his tongue at the black-clad, charcoal-smudged apparition of the Inamorata before him, with her equally sinister companion. But when we handed him our weapons, he recovered enough to send a message upstairs and promptly searched us for further lethal devices.

While we waited in the courtyard for Terem's summons, I saw a slender shape lying in the shadow by the wall. Snow had covered it, but I knew who it was and did not look at her again. Nilang gave the body one swift expressionless glance, but she said nothing, and neither did I.

Word came that we were to ascend. Sholaj took us to the upper floor to the council room. Three charcoal braziers warmed the low-ceilinged chamber; all the lamps were ablaze, although only Terem and his two bodyguards were there.

"So you didn't run for it, after all," he said. He looked at Nilang. "And her?"

"She's the Taweret sorceress I told you about. But Terem, she can't be here when I tell you certain things. I beg you to excuse her for a little."

"Why? What things?"

I hesitated, then said in a low voice, "She and I—"

Nilang made a quick movement of negation. I dared not go farther.

"You and she what?"

"Terem, I beg you, send her from the room. There's sorcery here, and it's for her safety and mine. Please."

I was sure he would refuse me, but perhaps the urgency in my voice and on my face made him think again. He gestured brusquely to one of the guards. "Very well. Avshan, take her to the anteroom and hold her there."

When the door closed behind them, Terem lowered himself wearily into a chair. "I have lost track of your loyalties. Whose side are you on tonight?"

"Yours. That hasn't changed. Nilang is also your ally, if you'll allow it. She helped me escape from the villa."

"She did, did she? Unfortunately for her, I do not consider that to be an act of loyalty, since I put you there." He looked me up and down. "Why should I not send you both back to Kurjain in mana-cles and throw you into the Arsenal cells for a very long time?"

"Because we've given you tomorrow's victory. Ardavan is dead."

The remaining guard made a startled noise. Terem sat up straight, disbelief written plain on his face. "Dead?"

"Dead. Nilang helped me cross the lines into the Exile camp, and then she took me to see him, pretending I was a spy for the Despotana. Ardavan thought Nilang was on his side, you see, and that gave me my chance to kill him. I did it silently, while he was alone, and his officers may not even know he's gone. If you strike at first light, you'll catch them leaderless."

"Why should I believe you killed him, assuming he *is* dead?"

"Because I'm as good an assassin as Dilara was. We had the same training." I fumbled in my pouch and the guard tensed, but Terem waved the man to stillness.

"Here," I said. "It's Ardavan's seal ring."

Terem took the ring and held it to the light. The ruby scorpion burned in its nest of gold and onyx. He studied the thing, then lowered it and looked at me. "Because of this, you expect me to trust you?"

"How much proof of loyalty do you need? Nilang and I could have been on our way to Tamurin by now, and Ardavan would still be breathing. And Dilara tried to kill you and failed, didn't she?"

"Yes."

"You're alive because of me. Without my warning, she would have succeeded."

Slowly, he nodded. "Yes, I think she would. She came at me as I was making rounds of the camp. I thought we were prepared, but she almost had me, even so."

"What of my loyalty now?"

He said dryly, "It seems to be to me."

"Exactly. But there's still the Despotana. This part should be for your hearing only."

I waited, wondering if he believed me enough to dismiss the guard and leave himself alone with a confessed assassin. But without hesitation he told the man to leave. When we were alone, he said, "Continue."

I did, telling him as much as I could without making a book of it: about Three Springs and about the wraiths, about Nilang's binding and its consequences, and about her rescue of me. And then I told him the core of it all, which was how Mother's grand design would have swept Bethiya into the hands of Ardavan and ultimately into hers. He was not quite as astonished as I had been, but I could tell from his face that it shook him.

"With Ardavan gone," I ended, "her plans to rule an Exile empire are ruined. But none of us will be safe while she's alive. Dilara may be dead, but the Despotana has plenty of killers like her."

"And Nilang?" he asked thoughtfully. "Why are you so certain she's on my side?"

"Because she hates the Despotana. She's a slave to the binding, Terem—she couldn't even stay in the room to hear all this or it would have driven her to kill me. All she wants is to be free of Makina Seval and to find her daughter again."

"And she hopes you will kill the Despotana for her, to make those things happen."

"Exactly."

"Which leads me back to you." He looked at me with pain in his eyes. "What am I to do with you? What?"

"I have been a traitor," I said. "I confess it. But I hope that what I've done tonight will help you forgive me."

"You betrayed everything," he said bitterly, as if I hadn't spoken. "The dream I thought you shared. My love for you. All the people who served me faithfully. You betrayed everyone and everything."

"I am most humbly sorry," I said, my voice breaking. "Do to me whatever you want. But first let me have revenge for my dead sister. Let me go with Nilang to Kurjain and give the Despotana the justice she deserves."

Terem frowned. "Why should I not simply order Halis to arrest her? Or go after her later, after she's back in Tamurin?"

"Because it would be better for us all if her end is quiet. If you allow her to return to Tamurin and later attack her, or if you arrest her in Kurjain and publicly execute her, you risk frightening the other Despots into combining against you. I don't think you'd want that. Even with Ardavan gone, there will be a lot of fighting before the Kingdoms are destroyed, and you don't want a war with the Despotates into the bargain."

He regarded me appraisingly. "And here I once thought you had no deviousness in you. So, if Makina Seval dies of natural causes, shall we say, there is nothing to frighten the Despots."

"Exactly so. One might suppose she came to Kurjain to offer you alliance, but sadly her health failed her. And when Ashken succeeds to the dais in Tamurin, you can deal with her as you deal with the other Despots."

Terem stroked his chin. He hadn't been shaved recently, and I could see the red-gold stubble agleam in the lamplight. At length he rose, still silent, and went to the map table, where he picked up a sheet of closely written paper. This he tore into pieces, which he then tossed into a brazier. Flames leaped high.

"That," he said, "was a dispatch to Halis, telling him you are a traitor. It seems to be out of date now, doesn't it? Anyway, I'll write a new one for you to take on the galloper. You'll leave within the hour, and you should be in Kurjain in no more than three days. I hope the Despotana will still be there."

"So do I. If she's not, our lives will become much more difficult."

"All the more need to be quick. As soon as you reach the Jacinth Fortress, send this new dispatch to the Chancellery. Don't deliver it yourself, just turn it over to the commandant and have him get it there. Then go and do what needs doing. You may decide you need a few men after all. If so, get them from the commandant."

"Yes, my lord. But the battle—" I wanted to see him win.

"I'll attend to the fighting," he said. "Go find Sholaj and tell him you are to be fed and clothed as necessary. You'll be given the dispatch for Halis before you sail."

"Terem," I entreated. I wanted a smile, a hint that he would forgive me, anything.

His face was impassive. "Go," he said.

Thirty-one

❧

It was a bright, sharp-edged winter morning in Kurjain, with a wind off the sea that smelled of salt and frost. In the streets the hems of the puddles were plaited with rime, and small icicles hung from the eaves on the shaded sides of buildings. In the canals the fishmongers and bread sellers sculled from door to door, and the breeze carried the tang of burning charcoal from a myriad break-fast fires.

Nilang and I had reached the Jacinth Fortress just after dawn, then delivered the sealed dispatch. Now, with eight soldiers in civilian dress coming behind us in a second craft, we were in a pe-riang on our way to find Mother.

According to Nilang, she had secluded herself in a small villa she secretly owned near the Salt Lagoon docks on Tannery Canal. This canal, along which I was now sculling our boat, was only half again the width of a slipper, and cloudy with runoff from the tannery vats. Over it hung the stink of half-cured hides and burnt animal hair.

"That is the one," Nilang said, "two landings along. There is a squid carved over the door."

I saw it. In spite of my apprehension at what was to come, I wondered for the hundredth time what had happened at Gultekin. Terem would have fought his battle three days ago, probably beginning at this very hour. But I was as ignorant of victory or defeat as anyone else in the capital; our galloper, with two crews of rowers keeping us on the move night and day, had outrun any courier in our headlong rush down the Jacinth.

I raised a hand to the soldiers in the second periang, which halted at a water stair behind us. The men scrambled ashore and disappeared into the alley that led to Lime Burners' Street and the landward entrance to Mother's villa. Watching them go, I thought glumly how much simpler it would be to have them kill her. But this was my very last resort, for I had promised Terem perfect secrecy in the manner of Mother's death.

Nilang wouldn't have agreed to using the soldiers anyway, because Master Aa and Instructor Harakty were also in the villa. If soldiers came for Mother, these two would defend her to the death, and Nilang refused to accept this. They shared her bloodline, and she would not buy her freedom with their lives. So we must try deception instead and hope that this would not awaken the horrors of Nilang's binding.

I would still have to deal with Tossi. But she wouldn't expect me to come as an enemy; if Nilang could get Master Aa and Harakty out of the way, I could take her by surprise. Or so I hoped. If she defeated me, Mother's fate would be up to the soldiers. They were to arrest anyone who came out of the villa, unless Nilang or I accompanied them, and take the captives to the Arsenal to await Terem's pleasure. This was a failure I wanted very much to avoid, since I'd already failed him in so many other ways. Nilang wanted to avoid it at least as much as I did; she did not want Mother in a dungeon but in a tomb.

We arrived at the villa. It was a tall building of three floors, with two of its windows winter-papered against the wind and the rest shuttered. I eased the periang to the water steps where Nilang secured us to the mooring ring. Then I followed her onto the landing, where she rapped in a complicated rhythm on the door. Several moments passed. I felt short of breath and edgy, just as I always did before going onstage.

The spy hole in the door slid open and a blue eye peered at us. The eye widened, then disappeared, and I heard the bar draw back. The door opened to reveal Instructor Harakty. He spoke to Nilang in Taweret; she answered, then said softly to me, "The Despotana and Mistress Tossi are upstairs. Harakty is surprised to see us, but I told him all is in order."

We entered. Inside was a dark kitchen storeroom with iron pans on a charcoal stove. Master Aa stood in front of it, frying small silver fish on a griddle. He turned around, delight on his face, and opened his mouth to speak. Nilang covered hers, urgently. Master Aa looked perplexed but remained silent.

Nilang spoke again in Taweret, keeping her voice low. Master Aa looked up at the ceiling, shrugged, and moved the griddle off the coals. Then, obediently, he and Harakty slipped out the door onto the water steps. Nilang followed, and I watched through the doorway as the three boarded the periang.

From upstairs, Mother called, "Who's there?"

Master Aa looked up. My heart almost stopped. Then Nilang spoke quietly but urgently and he pushed off from the landing. Harakty took the scull and drove the boat swiftly out into the canal, and Master Aa settled himself on a thwart. He did not look up again. I softly closed the door.

"Who's there? Master Aa?" Now it was Tossi's voice, closer, from the top of the stairs. And then I heard her footsteps descending.

If I'd been closer to the stairway I might have taken her by surprise, as I'd intended, but it was three paces too far. Her face came into view and her eyes opened wide.

"Lale?" she said in a sharp, astonished voice. "What are *you* doing here?"

If there was ever a time in my life to lie, this was it. "Nilang ordered me to come," I said. "She's still in Gultekin—she's ill. She tried a sending, but she was too weak, so I had to bring the news. Dilara succeeded. The usurper is dead."

Joy lit Tossi's face. She clapped her hands with delight and burst out, "Thank the Moon Lady! Now we can go home." Her gaze swept around the kitchen. "Where's Master Aa?"

"Master Harakty let me in, but then he said he had to go do the marketing. Master Aa went with him. They left a few moments ago."

"*Both* of them?" Her smile vanished. Clearly this was not supposed to happen. I edged a little closer to her.

"Tossi, who's down there?" Mother called. "Is that Lale I hear?"

"Yes, Mother," I called. "I've come in place of Nilang. But everything's all right."

"Come up and explain."

Tossi gave the kitchen an uneasy glance, then motioned me toward the stairs. She was very alert and maneuvered me into ascending ahead of her, something I could not avoid without looking suspicious. She gave me no chance to take her unawares, and the back of my neck prickled.

I reached the top of the stairway, which ended in a large room overlooking the canal. The chamber was well lit by morning sunlight streaming through the papered window, and a brazier radiated a welcome warmth. Near the brazier, Mother sat at a small table, on which were the remains of breakfast: fried fish on a large earthenware platter, a loaf in a basket, and a dish of beets pickled in vinegar. Wasting no time, she asked, "Is he dead?"

"Yes, Mother." To my relief, there was no suspicion in her manner. "Dilara did it, and she got away afterward. But Nilang's had a fever since she arrived in Gultekin, and when I left, she was very ill. She couldn't make the sending to Tossi, so Dilara and I decided I should come instead, and Nilang agreed."

"I see. And the battle?"

"I headed west the morning after Dilara killed him, so I can't be sure." I covertly studied her expression, which suggested she believed everything I was telling her; it was what she wanted to hear, after all. "Ardavan outnumbered the Sun Lord a good two to one," I added. "I don't think there's any doubt about who had the victory."

"Then we have won," she said quietly. She rose from the table and came forward to embrace me, and the delicate scent she wore filled my nostrils.

I could have broken her neck before Tossi could stop me. But I did not. Was it her scent, and the memories it woke in me, or the familiar warmth of her embrace? Whatever it was, I hesitated, and the moment passed. She slipped out of my reach and resumed her seat at the table.

Tossi said, "Mother, Master Aa and Harakty aren't in the house."

Mother went very still. Then she said, "Why not?"

Tossi watched me carefully. "Lale says they went to market as she came in. Both of them."

"What, both? Tossi, you instructed them otherwise?"

"Yes. They appear to have disobeyed me."

There was a frozen instant. And then Mother's face went cold, and Tossi said, "You told me Nilang ordered you to come here. If she was too sick to make a sending to me, how did she do that?"

Too late, cursing my carelessness, I went for her. But she was already on guard, and my first blow glanced harmlessly from her forearm. She kicked at my kneecap, I spun aside and slammed her in the ribs with my elbow. The impact would have broken her bones if she hadn't been so fast, but she was, and she merely grunted.

"Don't kill her, Tossi," Mother said in a strange harsh voice. "I want answers."

We faced each other, circling. I dared not drop my guard long enough to draw the Taweret murder knife at my waist. She'd break my arm if I did.

"I'll leave enough of you to feed the wraiths," Tossi hissed at me. "Remember Adrine?"

"Tossi," I said, in the faint hope that I might reach her, "I'm free of the wraiths. You can be, too. You don't have to serve her. She's *mad*, Tossi."

It was useless; she snarled and came at me. For the next few moments we did our best to kill or maim each other, dodging, grappling, breaking free. I was younger and faster than Tossi, but palace living had made me soft, and she was frighteningly strong. Once she got my throat and would have crushed it, but she must have remembered that she mustn't kill me, because her grip relaxed and I twisted free.

But I was no longer sure I could win. I'd squandered my chances. I should have gone for her in the kitchen. I should have killed Mother as she kissed me. The soldiers would still take them if Tossi won, but that would be small consolation, because I'd be dead. Or maimed for life; crippled, blind, paralyzed.

Tossi had my left wrist. I yanked her toward me, hand sweeping back to break her nose. This would do it—

Something hit the back of my head. Bright lights burst inside my skull and I dropped to my knees. An instant later, Tossi had yanked my wrist up between my shoulder blades and clamped my head in the angle of her right arm. I knew the hold and froze into stillness.

"If you move," she croaked into my ear, "I'll twist your head off."

Still on my knees, fixed in Tossi's relentless grip, I looked with dazed eyes at Mother. She'd left the table to strike me with the edge of the heavy fish platter, which now lay in two pieces on the floor. A hot rivulet of blood soaked into my hair.

"You've got her securely?" Mother asked.

"Yes."

"Good. Now, Lale, I'm sure you haven't come alone, and that you have men outside. If you call for help, Tossi will kill you. Do you understand?"

"Yes," I answered.

"Now, let's have some truth from you, shall we? Is the usurper dead?"

I didn't reply. Tossi rotated my wrist and agony speared through my shoulder. Just a little more and she'd dislocate my arm.

"No," I gasped, tears of pain filling my eyes. "But Dilara is. She missed him and his guards killed her."

"I see. And you? You were supposed to poison him if she failed."

"Well, I didn't."

She sat down behind the table again, like a magistrate about to pronounce sentence on a kneeling prisoner. The light from the windows made an aura around her head. Behind me, the door to the staircase was ten thousand miles away. I would never pass through it again, not living.

"I think you have betrayed me, Lale," Mother said. "Haven't you?"

My fate was sealed, but I might get a last satisfaction from telling her of the wreckage of her dreams. She'd ruined mine, after all.

"Yes," I said, "that's exactly what I've done. There's been a battle, all right, but I don't think the Exiles won it, because Terem's alive. Better yet, Ardavan's dead."

"Ardavan?" Shock passed over her face. "How do you know?"

"Because I killed him. I got into his camp and left him dead in his tent the night before the battle. The Exiles are leaderless." I took a deep breath. "And before I left Gultekin, I told Terem about you, and about Three Springs, and what you made of me and my sisters. I told him everything. He'll be coming for you as soon as he's finished with the Exiles."

Had I hoped she'd crumble at my words, at the ruin of all her intricately crafted plots? She did go pale, and her mouth tightened. But she was made of harder marble than that, and in her face I already saw the complexion of her thought, calculating, devising, scheming, searching out a way to retrieve the situation, to find a path to victory in the wilderness of defeat.

"It's not all lost," she muttered. "Ashken and he . . . perhaps." Then her gaze focused on me again. "But why, Lale? Why did you do it?"

"I fell in love with Terem," I said. "But it wasn't only that. I saw Ilishan Aviya in Gultekin, and he told me who Merihan was. You knew who she was, too. All those years, you knew she was my real sister, and you kept her from me. You kept us apart, when you could have brought us together. And then you murdered her. You murdered the last of my blood kin. And you *still* wonder why I've betrayed you?"

"Ah, I see. Who told you about the Surina?"

"Dilara. She was my best friend once, but then you made her a murderess, and now she's dead. You destroyed her. You destroy everything you touch." My voice was shaking now with sorrow and outrage and, yes, fear. I was going to die and I didn't want to. I tested Tossi's grip, just a fraction.

"Careful, Lale," she whispered. No hope there.

Mother regarded me thoughtfully. "I did what I needed to do, child. But what I would like to know is this—how did you wriggle free of the wraiths? Nilang said only she . . ." She trailed off and then said, "Oh, I see. Nilang released you. Yet more treacheries."

"What did you expect? You enslaved her and kept her from her daughter. All she needed was the chance to turn on you, and I gave it to her. And once you're dead, she's free."

"But I'm not dead," Mother observed. Her face was stony. "And when I get her back, I'll make her suffer. By the Moon Lady, I will."

"You won't escape even if I'm dead. There are men waiting for you."

She laughed. "Did you think I wouldn't foresee such a thing? There's more than one way out of this house. Tunnels. Even Nilang didn't know about them. That was wise, wasn't it?"

"Mother," Tossi said from behind me, "shouldn't we go?"

"I think we should. Very well, Tossi, kill her."

"Good-bye, Lale," Tossi murmured. She yanked at my arm to render me helpless with pain, and the vise around my head tightened.

"Tossi!" Mother cried, leaping to her feet.

The terrible, neck-snapping wrench didn't come. I heard two

soft quick footsteps, Tossi gasped, the vise loosened, and my throbbing arm dropped free. Still half blinded with pain, I almost fell
over, then looked behind me.

Tossi lay sprawled on the floor, facedown. A Taweret murder
knife jutted from her spine, just where I'd driven my own blade
into Ardavan. And beside her stood Nilang, who said, in a cracked
voice, "The binding has me. Kill her, Lale."

She dropped to her knees and toppled sideways; her lips drew
back to bare her teeth, and her back arched into a bow. I spun
around to face Mother, who was on her feet, wide-eyed and staring.

But it was not me she was looking at, nor Nilang, nor Tossi, but
at the doorway. Something shimmered beneath the lintel, and
then the air seemed to split like a snake bursting its skin.

A narrow door opened there, a gateway into somewhere else.
And I knew that place. It was the Quiet World, and a creature was
stalking out of it toward us. It seemed most like the thing that
wanted to devour me long ago, but it was worse, and I knew it was
coming for Nilang. Only that knowledge saved me from mindless
terror.

"Kill her!" Nilang groaned. And then she made a noise, a soft
noise, but it was worse than any scream I'd ever heard.

I struggled to my feet. My arm throbbed and my shoulder
blazed with pain. Now I had to turn my back on the approaching
horror. It was the last thing I wanted to do, but I did it. Then, winc-
ing, I drew my knife.

Mother did not move. She seemed to have no fear of the thing
from the Quiet World, for her attention was wholly on me. I
hadn't thought she'd run, for she had too much pride for that. But
I knew she would fight for her life somehow, and I was still very
dizzy. I must be cautious.

"Wait, Lale," she said softly. "Can you really do this, child? Can
you really kill me?"

"Yes, I can," I told her. "For my true sister. For Terem. For Nilang.
For everyone you betrayed."

Mother looked down at the blade in my hand. "Let me go," she said. "What harm can I do anyone now? I'll go back to Chiran and never trouble you again."

"Nilang will die if I do, and I owe her my life. And if I don't kill you, Terem will. There's no way out for you, not now."

She seemed to ponder this. I took a step toward her. Would she just stand there and let me drive the knife into her breast? And could I do that, in cold blood? But I had to. She had to die.

"Can you really kill me?" she asked again. "I'm defenseless, Lale. Can you really stand before me and stab me to death?"

From behind me, Nilang groaned, *"Lale!"*

It distracted me for a heartbeat, and that was almost our undoing, for Mother seized the dish of beets and vinegar from the table and dashed it into my face. The stinging liquid blinded me; sightless, I threw myself aside and felt a thin pulling sensation across my forearm. It instantly became a line of searing pain; fool that I was, she'd had a knife of her own. I saw a moving shadow through my tears, dodged, parried, clink of steel, her breath on my cheek, my training with me now, thrust the blade upward and twist. A resistance, then softness, a gasp, *ting* of metal striking tiles. She'd dropped her knife. Her weight slid away from me, tugged at the hilt in my hand. My blade pulled free.

On my left arm I felt the slick wet warmth of blood, but it seemed a shallow cut. I pulled my other sleeve across my burning eyes until the tears had washed the vinegar out. Then I could see her clearly, lying on her back on the floor with a red brook flowing from her bodice. My knife had gone in near the heart but had not struck it, for she was still breathing in husky gasps. But there was so much blood that I knew I must have pierced one of the great veins. She would not live long.

I spared a glance for Nilang and for the portal into the Quiet World. The dreadful creature had halted, and as I watched, the eerie doorway took on a translucent aspect and began to fade. The binding was loosening with the ebb of Mother's life, and the terror and agony began to slip from Nilang's contorted face.

I knelt beside the woman who had raised me. Spittle and blood trembled at the corners of her mouth.

"Why?" I asked. "Why couldn't you have been different? Why couldn't you have loved me?"

"Useless slut," she gasped. "Who could love you?"

If she hadn't been dying, I would have struck her. "I loved you once," I whispered.

She gave a strangled laugh. "Yes, you did, girl, I saw to that, didn't I?" She closed her eyes but she still breathed, and it came to me suddenly that the Mother I thought I knew had never existed. And to this woman who lay on the cold tiles before me, I owed nothing.

With a terrible effort she roused herself again, and in that beautiful voice, touched now with the rattle of death, she said, "Girl, I curse you with a mother's curse. I curse you and all that spring from you. You're the worst of daughters, and your own daughters will hate you."

A vast burden slowly began to lift from my heart. I had borne it for so long that only now did I perceive the weight I'd carried.

"You can't curse me," I said. "You're not my mother. My mother died in Istana a long time ago. I'm not your daughter, and I never was."

"Traitor," she breathed, and then blood came from her mouth. For a moment I felt her idu-spirit hanging in the air, seething with malice and hatred, and then it was gone like a bead of water on a sun-warmed stone.

Kneeling beside her, my blood mixing with hers on the cold floor, I felt a sudden strange sensation of lightness, as if I had become part of the sunlit air around me. I didn't understand it at first, and then I did.

I was free.

Thirty-two

❧

"There's much between us that we must face," Terem said. "And there is the question of what to do with you once we've faced it."

We were in the covered veranda of the Reed Pavilion, seated at the table where we had shared so many meals. I'd had my servants set it with cakes and wine, but the cups remained unfilled and the cakes uneaten.

He'd been back from the east for two days now, but until this evening I hadn't seen him. I'd worried that this delay was a bad sign, but I kept reminding myself that he had a lot to do at the Chancellery and the Ministry of War. His message that he would attend me had come as a relief of sorts, although it was mixed with a great deal of apprehension.

The weather was fine. We were halfway though the month of Rain, but the sky had been clear all day and the air was soft and warm. Spring had arrived in Kurjain, with the sea lavender and basket-of-gold coming into bloom at the margins of the pond, and small black and silver frogs chirring from the shallow places among the reeds. The slash on my arm had healed well, although I'd bear a faint scar to the end of my days.

"Then where should we start?" I asked diffidently. I didn't expect the worst fate possible, but I didn't expect the best, either. For I could guess how much pain I'd caused him, if only by measuring it against my own. All month I had lived with remorse and anguish; neither had diminished as the days passed, and why should they? I was the author of a hideous drama of deceit, treachery, lies, death, and love betrayed; and not an hour passed wherein I did not think of what had been, and what might have been, and what I had lost forever.

Terem didn't answer me, but gazed sadly at the young flowers at the margins of the pool. So I said, "But I would ask one thing from you. Will you let Nilang and Master Aa and the others go?"

They were still at Jade Lagoon, living in a pavilion uncomfortably near the Arsenal and its dungeons. The Chancellor had invited them to stay there, and me here, to await the Sun Lord's return from the eastern war. It was an invitation he did not intend any of us to refuse.

Nor did he leave us idle. Much of our time we spent being interrogated about the School of Serene Repose, Three Springs, and the web of spies Mother had woven throughout the Despotates and Bethiya. How the Chancellor would deal with that web, he hadn't indicated, at least not to me. But I reckoned that, with neither Mother nor Nilang to direct its actions, there was no immediate peril to anyone.

I often wondered, as he questioned us in his Chancellery office, with the clerks writing everything down, how my Three Springs sisters would be coping with the news of Mother's death and Nilang's disappearance. They'd certainly know about the former, because Mother had been entombed in state here in Kurjain, and Terem had sent condolences to Ashken on her adoptive mother's death. The new Despotana was no danger, for according to Nilang she knew nothing about the women of Three Springs. Also according to Nilang, with Mother's death the wraiths would no longer be a threat to my erstwhile sisters; perhaps they did not realize it yet, but they could now babble Mother's secrets as they liked and be none the worse for it.

As for Nilang, her new freedom had not appeared to change her a jot. When I asked her why she'd come back to help me, at such terrible risk, she'd given her usual Nilang shrug and answered, "If you failed, I was worse than dead. You were loyal to her for a long time, and I thought you might falter at the last moment, so I returned." The fact that her lack of faith had been justified had done little to improve my mood.

"Why should I let Nilang and her retainers go?" Terem asked. "Or let you go, for that matter?"

From his tone, I couldn't tell what sort of answer he expected or wanted. But my spirits sank even lower. I'd been hoping for exile, not imprisonment, but the latter seemed to be in the wind.

"Ardavan's dead and the Exile Kingdoms are doomed," I reminded him. "I had a hand in that and so did Nilang."

"Yes, you did. I would say that you very likely assured our victory at Gultekin."

I was glad to hear him admit it. That victory had been great indeed, greater than any of the past two centuries, because Ardavan's death had not only beheaded the beast that was the Exile army but also thrown it into turmoil. Some of his officers accused the allied Kings of contriving the assassination; then, on the very brink of battle, the King of Suarai demanded the army's leadership for himself. Ardavan's generals, beside themselves with grief and fury, refused, and the King ordered his men to withdraw from the field. And at that moment, in the faint light just before dawn, Terem hurled the Army of Durdane at the quarreling enemy ranks.

They were not ready for him, and his triumph was complete. The surviving Exiles fled toward the River Savath, with Terem in grim pursuit. But at the Savath, our brigades from Tanay blocked the fords so the Exiles could not cross, and the Army of Durdane took them from behind. Sixty thousand of their best soldiers died that day, with all three allied Kings and most of Ardavan's surviving generals. Of the hundred and twenty thousand men who had set out to destroy Bethiya a month ago, scarcely a battalion remained.

After the Battle of the Savath, Terem sent the army ahead into Lindu, and now he had returned to Kurjain to mobilize new forces and complete the freeing of the eastern lands. It would take time and much fighting, but it would come, for Durdana rebellions now flamed in Jouhar and Seyhan and Suarai, and few Exile troops remained to crush them. Better yet, it was said that Exiles by the thousands—man, woman, and child—were fleeing northeast toward the Juren Gap and the steppes from which they had come. If you listened to an easterly wind, you could hear the death rattle of the Six Kingdoms.

"It's going to be a different world," I said. "When and where will you proclaim the Restoration?"

"In Seyhan, before the leaves fall. We'll have the city by then. I will be raised as Emperor there, as it was in the old days."

"So we'll have our empire back." A frog was sculling across the pond, leaving an arrowhead wake. It risked sudden death from the carp beneath, but reached the bank without being engulfed. Lucky frog.

"Yes, we will, but that will be just the beginning of the work. We'll need two generations to rebuild what's been ruined, but rebuild it we will."

"Terem," I said, when he didn't go on, "please, what are you going to do with me and the others? We need to know. It's not like you to make us wait like this. It's cruel."

Suddenly he had an utterly unfamiliar expression on his face. It was an anguish such as I'd never seen in him, and it cut me to the heart; my throat closed up and my eyes stung with tears. I couldn't look at him and instead fixed my gaze on my lap and on my trembling, clasped hands.

"In the case of Nilang," he said in a strained voice, "she was never my subject, so there is no taint of treason. I would consider her a prisoner of war, but she fought Ardavan on my behalf, which makes her an ally of sorts. If she gives me her word, in the name of her gods, that she won't oppose me again, I'll release her and her companions."

At least the Taweret would salvage their freedom from the wreckage. "Thank you," I said. "But will you help her in the matter of her daughter?"

"I'll do what I can to bring the girl here. In the meantime, Nilang and the other two can move as they wish, beginning tomorrow. You, however, are another matter."

A dull ache settled under my breastbone. I was to be punished after all. Was it to be prison or exile? If exile, where would I go? It hardly mattered. When I reached wherever it was, perhaps I could get my hands on a little money and try my luck as a printer or bookseller. I had no heart anymore for acting. I had paid for its joys with misery and suffering, both my own and that of many other people.

Yet I knew I'd miss the life I'd led, my life in the palace, my life among the great and beautiful of Bethiya and Kurjain. Not so much the luxury and ease, though I'd loved that, too, but the excitement of being at the center of things, the sense of power over my own fate—illusory though that had been—and the feeling that I somehow mattered.

Most of all, I'd miss Terem.

"What do you want of me, Lale?" he asked.

"Don't torment me, Terem, even if I am a traitor. What choices have I? Exile or prison? I'll choose exile, if you'll let me."

"I'm not tormenting you," he replied quietly. "I've thought about you a lot since Gultekin. Yes, you were a traitor. But if it were not for you, I think that I would be dead, and so would all my men, and Kurjain would be nothing but smoking embers."

I tried to speak but could not. And then he said, "Lale, I love you still. I forgive you everything, if forgiveness is needed. If, that is, you'll forgive me for my harshness at Gultekin and for letting you go to face Makina Seval alone. I wasn't thinking clearly, or I would never have allowed it. I know that Tossi nearly killed you. When I think that she might have, and that you might be gone . . ." He spread his hands. "It would have turned victory to a heap of ash."

Dizziness washed through me. And then that hard knot of grief, which I had believed I must carry with me forever, began to loosen. But I wouldn't burst into tears, I wouldn't.

"You told me in Gultekin that you loved me," Terem went on, "but I didn't know whether I could believe you. I should have realized then that you spoke the truth, but I sent you away without a word. Do you still love me, even after that?"

"Yes," I answered. By now I *was* weeping, just a little. "And this time," I added, "just for your information, I'm not acting."

"Lale."

"What?" To my chagrin, I had begun to sniffle. Fortunately, the servants had left finger cloths on the table. I picked one up and blew my nose into it.

"Marry me, Lale," Terem said. "Come with me to Seyhan, and sit with me on the dais as Empress of Durdane."

The world became very still, as if time had stopped. One word hung in the air: *Empress*. Not Inamorata, not Surina, but *Empress*. It was the glittering dream of that ragged, determined child who marched up the road from Riversong so many years ago. How overjoyed she would have been at this.

"Lale? Do you accept?"

I didn't answer. I thought about the reality of that dream, for I'd seen enough to predict it. I remembered the stifling rituals of the House of Felicity, and imagined all the things I couldn't do if I were Empress: go alone to the theater or the Round, buy my own books in a bookstall, saunter around the Mirror with friends, decorate my own villa. Even as Inamorata I had been bound tighter than I liked. If I were Empress, those loose bindings would become manacles: golden ones, but still manacles. How would I put up with it?

But as I thought this, a sudden revelation swept through me. Why was I worrying about such things? For pity's sake, I'd be *Empress*. If I wanted to scull my own periang through the Round, who was going to stop me? If I wanted to spend an afternoon in the Mirror, who would tell me I mustn't? Terem? Hardly. He'd probably be with me in the boat or at the gaming table. So if I didn't like the imperial protocol, I didn't have to put up with it—I could rearrange it to suit myself.

There were going to be changes in the palace, and lots of them.

"*Now* what are you smiling about?" Terem exclaimed in exasperation. "How hard a question is it?"

"I'll be a very bad Empress," I warned him. "I'm willful and headstrong. I hate ceremony and I want my own way too often. And I like going places by myself. And I'm not likely to change, not even for you. Are you sure that's what you want?"

"I don't want you to change. I want the Lale I already know. Will you marry me or not?"

"Yes," I said.

And so, a year later, in the Hall of Heaven's Illumination in Seyhan, I became Empress of Durdane. Terem and I had already moved from Kurjain to the ancient capital. After our marriage and my ascent to the dais, we settled down together in a restored wing of the imperial palace.

Perhaps *settled down* is the wrong phrase. Ours was still a rough-edged, raw-boned empire, and already I sensed that it would be more than a mere continuation of the old, largely because of Terem. With the Juren Gap now secure against the Exiles, he bubbled like a hot spring with ideas. He refounded the Academy of Seyhan, then ransacked both empire and Despotates for men of learning and scholarship to teach there. He established the Imperial Printing Bureau, to replace the myriad books destroyed during the Partition, and ordered the printers to use the new technique of metal letters instead of carved pages. He reopened the Thousand Lilies Theater and attached to it a school for actors and musicians. He set up the Bureau of Original Devices and sought ingenious men to find new ways of doing old things, from glassmaking to canal construction. This was greatly needed, for so much in the east needed to be rebuilt after a century of ruin and neglect at the hands of the Exiles. And Terem seemed determined to do it all at once.

Even I could barely keep up with him. Halis Geray sometimes shook his head and grumbled, but I could see—though I never said it—that the student had overtaken the master.

I gave Terem as much help as I could, but I still wanted something to do on my own, besides be patroness of the Thousand Lilies Theater and the like. One morning, as we ate breakfast in the Opal Dining Room, I told him this.

"Hm. I do have an idea. I've been thinking about it for a while. Halis likes it."

"Oh, good. Does that mean I will?"

"You might." He pushed his plate to one side, waved the two servants out of the room, and put his elbows on the table. I perked up. This suggested something interesting.

"You're very skilled," he said, "at the profession Nilang and her instructors taught. You are extremely quick-witted and you can make people follow you."

"All this is true," I said modestly.

"Halis has finally brought himself to admit how inept his spies were, compared to the Despotana's. He's decided that a school like Three Springs would be very useful for training agents, not only young women but young men. But he needs someone knowledge-able to be in charge of it."

"Nilang?" She'd extracted her daughter safely from her home-land, aided by lavish bribes provided by Terem, and now lived qui-etly in Kurjain. The faithful Master Aa and the others were still with her.

"That had occurred to me. However, Halis is very badly over-worked these days, and within a year I want all secret activities transferred to the control of the palace. Along with that would come the school, which you and Nilang would have already or-ganized. You'd be in charge, with her as your deputy."

452   S. D. TOWER

"Me?" I exclaimed. "A spymistress?"

"Well, why not? Your experience and talents are too great to waste."

"But what sort of people would let their children enter such a profession?"

"There are more than enough foundlings in the world these days, sadly enough. Do as Makina did with the School of Serene Repose, but give the students a real choice and don't force them into the trade—give them another one if they want it. And you could call on some of the girls from Three Springs. They might be willing to help. Why not put their abilities to the best use?"

I considered this. I knew where most of my former sisters were, for Halis had spent the past year digging them out of their hiding places. I'd prevented him from punishing them, however, because there was no point in it. The few whom Nilang considered dangerous had been exiled to Abaris or the archipelagoes, but with Mother dead, most of them seemed lost and sad, not vengeful. I'd seen to it that they took up their trades again, for real this time.

But now I imagined them as they had been in the old days: beautiful Kidrin, saucy Tulay, Temile with her lisp, and all the others I'd known in the Midnight School: scattered now, and as alone in the world as they had been before Mother found them.

But I could have some of them back. Bring them together in Seyhan. Make a family of them again.

"All right," I answered. "I'll do it."

Epilogue

❧

The spring sun is warm. I gaze across the flowery expanse of the school gardens, where the students stand in expectant rows. They inspect me carefully, thinking perhaps that the Dowager Empress is too old and shortsighted to see their quick darting glances. But there is nothing wrong with my eyes.

Or with my hearing, happily, because the younger students will soon sing for me, and then the graduates will come up to my dais for their seal rings. Until then, I can sit in the warmth, ignore the speeches of the tutors and tutoresses, and gaze across the river to Stone Flower Hill, where the imperial palace gleams in the sunlight. There, on the great dais that Terem and I ascended long ago, our son sits in the thirteenth year of his reign. And Terem, whom I loved all the days of my life, lies now under his tall green mound at the Eternal Mercy Gate, where I will, I suppose, soon join him.

I look down at my hands. The brown spots on my skin are many, one spot for every summer of my age, perhaps, although I have never bothered to count. I have outlived everyone I knew in my youth, from actresses to Despots. But there are no Despots anymore; the Emperor rules north of the Pearl and south of it, too, from the Juren Gap to the sea, just as Terem and I dreamed so many years ago.

I still, sometimes, disbelieve my life. How could I have imagined, when the palace sequina carried me toward my first meeting with the Sun Lord, that I was to become an Empress and my son an Emperor? Or that I would become, like Makina Seval, Mother Midnight? For that, by some odd coincidence, is what my students call me, when they think I cannot hear.

The speeches have ended. I smile at the Music Tutoress and incline my head. She raises her arms, and there on the grass in the spring sunlight, like small bright birds in the wilderness, the children begin to sing.